KINGSLEY

M. RASHID

authorHOUSE®

AuthorHouse™
1663 Liberty Drive
Bloomington, IN 47403
www.authorhouse.com
Phone: 833-262-8899

Published by AuthorHouse 08/25/2022

ISBN: 978-1-6655-6875-3 (sc)
ISBN: 978-1-6655-6876-0 (hc)
ISBN: 978-1-6655-6874-6 (e)

Print information available on the last page.

This book is printed on acid-free paper.

CONTENTS

ACT TWO

CITY UNDER SIEGE

ACT THREE

SHADOWS & SECRETS

ACKNOWLEDGMENTS

WHEN IT'S TIME to get to the heart of it, I sometimes find myself drawing a blank. Spending a few extra moments thinking of all the people who have played a role in helping me to get where I needed to be. Helping to push me. Not only to create something interesting...but something memorable.

To my first strike reading team. Marcus, Jewel, Yitera, & B-O-B. Those nights at the round table, in one word...Unforgettable. Your thoughts, concerns, and opinions of the story provided me with an opportunity to better myself, and my work. Thanks in advance because we have more work to do.

There are many others who have gotten a chance to read the finished product early. Mrs. Bea, Tracie, Tanisha, Tammie, Tanya, Tish, and Toiya. Your reactions were guiding and helpful. Thanks for taking the time to read.

Sylene, I have to say it, you did a wonderful job. You may want to take up editing full time. I like the corrections you made without altering other parts of my work. That meant a lot to me.

To my brothers... Doyal and Marcus. Doyal, I know I've picked on you about not finishing reading the book and honestly that never really bothered me. I've been more excited seeing you enjoy what **you** do and getting paid to do something that you love. That is inspiring. We've talked about doing what we love. You've got it and now I'm going after mine. Marcus, we share more than just a passion for cars. We both look for our words to have an *effect on people whether someone is reading our words on a red eye flight trying not to wake up the people around them with small bursts of laughter. Or on stage in front of a crowd eagerly waiting for your words to affect them in the exact way you meant for your words to. I've watched the reactions to Red Pumps & Pastries. I've seen firsthand how your words have connected with the ladies who heard you recite that poem. I could only imagine how the reactions made you feel. Well, that was until I received that first late-night phone call with a few of the readers upset with me about the characters and their choices. It was at that point I received a sense of satisfaction. Hearing how something I created had an effect, positive or negatively on the person who read it. Exhilarated, that's how I felt. I realize that we take our thoughts, experiences, fantasies, and life expectations and put them into some medium of self-expression. Then...we share it with others. Now we are out there on that limb, hoping someone gets it. Someone understands what we're trying to say and gives us the validation of our work.*

However, we're able to reach others... Whether Spoken word, Cooking or Literary works, let's dig deeper within ourselves to always give the best of ourselves. Easier said than done, but the reward is always better when you must work harder to get it.

I've often asked myself who motivates me more...a skeptic or someone who has believed in me all along. The question and the answer are a bit bittersweet. I seem to be motivated by both. For some, a skeptic can give you that push you need... because there is no way you will ever let them see you fail. Yet on the other hand, having someone that believes in you ...will give you a sense of strength to draw from. Pushing you through those times you think you can't do it. So, for those who believe...Thank you for the encouragement. Thank you for the support.

Here I am again drawing a blank. So, let me say...Thank you to everyone who had a hand in making one of my dreams come true. No deed, big or small, should go un-noticed. It doesn't matter to me if you were a part of reading the first draft or putting paper in the copier that printed my work. Good work should never go unrecognized. Thanks everyone for all the Love, encouragement, and support. It will never go un-noticed with me.

MJ

In Memory of
Oswald L. Jones, Robert Lewis Sr., & William Tate (Men who have had a profound influence on my life)

DEDICATION

Thanks for helping me sharpen my claws.
Your wit is still inspiring.

ACT ONE

BETRAYED

A successful crime is planned, plotted, crafted and executed with skill.

A career criminal legitimately masks his or her crimes and will lethally eliminate anyone who endangers that livelihood.

I've been told that money is the root to all evil and those that don't have any will do whatever it takes to get it.

Those that have it...will do everything to keep it.

Money is only the start. Broken promises, lies and envy are usually very strong factors for someone desperately trying to survive.

In my case, when it comes to family and survival...trouble is hereditary.

Raymond Kingsley

CHAPTER ONE

Life Interrupted

IT ONLY TOOK a minute for me to realize that I was dying. Two bullets bounced around inside me as if they were playing tag. My head was resting against the hubcap of my car. My body was becoming limp, and I could feel my fingertips getting cold. My breathing became heavier and heavier as I began to pass out. I could hear voices all around me. There were people screaming, "Somebody help him! Somebody get help!" I couldn't move. I could hear someone saying, that both of my legs were in pretty bad shape. The left was bent back in the wrong direction. The pain to my right hand was excruciating. I had a gunshot wound to my chest and another in my stomach. I also had two defensive cuts to my right arm. My head felt like it was going to explode. I faintly hear the sounds of sirens, but somehow, I knew they weren't coming to help me. I felt like I was slipping away. There was no white light. There were no passed on relatives waiting to welcome me home. I was alone. Gasping for air and everything around me was getting dark. The only thing I could put my faith in, was hoping for the rumors about our city's emergency services were not true. They would get to me in time. I know they will. I hope they will.

I was losing a lot of blood and beginning to lose consciousness. I heard some woman asking me what my name was. That was right before I passed out. I remember my Grann (that's what we called her) telling me that I should always be ready. You never know when your last days on this earth will be. So, make sure you're ready. Well, I can tell you all that I wasn't ready if today were to be my last. I did everything wrong today. I was completely unprepared for the trouble that I knew was waiting for me.

I'm thinking about how life takes some strange turns. But don't worry about the state I'm in now. There is nothing anyone can do for me. I think I'm slipping into in a comma. So, while my body sorts things out, I'll take some time to think about how things got like they did. How I ended up next to my own car, my body badly damaged and in a pool of my own blood.

Now before I start, I have to say that love had absolutely nothing to do with what happened tonight. I fell victim to one of the seven deadly sins... Greed. "Only in America baby" ... isn't that what Don King would say. Take the bull by the horns and ride the beast until the meat is sizzling on my grill. There was a wealth of opportunity out in these streets, and I took advantage of everything and everyone who gave me a chance to do so. But when you ride hard, you sometimes fail to see the fall that's coming. You only concentrate on reaching your goals. No matter how you achieve it. It only takes minutes for things to go wrong, and you can never see it coming when it does. You never realize that someone you trusted would be the one person who would betray you. This is why you never see a situation like tonight coming. Blinded by ambition. Blinded by money and corrupted by power. I never thought that the crimes I trained to fight might possibly be the same things that may take my life.

I grew up hearing how the men in my family balanced business and family. I was taught to respect my elders, trust my feelings and to stay loyal to my family. I kept my end of the bargain, but it seems someone close to me didn't. I don't know whom, but they will reveal themselves just like Judas did. I just hope my body doesn't give out before I can learn the truth. Before I can uphold justice, and before I lose myself to the criminal activity that I've worked so hard to fight against. I'm looking for answers. I'm looking for justice. Unfortunately, I can't do much because of the state that I'm in, but it seems I'll have to think back into my past to find my answers and find the truth.

I'm still motionless but I can hear things going on around me sometimes. Nurses, Doctors, Cops, and my family, these are a few of the people I hear coming in and out of the hospital room. Sometimes I can hear a few of them talking to me, but I can't respond. I can't react. I can't move. I'm just lying here letting the beep from the heart monitor speak for me. It is the only auditory proof that I'm still alive. My body has these unexpected violent seizures that take me close to flat lining, but the closer to dying I get, the farther from the truth I become. I get vivid images sometimes. The person or persons that are speaking to me induce many of them. The others come in on their own. Images from my childhood and up to the moment that I blacked out on the street. I'm wondering ... when did things start to go wrong for me? I'm not sure if it happened the night I was attacked on the street or if things have been going wrong every day since my parents were killed.

I think I hear my grandmother at the bed next to me. She's telling me the same thing everyone who has come to see me has said,

"don't give up Raymond, you're strong and you're young. You can make it through this." Grann was asking me if I could feel her rubbing my arm. As she held my left hand, she was explaining how tragedy continues to affect this family. She spoke vaguely about how my father was viciously murdered and how my mother suffered a similar fate. Ironically, just shortly after my dad's death. My family never explained the details of their murders. As I grew up no one would answer any of the questions I had that related to my parents. When I was young, my Grann kept telling me to focus on my goals and let whatever misfortune happened with my folks...rest with my folks. That was something I couldn't do.

As I grew up my interest in what happened to them grew as much as I did. It became disruptive for me. It bothered me that my folks couldn't share in my accomplishments. I felt alone. I felt that way from high school until I graduated from the police academy. All my awards, all of my achievements would feel hollow to me until I found out why my folks died. Listening to Grann mention the murders of my folks brought up the anger I felt growing up. Although I was taken care of by my remaining family, I couldn't help feeling isolated. There were different expectations of me, very different from my cousin. The difference in expectations helped me to better myself, but the lack of closeness, proved to be more hurtful in my adult years. Losing the communication and the trust of my family was hard to deal with. I often wonder if it helped put me in this hospital bed. Well at any rate, I could still hear Grann's uncomforting voice. Her words began to run together as I began to fade out and reminisce about the past.

CHAPTER TWO

Uncle's Promise

(Years earlier)

I COULD HEAR MY Uncle Robert talking to Grann. They were sitting out on the porch. My uncle stops by...uh...maybe every two weeks or so to bring Grann a care package. I never actually get to see what he brings because I'm always asleep when he's here. I normally wake up hearing the two of them talking. And like clockwork, Uncle Robert is usually in his Navy blue '68 convertible Cadillac smiling and backing out of the driveway by the time I'm dressed and getting out to the porch. He normally acknowledges my appearance to the porch with an upward flick of his head. This is his way of saying hello and goodbye to me with just one gesture. I wanted to know why he never stays around to talk, but Grann just yells, "That man has got work to git done. He's got no time to be sit'en round. Listen to me... You can't move nowhere when your ass is stuck to a chair." Now that I think about it, she finished a lot of her sentences with that phrase.

"Don't you got somewhere to be Raymond?"

"No."

"Ya better find somewhere to be. Now! Go-on!"

I decided to do what she wanted. Find somewhere to be. Grann seemed angry and I didn't want her to take her anger out on me. Humm...The last few times Unck dropped in, she seemed mad just after he left. Something I observed to be a pattern as I walked out the door.

I came off the porch and grabbed my bike from the side of the house. I rode ten blocks to hang out with my cousin Sean. Being my only cousin, we spend a lot of time together. Most of the time we were nearly inseparable. As soon as I reached his house, I jumped off my bike and squatted on his front steps. Sean was coming out the door with his basketball in his hands. He almost had the door shut, but I could hear Aunt Kate calling to him.

"Sean, before you go and play... Did you do what your father asked you to do?"

(Whining)

"Can't I just go play? Momma, do I have to do it?"

"Now your father only asked you to do one thing today and he wants it done before he gets home. So be momma's big man and do what he asked you to do. The sooner you do it honey, the sooner you can go and play. (her eyes shift) OH, hey Rizz honey. How are you? I didn't see you there."

I got the nickname Rizz one afternoon after a mishap with a canned soda. I was drinking it too fast, and it backed up and came out my nose. Sean, in an attempt to be funny rushed his thought and got my name mixed in with his comment. Instead of saying, Ray has fizz coming out of his nose. He yelled out, "Rizz has fizz." Then sometime later it went from Rizz to Rizzo. I eventually got used to it. I turned my body slightly, looked to the top of the stairs and I answered, "I'm fine Aunt Kate."

"That's good honey. (Pauses) Ok Sean, don't make your father angry sweetheart. Go finish what you're supposed to do."

With a very disappointed look on his face, Sean handed the basketball to his mother and came down the steps.

"Hey cousin."

"Hey Sean, what's going on?"

"I have to do this chore for my dad before we can start playing. Just put your bike in the backyard and walk around the corner with me."

"What`cha gotta do?"

"I have to take this package over to Mr. Coleman. He's s'posed to give me some money for it."

"How much?"

"I think its fifty dollars. I don't remember. I think fifty is what pops said."

"You Think! I hope you remember before we get over there."

After I sat my bike down, Sean picked up a box from behind the garbage cans, tucked it under his arm and we began our walk to Mr. Coleman's house. As we walked, Sean told me how he doesn't want to waste his time doing these odd jobs for his dad. He said he'd rather be out playing basketball.

"My pops told me that when he and your dad were young, that they both did small jobs for Grann all the time."

"They did? I didn't know that."

"Yea, they did. But what's unfair is that I have to do these things just because he had to do it at my age."

"Ok, then let's hurry up and get rid of that thing so we can go play.

(Sean stops walking) How close are we Sean?"

"It's right over there Rizz."

"Then why are you hesitating?"

"I'm trying to remember what pops told me to say before we get inside."

"You don't remember?"

"Yeah, I remember Rizz. I got it. (Sean takes a deep breath) Let's go do this."

We approached this boarded up, abandoned looking house that I thought belonged to Mr. Coleman. The fence surrounding the house was an old wooden fence. It had planks missing from it. There were tall blades of grass and weeds sprouting through the few remaining and rotting planks. There was glass on the ground just below the windows that were busted out. The paint was aged, weather beaten and peeling away from the house. There was a gutter hanging and blocking the path to the front door. But the gutter wouldn't be the most obvious deterrent because with three of the stairs missing, you couldn't get to the front door anyway. So, we just followed several yellow spray-painted arrows that led us down the side of house to the garage. I noticed a bright orange extension cord coming from behind one of the boarded-up windows at the rear of the house. The cord was suspended across the driveway and entered the garage through the missing left garage door window. The right door was held open by a small stack of old newspapers. The closer we got to the garage; I could see a dimly lit bulb just inside the door. I could see the image of a husky man in the shadows, speaking to us in a deep raspy tone.

"You boys step in here and bring me my package."

Sean and I cautiously entered the garage and found Mr. Coleman leaning back in a folding chair. He was leaning with his legs resting on top of a folding table. The smoke from the cigar he was smoking filled the garage like the blinding fog of a three-alarm fire.

"Go on and take the envelope there. Then set the box on the table and leave."

Sean hesitated...so when he didn't move, I walked to the table and picked up the envelope. I backed away from the table, opened the envelope and counted the money that was inside.

"You only have half the money here. There's supposed to be fifty dollars.

Where's the rest of the money?" I asked with as much attitude as I could muster.

"Sean, your daddy knows that I'm giving him half the money now, and then the rest he'll get later. It's an arrangement we've already made. So, give me the box!"

(Mumbling to myself)

"I can't believe he just ignored what I said."

"Ok. If that's what you've got worked out, then I guess it's fine." Sean nervously spouted.

Sean was only able to take a few steps toward the table before I stuck my arm out and wouldn't let him walk past me.

"Wait a minute! Don't hand him anything Sean. Mr. Coleman, this isn't how this is going to play out. We'll give you this box when you come up with the rest of the money."

I got a little nervous when Mr. Coleman took his legs off the table and sat straight up in his chair. He took the cigar from his mouth, held it between his fingers, and turned and looked directly at Sean.

"Sean, I'm going to speak directly to you right now because (Pointing) I don't know that kid you brought with you. Your Dad and I go way back, ya hear. And... and... I want you to do right by him. So, let's finish what you came here to do."

"Don't give him that box until he gives you the rest of the money!" I said with angered confidence.

"WHO IS THIS KID!" Mr. Coleman yells, "Look kid, this isn't your business. Keep quiet and let me deal with Sean."

"Let's go Sean. Something isn't right with this. Let's just go!"

"WAIT SON, WAIT! Is this how you intend to take care of business? What would your dad say about what you're doing?

"My dad would say... Where's the rest of my money."

(Bobbing his head up and down) "Is that right? (Pauses) Then there's only one thing I should do..."

Mr. Coleman put his cigar down and sat back into his chair. He slowly reached into his jacket with his right hand. Sean and I could not move. My heart was trying to jump out of my chest. I stood there, looking at him with the meanest look that I could produce. Sean turned away from Mr.

Coleman and looked at me. I kept the same expression on my face. I didn't want to give the impression that I was afraid... even though I was terrified.

"If this is the way you boys want it, then here's how it's gonna be."

As he pulled his hand from inside his jacket, I noticed he was holding a huge wad of money. His hands were shaking as he snatched off the rubber band.

Mr. Coleman pulled twenty-five dollars from the roll and set it on top of the table.

(Speaking in an angry tone)

"Take the damn money. Give me the box... and get da fuck out!"

I looked over at Sean, but he never moved to get the money. He never took his eyes off Mr. Coleman. I was ready to leave. So, I took the box from Sean and exchanged the box for the money. When I began to back away from the table, I gave Sean a nudge with my elbow. My nudge seemed to reanimate him and together we both slowly backed out of the garage and all the way down the driveway. Once we were at a safe distance from any danger, we ran all the way back to Sean's house. We stood in front of his steps, bent over and out of breath.

(Panting)

"Do you always do jobs like that for your dad?"

"No! This was the first time. And I hope he doesn't ask me to do it anymore. Hey, I'm gonna get my basketball so we can go play."

Before Sean could move, the screeching tires of his father's Cadillac startled us.

(Yelling from the car)

"You boys come over here."

We both left the steps and stood alongside the driver's door of the car. Uncle Robert kept his right hand on top of the steering wheel and glared at both of us over the top of his sunglasses.

"Sean did you drop that package off like I asked you to?"

"Yes dad."

"Are you sure YOU made the drop?"

"Yes dad."

(Uncle Roberts points at me)

"Rizz, go get your bike so I can take you home. Sean, get in the car.

As Sean climbed into the car, I walked into the backyard to pick up my bike.

"Son, the next time I send you to make a drop, I want you to handle it. Not your cousin Rizz. I heard about you standing there and letting him take control. Your cousin should not have been there. Make sure that never happens again. Son, in our business you can't freeze up. (Pauses) and you can't be taken advantage of. First, I want you to learn from what Rizz did this afternoon. But do not involve him in any other job that I give you. Now, go in the house and we'll finish this when I get back."

When I returned with my bike, the black top was now up on my uncle's car and the trunk was open. Sean was heading up the stairs with his head down. Uncle Robert was now outside his car, leaning onto it with one leg crossed in front of the other and was puffing on his cigar. When I closed the trunk, my uncle uncrossed his legs and with one swift waving motion of his arm, instructed me to get into the car.

Uncle Robert was smooth. He was cool. He didn't try to be. His motions, his mannerisms proved that he was. The only thing that I thought was strange was how he never looked directly at me. I can't remember when he had. Even while he was driving me home, he either looked into the driver's side mirror or straight through the windshield. He also never had a problem speaking his mind. If it needed to be said, then Uncle Robert had no shame sayin' it.

"Before I take you home Rizz, I want to stop and show you something."

He turned the corner and pulled in front of the same run-down house that Sean and I had visited earlier today. It looked unbelievably worse as the sun began to set behind it. It appeared to be even more cold and uninviting. It sat nearly in darkness. Even the dim light from the garage was out. The only light I could see was the flickering streetlamp that sat in front of the house. Unck (My slang for uncle) shut the car off and with a new cigar between his fingers, began pointing towards the house.

"Rizz, I want you to focus on this house here. This house used to be the corner stone of this neighborhood. It used to be a place where people felt safe. It was a place that made strangers feel welcome and the neighbors glad that they lived next door. Everything that happened around this house was positive for this neighborhood. One thing both you and Sean must learn... that good and bad go hand in hand. You can't have one without the other. It was the same with this house. Under the surface, unseen by most, there were many bad things going on that made the good things possible. Severely worse things than what you and Sean experienced today. So, when the bad things that affected this family were unavoidable, your daddy and I found a way through it. And it was perseverance through the tough situations that shaped our characters, especially your fathers. He was a pillar for this family and for this community. So, when he died, life in and around that house died with him. Long before he passed, we made a pact. (Paused and takes a puff of his cigar) A promise we made to each other when Sean and you were both born. We decided that if either one of us died, we would keep the other's son from walking in his father's path. Unfortunately, he's gone. I miss your dad and I intend to keep the promise I made to him. So, I expect you do more with your life than we have. Rizz, I want your future to be much brighter than the darkness that engulfs this house. There are so many better opportunities out there. I appreciate you helping your cousin and your actions today remind me of your dad, but I don't want you involved with any pickup or drops that I send Sean on. If what you both had gone through in that garage today was real, you both might have been in some deep trouble. Although... I am impressed with how you thought quickly in

a tough situation. But Sean.... will have to learn the same thing without your help. Like it or not, ***my*** *work is Sean's future...not yours. I want you to be a pillar in this community just like this house used to be. Are we clear?"*

"Yes Unck, we're clear."

"Good. Now let's get you home."

Uncle Robert put his stogie in his mouth, grabbed the steering wheel and pulled away from the curb. I sank into the plush, couch like seat in his car and soaked in everything he had said. But I was still bothered by how he never looked at me the entire time he spoke to me. It was about a year ago when I first noticed that he wouldn't. I don't make a big thing out of it; I just know that it happens.

I leaned my head towards the passenger door glass and looked at the streetlights as we passed them. Before I knew it, Unck had bent a few corners and glided right in front of Grann's house.

"You remember what I told you Rizz, walk the right path."

"I hear you Unck, a straight path."

"That's right Rizz, you leave the crooked path to me and your cousin Sean."

I grabbed my bike from the trunk while Uncle Robert puffed on his cigar. After closing his trunk and putting my bike away, I received the customary head nod from my uncle just before he drove away. I went into the house thinking about some of the things Unck said about my father. Wondering why he doesn't tell me more about my parents or more about the past events that drive him to keep that promise to my father.

CHAPTER THREE

Arresting Development

I SAT IN MY seat, tapping my pencil on the desk. I always found American Government class to be boring. Today the classroom was silent, except for the shuffling sound of Mr. Winter's feet dragging across the floor. He paced back and forth throughout the class the entire period. He held his textbook in one hand and repeatedly adjusted his glasses with the other. I felt like the more he spoke, the harder I fought falling asleep. So, in an effort to keep from nodding off, I looked out the window into the school's courtyard. The ground displayed a huge silver X, which sat inside a huge black circle. Just outside the outer edge of the circle were the words: "By any Means Necessary". This was the attitude the school adopted when it came to providing its students their education. Many students use those words as a reminder of how to survive Malcolm X High School.

The school is just a common public high school. Full of poorly paid teachers with substandard materials, scarcely funded programs, and edgy, attitudinal, undisciplined students. It happens to be the only public school in this city repeatedly neglected by the school district. Not a fitting way to pay homage to an important figure of this nation's history. The school is filled with unmotivated teachers, babysitting students who won't focus on their studies. These kids need direction. Unfortunately, a few of them seem to be taking some direction from my cousin Sean.

I'm still looking out the window trying to overcome my boredom with class when Sean and four of his buddies came darting across the courtyard and disappeared into the building directly across from the one I was sitting in. I also watched two campus security agents and two Colver city police officers go charging after Sean and his buddies. Fifteen minutes later, the police were escorting Sean and two of his five friends off the campus in handcuffs. I didn't find out what happened to them until after the bell rang for lunch and I stepped onto the courtyard. As I took a few steps in the direction of the cafeteria, I noticed three guys running towards me. The first of the three to approach me was my friend Kevin James, who is now the High-school's star basketball player and has been my pal since grade school. The others were Kevin's teammate Kelvin and his girlfriend Sharon.

(Kevin excitingly about to burst)

"Man, what I just saw was crazy. Check it out. I was standing at the urinal in the bathroom...you know, handling my business when the bathroom door came flying open. There was a lot going on up in there. The way Sean and his boys came into the bathroom, you would have thought they were in a military operation or in some movie action sequence. It was amazing to watch. They moved quickly and nearly mistake free."

(With a confused look on my face)

"Nearly?"

"Yea, nearly Ray. Now shut up and let `em finish."

"Thanks Kelvin. Ok, so...I'm standing there, and the door crashes open. Sean and two of his four buddies run past me and then each prop open a door to a toilet. The tallest guy in the group stood at the door as a lookout, while the last guy ran to the middle of the room. He stood between the door and the stalls with an open duffle bag on his shoulder."

"So where was the school security?" Sharon asked.

"Wait a minute Sharon, don't rush me. I'm getting to that. (Pauses) Look...It was one of those situations that was happening so fast but seemed

to be moving in slow motion. Ya know what I'm sayin'. Ok... the guy with the bag kneeled, took the bag off his shoulders and placed himself so that he was facing the guys at the stalls. He started tossing bags that looked like they were filled with cocaine to each one of the guys standing at the toilets. From my angle, I saw each of them catch a bag, cut it open and flush the powder as quickly as they could. After flushing, they would reappear and catch another bag. The tall guy standing at the door would shout out the distance that the police and the school patrol were from the bathroom. Let me get back to the guy standing with the duffle bag in the center of the room. He tossed the first white package to the person in the stall that was the farthest away from himself. He didn't toss more than a total of two bags apiece to the guys who were doing the flushing. Sean happened to be the closest to that dude who was tossing the powdered bags."

"To whom Kevin?"

(With attitude)

"The one with the duffle bag! Now pay attention! (Pauses)

So, when Sean caught his first bag to dispose of.... he dropped it."

"He dropped it?" I yelled

"Yeah! I was surprised he did that too. Especially since he's the best point guard for our basketball team. Well, after dropping the bag, Sean fell behind flushing the powder. Then the tall guy at the door shouted that the patrol was coming down the hall. At that point the dude with the duffle bag was tossing a second package to the guy at the stall farthest from him. Then the tall guy at the door yelled out that the patrol was now just six doors away. Sean had just caught his second package and cut it open. At that point the guy with the duffle bag stood up, zipped it closed and put it on his back. Then he and tall guy both left their posts and quickly stood on each side of me at the open urinals. When the patrol busted into the bathroom, the dude in the stall farthest from the door tried to hide in the stall, the guy flushing in the stall next to Sean was just coming out with white powder on his hands

and clothes. Sean was caught holding a nearly empty package of cocaine. (Pauses) Man, If Sean wouldn't have dropped that first package; he might not have been caught holding anything. The police completely overlooked the two standing on each side of me. They handcuffed the guy who was hiding in the stall, Sean and the idiot standing in the center of the floor with the powder all over him."

"Why didn't they arrest you and the other two guys Kevin?"

"Arrest me? Are you crazy Brian? Man, all I was doing was taking a piss... and I couldn't do that because of all the excitement. The other two guys... well, the patrol, after intensely staring at us all, just assumed that they were taking a piss also. The police headed straight for Sean, found the guy hiding in the stall and grabbed the dude who looked like he just swallowed eight big ass powdered donuts as soon as they came into the bathroom."

"Kev, don't you guys have a game tonight?" I asked.

"Yeah. But the coach ain't gonna be happy when he hears about this."

"This is a little more serious than the coach losing his point guard.

Ya know what I'm sayin'."

As Kevin shook his head in disappointment, I threw up a horizontal peace sign and told everyone I'd holla at them later as I walked away. I headed for the phone booth that sat outside the cafeteria and called my uncle's pager. I only pushed in three numbers...1-1-1. The numbers one-one -one, they are our family's signal for distress. It means...Someone needs me to reach you, so help will come soon. I think that's how it goes. After my uncle sees the code in his pager, he immediately calls home or my grandmother's house to find out who's in trouble and how he can help. Uncle Robert set up this code and a few others. He wanted to keep the 9-1-1 code for injury related emergencies only. The 1-1-1 codes were basically for trouble with opposing competition, deals going bad and run-ins with the police. I was told that there should never be a situation where this code is to be used for me. Until I was an adult...it never was. Unfortunately, that code became second nature when it came to Sean.

When I got home after school, I was able to slip pass my grandmother undetected. Grann was sitting in the dining room with her back to the hallway talking on the phone. I tip- toed past the dining room, making sure that I was out of sight, just in case she turned around while she was talking. I leaned in and hugged the wall, attempting to hear bits of her conversation.

"He got caught with what Robert? (Pauses) Mm-hmm. Well, was he alone?

(Pauses) Uh-huh. Well, you can't just leave him there...Bail him out! (Gets quiet) and what's leaving him there gonna teach him Robert?"

Suddenly Grann got quiet. About two minutes had passed without her saying a word. I could hear her shifting her weight in the dining room chair, silent. Giving virtually no responses. She only mumbled under her breath until something she heard made her angry. She began to speak soft but irritated, almost as if she were speaking with her teeth clinched tightly.

"How do you expect that boy to learn anything if you don't give him the guidance that he needs. He will never learn from his mistakes if you don't show him what he's doing wrong. I agree that he must take a few lumps but not at the expense of losing sight on the real goal. Do you understand me, Robert? (Pauses) Good, do what you need to do. Go get that boy and we'll deal with the consequences of his actions when that time comes. Take care of family first Robert and take care of it now."

I stood frozen in THAT hallway, with my back pinned to the wall and my fingers digging into the wallpaper. I didn't want Grann to hear me move. I tried to relax my muscles and slowly back my way down the hallway to my room. I could hear the creaking of her chair as she stood. The heaviness of her footsteps as she approached the hall. I barely made it back into the threshold of my room when Grann reached the hallway.

(Calling out and still sounding angry)

"RAYMOND! I HOPE YOU'RE IN THERE WORKING ON YOUR HOMEWORK!"

I answered, "Yes ma'am", as the sound of her voice disappeared into another part of the house. I've learned that in moments like this, I should stay in my room and let Grann calm down. Get past her disappointment with Sean. Unfortunately, there would be more disappointments ahead for everyone.

CHAPTER FOUR

First Offense

THE COURTROOM WAS mildly quiet, except for the small group of people murmuring behind us. I leaned over to my aunt Kate and whispered, "It must be election time." There seemed to be a bit too many news people in the courtroom covering a small-time dealer like Sean. Normally when the charges given are as clear-cut and indisputable as Sean's are, it seems strange that they were taking so long to sentence him.

The judge banged his gavel and called for the courtroom to come to order. The chatter became disruptive as the spectators reacted to the judge giving Sean a lecture from the bench. I was sitting in-between Sean's three-month pregnant girlfriend Michelle and my aunt Kate, who both were among the many who were surprised by the judge's words. I looked in Sean's direction, but he showed no emotion, no reaction to what was being said. He sat motionless, as his lawyer jumped to his feet.

"I object your honor! I don't think my client is being treated fairly."

"Your objection is noted Mr. Mason and very easy for me to overlook counselor. Please take your seat. I have not finished speaking. (Clears throat) For anyone who is un-aware on how I disperse justice, let me take a moment to educate you. It makes no difference to me if it is your first time in front of me or your twelfth. If you are using, carrying, distributing, or selling any drugs (Pauses) and are caught and brought before me...you will

always receive the maximum sentence. First time offenders should be held responsible for the people that die after using the poison these dealers are selling. This isn't the first time this man has broken the law, it's only the first time he's been caught. So... if I can't punish the man who put you out on the streets to sell, (pointing at Sean) then I'll punish you for not being smart enough not to endanger yourself and this community. So, Mr. Reynolds, we will begin our renewed effort to clean up the streets of our fair city starting with you."

Sean was leaning back into his chair with his arms crossed and his chin pressed into his chest. And he still wore no expression on his face. He sat and gazed over the rim of his glasses, looking in the direction of the judge. I looked at Aunt Kate. Her hands were over her mouth and her eyes were wide open with disbelief. Flash bulbs were going off as the newspapers took pictures for tomorrow's headlines. The judge, the Honorable Richard Sheppard seemed to be on his soapbox. Making his run for office and using his bench as the platform to do so. He was clearly using Sean for his stand to wipe out crime in our city and win the Mayoral race at the same time. Judge Sheppard knew he had to clean up his image in order to win this election.

He was known to be an uncompromising hard-ass who gave lawyers, defendants and jurors an unbearable experience when they visited his courtroom. He became known as the "hang' em high" judge, who handed out his brand of justice...his way. It was this hard-nosed image that was hurting him in the polls. Judge Sheppard knew this, so he used Sean and his stand on crime to change his image. As the Judge spoke, the press hung on his every word. Sean paid little attention to the judge. He sat whispering to his lawyer as his future was being traded for winning votes. The Judge's monologue went on until he finally was interrupted. It was because of that interruption that caused Sean's verdict never to be shared with the media or the public. Let me explain what happped behind closed doors...

First, we continued to watch The Judge Sheppard Show. (Don't worry, it won't make syndication) But right before the newspapers could get any quotes for the front page, the district attorney approached the prosecuting attorney, tapped her on the shoulder and whispered something into her ear. Shortly after, she addressed the judge.

"Excuse me Your Honor, may I approach the bench?"

Sean's attorney had a perplexed look on his face as he left his seat to approach the bench with her. Sean turned towards his mother and hunched his shoulders. Signaling that he had no idea what was going on.

"Mrs. Bryant, what is the meaning behind your interruption?", asked Judge Sheppard.

"Your Honor, the state would ask the court for a delay in sentencing Mr. Reynolds."

The district attorney takes the opportunity to jump in.

"Your Honor, this is a development that can be better addressed in your chambers."

We looked on as all the attorneys babbled over each other in front of the judge. Then after about two minutes the judge addressed the courtroom.

"There will be a one-hour recess as I speak to all counsel in my chambers."

(Bangs gavel repeatedly)

[In chambers]

The district attorney took a seat as the judge rotated around in his huge leather chair to face him. Before he spoke, he took a cigar from a box on his desk, cut off the tip, lit it and took a few puffs.

(With a smug expression)

"So, Tom, what's going on? What brings you down to my courtroom to disrupt the proceedings on a case that you're NOT even working?"

"Well Richard, there's been a small development. We have a chance to nab a bigger fish if we dangle some bait at this Reynolds kid."

"What kind of bait?"

"We want to offer a shorter sentence for information on the person

he works for. A very good source tells me that this Sean kid wants to play basketball. Tells me that he's willing to do what he must do to be able to play. Basically, I think we can turn him and net a bigger fish like Robert Kingsley."

The judge took a few more puffs of his cigar and tapped his finger on the desk.

"Robert Kingsley Huh? (Bobbing his head up and down) The guys clean. No one has ever found any proof of anything illegal on that guy, Tom. (Puffs cigar) He's slippery, very hard to catch with his hands in the cookie jar. Now, do you really think you'll get his son to talk? Do you REALLY THINK he will give you something on his father?"

"Robert Kingsley would be great, but that's a long shot. (Clears throat) We believe we can get something more substantial from this kid if we make the pitch. He just might give up something or someone and still do jail time himself. Could be a good trade off and the break we've been looking for."

"How much time do you need?"

"Maybe a couple of days... at the most, Richard."

Judge Sheppard took a couple of puffs of the remaining half of his cigar and then leaned over to press the intercom button on his desk phone.

"Diana, would you ask the other lawyers to come inside and join us now."

(Stares out the window until everyone takes a seat) I'm going to hold off sentencing of this case and give the prosecution some Leigh way. The prosecution wants to offer a deal to the defendant and I'm going to grant the time for both sides to talk. Then we will reconvene in one week. Ok everyone. Then I will see everyone back in the courtroom in a few minutes and tell the public."

The judge snuffed out his cigar and began to put his robe back on. Everyone else quietly got up and made their way back to their seats in the courtroom. When the defense attorney reached his seat, he patted Sean on his forearm as if to let him know that everything is fine.

(Sean leans and whispers) "What's going on, Mr. Mason?"

"The prosecutor wants to offer us some kind of a deal. I'll fill you in on it after court."

The judge enters the courtroom, takes his seat, and then bangs his gavel.

"Will the court please come to order? Considering the new developments surrounding this case (looks directly at Sean) we will postpone these proceedings until these new developments can be sorted out. Courts adjourned." [Gavel bangs]

Aunt Kate looked on with a confused expression on her face, but we all were pretty confused about what was going on. Sean kept looking back at all of us as the bailiff came to take him away. As he left the courtroom he waved to his mother, blew a kiss to his girlfriend, and bounced a peace sign off his chest when he looked at me. I returned the gesture by giving him an upward head nod and bouncing a fist against my chest as he left the courtroom.

Three days had passed before the family was allowed to visit Sean. I stood at the back wall and looked over Aunt Kate's and Michelle's shoulders as they both sat and peered at Sean through the thick protective bulletproof glass. Aunt Kate spoke with him first. She apologized for his father's absence and repeatedly assured her son that things would be fine. Michelle would touch her belly while she described her doctor appointments. She told Sean how she and the baby were healthy. Michelle became quiet for about five minutes as she listened to Sean. I was looking around and watching a few of the other visitors while they talked. I needed to do anything that would ward off the boredom that was beginning to set in. Still standing against the wall I focused in on Sean. He was waving at me, encouraging me to come to the glass and pick up the phone. I made my way to speak with

Sean while Michelle and Aunt Kate went to find something to eat because Michelle was hungry.

"What's happening cousin? Everything all right?" Sean asks.

"I should be asking you that. We have been trying to see you for a few days, but they wouldn't let us see you."

"They kept moving me back and forth between my cell and one of the interview rooms. (Stops and wipes his nose with his sleeve) Listen, a couple of days ago they offered me a deal Rizz.

"A deal? What kind of a deal Sean?"

"They told me that they would reduce my charges from intent to distribute, down to just a possession charge if I give up the person I was working for."

" You didn't! Not your da... (Cuts me off)

"No! Are you crazy? I would never do that."

"So, what did you do?"

(Looking around)

"Well... I gave 'em Ronnie Ron. Pops had said that he had been fucking up lately. You know, stealing. Coming up short all the time. So, pops told me to give him up and get the reduced sentence."

(Surprised) "Your dad was here?"

"Yeah. He came in with my lawyer a few days ago. Pops said Ronnie Ron had to go and this was the best opportunity to do it. So, if we made the deal... I would be sentenced to six months and then the judge would sign the warrant for Ronnie Ron's arrest."

I asked Sean which judge signed the warrant and he told me it was the same one who was coming down on him in the courtroom.

"Sean, is this guy running for mayor or something?"

"Yeah Rizz, apparently, he and my dad are in some kind of cigar club together and my dad is helping to fund his campaign. So, dad says, this way the DA gets their guy, and we can keep business the way it is. It's more of a

win-win for us than the district attorney. Honestly, I'd rather have Ronnie Ron do the time than me."

"Only six months huh? Hello? Sean? Hello?"

When I looked through the glass Sean was pointing at his wrist as if to say that our time was up and that was exactly what was happening. Visiting time was over. So as Sean was being escorted out, we both pounded our fists at our chests and finished our goodbyes with a peace sign and a head nod.

I met Aunt Kate and Michelle back in the main lobby area. Wow, pregnancy must wreak havoc on a woman's hunger because Michelle was doing something criminal to a Kit Kat bar and some cheese n crackers. I began telling the ladies selected pieces of Sean's and my conversation. I felt that they didn't need to hear everything, so I just told them what I thought they needed to know. After hearing that Sean was only going to do six months brought a temporary sense of relief to Aunt Kate. You could tell that she, like any mother would rather not have her son behind bars at all. I think Michelle was happy that he only received six months also. She said that the sooner he comes home the better she would feel. Looking at my aunt, I think she felt the same.

CHAPTER FIVE

One step forward... Two steps back

SEAN HAD MISSED a lot during his six months in jail. The basketball team wasn't the same without its star point guard. Without Sean's scoring ability, it turned out to be the first year in the school's history that we didn't make the state finals. When the word got out about Sean's situation, the college scouts stopped coming to the games. They also lost interest in Sean. He now projected a bad image. Left with no scholarship possibilities, no college offers and no school that would even take him as a walk on. He became blacklisted, but even if all this hadn't happened, Sean still wouldn't be able to play basketball on any kind of competitive level for the rest of his life. Let me explain.

Three months into his sentence, Sean was on the yard of the prison playing a pickup game with some of the other inmates like he did every day since he went in. As they played a small crowd had formed around the court. Sean and another inmate named Anthony were showing out as if they were playing at Rucker's Park in Harlem. They were just embarrassing the other two guys that they were playing against. As you know...only the spectators like the showboating. It just doesn't sit well with the competitors. The following day, Sean and Anthony are out on the court again making an ass out of the other inmates. Anthony throws an alley-oop to Sean. He catches it and does a 180-degree slam- dunk. As Sean elevates into the air, one of the other inmates low bridges him. (Undercuts him while he's in the air) at the same time Sean begins to tumble. He's pulled violently to the ground and lies there moaning in pain until he is taken to the infirmary. We learned that Sean broke his ankle, cracked his kneecap, and tore the cartilage in his knee when he hit the ground. Now Sean is in a cast and is walking with crutches. With his hopes of playing again, being slim to none.

Ok...let's get back to what Sean might miss school wise as a senior. Possibly the Winter Ball, the second biggest dance of the year and maybe a few of the senior trips. He also might miss the graduation ceremony and may have to earn his diploma behind bars. He didn't get to see Michelle throughout most of her pregnancy although his mother did send him a few pictures and kept him well informed about her progress.

Michelle was well into the third trimester of her pregnancy. She was in her ninth month when Sean was released... and she was huge. Big enough that everyone thought she might be having twins. Sean got his chance to see how big Michelle had gotten when I brought him to the welcome home party Grann was throwing for him. Grann doesn't like huge numbers of people roaming through her house, so the party was restricted to family only. The house was pretty quiet until Sean and I came through the door. The yelling we suddenly heard came from my aunt Kate.

"Thank God. My baby's home!"

Then Michelle jumped in. "I've missed you too. (With her arms out) Come here Baby."

[Michelle has a tight grip on Sean]

Grann looked across the room with one hand on her hip and the other waving in the air. "All right you two...let's stop that. I'm not gonna have any of that public fornicating in my house. That's how that girl got all swollen like she is. Now, come on in here. It's time to eat."

Everyone came into the dining room for what looked like one of our family's holiday meals. We talked, we ate, but Sean remained quiet as he shoveled the food into his mouth. You could see that he hadn't had a good meal in six months. He just inhaled what was on his plate and continued to go back for more. I took a moment to look up from my own plate to see Uncle Robert standing in the dining room doorway. He lifted his hand, waved, and casually nodded his head to say hello. Then without saying a word, motioned to Sean to come over to him. Sean set his fork down, stood up and without his cane; he limped over to his dad. Uncle Robert opened his arms and embraced his son. I was stunned. I have never seen any kind of affection given to Sean by my uncle. I'M SHOCKED. As Uncle Robert held Sean, he was whispering into his ear. His words were as short as the hug he gave before he led his son into the kitchen.

"How's the knee son?"

"It's painful at times, but it's getting better dad."

"That's good. Good. (Pauses) Now I want you to listen to me, cause I could see how hungry you are, and I don't want to keep you from your plate. Look Sean, I want you to come by the shop tomorrow. We need to discuss a few important things. Be there around 11 o'clock. [Lights a cigar] Don't be late."

(Speaking softly)

"Yes Sir."

"Tell your grandmother that I'll be by tomorrow...and tell your mom I'll be home by ten."

As uncle Robert strolled out the back door, Sean carried out his instructions then buried his face back into his plate. Only lifting his head to breath, blow kisses at Michelle and answer Grann's questions about his six months in jail. Overall, the homecoming dinner with Sean was great... despite hearing about the overwhelming realism of prison life. After Sean finished eating, we tried to catch him up on everything and everyone as we washed the dishes and cleaned the kitchen. I don't know why Sean became angry about it. Just because Grann was happy, he was home didn't mean that she would change the things she has always made us do. As we cleaned, he was surprised how much weight Michelle had put on. Especially considering how thick her ankles had become. I could hear Michelle calling Sean from the living room, but he kept talking to me and ignored her. After the third call of his name, he slowed down his words then waved his hand as if to say that she could wait.

"Boy!" Grann yelled, "Don't you hear this girl calling you?"

Sean appeared at the kitchen door to find Grann standing in the dining room. Michelle was sitting in the living room with her legs up on the couch.

"How many times does that girl have to call you? I know it doesn't take that long for you to limp in here and find out what she wants."

"I was on my way Grann."

"Boy, you tell them lies to someone dumb enough to swallow 'em but for now...you go in that freezer, get that girl some ice cream and then you and Raymond hurry up and get out of my kitchen. I don't want to hear this girl complain anymore about her ankles, her swollen feet, or her hunger. You bring her what she needs to keep quiet until it's time to go."

Sean did what he was told and quickly came back to the kitchen. When we finished, we joined Michelle and Aunt Kate in the living room while Grann rocked in her chair on the porch. Sean sat next to Michelle and rubbed her belly after trying to rub out the pain in her feet. You could see the proud parents they were going to be as I watched them tease and play with each other. Aunt Kate broke up the party right after the Wheel of Fortune went off. As Sean helped Michelle to his mother's car, I told him again that I was glad he was home and before he got into the car himself, he tapped the roof of the car, pointed at me, and said, "I'm glad about it too."

[The next day]

Unck owned this building or structure that took up one city block. It used to be an old potato chip factory in its hay-day. When the factory went under the old owner boarded up the windows, locked the doors and left it to rot. Uncle Robert got the building from the owner's son. Here's how it went down. The original owner left the building to his son after he died. The son signed over the deed to my uncle in order to settle a debt. Unck began his renovation by letting an up-and-coming potato chip factory take all the equipment that they needed. Once the building was clear, Unck had a company gut out the inside and begin the renovation. Half of the building was split into three sections. The first section took up half of the block and was turned into a thriving auto body shop called, "Papa B's Rides". The next two sections took up the rest of the block. The second section was made into a sports bar and grill named, "The Popped Cherry". The bar is doing very well with the lunch and the dinner crowds coming in. The third section of that side of the block is still undeveloped. He could never decide what to do with the other half of the building, so he just uses it for storage. I've noticed my uncle enjoys watching the guys who work in his shop spend the money he has just paid them drinking in his bar. It was like recycling his own cash. My uncle Robert knows how to hustle. Realistically...it is the two thriving businesses that make Uncle Robert a respected businessman in this city. It also helps him cover up the most profitable way he earns his money.

It was a rainy Friday morning as Uncle Robert looked up from his desk and watched his son hobble into the shop from his car. "Take a seat, I'll be back in a minute", Uncle Robert told Sean. Unck left his desk and headed straight for his shop manager. Unck gave him some instructions and called into his office to Sean. "Sean. Come walk next door to the bar with me." As they walked in, the bartender handed Unck a cup of coffee and asked Sean if he wanted anything.

"Have a seat son. (Pauses) Look...here it is in a nutshell. I'm going to keep you inactive for a little while. We've got to let your injuries heal before I let you get back to work."

The bartender sets Sean's hot chocolate onto the table as his father continues talking.

"More importantly, I've been told that there's been threats from Ronnie Ron's people. I'm afraid they may want some payback. I'm not worried about his close-knit crew, it's his loose cannon little nephews that concerns me. They're both hot headed and trigger-happy. Those things combined with the fact that they are reckless are cause for concern.

"So, what do you want me to do?"

"NOTHING! I want you to lay low and take it easy. Run some errands for your grandmother (sips his coffee) and look after your girlfriend. Stay clear of all our money spots until we can get our version of the truth out there or get Ronnie's nephews off the streets. I'll let you know when things are clear. (Sips coffee again) My guys are pulling your car into the last stall inside the garage and covering it up. I want you to take the black Nissan Altima that's out on the lot. Drive it! It's not as flashy as your 67' mustang and should help you go unnoticed. I want you to keep a low profile until this thing blows over. Am I clear?"

"Crystal clear pops."

Two days had gone by, and Sean had been following his dad's instructions without a hitch. There still had been no word about Ronnie Ron's nephews. Although Sean didn't seem concerned about them anyway. He had mentioned something about learning not to live in fear. I knew that was a crock because Sean called me three days straight nagging me to come with him and Michelle to pick up some baby furniture. So out of pure frustration I gave into his pleas and agreed to go. When Sean arrived to pick me up, you could hear the loud music from the car inside the house. Apparently when he drove up, he didn't notice Grann sitting on the porch. I could hear Grann yelling at him as soon as he stepped out of the car.

"Turn that music down and hobble your dumb ass over here. Boy, what have I told you about coming over here wit that music up loud like that!"

"I'm sorry Grann. It... It... won't happen again."

"Boy, I don't need you to be sorry. I want you to stop that shit. (Speaking loudly) Do...You...Understand me?"

"Yea Ma'am."

[Grann yelling]

"Raymond! Raymond! Hurry up out here. Sean's ready to go."

Grann leaned back and continued to rock in her chair. When I finally came out the front door, Sean greeted me with his customary head nod then began to head back to the car.

"Thanks for ridin' with me Rizz. I could not do this without you man. Michelle's been a handful. The baby keeps her cranky."

"I heard that Sean, I'm not cranky. Now hurry up and let's go. We need to stop and get something to eat. I'm hungry."

"That's cool Hun, I'll get you something when I stop for some gas."

Sean started the car and waited to get around the corner before he turned the music back up. When the coast was clear... he blasted it.

[Michelle yelling]

"WILL YOU TURN THAT SHIT DOWN? DAMN! IT'S GIVING ME a HEADACHE. TURN IT DOWN!"

So, with a frustrated reluctance, Sean extended his arm and turned the radio down. Then gave me a glance through the rearview mirror and said, "You see what I'm talking about Rizz?"

"Don't start with me Sean Kingsley Reynolds. I'm hungry, I'm not in the mood for your bullshit and we need to get this done. So, don't start any SHIT with me today."

[Sarcastically]

"Yes Dear." (As he looked into the mirror at me winking and smiling)

[Still angry]

"You can keep being a smart ass if you want to, but you are trying my patience."

Suddenly Sean wiped the smirk off his face and began concentrating on where he was headed. "Where you going cuzzo?" I asked. He told me that he was going to make a left and go to the gas station on Attwell Avenue. This was one of the city's busiest gas stations. So consequently, it was also one of the biggest, housing fifteen pumps and a mini mart. It used to be a Chevron but somehow became independently owned. Almost seems like it happened overnight. I think it's called "Gas n Go" or the "Fuel Depot" now. Well anyway, ever since it became an independent and lowered the prices for gas, this place stays crowded. Sean drove in and stopped next to the center pump on the last row of pumps. I think it was pump number ten. Yeah, it was because we were on the side closest to the street. After stopping abruptly, Sean slammed the car into park and quickly hopped out. "Hey! Don't forget to get me something to snack on," Michelle shouted. Sean just nodded and headed into the Snack Shack. I stepped out of the car to stretch my legs a little bit. Small cars are sometimes uncomfortable for tall guys like me. I turned and noticed an old guy struggling with the computerized gas pump. So, I went over to see if I could lend a hand while Sean was still inside.

(Shouting)

"Rizz! Rizz! Come here. Quick, come here!"

I peeked around the old guy and noticed Michelle waving frantically for me to come to her. I finished setting the old guy's pump and walked over to the passenger side of the car where Michelle was sitting. "What's up Miche..." (As she cuts me off.)

"Rizz, can you go tell Sean to bring some Oreo cookies?"

"All you want are some cookies. I thought you were hungry?"

"Well...make sure he gets me something to drink."

"Aw right."

As I turned to make my way to Sean, he was just coming out of the Snack Shack. I stopped where I was so that he would have to keep coming towards me. As he got closer, I noticed that he suddenly had a frightened expression on his face. He yelled, "OH SHIT!" As I rotated to face the street, everything and everyone began to move in slow motion. I saw that an old 1969 Lincoln Continental had abruptly stopped in the middle of the street. The cars suicide doors flew open and immediately bullets began to fly. But before I ducked behind the first car that I hoped would shield me from the bullets, I saw Sean drop the bag of snacks and pull a Glock 9mm handgun from the small of his back and begin to return fire. I'm not sure if any shots hit because we had to take cover quickly. I yelled, "No Sean, not there!" as he ducked behind one of the gas pumps. I could hear the bullets cutting through the air and violently striking the objects around me. The tires of the car I was hiding behind were going flat as the slug's ripped holes through them. Glass sounded like it was shattering all around us. I heard the man I was helping earlier shriek. Then I heard a big thump as if his body hit the ground just behind his car.

"SHIT! SHIT! Rizz, can you see 'em?" Sean yelled.

I looked over at Sean and answered by shaking my head "no". I tried to peek over the fender of the car. Hoping to see which direction the guys were shooting from, I hesitated to look around. I was afraid I would put myself into the line of fire if I moved. The bullets were loud. The sound of them slamming into the metal around us reminded me of the opening scene of the movie "Saving Private Ryan". Sean was aimlessly sticking his gun out, pulling the trigger, shooting blindly, hoping to hit something. I began to hear sirens faintly in the distance. Then suddenly... the rapid fire of bullets stopped. And then, (bang) (silence) (Bang- bang) I heard shots fire that sounded as if they came from separate guns. I didn't hesitate this time. I had to peek. When I looked over the fender of the car that I was hiding behind, there was a guy standing at the side of the car where Michelle was, holding a pistol in each hand. When he saw me, he turned his guns on me. As I ducked, I didn't hear the guns fire. Just the firing pins clicking because he was out of bullets. Realizing that his gun was empty, the guy ran and jumped into the Lincoln as it began to speed away. This is when things seemed to return to a normal speed.

I hollered in Sean's direction, "OH SHIT... SHE'S BEEN HIT! SEAN, MICHELLE'S BEEN HIT!"

Sean begins pacing in a small circle cursing.

"SHIT...FUCK... ***DAMN IT!!!****"*

I'm already at the car frustratingly signaling Sean.

*"****Fuck****, Sean...get over here!"*

Sean dropped his gun near the gas pump that he had been hiding behind and ran over to the car. Michelle was slumped over in the front seat. She had blood around the corner of her mouth and was taking crisp, short breaths. Sean lifted her upright and was trying to get Michelle to respond to him. She just looked at him and continued to take those short breaths. Sean yells out, "Somebody get some help!" A stranger from the crowd responded, "Don't worry, help is on the way." Michelle's breathing began to slow down. "Stay with me baby," Sean said, "Help is on the way." Michelle looked at Sean, reached for his hand and began to rub her stomach with it. Then placed that same hand over her heart. She patted her chest twice and then put her hand over his heart. She gazed into his eyes, short of breath and said, "I love you." Then she made one huge gasp before she stopped breathing. ***"Come on baby...come on baby, don't leave me****," Sean screamed, but she never moved. She didn't respond. Some guy standing close to the car began saying how her last breath was actually her spirit leaving her body.*

"She's not coming back. "When something violent happens, the spirit needs to be free. (Looks around) Um huh, he's got to let her go."

*"****I don't want to hear that shit!****" Sean shouted. Withstanding that guy's comments and Sean still speaking to Michelle, I moved out of the way, so the paramedics could go to work on Michelle. As I stepped out of the way, I noticed that the police were already collecting evidence and speaking to witnesses. Michelle was now on a gurney with Sean at her side. The*

ambulance raced away (if you believe ambulances move that fast) while the EMT'S worked to revive Michelle.

With Michelle and Sean heading towards the hospital, the police questioned me while they continued collecting evidence. After they were done with me, I sent a 9-1-1 page to my uncle who then came and quickly picked me up. As we drove to the hospital, I told him every detail I could remember along the way. He reached to turn off the radio; puffed on his cigar and told me I had his undivided attention. We rode for blocks without my uncle uttering a word and then he surprisingly pulled the car over next to a bus stop.

"Is that all? Is that everything you can remember Rizz?"

"No. (Swallowing the lump in my throat) There is something else."

(In an unsure tone)

"Uh-Huh"

"Sean dropped his gun at the scene and the police picked it up before I could get to it."

Uncle Robert's expression remained blank. He looked into the rearview mirror, tossed his cigar onto the street and bent the corner with an unexpected urgency that I have never seen from him. Although I saw no anger, no visual signs of concern, I would look over at him occasionally, but like I said...his expressions never changed. I watched him lean back into the plush seat of his Cadillac, hang his arm over the door as he continued bending corners until we reached the emergency side of the hospital. When we stepped into the emergency room, it felt like we were stepping into the most dramatic scene of a made for TV movie. Doctors, nurses, patients, and my aunt Kate were all creating an increased amount of hysterics. We stepped into the lobby and heard two ladies screaming simultaneously.

"OH GOD...THEY TOOK MY SON!!", Aunt Kate yells.

Ms. Capshaw is attempting to yell over Aunt Kate while trying to speak to the nurse.

"NURSE...WHERE'S MY BABY? ARE YOU HELPING MY DAUGHTER?"

Ms. Capshaw is Michelle's mom and Michelle is an only child. And let me tell you, between Ms. Cap (that's what Sean and I call her) and Aunt Kate...things became intense.

"Ma'am, the doctor's in with your daughter now." The nurse says to Ms.

Capshaw.

"I need to see my daughter. Right Now! RIGHT NOW!"

"Ma'am. Ma'am, please have a seat. The doctor will be with you as soon as he can."

Aunt Kate was now shouting at Uncle Robert at the same time the nurse was trying to speak to Ms. Capshaw.

"They came up in here and snatched OUR boy. TOOK HIM! Pushed him into the wall, handcuffed him and dragged him away. FOR WHAT? Nobody has told me anything. JUST HELD ME OUT THE WAY AND TOOK HIM!"

Uncle Robert reached out, took Aunt Kate by her hands and spoke very softly to her.

"I need you to calm down Kate. I'm having trouble following you. Please, come sit over here and tell me what happened."

"Sean called me from the ambulance and sounded really upset. I happened to be right down the street from here. They were just bringing Michelle inside when I drove up. Sean and I came inside and gave the admitting clerk some information. A few minutes later an officer walked in, and the clerk pointed him in our direction. He said his name was Officer Harmon and that he needed to ask us a few questions. (Pauses) Robert, that man didn't ask me SHIT! He focused on Sean baby...and Sean only. You know how they do! Ask you questions, then half ass listen to your answers. Every time Seam would try to answer him, the officer would put his ear to his shoulder. Trying to hear what was being said on that DAMN radio of his.

So, when he was done playing with his radio, he looked up and asked Sean what his name was again. I mean he just kept repeating the same questions. The cop wasn't even paying attention each time Sean would try to respond."

Uncle Robert leaned a bit closer to Aunt Kate, so she could speak directly into his ear. He was having a hard time hearing her because of all the noise Michelle's mom was making. Ms. Capshaw paced up and down the floor, clinching and balling up her fists. Occasionally chanting, Oh Lord, My Baby. How's my baby?" When Ms. Capshaw shouted out, she spoke rapidly and would repeat herself over & over. I noticed she was holding onto the cross that she was wearing around her neck. Pushing it up towards the heavens with both hands and mumbling to herself. This behavior continued until the doctor finally arrived. All the voices became quiet as the doctor walked into the room.

Ms. Capshaw slowly lowered her cross but still held onto it tightly between her two hands. Aunt Kate nervously grabbed Uncle Robert's arm as they both focused on the doctor. The doc came into the room with an expressionless look on his face and approached Ms. Capshaw. Motionless. That's how everyone was. I stepped behind Ms. Capshaw just as the doctor told everyone that Michelle didn't make it. Good thing that I did, because Ms. Cap threw her arms into the air and fell backwards. The doctor and I were able to keep her from hitting the floor. She looked like she was out cold. The doctor began to check her vitals. My aunt left my uncle's side and began to hysterically shout questions at the doctor.

"OH MY GOD. OH MY GOD! What about Michelle's baby? WHAT ABOUT THE

BABY?"

Another nurse brought a wheelchair into the room and the doctor and I set Ms. Capshaw into the chair. The doctor instructed the nurse to take her to an examining room until she came to. He then turned and continued to address everyone else.

"I will take a moment to answer what I can. Miss. Capshaw [Michelle], (pauses)

came in under duress but was still breathing. We began doing what we could to revive her but her vitals became dangerously low for the survival of the baby.

We did a c-section to save the child. Miss. Capshaw held on long enough for us to retrieve the child. It was just after that when we lost Miss

Capshaw. (Pauses) The baby is breathing. The baby is healthy...and it is a girl."

The Doctors words began to fade and at some point, I hadn't heard anything more of what he was saying to my aunt and Uncle. My attention turned to thoughts of why any of this had to happen. I was playing the entire incident back in my head. Wondering if there was anything I could have done to change the outcome of this afternoon. That's all I did was wonder. I stood motionless in the emergency room with hands in my pockets, my head hanging sorrowfully and my thoughts shouting louder than the disruption and despair that was happening all around me. Grann would speak sometimes about how fast our lives can change for the worst. She would say, "Baby, pain comes unexpectedly. It's swift and unkind. Strength comes from overcoming it and there's no way you get stronger from it if you know it's coming."

Suddenly my thoughts screamed out the obvious. That Sean might go back to jail and how Michelle will never see her baby grow up. I stood there frozen. I stood helpless. My thoughts...were thoughts of wasted lives and squandered opportunities. Of how I could have and should have made some kind of a difference today. I stood engulfed in the suffering of two families, unable to comfort either one. I stood thinking about my own fate, my own destiny. Affected by my own indecision and how things are complicated by the reality of my family, their lives, and the imposing danger of being related. I just stood there... thinking how useless I felt.

CHAPTER SIX

Strained Relations

GRADUATION CAME AND went with Sean still behind bars. My Uncle was a no-show to watch me walk across the stage, but Grann and Aunt Kate were there to see me get my diploma. About a week after our graduation, a bunch of us got together and went to visit with Sean. Once we were there, we all could not go in at the same time, so we entertained each other until we got a chance to see him. Kevin brought his Yearbook and pictures from the graduation to share with Sean. Justin and Eric, who were both on the basketball team with Sean, tried to explain how the team lost the state finals without him. I made sure that I went in last. I knew my visit with him would take up a lot of time. We began with our normal hellos and then he started in with the questions. He began asking about Ronnie Ron's cousins and wanted to know if they had been caught yet. He told me that it didn't make a difference whether they were caught by the police or by his father's people. Sean did mention however that he preferred street justice over the court system. I asked him why and he replied, "The courts just drag shit out. Street justice is swift." Sean stopped speaking for a moment and seemed to be staring off into space. "Are you alright?" I asked.

"Uh, (pauses) yeah I'm fine. So... what kind of justice was there?"

"Nothing has happened at all...not yet. Ronnie Ron's cousins haven't been caught. They've gone into hiding. They've disappeared."

(In an angry whisper)

"That's fucked up."

Sean sat with a sad but angry expression on his face, barely moving his head. Although his eyes moved all over the room until he looked back at me.

"So... what's my dad doing about it?"

I responded in an equally frustrated tone. "Man, I don't know. Whatever it is

Sean, he's not telling me. If I hear something...I'll let you know."

(In a solemn voice)

"And how was the funeral?"

I watched him get a bit misty as I went into as much detail as he could handle. As I spoke, you could see the pain welling up inside him. It was hard to look at him. It was tough to keep talking about it, so I found a way to change the subject.

"Hey... your mom asked me to give these to you."

I reached into my pocket and handed Sean a few pictures of his daughter. He said with surprise in his voice, "This is my baby girl?" I nodded "yes" as he flipped through the photos. He had a proud expression and an even bigger smile on his face.

"Can I keep these?"

"Yeah Sean, those are for you. Your Mom sent them for ya."

"WOW cousin, she's beautiful. (He pauses) So... who's takin' care of her?"

I didn't speak right away. Mostly because I was unsure how I should explain things to him. Sean noticed my hesitation and slowly raised his head from looking at the pictures to see why. It took me a moment to get my thoughts together. I wanted the details to be specific. I began by telling Sean how Ms. Capshaw fell out in the hospital and how she had to be looked after for a couple of hours. I told him that his mom was told that the baby would be held a few more days than usual, mainly for observational purposes. This was due to the traumatic birth. It was a day or two before the hospital released the baby. I was unfamiliar with the procedures or whether there was any paperwork even filled out. The only thing I knew for sure... was that the baby was released to the maternal grandmother, Ms. Capshaw.

[Tapping his fingers on the table]

"Hang on a sec cousin, you keep referring to my baby girl as YOUR daughter or the baby. Does my baby girl have a name? and who named her?"

"OH SHIT! Damn, I thought I told you the baby's name."

"No cousin, you haven't."

"I'm sorry. It's Cheyanne Janey Reynolds. Ms. Cap came up with your daughter's first name and your mom provided her middle one. Everyone just calls her Cee-Jay though. It's her new family nickname. You know how it is, everyone gets a nickname."

"You would know more about that than I would. RIZZ!"

"Don't be jealous. Anyway...I don't know about the legal aspects of things, but what I can say is that Ms. Cap somehow was given custody of Cee-Jay after

Michelle died. So, for now she's taking care of your baby girl."

A security guard interrupted everyone. Announcing that there were only five minutes left before visiting time was over. Sean wasted three of them asking about his dad, his daughter, and then squeezed in a few other subjects that I didn't have enough time to answer with any detail. Now with visiting time over, Sean headed back to his cell. But before he hit the door he yelled, "Hey cousin, we'll finish where we left off next time." He then pounded his fist to his chest two times, gave me his usual head nod and then he disappeared from view.

[Days later]

I felt so isolated, confined, and slighted while Sean was in jail. Not just this time, but also during his first arrest. There was no one to talk to and no one to hang out with. Without Sean, it just left the adults of the family. Uncle Robert only spoke with Grann when it was necessary, so you can image how much he spoke with me. I have said before that I think my uncle avoids me, but it doesn't bother me as much as it used to. When it comes to my grandmother...she's reminiscent of most inner-city elderly who take on the responsibility of raising other people's children. Ok, what I'm trying to say is that I know Grann loves me but there is no closeness. It doesn't seem like the same thing that Sean shares with his parents. Grann has always provided the things that I've needed but somehow seems a bit distant. Oh, she would yell at me from time to time but most of the things that I have learned, I've learned from trial and error. On the brighter side of things, the seclusion has helped me sharpen my instincts. I'm thankful for that. Sean is often spoiled and seems to be babied a bit by my aunt and overprotected by his Dad. Some days I can't decide if I'd rather be in Sean's shoes or be thankful for the serene isolation.

It was late afternoon, and I was sitting on the porch gazing out at nothing. Focused on my daydream. Grann had just come out onto the porch to have a seat. As she started rocking, she began to speak to me about my future. She mentioned how it had been a couple of months since I graduated and that I was wasting my life sitting around here gazing into the air every day. She told me I had to decide what I was going to do with my life, then get to it.

"Raymond, I remember when I was coming up and my momma, your great grandmother, seemed to always be upset with my daddy quite a bit. He came home every day smelling like the fields. Working hard, so another man could collect good money on my daddy's hard work. Momma used to ask him why he worked so hard on another man's land. Especially since he had enough land to make money for himself. Sometimes at supper he would tell mamma that this was the last harvest he would work for that old farmer Mr. Patrick. He would sit there stewing over his plate nearly every night and talk about how he planned to make some good money with his own land. I watched how angry she got night after night listening to my dad give her

detailed plans on something that he would never get started on. Then one night she told him that he would never get anything done with his ass stuck to that chair. Told him to get started doing something or stop complaining. Every year my folks argued over his reasons for not getting things going and eventually momma got tired of hearing it season after season. I watched how she bottled up her frustrations as she tried to feed and clothe my three brothers and me. I never understood why she stayed so quiet when it all bothered her so much...I never understood that. (Adjusts herself in her chair) The very next year my daddy was still working Mr. Patrick's fields and momma was keeping us in the house because of how unbearably hot the sun was that summer. It was around noon when momma went to call him in for lunch but walked out and found him dead in the field. He died and never farmed anything more than pretty grass on his own property. Long story short Raymond...we struggled after he was gone and somehow, I feel it never had to be that way. As I grew up, I decided to never let an opportunity to better myself get away from me or for that matter, my situation either. I vowed I wouldn't let my children sit around contemplating or squandering any opportunities and I won't let you sit around and do it either."

I remember her specifically saying that she wanted me to find a job or get back into school. She told me that my days would not be spent on her porch gazing at nothing or falling into the same fate that Sean has. She mentioned that I was old enough to take care of myself and that's exactly what she expected me to do. Grann rocked back and forth in her chair saying, "Your future starts ta-marra, you hear me. You can't move ahead in life with your ass stuck to a chair." Grann repeated that statement twice. She made her feelings clear and assured me that I was bright enough to make the right choices. She made it perfectly clear that I needed to move quickly because time will not wait for me to do something with my life. She repeated, "Time will move with you... or without you. It's up to you not to let it pass you by."

CHAPTER SEVEN

New beginnings/Old Pains

MY LIFE GRADUALLY changed over the next couple of years. I still went to visit Sean when I could, but I seemingly began to grow apart from the rest of my family. I moved out of Grann's house and moved into the house that was left vacant when my parents died. As a small gesture towards my independence, Grann had Uncle Robert send some guys over to repair the front porch, the loose floorboards, some electrical wiring and every broken window on the house. She told me that this was her gift to me. It's a house-warming gift. Her reasoning was simple; she said that I helped restore the silence that she's always loved when I left her house. Still... however humorous she sounded; I knew she meant every word. "Raymond, you will learn how the silence of your home will shield the disruption that this world can cause.", she began. "Listen to me," she said, "You'll grow fond of the peace you find, just like I have." Grann suggested that I find a spot in the house to shake off the dirt of the world and re-center myself. So, in honor of Grann's wisdom, I had the words: (Find Your Center) framed and hung over the entryway of my den. I didn't have much, but the house that once looked dead began to slowly regain life after a few months.

It felt good being out on my own. As my house grew to look better, my family saw less of me. I kept my distance because I have been lying to Grann and Uncle Robert. I led them to believe that I had been attending the local college and supporting my tuition by working nights. Although truthfully...I was secretly studying police work at the academy. My distance from my family helped make my cover more believable. My uncle and Grann were both happy with my decision to further my education and staying clear of the family business. (Not that I was ever involved anyway) Surprisingly, hiding what I was really doing wasn't very easy. Especially when I go to the prison to visit with Sean. I didn't want him to see how my mannerisms were changing. I was a cadet now and was becoming more cop like every day. I knew acting cop-ish around Sean would raise some suspicions. I couldn't risk having that pipeline run directly back to my uncle and spoil what I was trying to accomplish. So, I tried to be my old self when I went to see Sean. Showing the homeboy, street image that he was used to seeing in me. But after watching Sean walking, I noticed that I wasn't the only one changing.

I sat at this circular table in a heavily guarded room waiting for Sean to pop out. As he emerged from the doorway, I noticed Sean had a different motion, more of a swagger in his walk. His mannerisms were a bit rougher and the look in his eyes was surprisingly different. They commanded more respect. He seemed confidently unafraid of the other inmates. Unlike the first time he went in. He no longer appeared to be the Momma's boy that he once was. He still walked with a limp but looked more mobile than before. "Don't get up cousin," he said as he sat down. He wore a goatee now but still wears his hair cut low to his head.

"Look at you cousin...What happened? Did you get hooked up with a cell-block make-over or what?"

(Holding one hand in front of his face)

"Oh shit, you got jokes!"

"We'll look at ya Sean, something's different."

"Cousin, I'm exercising my potential to evolve. Finding that guy in me that I never knew. Ya know?"

"Ok, that must be some of that old jail house bullshit. Anyway...what's going on wit-cha Sean? Are you alright?"

"Couldn't be better."

Sean leaned forward, motioning me to lean forward also across the table. He began to tell me about how all the prisons were overcrowded. How they were stacking three inmates into a cell that normally housed two. The word on the cellblock was that the state might begin to set some inmates free. Basically, any of the people they considered low risk criminals. Every inmate is waiting to see if they are eligible. Hoping for an early release. This process may take a while but that's because of all the cases that the state has been working through, and they aren't working fast. "I've got as good of a shot as anybody else." Sean replied with an unworried look on his face. I asked him what he had been doing with his time now that he couldn't play basketball anymore. "Rizz, I've been getting schooled," he said. I sat quietly, surprised as I listened, looking confused. "Schooled at what?" I wondered. What could he possibly be learning? So, I asked him. Sean mentioned that he had been moved to a new cell about a month ago. The move happened shortly after his mother's last visit. He had been complaining both about his cell and his cellmate to his mother. So, then his mom went home and chewed my uncle's ear off about her son's accommodations. Unofficially, Uncle Robert made some phone calls and somehow Sean was being moved to a low security cellblock. This wing of the prison is designated for the white collared criminals and ex-police officers who are serving time.

Sean's new cellmate was an ex-1970's pimp/hustler who is also a recovering PCP addict. He's 6ft tall, 155lbs and wears a frizzed -out perm. Normally he wears it combed towards the back of his head and it is usually streaked with very thick grease. He loved to smoke cigars but never discriminated from any forms of tobacco. He'd puff on a pipe, chewed tobacco, even rolled his own cigarettes. When he talked to somebody, he would often hold the cigar in-between his fingers and point it at you when he spoke. He is also a man of very few words. It was his actions that spoke the loudest. On the streets he is known as "Slicky-Bo", but in prison he's known simply as Slicky 4-1-1. Slicky is the best, the only pipeline for information inside and outside the prison and he is paid well for it. He has transformed many of the racial barriers in the prison. Information is important. Important enough that any prisoner, outsider, guards, or wardens will come to this man because he knows what they want to know. And he may tell them...especially if the price is right.

Now that Sean has become Slicky-Bo's cellmate, Sean has become part of the prison information superhighway. And incidentally, that commands more respect than other inmates used to give him. According to Sean, it all wouldn't have happened without some training from Slicky.

Slicky was sitting in a chair reading when Sean first entered the cell. Slicky looked over the top of his glasses and in a soft tone, welcomed Sean to his new digs (home/cell). "He's a down to earth dude. He's easy to talk to and easy to learn from," said Sean. He mentioned that he had learned to play chess. It's one of the first things Slicky taught him. The game is all about strategy. It teaches patience and how to play against your opponent, not just the board. You would often see them both playing a lot of card games. Mostly poker. Slicky proclaims that both games are good tools for teaching anyone about strategies, but with poker you must rely on more than just the luck of the cards. Slicky's buddy Jimmy Donte would keep repeating that the game of poker is the best way to learn how to tell which of your opponents is just full of shit. You must watch mannerisms and try to pick up on the other tell signs. I mean when they're trying to bluff. Looking for any edge while trying not to give anything away yourself. Poker teaches how to recognize who's bluffing, while honing your skills on how to fool others. Both games, Chess and Poker were essential first lessons for Sean.

Just weeks after Sean moved into a cell with Slicky-Bo, Sean was forced to use what he had learned from Slicky so far. Sean was telling me how this cocky, six- foot, 235-pound muscular inmate had approached him. A man who apparently woke that morning and decided that he had a problem with Sean. This bearish sized inmate came across the exercise yard, right up in front of Sean as he and Slicky were talking. His name was Roderick, but he's best known as "Big Guns". If you're thinking he has that name because of the size of his arms, ok...then you would be half right. He first received his name because he became the biggest dealer of illegally sold military issued weapons. And not just the U.S. issued ones. It's said that he makes more money now than he did before he was put in prison.

Sean sat alongside Slicky in the courtyard and watched as Big Guns approached. He was alone, but someone his size doesn't need an entourage. A one-man gang, who is respected and feared. His head eclipsed the sun, and his anger is evident in his glare. "Ronnie Ron tells me that you're R. Kingsley's son," he began to say. "I also know that your father was principally responsible for the loss of a big chunk of hardware and money I was expecting. So, here's what's gonna happen youngster...You and I are going to decide how ***you're*** *gonna pay both me and Ronnie Ron back for our losses. Are you wit me? Or...I'm gonna have to whoop that ass every day until you're released or until I recuperate from my losses. So, what's it gonna be youngster?" Sean said that he never moved. He looked up at Big Guns and calmly said, "I think your walk over here was a waste of your time. There will be no payout to you or anyone else. There is no chance in hell that it will ever happen."*

"Tell me, please tell me you're joking with me youngster? Before I put my foot up your ass." He angrily yelled.

Sean tapped Slicky on his arm, and then arose from his seat. Uncharacteristic of Sean, he approached this angry mammoth and began to use what he had learned from Slicky.

"Ok, let's make a deal. Here it is, I'll prove my family had nothing to do with you losing any product or money."

Big Guns clinch's his fists and took a step towards Sean.

"Whoa!!! Now wait a minute big man. Hear me out for a moment. Big Fella, you have been mis-informed. I can prove that Ronnie Ron has been stealing your product and your profits. Here's what they do...(pauses) Ronnie Ron and his nephews highjack your shipment before it can reach the regular drop point, then Ronnie undercuts you on the price. He sells ***your*** *weapons to the original buyer that you lined up at the cheaper price. That's how he's doing it man. Like I said, he has his nephews intercept it and when your regular guy finally shows up, he must explain to Ronnie how the shipment was jacked. Not knowing that Ronnie's people did the jacking. Think about the times he has told you about the missing shipment and how he's working on the problem."*

"You think trying to sell out Ronnie Ron is going to save your ass? This sounds like some bullshit to me. A lot of talk and no proof."

"I don't have to prove anything. You can find out the truth for yourself. Have your people check out the garage over on 1087 Hesston Lane and that will tell us who's ass will need savin'. (Pauses) Here's my offer big fella. Take a moment and check my story out. If what I've told you is bullshit, then I will find a way to make things right with you. But...If I'm right, then I would ask for a favor from you as a gesture of your gratitude."

"Ok, Junior. You've got me a bit curious. It won't take long for me to check this out. You've got twenty-four hours, and then we will see if your shit swims or sinks. Twenty-four. Ya here me junior?"

Sean stood there smirking and watching as Big Guns walks away. He told me that Slicky was smiling at him as he came to sit back down. [Sean looking at Slicky] "What?" Sean said. "What's the smile for?"

"I want you to tell me what the four most important principles of dealing information are." Slicky asked.

Sean put his hand to his chin and took a moment to think before he began to speak. "First, your source of information must be reliable. Second, what is the information worth? Third, who is the information worth the most too? And last...how long can I benefit from it?" Slicky sat, looking at Sean, shaking his head up and down and said, "You're right. You're right. Now apply what you know. (Stops to puff his cigarette) Looking at what just happened, are you at all concerned about the big fella returning?" Sean leaned back into his chair, folded his arms behind the back of his head and crossed his legs. Showing he is seemingly unconcerned by Big Guns. "I look at it like this," Sean began to say, "He's gonna learn the truth just as soon as his goons open that garage. Once it gets back to him, the rest will take care of itself. He won't be concerned with me at all. If he does come back, it will only be for more information. That's when what I know becomes more valuable to the big fella."

"Good." Replied Slicky. "You have learned something these past few months."

I sat in front of Sean, watching his mouth move but I hadn't heard much of what he had been saying, maybe just bits and pieces. As he spoke, I was more pre-occupied with avoiding talking about all the things I have been up to. I kept asking Sean questions in hopes it would push him to continue telling his story. He shortly soon began to rush things a bit in order to finish his story before visiting time ended. So, the last thing he said before being escorted out was...that everything had worked out with Big Guns. The entire ordeal was now a dead issue. Everything Sean told Big Guns about Ronnie Ron robbing him was true and now he's negotiating with Sean for more information. More importantly, Sean says he wants to hear more from me the next time I come to visit. More about what I've been up too. But like I said about the last time I came to visit...as he exited, he gave me that head nod, pounded his chest and in just moments ...he was gone, and I was relieved.

CHAPTER EIGHT

Juggling Act

I BEGAN MY ROOKIE street training shortly after becoming a full-fledged police officer. I was partnered with a fifteen-year veteran who would teach me the ropes. Officer Kent Crosby was a middle aged, happily married, father of two, balding white man who took me under his wing. I had been the fifth rookie the department has put with him for training. Crosby (what he prefers to be called) doesn't believe in coddling any rookies. He believed that the best way to teach was to let us learn with hands on experience. So, he had me take lead on every call we answered. I took the lead for calling in our location and I was also first contact with the citizens. Crosby showed me the proper ways to complete or get around the paperwork. It went on like that for the two years riding with him. He quickly gained my respect.

As the days went on, I began noticing how some of the other white officers appeared to be a bit indifferent when it came to minorities. Crosby felt equally bothered with society, entirely. I never saw any prejudice towards any nationality from him. He seemed to be disgusted with everyone we encountered. He always said that ninety percent of the calls we answered were an incredible waste of time. "People are genetically stupid." He would say. "If people could learn to control their emotions, there wouldn't be a need for us to intervene. But then again... If people could be calm, rational, honest and peaceful...there would be no need for us to keep the peace." Crosby would spit out little gems like that all the time. The one I remember the most is what he told his wife every day before he left for his shift. Every day she would ask him what the most important thing he had to do that day was. He told me that his response was the same every day. He would tell her that the most important thing he had to do was to come home and kiss her goodnight before bed. He told her that nothing that happened throughout the day would keep him from that kiss. It's a promise he has kept for the fifteen years he has been on the force.

It was early into our shift when we began to patrol around the Rockport Galleria. A renovated auto plant that was recently completed two miles out on the south side of the city. It was one of those strange fall days where it was hotter than it should have been. We were instructed to patrol the mall during the first hour of our shift. This mall has had problems lately with groups of high school kids doing "Grab and runs". We were there to assist the mall security team and to act as a visual deterrent. The first hour of the shift was quieter than we had expected so Crosby decided that we would move on from the mall and continue with the rest of the territory that we were to patrol. I had started driving the squad car two weeks ago, just after Crosby bruised his right foot doing a repair in the basement of his house. He couldn't apply much pressure. Said that it still hurt terribly, even driving into work. I didn't mind driving; it was a new experience to me on this side of the car. We pulled out of the mall onto Rockport Drive, and we're almost hit by a burgundy Chevy Lumina that had just run through the red light. Immediately we pulled behind the vehicle and flashed our red light signaling for the car to pull over. When the car didn't, I turned on the siren and pulled up close behind the car. I watched a passenger in the backseat turn and look right at me. He must have told the driver that we were behind them because after traveling five extra blocks they finally decided to stop. As instructed by Crosby, I followed protocol. After both cars came to a stop, I opened my door and began talking on the loudspeaker as Crosby took a power position with his gun drawn. We took this approach for safety reasons. First, we had to assume that there was a suspicious reason that they would not pull over and until we ruled that out, we couldn't take any chances.

"Driver!" I began. "Turn off the car. Take the keys, put them in your left hand and stick your arms out of the window. (Waited for the driver to comply) Now, you, the guy in the passenger front seat...stick your arms out of the window and use your left hand to open the door. Slowly get out and kneel on the sidewalk with your hands behind your head. (I paused until he carried out my directions) Ok...You there in the backseat; it's your turn. Do the same thing your buddy just did. (I paused again) Driver, drop the keys on the ground, come out of the car and lay down on the street. (Looking to my right) Do you have the other two Cros?"

He answered, "Yes" as he began to limp towards the suspects kneeling on the sidewalk. I slowly approached the driver, told him not to move, pulled his hands behind his back and handcuffed him. As I stood him up to take him to the squad car, I heard the screeching of tires as a car came violently to a stop. When I looked around, I noticed the skidding was created by what looked like my aunt Kate's bright red Range Rover. I quickly and uncharacteristically as a police officer, turned my head and looked away from the truck. Making myself focus on getting this guy into the car and running his information.

"Raymond? (Almost loudly singing my name) Raymond! Is that you? Raymond!"

I never turned around. Hoping that if there was no physical response from me. Hoping that she might think she made a mistake and leave. She didn't leave; she sat there in the middle of the street and continued to yell out my name. As I ignored my aunt, an additional squad car pulled up and shaded me slightly from her view. I walked the driver over, leaned him against the car and searched him for weapons. I pulled a snub-nosed 38-caliber handgun from the small of his back. I removed a bag of marijuana and a switchblade, and then I set everything on the hood of the car. My aunt Kate was now outside of her truck, calling my name and heading in my direction. Officer Jeremy Ashley, who graduated from the academy with me intercepted her a fairly good distance from where I was patting down my suspect. I placed my suspect into the back of my squad car and Officer Ashley began to sternly tell my aunt to get back into her truck.

"Ma'am, you cannot stop your vehicle and hop out of it on a busy street."

"Officer!" She started as she pointed in my direction. "I think that's my nephew right over there. I need to speak with him."

"Not possible right now ma'am. I need you to get back into your truck and move it now! You are holding up traffic, and even if that officer were your nephew there would be no way he could speak with you right now. You will have to catch him later. So... please, get back into your vehicle and move it."

Aunt Kate tried to look around Officer Ashley a couple times, hoping to get a better look at me. I was now sitting in the car, trying to keep my head down as I called in the information of the driver we stopped. I sighed briefly in relief as she got back into her truck and drove off. As I watched the other officers dealing with the other two guys, my thoughts quickly became fleeting hopes that my aunt didn't recognize me. It would become an awkward situation if she knew I was a cop. There would be no way to stop her from telling everyone. My aunt is the biggest busybody I've ever encountered and apparently a skilled gossip as well. I don't need her throwing a wrench into my attempt to be successful in this profession.

Information was coming in on my suspect as Officer Ashley searched their car. Turns out that the man I have in custody is Jerome K. Watkins. Better known on the streets as "Lil Rome". The other two who were placed into the back of both Ashley's and Officer Mill's (Ashley's partner) car was Stanley Watkins and Melvin Wilburn. All three were cousins. I flashed back, remembering how Sean mentioned the Watkins brothers the last time I went to visit him. They were Ronnie Ron's nephews. Sean said that he had heard how they had possibly snuck back into town. Jerome was the only one of the three who had any priors and warrants. He was wanted on aggravated assault charges. He went missing after skipping out on bail. My first thought as Crosby approached the car to talk to me was... "We will definitely hold on to Jerome but will have to release the other two because they had no warrants and were only passengers". That's what we were discussing until Officer Ashley opened the trunk of their car. He waved us over and began to speak into the radio clipped to the shoulder of his uniform.

"Base this is unit three -two- seven."

"Go ahead Three-two -seven."

"Need an ambulance and a crime unit at the corner of 3201 Rockport Road."

"Copy that, Three-two-seven. Medical assistance is in route."

As Crosby and I joined Ashley at the rear of the suspects Chevrolet, we found two people bound and gagged in the trunk. A man and a woman who both looked to be in their mid-twenties. Their arms, legs and mouths were wrapped with duct tape and neither one was conscious. We documented what Officer Ashley found but didn't touch the people lying in the trunk until the paramedics arrived at the scene. It didn't take the EMT'S long to tell us what we had already suspected. They confirmed that the two in the trunk were both dead. Shortly after knowing that, our trafficstop quickly turned into a crime scene. The area was roped off and we turned over all evidence we collected. The suspects were moved to a paddy wagon and the new crime scene was turned over to the homicide department. We were finally dismissed from the scene and began to head in because our shift had ended three hours ago. As we headed in, Crosby began to tell me what he found out about the two-people found in the trunk. The girl was Christine Kennedy and the guy was Alex Dunbar. Christine had been dating Stanley

Watkins until he beat her up and she had him served with a restraining order. Alex Dunbar began dating Christine and had a few incidents with Stanley himself according to a few reports that were made. Then with a strange turn of fate, we pulled the Watkins boys over on a traffic violation and then found Christine and Alex in their trunk. Crosby was discussing how often he has had days like this one throughout his career. He keeps reminding me not to get emotionally involved. As he spoke, I was thinking back on that shootout in the gas station with Sean. I wasn't sure how I felt about catching the guys who might have possibly killed Michelle. I never saw any of the shooters faces that day so it's hard to feel anything either way. Just at that moment Crosby reminded me that I should keep my work life and my personal life separate. It's always better if you don't take this shit home with you every night.

I thought about Crosby's words during my drive home. I knew he was right. Seeing my aunt today made me wonder how I could keep my family and my work separate. I didn't have a choice. I have to keep those two worlds from colliding. I missed lunch today, so on my way home I pulled into this chicken place called "Flightless Wings" to pick up some dinner. As I was standing in line, I could hear my cell phone ringing.

"Hello."

"Hey nephew, where are you?"

"Oh, hey Uncle Robert. I'm over here at Flightless Wings picking up some dinner."

"Which one Rizz?"

"The one over on Webber Avenue."

"That's fine. Look, I'm two blocks away from and I need to talk to you. Stay put and I'll meet you over there."

"Ok Unck, I'll be in the parking lot."

[We both hang up]

I could feel the cold air attacking my face as I walked out of the restaurant. I could see my uncle pulling into the lot with the smoke from his cigar escaping through the slightly cracked window like smoke from a chimney.

"Get in the car for a minute nephew."

I opened the door to his Cadillac and slid in. I heard the song "Back Stabbers" playing on his radio. I noticed that Uncle Robert wasn't even wearing a jacket. He's been riding in his car with a thin shirt on. He had the climate control in his car set somewhere close to ninety degrees. Unck was always fonder of summer days. He never liked cold winters, hated the snow and more importantly hated driving his Cadillac out on days like this. He left the car running as I made myself comfortable.

"Let's not mince words nephew. I'm going to get straight to it. Your Aunt Kate called me and was all worked up this afternoon. Said she saw a cop that looked just like **you** *over near the Rockport Mall. Swears by her mother that it was you! (Puffs his cigar) Tell me nephew, got a new job that I should know about?"*

"No. I'm still working at my part time job in Safeway's main warehouse. That is until I can find a better paying job. I wasn't anywhere near the Rockport today."

"Kate told me it was pretty hectic out there. How many of your fellow officers were out there with you today?"

"Come on Unck, how would I know! Especially if I wasn't anywhere near the mall!"

"Just testing ya nephew. That usually works on your cousin. My mistake. I shouldn't have tried that with you. (Takes another puff) Alright Rizz, I believe you. (Pauses) And even after your aunt called me, she drove past your job to see if your car (my decoy car) was in the parking lot. That should have satisfied her, but it didn't. The things we see with our own eyes sometimes still aren't enough to give some folks the satisfaction they're looking for. (Under his breath) I don't know about the woman sometimes."

Uncle Robert paused just long enough to look at some guy who was passing in front of the car. I was holding my chicken close to the heater vent. I figured if I was breaking a sweat, then the heater was hot enough to keep my food warm. My uncle cleared his throat and brought his attention back to me. I assumed that the guy he was watching had passed because he was looking at me strangely. I wasn't sure if he was trying to figure out why I was holding my bag up to the heater vent or if I was lying to him.

"Ok nephew, we're done here. I'm taking you at your word. And Raymond... Your word is the only thing that stands between you and anyone trusting you. Don't fuck that up! We clear?"

"Crystal!"

"Good!"

He said nothing else to me. I said, "Goodbye" with a gesture, grabbed my lukewarm dinner, left my uncle's summer climate, and braved the cold air back to my car. I headed for home again confident that I would never hear anything more about whether I was a cop or not. If I can count on anything from my uncle...when he says a subject is dead, that's exactly how it stays.

CHAPTER NINE

Going Under

I'M SITTING AT a small curbside café having a cup of Earl Grey, thinking about the last few years. It's funny how things have gradually changed in our lives. I'm enjoying my drink, thinking about how Sean's not getting the early parole and how he might have to do his entire sentence. That is unless Unck's lawyers can work some magic. I haven't had time lately to go and see Sean and even when I did... I keep him distracted with stories about how his daughter is growing. Just to keep from having to explain all the things that I have been doing. Even with him, I'm still dodging that bullet. But again, I've been too busy to visit with him. So, I'm stirring my tea, reminiscing about what I've been through the last four or five years. Graduating the academy, then becoming a cop. Being assigned as a patrolman and working the Upper East Side of the city. My tea was too hot to drink so I sipped on it and revisited old events until it was cool enough to drink. I needed to come up with some fresh ideas for a new assignment that I'm now on. My mind must be sharp so I can handle this narcotic undercover job. I applied for the position two years ago but never thought I would be considered for it or even get the job. But...despite some self-doubt, surprisingly I was given a chance. I was finally out of those dark blue uniforms and into the stylish and casual clothes that I normally enjoy wearing. It seems that I'm always working, always in character and trying hard not to blow my cover.

Who knew that I would be such a natural at undercover work? There was something instinctive in the way I talked, with my movements and how I handled things. Using my family as an example made it easy for this schoolboy to fit in on the streets. I had no problem with my street credibility. I quickly built my crew and earned respect. I was a natural. Plus...with the help of the department, I could step in and take over the territory left from other dealers as the department took them down.

I've been sitting here still stirring this tea, waiting on a kid from the lower east side to show up. I'm told he's this over- talkative, cocky little punk who is the next mark on my departments take down chart.

His name is Eugene Earl Jenkins. A.K.A.... "Jenk". His jacket (file) says he is a 5ft 7inch African American male, with short dark black hair and gray eyes. He had been arrested twice for aggravated assault but somehow has escaped prosecution for both offences. Jenk controlled the two- block area between Henry Boulevard and Central Street. Which is right around the corner from where I was enjoying my tea. As my bagel arrived to my table, I heard some music in the distance getting louder as it got closer. I turned around in my seat and watched this old two-toned Ford Falcon approaching the café. The car has a two-tone faded white and midnight blue paint job. The Falcon had two spoke rims with dirty white walls on the front of the car and black steel rims holding up the back of the car. The music was distorted but loud enough to vibrate the trunk and cause an annoying rattle from the license plate. The Ford looked like a project that someone else had taken on and then stopped caring about. It looks like something Jenk might have picked up cheap. Anyway...he pulls up and stops a little way from where I was sitting. Then he motions for me to come over to the car. I looked back down at my bagel, adding the strawberry creamed cheese, with no intention of moving. He finally found a spot to park before he shuts the car off and walks over to me.

"Hey man!" Jenk yelled. "Damn Rizzo, didn't you see me waving you over to my car?"

"I don't do walk over's Homey! Have a seat."

I gave him a motion to sit then tried to offer him something to eat. He looked around, checking out his surroundings and began to shake his head in a "no" motion. Then turned back to me and said, "Naw...I'm good." "Suit yourself," I replied, "Tell me what-cha got."

(Looking around)

"You want to do this ***here****?"*

"Is there a problem? I mean...This is your neighborhood Jenk. Is there a reason why we can't talk... here?"

(Hesitantly)

"No, uh...naw. (Still looking around) I guess not."

"Then have a seat and start talking."

"It's like this, Double Z. (Even shorter for Rizzo) There's been a setback. Your bird, um (short pause) ain't ready for delivery. Now before you say something...the package is being put together right now."

[Sighs]

"How long before the bird flies Jenk?"

"It's like...Ummm...we need a-notha Twenty-fo."

"I've got someone to answer to just like you do Jenk! (I take a sip of the tea) I've got my own deadlines!"

"Yo, don't trip. It's ***our*** *fuck up. We're gonna fix it, ok. We're sending the bird with some extra feed. You know, to make things right."*

"How much feed?"

"About a quarter extra will be sent with the original order."

"That'll work! Tell your folks...That'll work. But listen there's a new

drop spot Jenk. The old one's too hot. I'll call you in twelve hours. I'll expect a progress report and then you'll get the new drop location."

Jenk nodded as if he understood and then he walked to his car, turned up the music and drove away. I continued sitting there, still in character, watching him, drinking my tea, and contemplating my next few moves.

The department has a problem with me changing the drop spots as frequently as I do. Something about giving them enough time to set up the surveillance. What I was most concerned about was being believable to these knuckleheads. I needed to get closer to people who are pulling Jenks' chains. They had to believe I wanted to be as cautious as they are. Caution has kept them out of jail so far. Caution has me working on Jenk so I can get to the others and I'm still building trust. I'm told that Jenk is a small part of this bust, so we're trying to use him as bait to reach the people ***he*** *works for.*

We've had several successful drops with Jenk but have yet to see anyone above his level. So, two weeks after my last pick up with Jenk, I called and asked him for an amount of dope that was too much for him to handle. Jenk explained, although I already knew, that he couldn't handle it but would try to set up a meeting with someone who could accommodate me. Jenk wouldn't make any promises to me and that was to be expected. "I'll let you know something in a couple of days," he said. So, I kicked back and waited for his call.

After a few days Jenk was able to put a meeting together. Tuesday around 1:00 o'clock, over on the Westside of town, at this small old, abandoned airfield. As instructed, I parked my car across from runway number six and waited for whoever was going to show up. Standing with me was Terry, another undercover officer posing as one of my boys. We were both leaning against my car watching as another came towards us on the runway. The sun was setting just behind us as the car came to a stop and three guys stepped out of it. The first person and the easiest person for me to recognize was Jenk. The second guy was about 5"6" and looked to be about twenty-four years old. He had a light complexion, wore his hair brushed back into a ponytail and seemed to wear clothes that are two sizes too big for him. His name is Angel and when he spoke, his English seemed better than mine. The third guy looked big, but I couldn't get a good visual because he stood behind the open car door as Jenk and the Angel dude approached Terry and me. As they got closer, I never moved. I just leaned against the car with my arms crossed, a scowl on my face and a toothpick resting in the left side of my mouth. Strangely, it wasn't how well he spoke that surprised me the most, it was how quickly this guy got down to business. He didn't mince any words.

(Standing with both hands in his jacket pockets)

"My man here says you're looking to increase your dose. Well...let me be straight with you. ***I*** *don't know* ***you****; don't know if* ***I*** *can trust you or if I even want to do business with you. Do you know what I'm sayin'?"*

I never responded. I just looked at him and then shifted the toothpick to the other side of my mouth.

"Hey, I aint tryin' to make any enemies here. I'm just being a bit cautious before I decide to do business with you. My man, vouching for you isn't enough. I need to know a little bit more about you. Like...where'd you come from and why after such a short time do you suddenly need so much weight?"

I waited a second before I spoke.

"It seems you want to know things that really aren't any of your business but if you need my personal profile, just ask around and you'll find out what you need to know. Although I appreciate the caution, it's all very simple for me. ***You*** *have a product,* ***I*** *have the money, and you're either going to sell to me or not. Ultimately, it's your decision. But let me add that I know you're not the only one I can take my money to."*

"Well, you're welcome to give your money to whomever you like. Money will always remain credible, meaning good... but you cannot say the same about the product that you receive."

(I nodded in agreement)

"No question. You're right about that. No doubt. So, in an effort not to waste any more time here, let me say this... I have a few days until I need more product. So... you do what you need to do and if you decide you want to do business...cool. Jenk knows how to find me. And if after two days I don't hear anything, then I will take my money somewhere else."

(Angel slowly nodding his head repeatedly)

"If things check out, I'll be glad to take your money."

At that point nothing else was said. Angel and Jenk returned to the car and drove away. I turned to Terry as we were getting back into the car and asked, "Do you think we're in?"

"Hard to say", he said, "You were both sizing each other up and both were trying to bluff a bit. Let's hope that your reputation on the street will be enough to get him to play."

"Let's hope so." I replied.

Twenty-four hours later, I received a call from Jenk. He told me that the deal was a go. He said that his people would need a couple more days to fill my order. At that point I gave him a drop location and told him that I'd see him in forty-eight. Which gave us more than enough time to get things set up.

The following afternoon I was sitting outside of that same little curbside café having lunch. Normally on my day off I don't spend it in a place we have been using for the undercover work, but the café has a great crab salad sandwich. The sun was out bright today, so I had on a nice pair of designer sunglasses, and I wore a slightly oversized baseball cap. Pulled low on my forehead to mask my eyes from the sun as I ate. Halfway through my lunch, I heard the faint ringing of a telephone. The ring began to bother me, probably because I was the only one eating outside and the ringing was coming from somewhere close. It wasn't the phone I had on me that was ringing because I checked. Then it suddenly hit me...it must be the cell phone I use for work ringing inside my car. The good thing was, I had parked right in front of the café. I left the table, sat in the car with the door open and answered the other cell phone. "Talk to me." I responded as I answered the call.

"You're a tougher man to contact than I anticipated."

"Who is this?"

"A potential supplier. Remember? It's ponytail. Are you ready to talk? Cause I'm ready to do business wit- ya."

*"**Really**? I thought we were already doing business Angel. There's twenty-four hours until the drop according to your man."*

(Surprised)

*"**Really!** Twenty-four huh?"*

"That's right. That's what I was told."

(Hesitant)

"Ok Rizzo...well let's do that then. Check with me if there are any problems."

"Cool. I'll get at ya if there are."

I set my phone back down and was heading back to my crab salad sandwich until my phone rang again. It was Jenk calling to let me know that my package was ready for pick up and that he would meet me at the drop spot tomorrow at 8pm. I agreed, hung up, and then went back to eating my sandwich.

I was supposed to meet Jenk on the backside alley of this old, abandoned brick four-plex building. It's been vacant for thirty plus years and served as a great out of the way place for these kinds of meets. As I parked and looked around. I was somewhat bothered with the amount of people that were walking near the drop spot. This was an abnormal amount of folks just hanging around. I took a few minutes to make sure this wasn't some kind of ambush before I would get out of the car. I watched several people cycle back and forth from the front of the four-Plex to the back. So, I decided to follow the crowd. When I approached the rear of the building, I saw a big crowd standing behind a yellow line of tape. The police were moving around like ants whose hill had been disturbed. Lights, cameras, and non-stop action kept the crowd glued to the activity going on in the four-Plex's rear parking lot. I inched my way closer to the front, trying to get a better view. I noticed the coroner had what looked like two bodies covered while others were gathering evidence. Some other officers were questioning people from the crowd, so I took a few steps back to quickly blend in with the back of the crowd. But as I took my first steps backwards, a plain clothed officer pointed towards me and yelled," ***Hey! Yeah you! Don't Move!****" Two uniformed officers surrounded me as the other guy continued to yell. "****I've got some questions for YOU. Bring him here****." I was escorted away from the crowd and was taken near the coroner's van. As I stood waiting for this officer to speak to me, I took a glance over at the crowd. They were looking the same as I was...wondering what exactly had happened here. The cop that had been yelling was now standing in front of me.*

"My name is Officer Douglas Richard and I want to take a few moments to ask you a couple of questions."

"Questions about what?" I asked with a strange look on my face.

"Specifically, what you might be able to tell me about what may have happened here tonight. But first...Let's start with your full name."

"My name is Ryan "Rizzo" Walker, and I can't tell you any more than anyone else here can."

As I spoke, another officer was calling in my name over his walkie-talkie. I stood, waiting for Officer Richard to ask his next question. That's when the guy talking on the radio walked up and whispered something into Officer Richard's ear. Next thing he did was come and stand directly behind me.

"Sir, I'm sorry but we're going to have to detain you."

"FOR WHAT?" I said with an angry tone.

"First, to question you about your ties to this murder victim but most importantly for the two warrants out for your arrest."

I heard someone from the crowd yell," THAT'S FUCKED UP! He wasn't doing anything but standing here with the rest of us." As people from the crowd continued to yell about the injustice, they cuffed me, walked me over and put me into a squad car. I sat in the hard- cramped space they called a back seat, with my arms uncomfortably cuffed behind my back, waiting to be questioned or taken in on those so- called warrants they had. I sat watching as the bodies were removed from the scene, while all the evidence was collected, and the crowd was dispersed. Finally, I was let out of the back of the police car, led behind a police van that had just pulled up and taken to my awaiting Sergeant.

"You understand we had to take some precautions, so we wouldn't blow your cover." Sergeant George asked.

"What happened here Sergeant?"

"That's what we're trying to piece together. What I do know is that we lost the guppy tonight."

"Jenk?"

"Exactly. It was him. (Looks around) We know he was coming to meet you and we can tell from the time of death that he was here two hours before the scheduled meet."

"I saw the coroner carrying two body bags over there. Who else was killed,

Sergeant?"

"Only our guppy. That kid... Jenk."

I closed my eyes, placed my fingers at the bridge of my nose and focused on the boss's voice as he explained what he thought happened here tonight. He began by saying that each of Jenk's wrists were handcuffed and chained to the bars covering the windows of the abandoned building. His legs were bound together with a thick chain. The chain was woven around his ankles, locked with a dead bolt, and then secured around the axle of that Mack truck that sat just a few feet away from us. The truck was slowly pulled forward until there was no slack left in the chain that held his arms and legs. Looking at the skid marks, the truck must have hit second or third gear. Completely pulling his body apart. "It must have been excruciating to be stretched like that." I added.

"The building's structure is weak. So, as the truck pulled...the wall collapsed and the bricks gave way."

"Then how did he end up in two pieces, if the wall collapsed Sergeant?"

"Withstanding what the report might say... we think he was cut in two.

Although there was no evidence left at the crime scene to support that theory, we are sure the autopsy will. (Reaches into his pocket) Raymond, what do you make of this?"

He handed me a folded plastic bag that contained a blood- stained note that was left on the body. It read, "To be loyal you must choose a side. This is what happens when you straddle the fence. Bad choices can tear you apart".

"So, what do you think? What's the possibility that his own crew committed this murder?"

"It's possible, definitely possible. I thought Jenk was still working on behalf of that Angel guy until... I heard Angel's reaction to me explaining how the deal with him was already in motion according to Jenk. He seemed a bit surprised."

I stopped talking for a moment to clear my throat. That is when the old timer who was driving the police van jumped into the conversation. Adding his take on what happened tonight. This older officer was a thirty-five-year public servant who is two weeks from retirement and spending his remaining days driving the city's crime scene recovery van. Everyone calls him "Old Jack" and he leaned his head out of the van window as I was clearing my throat and jumped in with his thoughts.

"There was a similar murder to one that happened across town nearly

twenty-eight years ago. It began with this guy's wife being kidnapped. Then somehow, he...uh... tracked down the people who had kidnapped his wife. They had taken her to an old, dilapidated warehouse that used to stand... maybe...six blocks from here. Anyway... a few days had passed with no word from either one of them. Not until their bodies were found. It's said that the entire kidnapping was just a setup, a way to draw him out. With his wife in danger, he would do just about anything they wanted him to do to keep her safe. According to the report, this man was found lying among a pile of bricks on the other side of that old warehouse's outer wall. Now they say that his body was strapped to the front grill of some old Mack truck. His arms had been pulled behind him and fastened to the truck's front fenders; his legs bent at the knees and pulled beneath the front bumper, with both his ankles secured with rope to the undercarriage of the truck. Witnesses say that they drove that truck...with his body strapped to the front... right up to the edge of that wall until his nose barely touched the bricks. They, the kidnapers, then pulled his wife out of the cab of the truck and held her at gun point. Forcing her to watch as they slowly drove both the truck and her husband's body into the wall of that old warehouse. Some folks thought they heard the man screaming, but others say the loud screeching everyone heard was coming from the tires of the truck. Now... the force created by the truck and the uh...seemingly un-giving wall was a horrific way for this woman to watch her husband die. His moaning abruptly stopped as the big truck broke through to the other side of the brick wall. Some believe that his wife was given the opportunity to walk away but was shot in the back as she tried to climb pass the truck to get to her husband. Her bullet filled body was found lying on top of the rubble and her husband was found beneath it. Look gentlemen...I've seen many crime scenes over the years and in my opinion, there are just too many similarities between the one I just described and this murder here tonight."

"Any connection between this kid here tonight and those folks you've spoken about? Are they...possibly related Jack?"

"I don't think so. That kid tonight... his last name is Jenkins and those other folks...um...they were the Kingsley's."

As they continued to talk, I was lost in a barrage of thoughts. Flooding my mind like water into a cracked hull. Did this old timer just describe how my parents died? I stood next to the van in shock. How does Jenk's murder relate to my parents? Why didn't Grann or Uncle Robert eventually tell me that my parents were killed? I dropped my head into my left hand and rubbed my temples. Frustrated, I felt overwhelmed. Just too many unanswered questions. Confusing questions and many of them totally unrelated to the case I'm working.

With the crime scene nearly cleaned up, I was dismissed by my Sergeant and began to head back through the alley to my car. I'm thinking about what the old timer had just told us all. Once I was in my car, I leaned back into the seat wondering why no one in my family had told me how violently my parents died. I was led to believe in my younger years that they were gunned down in a robbery attempt. Hearing what I heard tonight was a hard way to learn the truth. I sat there feeling like I was going to burst. Overcome with a painful rush of emotion, bursting is exactly what I did. I broke down, crying uncontrollably, thinking about the only family I knew who loved me unconditionally. I sat on that dark empty street and let it all out. My tears won't cleanse my anger. It only motivates me to dig for more of the truth. My tears began to dry as I closed my eyes and remembered an image of my parents smiling at me. I was tired. My thoughts were still bouncing back and forth between my parents and my case. I needed answers. Answers I know I will not get overnight. So, I focused my thoughts on getting some rest and hopefully getting a fresh start in the morning.

CHAPTER TEN

Old Demons...New Start

I WAS UP LATE trying to figure out our next few moves now that Jenk was dead. He was gone and I don't know why or who killed him. Now, that just left Angel. I also wondering how could get the case file on my parents without causing any suspicion with my superiors. What was also keeping me awake were the conflicting thoughts of my parents. This went on for another hour, but somehow, I eventually found my way to sleep. My mind was unsteady as I juggled thoughts of work and finding the truth about my parents. It happened to be a very long night. I opened one eye, trying to focus on the bright blinking numbers of the alarm clock. Every sound seemed amplified as my head pounded. The last thing I remember doing was hitting the snooze button and maybe knocking the alarm clock to the edge of the nightstand before I passed out again. It was hours later when I decided to open my eyes again. Strangely, I focused to find my Rottweiler "Bane" looking right at me. How did I get on the floor? Damn my head hurts. Even on the floor the sun was too bright for my eyes. I felt exhausted. I didn't feel like moving, but I needed to get up and salvage the rest of my day. Before heading to the shower, I took a moment to let Bane out into the yard and to check my messages. [Beep] "No new messages." I was a bit surprised after hearing that. No calls from any of my superiors, or any from the knuckleheads who are still a part of my case. It is a bit odd to me. I just shrugged it off and got into the shower. The steam and hot water helped to me relax but my mind remained foggy for more reasons than just my hangover. Normally it never takes me this long to get dressed, especially with hunger as motivation. I couldn't find my car keys. I could hear my stomach growling as I searched. I was looking in my living room when I heard Bane begin violently barking and jumping at the fence out front. When I peeked out of the shade, I saw this old truck blocking my driveway and someone under the hood of my 1967 Mustang. I drew my weapon, crept out the back door and tiptoed my way past two of my other cars, so I could confront whoever was stupid enough to tamper with of one of my cars. I aimed my gun and yelled, "Put your ***fucking*** *hands up and move away from the car, before I blow your* ***Damn*** *head off!" I heard a nervous voice reply, "I... I... was just checking it out." He began to lift his right arm.* **"DON'T FUCKING MOVE"**, *I yelled. I watched his eyes. At first, he wasn't looking at me, but he suddenly started looking towards my front porch.*

"Whoa Cousin...What the hell do you think you're doing? That's some serious hardware you've got there. If...my ...dad knew you had that...You know that would be your ass. He'd be pretty pissed."

I kept my gun aimed at the guy closest to my car as I turned to see who was speaking to me from my porch. It sounded like my cousin Sean, but I knew that couldn't be possible. I turned slowly and positioned myself where I would have a better view of both guys. But as I circled around, I couldn't believe my eyes. It was SEAN.

"What's up Cousin? I knew you'd be surprised. (Speaking softly) Hey, do you mind lowering the gun. (Pauses) Unless (Pointing) making him piss his pants isn't all you were planning to do."

I slowly lowered my gun as Sean's buddy moved closer to the truck that he had blocking my driveway. Before addressing Sean, I holstered my weapon and closed the hood on my Mustang.

"Damn Cousin, how many cars do you have?" Sean asks sarcastically.

[Bane's still wildly barking]

"BANE, QUIET! Go...Go to the back!"

(Turning to answer Sean)

"Just what you see. Hey, why was your potna under the hood of my car?"

"That's my fault. I opened the hood, so I could look at it and then left him there to come knock on your door. I didn't expect Dirty Harry to come down his driveway like he was on S. W. A. T. Man, you'd better stop watching all those cop shows. ***You*** *sounded a bit too real for a minute there."*

"What-ever man. Quit playing."

Sean descends the stairway, and we give each other a hug.

"Fo-real...you'd better not let my pops see you with that cannon."

"Forget about the gun Sean. When did you get out?"

"I've been out for a few days now. My dad told me you were living here now. I just haven't been able to catch up wit-cha. I also had to take care of a couple things as soon as I hit the streets. [Pulls out his cell phone] Look Ray, let me get your number. I was just on my way to pick up a bed for Cee-Jay. That's why I'm with Darryl in the truck there. [Punching numbers]

I begin. "Two, eight...zero...."

Sean cuts me off.

"Four, three, seven, zero...Uh-huh, yeah, I got it. Cool. [Closing his phone] We'll pick this up later Cuzzo. I'll hit you up later. We'll get into the details then."

We said goodbye with a handshake and a hug. As he climbed into the truck, I just glared at his buddy as they drove off. It wasn't long before my stomach began to grumble again. So, after locking Bane up in the backyard, I hopped into my Mustang and headed somewhere to get something to eat.

I needed some time alone. I tried to go somewhere a bit out of the way. Attempting not to run into any family and definitely not anyone associated with my job. I decided I wanted two old style tacos and some chips from this out of the way spot that was an hour's drive from my house. I hadn't been in the place long enough to order more than a soda before I noticed Jenk's former employer come walking through the door. I had seen him before he noticed me. He walked in alone and headed straight for the front counter. He spoke with the hostess before checking out his surroundings. When Angel finally saw me, with one hand motion I threw up a sideways peace sign as a hello and invited him to come over and have a seat. He responded with a very slow head bob and held his finger up as if to say... "One minute". As Angel was waiting at the counter, the waitress came back over and took my order. After receiving what looked to be a to go order...Angel grabbed the small box the hostess had handed him and turned and walked towards my table. Angel stood in front of the table and waited for the waitress to walk away.

"We have a few things to talk about." I began.

"I heard." He replied. "Can't do it now though, but definitely has to be soon," He added. I asked when and Angel suggested tonight at the club over on twelfth Ave.

"How about eleven-thirty", I asked.

"Cool, meet ya there. VIP section. See ya."

The timing of the waitress couldn't have been any better, as Isabella arrived with my food, Angel picked up his box and headed out the door.

[Later that night]

The rain had let up earlier in the day. The sky suddenly dried up. Just in time too. Most people don't hit up the clubs when it's raining. You know how it is. Women want to be cute; guys have to be fly and honestly...who wants to put out all that effort if you're going to have to stand in the rain. Easiest answer? No one. That's why I'm glad the rain has stopped.

On the corner of Twelfth Ave and 2nd Street sat Club Misery. Not even the possible threat of more rain had dampened anyone's intentions of coming out to party tonight. The line started outside the club and rounded the corner. I never worry about standing in line. I have been a V.I.P. since this club opened. It is one of the perks of my undercover identity. Since I arrived at the club forty-five minute's early, I found a table off to the side and watched the door waiting for Angel to arrive. I wanted to see what I was up against before I sat with him. Angel came through the door ten minutes early with two women on each arm I happened to see standing in line. They seem delighted to follow him up to the secluded section of the club. Once Angel got comfortable, I grabbed my Coca-Cola on the rocks, which masqueraded for a Rum & Coke and passed through the crowd towards the V.I.P. section. From Angel's angle he could see me coming so he had one of the women slide over on the sofa to make room for me. "Glad you could make it", he said as I sat down. The music was loud, so we had to lean close to each other if we were to hear anything.

"I'm wondering if you are still interested in us doing business", I began. "Your boy never made the drop. The police were scraping what was left of him off the street when I got there."

Angel's expression never changed as he rubbed his hands together in front of his face. "I was told that it was brutal. He was also robbed." I leaned in closer with a scowl on my face and an intense curiosity as Angel continued.

"The youngster doesn't make drops like that one. It's below his pay grade. If he was there...it wasn't on my behalf."

Angel took his drink off the table, sat back, and took a few sips. I sat, leaning forward with my elbows on my knees, my fingers interlaced and resting on my chin. Angel continued but tried not to discuss the personnel problems of his organization. He did mention that Jenk would only have been carrying half of what I was expecting to get. There's no way he could fill my order.

"Unless... [Angel pauses] he bought the other half from my competitor."

He sat back and took a few more sips. I don't think he meant to say that out loud. After being quiet for a few seconds, he just went on to tell me that he would be making the drop to me personally.

"Give me a week.", he said. "Let's let things die down some and then we'll meet out at the air strip. Cool?"

"It's cool."

I picked up my drink and bobbed my head to the music as I stood up from the sofa. I hit Angel with a sideways peace sign, a head nod, then started to make my way out of the V.I.P. lounge. I hadn't made it halfway out of the room before this wanna-be club gangsta wearing a white t-shirt and sagging pants bumped into me and knocked my drink out of my hand. He turned towards me with this staged angry look on his face and these horrible looking gold pieces scattered throughout his open mouth. Obviously, a weak attempt to intimidate me.

"A Yo mutha-fucka, ya betta watch who you're bumpin' into before you catch a slug or a beat down!"

Before I could respond, he had handed his drink to some guy standing next to him and continued shouting and pointing. All eyes in the lounge turned to us.

"Yeah motha-fucka! I'm talking to you!"

Police training made me want to give him a pass, but instinct had me wanting to fuck him up. And as he continued to talk shit, I thought about the street image I have to uphold. So, I decided to give in to a little violence as he continued.

"Bitch motha-fucka. Ya lucky you caught me short tonight or I would-a put a hot one in... your...bitch ...ass."

My expression was cold, un-wavering and mean. I looked at him and said, "Don't just talk...make your move!" He lunged towards me and threw a punch. I side stepped him, grabbed him by the neck and put him down hard into the floor. I pulled my gun and jammed the barrel into his chest. With a quivering voice he asked, a Heh...how di...did you get that in here?"

"Part of the perks of being a true V.I.P. and not just some peon wanna-be gangsta who had to sneak in. You'll learn that all that loud talk don't mean shit to a real killa. [Slowly pushing the gun harder into his chest] It's real motha-fucka's like me who will silence your bitch ass in front of your hommies.All that loud talk only brings unnecessary attention. If you're real about yours... no one should hear you coming."

The room was silent except for the music that was still playing in the club. I felt a hand touch my shoulder and I turned to see who was standing over me. As I turned Angel said," Not in here big dog. Not here." Angel had somehow signaled security. I was standing erect and walking away before security arrived. Dumb ass was still lying on the floor shaking and too afraid to move. When security realized that they had thrown him out last week for causing problems with one of the waitresses, they became more aggressive with him. I had reached my car and was closing the door on my Mustang as security was escorting the knucklehead out. He was yelling," Fuck dis club! It aint shit anyway! Bitch ass motha-fucka's!" He kept ranting out in front of the club with the people waiting in line staring at him. As I watched him, I couldn't help but think how he has a dirt nap waiting for him sometime in his near future. Unfortunately, it will only take someone just a bit short tempered and trigger-happy. I continued watching him, shaking my head in disgust at his theatrics. Eventually after becoming bored, I started my car, put Luther Vandross's "Superstar" into the CD player and headed home.

There was definitely a different look in Sean's eyes as we sat in his 1978 Chevy Caprice down by the lake. We were parked in a dark blind spot next to the boathouse, waiting and talking. As the glimmer of headlights from the passing cars bounced off the side view mirror and hit his face, I noticed he had a cold unforgiving expression. One hand squeezed the steeringwheel and he was rolling his window up and down with the other. It was strange to watch him do things that normally only came naturally to me. He was checking blind spots, was suspicious about the people walking by, and was making sure that his escape routes weren't blocked. That squeamish momma's boy I used to see... is gone. He now seemed sly, cunning, and smarter about the things he was into. Sean turned his head and looked out the side window as he spoke.

"I'm glad you could come hang with me tonight, but I am sorry about it though. I know Pops wouldn't be happy if he knew I had you with me while I am taking care of some business. It's all right though...this won't take long."

Sean was checking his sight lines and repeatedly looking at his three hundred dollar watch as we sat, waited, and talked in his car.

"So how did it happen?" I asked. "How did you get out so early Sean?"

He began telling me how the warden had moved him to the minimal security level of the prison where he was surrounded by bad cops, crooked accountants and lawyers who were in contempt of court. Things were a lot easier because the guards didn't bother him as much as the used to when he shared a cell with Slicky. With his new surroundings, Sean had a new wealth of information that prisoners in the general population might never get a chance to pay for and this made the information business he and Slicky ran, more profitable. Also, the prison was getting crowded and with no state funding to build additional facilities, the prisons began to release a vast number of inmates to make more room.

"I was surprised myself when I got the word of my release." Sean said. "I thought they were going to send me to a half-way house but that didn't happen. I just have to see my Parole Officer once a week, don't get caught with a firearm and prove that I'm working. Not a problem since I'm on the payroll at my dad's shop."

He bragged about only spending a couple of hours down at the auto shop and said that he spends most of the day taking care of things for his dad and trying to re-connect with a few people he met in prison who had also been released. As we sat in the darkness of the parking lot, Sean complained about how he couldn't get a real job if he wanted to because no one will hire a felon. It is one of the biggest reasons he is now giving 100% to working with my uncle.

"Pop's is handing me a lot of responsibility and I'm learning quickly to pull my weight. I don't want to disappoint my dad."

Sean would occasionally lean forward in his seat when he thought he saw whoever it was we were out here waiting on. "I'm so glad to be home.", Sean continued as we watched a police car pass us slowly then keep going. "I love being around my daughter, family and friends again." His smile left his face as we began to be flashed by a car's headlights in the distance. Sean flicked his own high beams as a sign to the other car that it was ok to approach. A two-door hatchback Ford Fiesta pulled right up to Sean's side of the car. Inside were two of the largest guys I had ever seen squeezed into any little shit box. Sean said "hello" with a head nod as he rolled down the driver's window.

"What the fuck are you driv'en'?" Sean asked.

The big guy didn't hesitate to answer. "It's a rental from one of my new businesses; "Rent Some Junk". It's exclusive to keep a low-key ghetto profile, ya know."

"You are one big ass crazy motha fucka man. You know ya'll are too damn heavy to be in that little ass car." Sean said as he laughed.

"Look man...I'm more incog-negro in this piece of shit than I am in my Buick."

Sean laughed, shaking his head. "You're fucking crazy man." As the headlights of another car passed, Sean's laughter ended, and his face took on a more serious expression. "So?" Sean inquired as he leaned back into the seat with his arms crossed, head back and his eyes closed. I leaned forward slightly and noticed the big dude in the driver's seat reaching into his jacket. He pulled out an envelope and reached out to hand it to Sean.

"Everything you need to know about the drop is right here. Times and locations, just as you wanted."

Sean read the information in the envelope and handed it back to the big fella. "What did I tell you about paper trails?" Sean said in an aggravated tone.

"I'm working on it boss. I'm working on it," replied the big fella.

The big fella took out his lighter and set the paper on fire, then let it fall to the ground as it burned. "Good work. We'll get on this tomorrow. Peace Out." Sean through up another head nod as the big fella's drove away in the sardine can size piece of shit. Sean started up the car and then turned towards me.

"Where do you want to eat Cousin? I think I want to try that soul food place over on Twenty-second Ave."

"Are you talking about... that Lady's Gravy place?" I asked.

"Yeah. That's it. Yeah, let's go there."

We pulled out onto Vessel Street and then made a right onto Segal Ave on our way to the restaurant. "Sean, that was a big ass dude. I don't remember him from the neighborhood?" Sean leaned into the door panel with a jovial smirk on his face. "You wouldn't have remembered him Ray, we met in prison. That's Roderick, but he's known as... "Big Guns". I will tell you more about him some other time. Hey, right now my only focus is on getting something to eat. I'm starving."

CHAPTER ELEVEN

Pressures of the Job

I COULD SEE A stream of dust floating pass the sealed beams of my headlights while I leaned against the front of my car. The airstrip was a bit breezy tonight as the cool night air chilled the tips of my ears. It gets dark on the airfield after the sun goes down, so I decided to turn on my lights so that I could see when Angel was approaching. Angel was an hour and a half late. I tried to call him thirty minutes ago, but he wasn't answering his cell phone. I was sure that something was wrong or went wrong. Regardless, I wasn't going to sit out here and wait much longer. Lately this case has been awfully frustrating. Look, it's hard to build a case when the target won't do anything criminal. I've been wasting a lot of department hours and I'm not coming up with many results that will help provide an arrest. My superiors want results and now they're telling me that if I don't produce a better outcome...I will be replaced. It's amazing to me how quickly shit rolls downhill but when you deserve accolades for your work, the praise climbs up the ladder without you. I'm just saying that it's fucked up. Everything was moving just fine for my superiors, up until Jenk's murder. But now... now that the investigation has hit a bit of a snag... they're questioning my training, my tactics, and my judgments. Shit, I can't be held responsible for the way these streetwise hustlers run their businesses. These low budget millionaire wanna-be's can't get their shit together. That is why they will live, sell & die within a five-block radius of where they make their money. This is the reality. It's just how things are. Hey, by no means am I asking for any handouts out here. I want this bust to be a bit challenging but that can't happen if these self-proclaimed tycoons won't show up to make the deal. It's frustrating... fucking frustrating! Truth is...I've got people to answer to and they expect results.

The night air was getting too cold for me to keep standing out here. I looked down at my watch one more time before I decided to get back into my car. He's not coming. "Got me out here beginning to freeze my ass off... and for what?" I thought. I have a sense that something isn't right. I'm glad I have a couple days before I must report in. It might be enough time to find out why Angel didn't keep his appointment. I tried his cell phone one last time then waited five more minutes before I angrily drove away.

(Two hours earlier)

Angel sat on the couch in his three-bedroom loft, waiting on his boys to show up with the four bricks of cocaine that he was going to sell to Rizzo. The sun was going down and he wanted to make the drop before it got dark. Feeling a bit nervous, Angel turned off the TV and switched on his CD player as he began pacing his living room floor. It wasn't like his guys to be this late and Angel felt that something might be wrong. As he circled his living room, he was hoping that the music would keep his mind off what was taking his crew so long to show up. Midway during his second pass around the back of the sofa, Angel's cell phone began vibrating on the coffee table. "Who dis?", asked Angel. The voices on the other end of the line were yelling franticly, and almost out of breath. Angel could hear horns honking, guns firing and screeching tires in the background. All the noise almost drowned out everything one of his guys was trying to say. [Gun shots]

"We're under attack Angel! ***These*** *Motha-Fuckas came out of nowhere.*

TURN...TURN! [Screeching tires] We came out of the lab and was under attack as soon as we got into the car."

"Can you tell who it is?" Angel replied.

*"Best guess...looks like two **big** ass Motha-Fuckas in a Buick."*

[Someone shouts from the back seat]

*"I can't get a clear shot! **Damn it!** I can't get a shot!"*

Angel stands on his balcony staring down at the street, listening, and feeling helpless. "Can you shake em?", Angel shouted.

*"Shit ain't easy dog. It's hard to shake these fuckas. **Turn...shit...turn HERE!** [Tires screeching] Damn it! Keep this shit on the road! **Watch the curb. Watch the...**"*

*There was a very brief silence before the distracting sound of thunder. Noises like metal making brutal contact with something un-expected. **"Don't hit those parked..."** Then screams as the car violently slams into the occupied tables of an outside Café. Angel could hear the faint screaming of people in pain and then the sound of somebody gasping for air. He pushed the phone deeper into the side of his face after hearing...*

"Stop fuck'en around and grab the shit! Damn, these Motha-fuckas ain't gonna make it. You got what we came for? Good, Rizzo will be happy. Get back to the car. I'll be there after I put these Motha-fuckas out of their misery."

[Bang, Bang]

Angel clenches the balcony railing tighter with his free hand and flinches as he hears two gunshots. Suddenly the voice he was hearing became gruesomely clear.

"Oh yeah Bitch...regarding that Angel Motha-fucka...Let me give you a taste of what he's gonna get. Yeah motha- fucka, here's one to grow on... Bitch!" [Bang]

Angel folded his flip phone and threw it clear across the street. Watching it slam into a telephone pole before decelerating and crashing onto the *sidewalk. He staggered from his balcony, back to his sofa and collapsed, banging his knee on the end of the coffee table. He leaned his head back, stared at his ceiling and screamed out in a frustrated tone, "**What the fuck!**" He rubbed his face with his hands completely overwhelmed by what he had just heard. He wondered if it was actually Rizzo's name that he had heard. He didn't want to believe it, but there was no mistaking what he had heard. Angels sat shaking, angry and confused. He had no explanations, no answers and the reality of a new threat to himself and his business setting in. A new enemy? He knew he would have to get his hands dirty in more ways than he knew he would want to and that just comes with the job. He also knew that not much of what had just happened made any sense. He would have to verify what he thought he heard before he made any moves and definitely before he would retaliate.*

(Two days later)

Sean has been sitting inside his car outside his father's shop, worried about why his father wanted to speak with him. Sean's dad has been giving him small jobs every day since Sean has returned from prison. They have been odd requests that someone else...shit, anyone else could have done. Sean believes that his father is still testing him, trying to determine how much responsibility that his son could handle. He wondered when his Father would realize how he has changed. How his connections from prison can help the family with the expansion of their business. Sean had been keeping his frustrations to himself and decided to just jump through the hoops until his father found confidence in him and his new crew.

"I don't know about this new crew of yours Sean. Son, I don't think they wield the kind of discretion we need to have in this business. They're a bit uncouth. Don't lose control of them..."

Sean reassures his father that his crew does exactly what he tells them to do and that there will be no problems.

"We handled things a little differently in my day son. Your Uncle never had to use brute force or guns to get the job done. He had a way with intimidation that was just so damned impressively effective."

"Well Dad, styles of intimidation have changed over the years. It's... um... a bit more intense, and that works for me."

Sean's Dad took two long puffs of his cigar and leaned back into the leather of his office chair. He looked at his son with an expression that was partially proud but was mostly smug.

"Don't get comfortable and don't be cocky. We still have plenty that needs to be done and we can't afford to have anything blow up in our faces. Do you understand?"

"Yes dad." Sean replied.

"Good. Now how's our little project across town going?"

"Pop, we have effectively reduced the amount of people working for him and have increased our inventory at the same time. It won't be long before we have complete control of his territory. Once he is eliminated."

"Ok, I want you and your guys to focus on that. We won't move forward on anything else until this is done and our people are in place. Son, (he puffs his cigar) initially I need you on the streets for this move. Be careful, you can't afford to be sent back to jail for any stupid reasons. Make sure you attend all your meetings with your parole officer. Let your boys carry the weapons. I don't want you to get caught dirty... for any reasons. (Takes one long puff then blows the smoke out slowly) If you want to be an effective leader, you will have to start delegating more of these jobs to your crew. Give them more of the responsibility. Just like you did today. Do you understand?"

Sean looked at his father, twisted his lip slightly and shook his head in agreement to everything his father has been telling him.

"Son, I want you to be able to take over for me some day. So, watch what I do and learn from it. You also need to be careful with who you

confide in. Even your closest friends can be untrustworthy. Given the right opportunity anybody could betray you. Watch your crew, do what I tell ya, and watch yourself out there. If these streets are going to be dangerous...I want "us" to be the ones making it that way."

"Ok Pop."

Sean's Dad dismissed him from their meeting with a wave of his hand, as Sean jumped onto his cell phone to rally his troops. He needed to brief them about the new plans and stop the grumbling in his stomach at the same time. So, he told his boys to meet him at the Burger Buddy on Broadway. After listening to his dad, Sean wasn't as frustrated as he had been just before he walked into his father's office. He decided to be comfortable in his dad's shadow for a while. At least until his dad retires and gives him the chance to run the business. But for now, he'll rally his boys, do what he's told and help make the family more money.

[Across town]

Angel had gotten word that one of his guys (the one in the backseat) had escaped the car crash, while the driver and the one who was talking with Angel on the cell phone were both heading to the morgue. Angel sat at his office desk inside an abandoned Mobile gas station waiting for members of his crew to report in. Angel had just opened a can of Ginger ale to help settle his stomach when he watched three of his guys approaching the gas station on the video monitors, he had been watching. As his crew entered the office, one of the three appeared shaken, twitching, and scratching as if he was having Heroin withdrawals.

"Have a seat Anthony and tell me what happened." Angel said with a low angry tone in his voice. Anthony took a seat and nervously moved around in the chair as he spoke.

"Yeah, yeah boss. It went down like this here. We stepped out of the lab with the package, and all jumped into the car. I was in the backseat and

kept asking Leon to turn the music down because that shit was too loud. But he wouldn't..."

"I don't care about any of that shit." Angel barked. "Get to the ambush part."

"Well, um...like I said we had left the lab and Dwayne saw this old Buick hanging with us at every turn. He had Leon deliberately make two left turns just to prove that we were being followed. Leon tried to put some distance between us, but that Buick was fast. We couldn't lose it. Then I heard gunshots. The back window shattered, and Leon was hit in the shoulder. Dwayne was barking orders and taking on the phone at the same time. Once Leon took a hot one, he was having trouble concentrating. His reaction time became slow, and the Buick was gaining on us. I shot back at them through the broken back window but had trouble hitting anything because of the erratic way Leon began to drive. He was swerving all over the place, trying to avoid the gun fire and attempting to keep control of the car with the only arm he could lift to hold the steering wheel. We continued to pick up speed and I still couldn't get a clear shot. I kneeled on the backseat, turning my body to face the rear of the car, and tried shooting left to right in a sweeping effort to hit something. I saw a few of the shots ricochet off the trunk lid before hearing one whiz pass me. It struck Leon through the back of his neck. Dwayne was still yelling, and we suddenly hit something. The impact sent me flying out of the shattered rear window. I rolled across the trunk, hit the ground and tumbled uncontrollably until my momentum was stopped by the front tire of a parked car."

Angel sighed frustratingly and shifted in his chair as Anthony continued.

"I was... for lack of a better expression, punch drunk as I laid on the ground. I didn't know where I was, but I thought I heard people screaming, gunshots and then I blanked out. Sounds of sirens made me come to. I got up, slowly stumbled and staggered three blocks before collapsing again on a bench outside the 8th street rail station."

Angel rose from his chair, walked around to the front of the desk, and leaned comfortably against it. He had casually crossed both his arms and legs before lowering the tone in his voice.

"So, what happened next?"

Anthony sat with his head down. He still looked a bit punch drunk and Angel was waiting for Anthony to respond.

"Is that everything that you can remember?" Angel asked.

"Um...uh...yeah. That's it."

Angel seemed concerned about Anthony. He was leaning in the chair favoring his left shoulder and wasn't looking well. Angel gave his boys an address to this private doctor that he frequently sees so he can avoid hospitals. He told them the doctor would be expecting Anthony, and to make sure he gets there. Shortly after sending his crew out, Angel worked his way back to his seat behind the desk. Leaning, he gently rocked in the chair. His mind wandered. He was unsettled about what he thought he heard. He was sure he heard Rizzo's name, but nothing was making any sense. He knew Rizzo was out at the airstrip waiting for him to show, so how could he have followed his boys, killed two of them and stole the package. It doesn't seem possible. That airstrip is a good forty-five-minute drive away from where his crew ended up. It didn't make any sense. Angel just sat there ... "This shit doesn't make any sense."

CHAPTER TWELVE

Let's Stir the Pot

THE MUSIC IN the Buick was shaking the windows of the buildings as it rolled along. Big Guns was out doing his ghetto re-con and turned his music down just as he was passing the abandoned gas station that Angel and his crew occupied. With one pass he noticed the station was on a corner lot, all the windows were blacked out and the cars on the lot were blocking both driveway entrances except for the one car parked near the cashier's entrance. As he came around for his second pass, he saw a huge propane tank sitting alongside the garage. There were still no signs of Angel or any of his crewmembers so Big Guns carried out this task and moved on to his next.

(Cell phones rings)

"Who dis?" I asked as I poured dog food into Bane's bowl.

"What's up Play-ya. This is Angel. We need to talk."

"You damn right about that!" I replied. "What the fuck happened to you?"

"Hold on Folks...how long were you waiting?"

"Two or more hours."

"Damn. (Pauses) I fucked that up and I need to holla at you about it. Can you make it to Jackson & 5th around 8:30?"

"What's up?" I asked.

"Can you be there?"

"Yeah, I can be there."

"Cool. We'll work this shit out when you get there."

After hanging up the phone, I stood in my kitchen daydreaming and spinning the glass I was using in circles by its rim. I was thinking that his explanation had better clear some shit up. I expected it too. Leaving me stranded the other night made things a little complicated with my superiors. It seemed like my boss's boss was questioning my integrity. He didn't say it, but he was making it appear that I wasn't being honest in my reports. He looked at me as if I was hiding something and I felt like I needed to fix things before they get out of hand. More importantly, I'm hoping that this meeting tonight with Angel will give me something tangible I can use to help resolve this case.

I turned the corner onto 5th street and headed two blocks up towards the gas station. The corner it sat on was dark. The only light shining came from the building across the street. Providing a white glimmer of light on the windshields of the only two cars on the lot. I pulled in and parked my car as close to the street as I could, trying to provide myself a quick get-a -way just in case I needed one. The rest of the businesses in the immediate area were already closed. It was quiet. I felt the same eerie feeling I had felt when I was twelve. Sean and I had snuck out to a party and missed the last train going in our direction. We were downtown at 3:30 in the morning waiting at a bus stop. The cool morning air whistled against the backdrop of the dark, abandoned, and uninviting buildings. I kept looking around because I felt like we were being watched. I had an overwhelming sense of uneasiness standing at that bus stop that night. And as I checked my surroundings, I got the same feeling of uneasiness as soon as I stepped out of the car. After a quick scan of the area, I followed Angel's directions and made my way to the men's bathroom door on the side of the station. I pressed a button that sat to the right of the door. I twisted the handle as soon as I heard a buzzing sound and then I entered. The old bathroom had been gutted out and turned into an entry way or lobby to Angel's office. I was surprised as I walked in. His office looked like something you would see on a 21st floor VP's office. Decked out with the big desk and conference table. Angel was sitting in the middle section of the conference table facing me with a brief case in front of him. One of his boys stepped up to me with the intent to frisk me for weapons.

"Let me save you the trouble." I began. "I wouldn't have gotten out of my car un-strapped."

Angel motioned to his muscle with a hand gesture, letting him know that it was ok and to back off.

"First, let me apologize for the delays Rizzo. But as you know in our business…shit happens. You know how it is...personnel problems, product misplacement, police interventions and the unfortunate eventuality of being robbed. But still, none are good excuses for a man not to keep his word. Right? (I nodded) Right! Ya see, although shit sometimes happens to us...to be successful we still must make shit happen. So, if you still want to make a deal...I have your product right here."

I put my hands up in front of myself before I began to slowly reach into my jacket with my right hand. I pulled out a thick envelope with two rubber bands around it and tossed it onto the table. The money slid and came to a stop in front of Angel. He picked it up and handed it to the guy standing behind him on his left.

"Make sure it's all there. (Looks at me) No offense."

"None taken." I replied as Angel's crony left the room with the money.

"I didn't mean to leave you stranded out there on the air fie...."

"Don't worry about it.", I interrupted. "We're here now making it happen so…let's both let it go."

Angel's guy had walked back in and whispered something into his boss's ear.

"So, everything alright here?" I asked.

"Oh, we straight Play-ya. We are straight."

He reached out and slid the briefcase across the table to me. I popped it open and smiled. "You damn right we straight.", I mumbled as I closed the briefcase and lifted it off the table. Angel stood while scratching at chest. "Good. (Pauses) Cool!"

I traced my steps back out to the front of the station. Angel and his crew were dragging their heels behind me. I had made it into my car as they were just coming out of the side entrance. As I turned the key to start my car, I still had that nagging uneasiness that caused me to look around before I drove off.

(In a dark corner across the street)

"Who was that getting into the car?", asked Slim Nate who was sitting in the Buick with Big Guns.

"Slim we'll ask our snitch about that later. Now let's get this done before anyone else gets into another car."

Big Guns reached up and pulled the bulb out of the overhead light of the car before he and Slim Nate quietly propped open the car's doors. Gradually they positioned themselves, taking aim as Angel and his crew emerged for the side entrance of the gas station and headed to the front. Slim was always quick on the trigger and before Big Guns could tell Slim to wait a second, he had already begun to shoot. I had just pulled onto the street, heading north on 5th when I saw a flash of light in my back window. I could hear the bullets ricocheting and I didn't let up off the gas to find out where they were coming from or if they were shooting at me.

The first few bullets ricocheted off the bus stop's bench, alerting Angel and his crew that they were under attack. As Big Gun's joined in, they both began shattering the windows of the gas station and putting a few holes into the car that was out front. Angel took cover but not before watching me speed off. Slim Nate moved his weapon from left to right putting holes in any soft metal that came across his cover fire. He didn't leave much of the car that was out front of the station. One of Angel's boys made a run for the other car but got hit by a single shot from Big Gun's sniper rifle. He fell quickly, banging his head against the fender before hitting the ground. As Slim continued to recklessly shoot, Big Gun's put his rifle down for a moment and reached into a box that was on his back seat. He pulled a pin out of the small green granade that was in his hand and hurled it across the street. It fell out of the night sky like a badly thrown football, tumbling and rolling towards the old propane tank at the back of the lot. [BOOM.] The propane tank exploded, sending reddish-yellow flames high into the night sky. The back fence went up like a camp bon fire and the back portion of the station went up as well. The blast froze Slim as he cheered with excitement, but as Slim jumped up and down, Big Guns pulled his 9mm from the small of his back and was still scanning the area for Angel. Without anyone noticing, the last one of Angel's guys standing found his way into the car that his dead buddy was laid out next to. Slim Nate stopped celebrating when he finally notices that the car door was open and began illuminating the barrel of his gun again. Angel was wearing all black tonight and neither Slim nor Big Guns were able to see him squatting and crouching his way around the back end of the car his buddy had just climbed into. Slim focused his gunfire on the open car door as Angel crawled into the back of the car. "Go...Go! Get us out of here!" Angel barked. Big Guns heard the car turn over and lobbed another grenade across the street. The oblong metal powder keg drifted over the top of the car just as it moved. The grenade dropped out of the night sky, hit the curbing for the gas pumps, then bounced and rested on one side of the burning station. "Ka-BOOM". Big Guns was cursing at himself because he lost his grip, causing the grenade to go where he hadn't intended for it too.

"LET'S GO. LET'S GO!" Angel screamed as he ducked in the back seat. And with reckless speed, Angel's transport knocked over a mailbox as the car jumped the sidewalk and onto the street. Swerving and slamming into a parked car before straightening and racing down Jackson Street.

"The tires Slim...the tires. You should've flattened the damn tires!"

"I was tryin' to hit the motha-fucka driving."

"Well, how'd that work out for ya? Ya target missin' motha-fucka! (Twists his lips up at Slim) Get ya ass in the car and let's go!"

I never looked back. I heard the shots and laid my foot onto the gas pedal. I slowed down only when I realized no one was shooting at me. When I didn't hear any more gunfire I relaxed, drove to a safe spot, and called in. My boss was pleased with the pickup I had made from Angel but asked me what I knew about the buildings roasting over on 5th. He knew I was working in the area tonight and figured I had to have seen something. I held the phone, was quiet for a few seconds before telling him that I was working in the area, but nothing like what he was describing had jumped off while I was there. He tried slipping in the same question during his recap of the fiery scene and I didn't hesitate to reiterate that I was nowhere around. I was becoming annoyed with his tactics and questioned him about what the real problem was. "Look Ray", he began, "One of the city's oldest libraries was burnt to the ground with that gas station and a couple of other surrounding buildings. Excuse the play on words but... the heat is on about that library. Apparently, it was a historical building undergoing restoration and millions of dollars was lost now that it's nothing but ashes. Heads are going to roll over this one and I want to keep any blame off our department if at all possible. So, I need to know every detail from the time your night began... up until the moment it ended."

I did exactly what he wanted me to do. I told him everything except that I was out there when the shooting began. Why did I leave that out? I don't know. Not sure what purpose it served but I do know I don't want to take the fall for that library burning down. I was ordered to find out what I could about anything that happened after I left. Instructed to get the information from Angel if I could, but most importantly, come back with something.

Angel was now safely sitting in the comfort of his living room. Although his surroundings put him at ease, he had felt an unfamiliar sense of fear tonight. His hand shook as he sipped the Rum & Coke, he had fixed to help calm his nerves. The violent images from earlier were vivid and replayed in his mind as he leaned back onto his couch and closed his eyes. Un-escapable thoughts of his buddy Brian falling to his death as his skull shattered not far from where Angel was crouching. With images so bloody, it was hard to keep his eyes closed. He sipped, trying to find some comfort in his drink not understanding the reasons for these attacks. Not understanding why after five years of hard work, negotiations, and street treaties he has become a threat to someone. There was an agreement and he had lived up to his part of it. All the head dealers in town made the treaty two years ago. Simply, they would split the city. Everyone knew who was selling and who was supplying, and everyone knew not to cross the boundaries that had been agreed upon. There was never supposed to be any blood spilled on the streets. If anyone had a problem with the preset arrangements, then the parties involved would set up another meeting to discuss any changes wanting to be made. No one sent word about wanting a sit down and there was nothing done on Angel's part to warrant these attacks. Angel sat his drink down and picked the TV remote up from the table. Nervous and with his hands still shaking, he began clicking the TV on and off in a rhythmic fashion. "Let's look at what we do know." Angel said aloud to himself as he dropped the remote, stood up and walked over to his balcony window. He stood; staring at the city lights with his arms crossed running different scenarios in his head. His anger grew as his thoughts kept bringing him back to one person...Rizzo. That's where the problems began. Since meeting and dealing with Rizzo, he's lost three-fourths of his crew, lost the gas station, and has had his business temporarily crippled. It also was awfully convenient for Rizzo to get away without being harmed. "Shit!" Angel said as he came to a few realizations. It's no coincidence that Jenk, Dwayne and Leon were all robbed and killed. All on days there were drops set up with Rizzo. And tonight...those gunmen never turned their weapons on Rizzo's car. Just on him and his crew. That's just too damned convenient Angel thought. "What else could it be!" Angel yelled as he continued to gaze out his balcony window. (Softly) "What else could it be?" The entire thing seemed to be an elaborate set up and Rizzo seemed to be at the heart of it.

CHAPTER THIRTEEN

New Hang ups, Another Obstacle

I WAS DRIVING ON Benson Avenue when I noticed the bright red lights shining in my rear-view mirror. My music wasn't loud, I was wearing a seat belt and the signal was green as I went through the intersection. It had been a while, but I had been through this before. Every time I'm riding in what is considered a ghetto neighborhood it's the same routine. Pull me over, check me, ruff me up, tow my car and put me in a paddy wagon headed to the city jail. This was the department's way of keeping my street reputation intact and bringing me in to swap information. Today began with a formal debriefing about my participation in last night's Bon fire. It didn't take long for my superiors to become aggravated and move on, especially after hearing the same details that I told them last night. It seemed more like department procedures uniting in an effort not to take the fall for that library burning down. So, they concentrated on getting accurate and detailed descriptions of my undercover work last night. We were at it for more than an hour. They kept asking me the same questions over & over. It felt like they were trying to trip me up on something, but they finally gave up because my answers never changed.

Next on the agenda was collecting the drugs that I bought from Angel. After being asked, I explained that the drugs were in a briefcase in the trunk of my car. My captain smiled and asked, "Did we impound your car again

Ray?" I nodded my head in a "yes" motion. He turns and points at an officer standing in the doorway. "Call down to the impound lot and have someone secure the evidence. (Pauses) Do you...or do they have the keys, Ray? I would hate if they're forced to break into it." The captain had a sarcastic smile on his face as he spoke. I quickly spoke up. "No need to damage my car Captain, they already have my keys." He then turned to me and everyone else in the room with an intense expression on his face. It seemed to me that whatever he had to say would be serious. "Gentlemen our new objective will make things a bit more complicated. The powers that be, not only want us to take down our first target (Angel) but now they want us to use our investigation to find the folks responsible for torching that library."

"Isn't that the arson investigation team's responsibility Captain?" Asked officer Hawkins.

"Normally it would be...but somehow, they feel it crosses over into our investigation. They're dropping it in our laps. Ok...with that being said, here's how we want to go about it. Raymond, we want you to set up another pickup with the mark. Tell him that you heard what happened and try to find out if he knows who attacked him. Let him know that you're ready to re-up and willing to lend him some back up if he needs it. Maybe we can draw his attacker out and take them both down at the same time."

"Are you sure this is how you want to do this?" I asked.

*"This isn't how **I** want to do this; this is how **my** superiors want it done Ray. So, don't question everything, just go get it done."*

I didn't agree with my captain or the higher ups. I thought their decisions would be a bad move on our part. Whoever came up with this new strategy obviously hasn't spent much undercover time on these streets lately. They can't see the difficulty in what they're asking me to do. They don't see things how I see them. I can't help but assume that I may be under attack by Angel, that he might believe that I was involved with the assault on him and the death of some of his crew. Without knowing what he knows,

I must be cautious before I approach him. I must decide what my next few moves will be.

Sean had just sat down in his living room placing his daughter on his knee. Big Guns and Slim Nate had been sitting and waiting nervously for Sean to finish dressing Cee-Jay. They have been waiting for about thirty-minutes sitting quietly on his couch. Sean left the room leaving them with nothing to watch or listen to. Sean thought that the silence would help them concentrate on the responses he was expecting from them. Sean returned to the room and sat in the chair that was to the right of his couch and began to bounce Cee-Jay on his knee.

"What happened out there Nate? I hear you had trouble hitting your target."

Slim Nate was nervously fumbling with a magazine that he had brought with him, and his voice cracked as he responded.

"Um...Ok, yeah. I had some problems with the sight on my gun. Yeah, some trouble with my sight."

Big Guns looked over at Nate shaking his head and twisting his lips.

"Am I mistaken? I thought you always used your chrome nines?"

"Um...Ok, yeah, my 9's. You're right. Um...guess I had a bit of an off-night Boss. Sorry bout dat."

Sean shifts his daughter to the other knee before he speaks again.

"SORRY! (Pauses) Nate...do me a favor."

"Anything Boss man." (Covers his daughter's ears) Sit there and try not to say anything else...Please!"

Sean turns toward Big Guns and asks him to explain what he knows about the car that got away.

"I got no ID on that car.", Big Guns began. "I was concentrating on the three guys coming out of the building. I was trying to get set up until El Trigger here (pointing at Nate) started lighting shit up before I was ready."

Sean glares back over at Nate before he speaks.

"Ok. Here's what we gotta to do. We need to know if that person is part of his crew or one of his buyers. Cause if he's a buying from Angel, then he's moving a lot of weight. And…since we broke the treaty, it doesn't matter what his roll is. Eventually he's gonna have to die also. Let's find out who he is. Alright?"

As Sean tried to make eye contact, both Big Guns and Nate mumbled out an "Ok". Then Sean continued talking to them about a few other things that his father wanted them to get done.

An intricate piece to Sean's part of the operation was using what he had learned in prison. Simply, his ability to get information, and it didn't matter how he came by it, just as long as he did. From monstrous to modest, no method was ever frowned upon. Sean was always looking for the most effective way to find out what he needed to know...or what others will pay to know.

Big Guns and slim Nate had kidnapped two guys and brought them in a van to the rear of an abandoned Raley's grocery store. They backed the van down into the receiving dock and made sure the coast was clear before they dragged the two into the building and lowered and locked the gate. Following Sean's instructions, Big Guns separated the two men and began to work them both over one at a time. As Slim Nate locked one of the guys in the abandoned refrigerator, Big Guns was dragging the other to the open area of the store where all the old shelving and racks used to stand. Sean was sitting at a table in the darkest part of the store just out of reach of a small ray of light that came shining through the boarded- up windows of the store. Darren, the guy being dragged by Big Guns, could tell he was in a fairly big and empty room. He could hear the voices carry to the other end of the room, bounce off the wall and then reverberate into the empty space he was hostilely brought into. He was placed in a chair with his arms pulled behind it and secured with plastic tie straps. His eyes had been covered with duct tape and his ankles where also secured to the front legs of the chair.

Darren never expected to be where he now was, bound and scared shitless. He could hear the faint screams of the other man as Slim Nate unnecessarily hit him in the stomach with a crowbar. Darren began to shake. He was frightened and wondering what his captors wanted with him. Darren nervously struggled to get free but while trying began tearing the skin of his wrists against the tie straps. He decided to stop moving. Especially when he heard the loud footsteps coming towards him. "Here's how it's going to work" Sean began. "You have a choice. A very simple choice as a matter of fact, and it all depends on your response. Your choices are...with pain or without pain. Like I said, it all depends on how you answer me. Shake your head up and down if you understand. (Moves his head up and down) Good. G... you can remove the tape from around his mouth."

Big Guns grabbed the guy's chin with one hand holding his head in place. He then took his switchblade out of his back pocket and flipped it open. Darren sensed what was about to happen and began to tense up. Big Guns never lost his grip of Darren's chin and raised the knife to the tape that covered his mouth. His mumbles became louder as the knife put a small cut into the tape covering Darren's mouth. "Hey!", yelled Sean, "Just pull the tape off him so we can get on with it." While applying more pressure to Darren and with a disappointed expression on his face, Big Guns reluctantly put his switch blade away, gently grabbed a corner of the tape and with one abrupt motion, he smiled, then violently tore away the duct tape. Doing so while digging and scraping his fingernails across his face as he pulled. As Darren yelled out in pain, Slim Nate had finally entered the area wheeling in a cart of assorted tools for Big Guns. After smirking at Darren, he returned to the freezer to keep an eye on the other guy they had tied up.

"I'm going to ask you a series of yes and no questions. Ok? (Darren nods) at this point... I want a verbal response for you. Are we clear?"

"Yes." Darren answered reluctantly as if he had a choice.

"Do you work for Angel?"

"Huh? Umm...Who? Uh, No."

"G!"

Big Guns grabs Darren's arm and began to scrape across his skin with a wood file. The pain comes swiftly, causing him to yell out.

"AAAAAAAHHH. ***Got Damn! Stop! SHIT!"***

"If I'm not mistaken, you were picked up off one of Angel's corners. Am I right?"

"Yeah, yeah!" He answers breathing heavily.

"Were you at the gas station with him two nights ago?"

"Yes."

"Who was the motha-fucka who left before you did the other night? I know someone was meeting with Angel."

"What? Who the fuck are you talking about?"

Big Guns took a rubber hammer from the cart and smashed it into Darren's thigh as Sean continued to speak.

"Next time he'll do it with the claw side of a roofing hammer. Now, do I need to ask again?"

"No." He answered as he grimaced in pain.

Darren sat, rolling his head and neck around for some seconds, trying to adjust himself to the pain that pierced his leg. Anticipating that he was taking too long to answer, Big Guns popped him on the back of the neck with one of those childhood Mammy-greases. The sound of his hand hitting the back of Darren's neck was so loud that it caused Slim Nate to lean into the room to see what had happened. Sean decided to pick up the pace of his interrogation, as Big Guns stood ready to inflict more pain. "Let me be clear." Sean bellowed impatiently as he began to pace back and forth behind Darren.

"Your life is at stake here...and I have never been known for my patience. So, either tell me what I want to know, or I'll just let the big man go to work on ya."

Darren slowly raised his head as Big Guns cracked his knuckles in front of him. Darren's breathing was heavy, and his expression was filled with anger.

"Alright...Damn! I think I heard someone call him Double Z. I heard he opened up shop over on the south side. He must be moving some major weight. He and Angel were s'posed to meet somewhere else, but something happened with the drop. That's why he was at the station picking up his package."

"How long has Angel and **this** *Double Z been doing bidness?" Sean asked as he continued to pace.*

"Not very long. (Adjusting his neck) Umm...Not long at all."

"How much weight did you say he was moving?"

"I don't know! (Takes a hard slap to the back of the head) I'll just say... looking at the size of the package he picked-up, he must be moving a lot."

Sean took a few steps away and began dialing his cell phone. "Hey it's me. Check it, I need some Intel on a guy on the south side going by the name Double Z. (Pauses) Yeah, A. S. A. P. Call me back on the other phone as soon as you get something. Thanks."

Sean hangs up the phone and just paces back and forth before he turns toward Big Guns.

"Here's what I want you to do. Give this guy the message we want delivered. Finish working him over and then call me after you dump him."

"You got to be shittin' me! That's all you wanted to know! You Fuckin' Kiddin' me!" Darren shouted as he began struggling to get free again.

Sean turned to face Darren just long enough to say, "If I were you...I would value the fact that you will live through this just as much as I value the little bit of information that you have provided. Please give Angel my regards." Then with nothing more than a glare, Sean turned and began to walk towards the rear of the abandoned grocery store. Leaving Big Guns to do what he likes to do...the dirty work. As Sean approached the rear entrance, he stopped at the freezer and called Slim Nate to come to him.

"Hey boss. Um what about this kid here?"

"Slim...He's a cousin to my daughter's mother. He just turned seventeen and has been trying to get into the streets. Been hangin' on corners trying to run dope for Angel's crew ever since he's been recruiting new runners. He has also been disrespectful to his moms and to my daughter's grandmother, and we can't have that! He's good at basketball and could probably do well at it if he was focused. So, I decided to start my very own scared straight program. (Hands Slim a folded piece of paper) I want you to leave him tied up, pull him out of this freezer and make him watch what Big Guns does to homie in there. I want you to randomly hit him and tell him he's next. I want to make him feel like he is a real part of what's going on here. Then, while Big G is carrying homeboy out, I want you to leave him tied up and blindfolded in here for a couple of hours. Ok? (Slim nods) Then come back and pick him up. Throw him out of the car about two blocks from the address I just gave you. Tell him someone will be watching him. Maybe what he's gone through will be enough to convince him to give up the streets and go back to basketball practice. Alright?! (Slim nods again) Ok. Let's make it happen."

CHAPTER FOURTEEN

A change of pace?

THE 1960'S LINCOLN'S acceleration had slowed down to about ten miles per hour as it approached the middle of the block. Darren sat in the backseat next to Big Guns with his ankles, arms, and hands still tied up and his mouth was re-gagged. Big Guns leaned against the rear door panel looking and smirking at Darren. He had a crazed look in his eyes, an excited expression as if he was anticipating what was about to happen. When the car reached the middle of the block it slowed down to ten miles per hour. Big Gun's tapped Terrell (who was driving) on the shoulder and told him to keep the car steady and in the middle of the road. "Welcome home, bitch!" Big Guns said laughing as he opened the rear suicide door of the Lincoln. He continued to laugh without hesitation before he tossed Darren out. Darren's already battered body hit the ground and tumbled a few feet before the rear tire of a parked car stopped his momentum. There were only a couple of youngsters hanging on the corner as the Lincoln sped off. Normally a body dump would be handled more discreetly. Usually in the wee hours of the morning, but Sean was trying to send a message.

Two weeks had passed and the swelling in Darren's face has gone down enough for him to speak. Angel stood over Darren's battered body as he sat on a couch and stumbled through the explanation of what had happened to him. With his jaw and bottom lip still swollen some, it wasn't easy understanding what he was saying. Angel was patient as Darren stopped to catch the saliva that fell from his mouth with a couple of balled up paper towels. After wiping his chin for the third or fourth time, Darren began to give Angel the message he was sent back with.

"He said what!" Angel shouted. "So, you're telling me he's offering me a choice? (Pauses) And what are my choices?"

"He didn't tell me, Angel. Only mentioned setting up a meeting with you. Said he wanted to discuss... Man, never mind."

"To discuss...What?!"

(Sighs frustratingly)

"The terms of your surrender. That's how he put it."

[Almost out of breath]

*"Wha...**What!** Did you just fuckin' say...surrender? Are you joking? This ain't the **fuckin'** movies."*

[Mumbling]

"He...He...he said he wants to have a one on one with you to discuss his terms."

"A one on one, huh? Good. Cause I've got to set this motha- fucka straight. (pauses) Is that all that he said?"

[Voice quivering]

"No. He wants you to call this number, so arrangements can be made."

Before Angel could get the words "What number?" out of his mouth, Darren raised his shirt. Revealing a jailhouse style tattoo of a phone number that Big Guns carved onto Darren's stomach. After seeing the tattoo, Angel let out an exasperating, "SHIT!" Darren pulls his shirt back down as one of the other guys in the room asks, "Who is this Motha-Fucker?"

[Three nights later]

I was late. I was supposed to meet Sean and my uncle Robert over at Estelle's, the best soul food restaurant in the city. Sean wanted us to treat

Uncle Robert and celebrate his birthday. I was late, so I found my way through the restaurant looking for the guys. As I approached, I was a bit surprised. I thought it was only going to be me, Sean, and my uncle but I was obviously mistaken. My Aunt Kate was sitting across from my uncle trying to get little Cee-Jay to wave in my direction. Sean was sitting next to my grandmother shaking his head up and down as a response to whatever she was saying to him. The waitress stood next to Sean's new girlfriend Aprielle who was sitting next to the chair that I assumed was left for me. Once the waitress noticed me, she stepped aside so I could sit down.

"Ray, we done went on and gave our orders already." My Grandmother began to say with a disconcerting tone. "Can't be waiting for you all evening Raymond. You know better than to come here late like you are. You been taught better. Folks can't just be waiting...so tell us what it was that made you forget where you where s'posed to be."

I pulled the chair out and sat down as the waitress handed me a menu. After finishing everyone drink orders, she told me she'd be back in a bit with the drinks and then take my order.

"My last class let out late Grann. That's why I'm late. (Pauses) Oh, Happy Birthday Unck."

My Uncle's nod was his way of acknowledging what I had just said. But if he were going to reply, Grann wouldn't have given him the chance.

"If you had to give an excuse for being late Ray, that would be a good one. You're doing what you're s'posed to be doing. Good."

"Is that why we haven't seen much of you lately?" Aunt Kate asked as she put Cee-Jay into a highchair. I took a page from my uncle's book and just nodded my head. I was sitting next to Sean and elbowed him in his side.

(Whispering)

"I thought it was going to be just the guys?"

"It was going to be, but you know how my mom doesn't like to be left out. So here we all are."

The waitress returned to the table with a few of the drinks for my family but still wasn't ready to take my order. I started hearing a faint ringing sound over the people talking around me. I noticed Uncle Robert, Sean, Aunt Kate, and myself all looking down to see which of our phones were ringing. It just happened to be both Sean & my phones ringing simultaneously.

"You boys take dem phones away from the table. I don't want your loud talkin' to interrupt my dinner."

Grann hated for dinner to be disrupted. She always said that the fellowship of families eating dinner together was ruined with the invention of the cell phone.

"Sean, both you and Raymond go answer those calls closer to the bar. While you're there, get me something on the rocks."

"Like what Dad?" Sean asked.

"It doesn't matter, just as long as it's dark and strong."

We left our seats heading towards the bar when I noticed the call coming in for me had gone to voice mail. So, while Sean answered his call, I ordered Uncle Robert a Rum on the rocks. Sean answered his phone like he recently has been answering his phone. "Yeah, what-cha need?" Sean leaned his back up against the brass railing of the bar, as I made myself comfortable on one of the bar stools. His expression went from a jovial smile to damn near none. Everything I heard was fragmented, obviously because I could only hear his end of the conversation. Whatever he was being told appeared to be important. I decided to prepare myself to ear hustle, so I ordered myself a drink and tried to listen in.

"You got the info I wanted? Uh-Huh. What! A cop! Are you sure? Um-Hum. Did you find out who he is? But everything else is confirmed. Right? Cool. Alright...I'll holla back."

Sean slipped his phone back into his pocket, turned around and then sat in the open seat next to me. He got the bartenders attention and ordered himself an Alabama Slamma.

"You know Cuz-zo, the more I work for my Pops...the more interesting... No... crazy all this shit gets."

"What's the problem Sean?"

"First, it was that Motha-Fucka across town. Now it's a cop. Man, Pops ain't gonna like this. He puts up way too much bribe money to have any problems with the Police department."

"Is there something I can do? Maybe I can look into it. Find out who this cop is for ya."

(Sean shakes his head)

"See what I'm sayin'. A brotha watches one or two Colombo episodes and thinks he's a detective. Man, leave playin' Kojak to Telly Savalas or Ving Rhames. Besides, you ***KNOW*** *Pops don't want you doing nothing when it comes to* ***this*** *part of the family."*

"I know. I just thought I could help."

"And I love you fo dat, but ain't no way I'm taking any heat for getting you involved when they don't want you to be. I appreciated your help when we were kids. I know you got some skills, but I'm not letting Pops get angry with me like that ever again. Thanks Cousin...but no thanks."

We let the awkward moment pass and then began another humorous conversation as we continued to sit at the bar. We decided to finish our drinks. We knew that Grann wouldn't approve of us drinking, so we saved ourselves the tongue bashing and enjoyed ourselves at the bar. Before returning to our family, we ordered Uncle Robert another drink. Seeing how Sean drank the first one. When we returned to the table, we got an earful from Grann about being away from the table for so long. She went ahead and placed my order, but my food was already getting cold because we were away from the table so long. I picked over my food until the waitress brought out a single serving size peach cobbler with one candle in it and set it in front of my uncle. We sang along with the staff of the restaurant as they sang Stevie Wonder's version of "Happy Birthday" and waited for him to blow out the one candle before they all walked away. We joked, and we laughed for a couple of hours. We hadn't had fun like that as a family in a long time. Felt great to take my mind off the pressures of work for a change. I really enjoyed myself tonight.

CHAPTER FIFTEEN

Two Meetings/One Purpose

I WAS CALLED IN for what I was told was a special briefing. When I arrived, I sat in the briefing room for about thirty minutes before I realized I was the only undercover agent here. I thought it was a bit odd because the department has different operatives working different parts of the city. So as urgent as they made this briefing out to be, I just wondered why I was the only agent here. It was around 10:10 am when my commander came into the briefing room. No handshakes, no smiles, none of his normal joking around. He was all business. He came in and got right to it.

"We received an anonymous tip; it came in yesterday. It's a possible lead on the guys who torched that historic library. Our potential suspects are two black males. The best description we have is that they look like the ghetto versions of Laurel & hardy. I know that description is crudely vague, but the suspects are big and thin. One even seems goofy while the other is efficiently serious. That includes the big guy smacking the thin guy around sometimes. Intel has given us (hands me a piece of paper) a location for the library perp's. They seem to be hanging around in Angel's four-block empire. We want you to follow up on it. We also need more evidence on Angel. We must have audio or visual proof of any big transactions. The D.A. will not go forward without it. So, if you can...try to kill two birds with one stone

on this one. The city wants results and surprisingly, they want the library guys taken down first."

He noticed the reaction on my face.

"I know...I know. You've been on this case for a while now but trust me when I say...their priorities are not the same as ours. I want you to set up another meeting or something with Angel. Inadvertently run into him at one of those restaurants he likes. Maybe he can give you something on the library guys. But remember...He's our first priority. (His voice lowers an octave) Look Ray, one of our other agents blew his cover two or three nights ago. A couple of people died, and we came out of this debacle with no tangible evidence to show for it. We need work smarter from here on out. The department is making sure the other operative's covers haven't been compromised. (Clears his throat) You're on your own out there, and the neighborhood may not be very responsive to being questioned. Just play it cool. When we know the status of the others, we'll send someone in to help cover you. Report in a few days and we'll exchange information. Any questions? No? Ok...remember this is nothing more than a hands-on surveillance job. Do what you have to, but we want you to report in before making any major moves."

As he stood up, he gave me a wink and quoted and old line from the old Hill Street Blues TV show before he walked out the room. I think you can remember... It was simply, "Let's be careful out there."

[One week later]

The phone rang over on 1671 Delview Lane. That's the block where Sean's new girlfriend lives. When she answered the phone, she did exactly what she was instructed to do. Just follow the script she was given to read. She answers, "Hello. Snitches and Bitches hotline."

"What did you fuckin' say?" Angel interrupts. "Snitch...Bitch...I know that's not what you just called me?"

Aprielle cuts him off, "I'm sorry Sir, I've been told to assume that whoever calls this line is either one or the other. So please...I don't have the time to decipher which one ***you*** *are. Remain quiet and listen for your instructions. Also...hold your comments until I'm finished. Thank You. Your meeting is scheduled for 10:00am tomorrow morning. That's tomorrow morning. On the corner of 8*th *and West Bolten Ave. Come to Cantelli's Bar & Grill, there will be someone at the door to let you in and lead you to where you'll need to be. The meeting will begin as soon as you're seated and lasting only as long... as* ***your*** *need to ask questions. If you need any of these directions repeated for you...say yes now. (Pauses) If not, this will conclude our business."*

"Wait, wait." Angel yelled into the phone. "Who are you and what is this shit about?"

She began to speak in a soft, sarcastic, contemptuous tone that seemed to make Angel even more agitated.

"I am the messenger! That's all you need to know about me. Everything else you will find out when you show up. Okay! I've given you your directions, thank you for calling."

[The next morning]

The lighting in the restaurant was dim. Slim Nate was at the bar nervously humming and stacking shot glasses, while Big Guns and Sean were seated at one of the tables facing the door. It was about 9:50am. Sean was talking on his cell phone, while Big Guns sat calmly reading the sports page from the local newspaper while repeatedly telling Slim to shut up. The bar was quiet, except for Slim Nate and the sounds of the Cantelli family preparing things for the lunch crowd. Joey Cantelli, son of owner Paulie, was fixing table settings near the front when he heard someone knock at the front door. Joey unlocked the door and was almost knocked over as Angel and Darren barreled through it. Paulie, who was standing near yelled,

"What da fuck? You two's... watch dat shit!" Joey re-locked the door as Angel made his way to the table where Sean and Big Guns were sitting. Darren stopped at the bar and sat at the stool next to Slim Nate. Sean had just finished his call and set his phone on the table in front of him as Paulie was yelling. Big Guns slowly looked over the top of his paper at Angel. Sneeringly watching as he approached the table in front of them.

"I'm here, so what da fuck is this about?"

Angel asked in an aggravated tone. The scowl on his face motivated Big Guns to fold up his newspaper and be a bit more attentive. Before Sean politely began to answer but Angel cut him off.

(Pointing at Sean)

*"**YOU...**You must be the one running this circus."*

"Not exactly, but I am the reason you are here today. Please, have a seat." Sean replied.

"That's alright, I'd rather stand. Let's just get to it...what do you want?"

"It's simple...your territory. We'll run it and you... will... work for us."

(With contempt)

*"Young-sta you must be out of your fuckin' mind. Don't you know that there must be a sit down with the council? You can't just torture my people, then call me to come see you. You're a virtual nobody and expect me to hand over my cash cow. You must be as **stupid** as your guy sitting at the bar **looks**."*

(Sean clears his throat)

"I used the word "SURRENDER" for a reason when I sent you the message about this meeting. What you don't understand yet, is that you don't have a choice. This is going to happen whether you want it or not."

"Shit yeah! Tell him Rizzo!" Slim Nate shouted.

Angel immediately tightens up. Nodding his head as he gives a quick look to Darren. Suddenly the room was eerily silent. Then simultaneously

Angel draws two chrome 9mm's and Darren grabs Slim Nate by the collar and puts a snub nose thirty-eight to his head.

"Rizzo! That motha-fucka called you Rizzo! That makes you the MOTHA-FUCKA that killed my cousin and half my crew."

Big Guns slips his right hand under the table and turns off the safety of the gun he has in his lap. Sean never flinches. He signals his guys not to move. He continues to look at Angel but directs his next words to Big Guns.

"See G, how can we effectively take over ***this*** *man's business and not get sidetracked when he's accusing me of murder. The problem... (pointing in Angel's direction) I mean* ***your*** *problem. Simply, is you not knowing what's going on around you. If you had been the least bit aware, then you would have known that "one man" has been slowly taking your crew apart over the past six months. One man. Stealing your dope, buying what's left, and using my name while he's been doing it. One man. One man who happens to be a cop. That's why your about to lose your corners."*

"That's bullshit! (Aiming his guns) You expect me to listen to this shit! Especially when my boy damn neared died from a beat down from that motha-fucka! (Points one gun at Big Guns) One man my ass!"

"Your boy? That was just to show you how weak your crew is. You now know how serious we are."

"Let me kill this bitch, Angel." Darren yells as he pushes his gun into Nate's temple.

"Hang on D. He mentioned…SURRENDER. That shit just ain't gonna happen! (Points) You don't have that much power! Right now, I don't give a shit whether you're lying about everything or not. Ya see...no matter what you say, I ain't giving up shit."

(Sarcastically)

"Uh-huh, is that what you think?" Sean asks before putting a stick of gum in his mouth.

"You Damn right! And what would stop us from killing your man and walking out of here right now?"

The room becomes silent again after hearing the noises of a table scraping the floor in one of the darker corners of the restaraunt. Sean's father stood up from one of the nearby booths. In that moment every gun in the place came out, as he walked over and froze all the tension with his presence.

(Confused and frightened)

"Mr. Kingsley?" Angel stuttered.

(Lights a cigar)

"Sure, you could kill Slim. You probably have every right. But...right now I want you to be smart. I know you can be. Your choices aren't difficult to understand. First, if your buddy pulls that trigger...neither of you will walk out of this restaurant alive. Second thing... my offer is non-negotiable, and here's is why. (Puffs on his cigar) You have been doing business with an undercover cop for the past six months. Unknowingly bringing heat down on everyone else. Heat that as head of the council, I pay big money not to encounter. In my efforts to keep my businesses running smoothly, we ousted another undercover just two nights ago. Which I'm sure has hurt the police's ongoing investigations. So, if you don't believe anything else, know that it won't be long before they come after you with everything they have already compiled. That burning library, no pun intended, has shined a very bright light on you. (Stops and looks around at some of us) Here's how I see it. This entire thing is a potential problem for everyone. Something has to be done before anything else gets out of hand. So, I decided to offer you in order to fix things but...for a price. I can see by your expression that you are wondering how. How is he going to help? Well, either I could kill you now and take all of your territory or you can kill the cop and give me 40% of everything you make until your debt to me is paid. (Puffs his cigar) Things are in motion Angel and people must be paid off for us to have the outcome that we want. Payoffs aren't cheap. (Points fingers at Angel, still holding cigar) So! Your

decision...here...now! It isn't complicated. Kill the cop. Pay me 40%. Or... die within the next few moments."

Mr. Kingsley began to walk away, and in the distance, we could faintly hear him say, "So what's it gonna be?" This was said just before he stepped out of the restaurant's front door. Slowly everyone began to lower their weapons. Darren let go of Slim Nate and the two red laser dots that were on both Darren's and Angel's foreheads suddenly disappeared. Angel gently un-cocked his 9mm's. Angel's anger was strangely overshadowed with a nagging sense that something other than this new deal was fucked up. A piercing irritation that was centered on coincidental times, places and trying to figure out which Rizzo had cost him the most. Because there are clearly two. But it was an irritation that would have to wait, cause there's a little voice in Angel's head that's saying, "Live today, fight again tomorrow." So, for now he humbly asks, "What do I have to do?" Sean jumped right in giving Angel his directions. Everything including where to begin dropping the 40% he owes. To the location, day & time he should kill the undercover cop. Every other detail was already in motion as Sean laid out all the details.

[Just across town]

I was sitting on of my corners inside my car when the call came in from my captain. Undercover officer Roslyn Moreno, who has posed as my girlfriend every day since my assignment began, was sitting in the passenger seat. Roz had my sides hurting with the jokes she was telling me, but I had to pull it together to answer the phone. My captain was surprisingly brief, again. He began by telling me that the department has changed my orders. I asked him to hold for a moment as I motioned Roz to turn the radio down. Once I could hear him better, he instructed me not to waste any more time looking for the library arsonists. There was something much more important that was about to go down. He began...

"We have another agent in trouble, and we need you to give him some

back-up. There's an exchange-taking place between the corners of West Texas Avenue and Virginia Street. We want you to be somewhere nearby to provide back-up if the agent needs it. Otherwise just lay low. If he doesn't... just stay out of sight until the bust is over. We don't want you blowing your cover for any unjustifiable reasons."

I was waiting for a chance to interrupt. It seemed like he was leaving out a few key details.

"Ray the whole thing is happening tomorrow night about eight or eight-thirty. I want you to report in afterward. Immediately after! No matter what the outcome." [Hangs up]

I sat quietly for a few moments after hanging up the cell phone. Roz broke into my day- dreaming asking me if everything was ok. We sat for another forty minutes discussing everything that was bothering me about this case. But more importantly...everything that's bothered me with-in the last forty-eight hours. I'm uncomfortable. I have no confidence that this operation is still organized. There are just too many decisions changing too rapidly and we as a department have never worked this erratically in the past. It bothers me, but Roz has reminded me that no matter what the department's wishes are, I still have a job to do. She also reminded me that whether we are undercover or uniformed, we have an obligation to look out for each other.

"We may not completely understand our assignments, we may not even like them, but we should never be alone out here. Although we do have a responsibility to protect our own Asses, they would never send us into a compromising situation."

I looked at Roz and assured her that she was right, but the more I thought about things, the worse the feeling in my stomach became.

CHAPTER SIXTEEN

One Bad Night

SOMETHING CONTINUED TO bother me as I parked in the center of the block. The street wasn't as deserted as I had expected. Honestly, that may possibly be the best thing. The more people that are out here, the better I'll blend in, especially if I'm supposed to go unnoticed. The two streets where this meeting is to take place, West Texas and Virginia Street, run into each other like a capital "T". Virginia is a one-way street that ends at or meets West Texas. As I looked around, I didn't like where I had parked and decided to move two spaces back. That way, I still have a good visual and I could still go unseen. I took a few moments to prepare my gun. There's twelve in the clip and one in the chamber. That'll work, I thought to myself. When I looked up after setting the safety, I noticed an elderly woman waving her hand (the one that wasn't gripping her purse) and now she's coming towards me. Although I'm wearing a badge that's hidden, I'm not dressed like your typical police officer. I'm dressed like most thugs in this city would be. So, as she approached, I slipped my weapon between my seat and the center console of my car. Mostly to keep her from being startled or causing a scene if she just so happens to see it. As I began to roll down my car's window, I could hear her saying, "Excuse me, young man. Can you help me?" As she continued to overtly wave her hand.

"Young man can you help me? I am looking for the bus stop. I'm not

too familiar with this area. Can you show me where to find the number fifteen bus stop?"

I began pointing towards the end of Virginia Street but realized she couldn't see where I was trying to direct her. "Ma'am." I began as I led her across and down the street.

"Ma'am, at the end of this block... make a left and walk one more block. You will find the bus stop there."

She nodded her head, smiled, and told me "Thank you" as she headed in the directionI had just pointed her towards. After I turned away from watching the old woman, I hadn't realized that I was more than half a block away from my car. I was out in the open and had to hurry back to my post before I ruin someone's operation. When I checked my watch, it was only a quarter to eight. Which gives me enough time to get back to the car and get set up. I relaxed, slid my hands into my pants pockets and slowed my pace as I walked back down Virginia. The evening was warmer than it has been the past few nights and I always enjoy it when it's warm like it is. The streets are beginning to clear a bit. I was able to buy a soda from a hot dog vender before he shut down for the night. I continued walking towards my car, drinking my soda when I could hear someone call out my name. Not my real name, but the one I use undercover.

"Hey Rizzo!" He said with a thick New York accent. "Yo Son, over here."

Standing on the other side of the street was a 5"10", medium built, dark skinned kid with short dread locks who I don't recognize. He's wearing a Nike sweat suit with his right hand just inside his slightly unzipped jacket and the left pointing in my direction. With my hands still in my pockets I turned to face this guy with a glaring look on my face waiting to see what his next move would be.

"Yo Son!" He continued to yell. "Hold up. Hold up! My boy wants to holla at cha."

"Your who... wants to do...WHAT?" I yelled.

The guy didn't respond. He just stood out of the way as Angel came walking out of the store the guy was standing in front of. I noticed Angel throw me a head nod when we finally made eye contact. We both walked in-between the parked cars and met each other in the middle of the street.

"What's up Rizzo."

"Hey Angel, he with you?"

"Oh, don't mind him; he's one of my new associates. (Lowers his voice and partly covers his mouth with his hand) But he ***is*** *a ruthless killer. We call him "The Predator"."*

"Ooo...kay. (Pauses) Hey don't take this the wrong way Angel but you were on my "to do" list for tomorrow."

"Then it's good that I ran into you Rizzo. Cause I needed to holla at you as well.

Let's walk."

We began heading towards my car, leaving The Predator standing on the street where he first shouted at me. As we walked, I was trying to scan the area because it was getting very close for that other operation to go down. I was trying to multi-task by observing my surroundings and listening to Angel, but I was a bit distracted by the things he was saying. It wasn't until I leaned against the fender of my car, on the street side when I paid closer attention to him.

"Riz, did you hear me? Man, I just said I'm gonna have to lay low for a while. Got a few things to take care of. (Reaches into his jacket and then slips a piece of paper into my shirt pocket) That's the name of someone who can fill your orders. Don't worry bout it, you'll still be getting ***my*** *product. Just check with him when you're ready. Look here, like I said earlier...I've got a few things I have to handle. So, for now Double Z, stay sharp and keep your head on a swivel. (Pounds his fist two times to his chest.) I'll get at ya. I have your number, so I'll call ya when I resurface."*

Angel stepped onto the sidewalk as he was ending our conversation. Turning away, he began to head to West Texas Street. I reached into my pocket for the folded piece of paper as I continued to lean on my car. I unconsciously looked around before looking back at the paper. There was still no sign of the other undercover agent, just Angel talking to someone else up the street. I focused on the paper and then felt like I had been punched in the stomach when I saw my own name on it. I quickly looked back in the direction where Angel was. Now he was standing with two guys, and he was smiling and pointing right at me. The bad feeling, I felt came quickly and before I could react... [CRASH]. I never heard the screeching tires, never saw the driver, just an instant excruciating pain as the car violently slammed into me. Pinning my legs, causing me to writhe and yell uncontrollably. I slumped over onto the hood of the car. I could hear someone hollering. Yelling... at me... I think.

"Yeah Motha-Fucker! Ha! Time to get yours."

Darren backs that piece of shit out of the way as someone yells, "Hold that motha-fucka up!" I felt someone grab the collar of my shirt and pull me up off the car. Angel was standing in the street pointing his 9mm at me. [BOOM! BOOM!] I took one bullet to the chest and one in my right shoulder. I thought I would fall back over onto the car that ran into me, but it was backing away, and I fell face first into the street.

(Angel's yelling)

"Did you think ***YOU*** *could steal my dope, kill my boys, set me up and I would just walk away? Ya piece of* ***shit*** *cop."*

My chest and stomach were only stinging (thanks to my vest), but I think the bumper of the car broke my leg at the knee. I don't know why I was trying to get up. I was face down on the asphalt, wincing and couldn't make out everything Angel was saying. My left arm was parallel with my body, but my right arm had been dislocated and was being held down by Angel's foot. I heard someone yelling in excitement, "Yeah Predator, do that shit!"

I could hear something cutting through the air. It's the same noise swords make in any of the karate movies that you've ever seen. I didn't feel a thing... at first. Strange how the body doesn't react until you become aware of what's happening. When I turned my head, I could see blood dripping from the sword and Predator was watching as my right arm began bleeding badly. He made more swiping motions but was waved away by Angel. Almost in shock, my blood came gushing past the bone and tissue where my arm was sliced open. The pain was unbearable, but I still pulled my belt off, wrapped it around my arm and tried to slow down the escaping blood. I could still hear Angel, but I don't think he was yelling at me anymore. I also heard two other voices.

"He don't look dead to me Big Guns." Giggled Slim Nate. "He looks fucked up, but he ain't dead."

"Well, he better be before the younger boss walks up. That's part of the deal." Big Guns added.

"I know what the deal is!" Angel yelled. "I don't need **your** *big ass to remind me."*

"What's with all the theatrics man? You could just kill him quickly like most cops kill. Use one bullet to the heart then another to the head. All this extra shit is unnecessary."

"Nobody asked your big ass for tips. (Angrily) And where did ya'll come from anyway?" Angel asked.

Big Guns just glared at Angel and didn't respond. I, on the other hand was able to prop myself up against the front tire of my damaged car while they were barking back and forth at each other. I felt heat coming from the bullet wound in my leg. The belt around my arm was unbearably tight, my leg was twisted in the wrong direction and I believe my adrenaline was the only thing keeping me from blacking out. The weird thing to me...with all my moving, I seemed to go unnoticed as they continued to insult each other.

(With contempt)

*"Come from! Where did **we** come from? We've been watch'en this sloppy shit since it began. Is this what **you** call killing a man? It's a good thing we were sent to check on this shit! Cause this bullshit **you're** doing... (disgustingly shaking his head) is the work of an amateur."*

"You know ...you talk too fuckin' much Big Man.", Angel replied as he pointed his weapon at Big Guns.

Big Guns was looking down at his hands, cleaning his fingernails with a folded scrap of paper and hadn't noticed that Angel was now pointing a gun at him. Big Guns was concentrating on his nails and had never stopped talking.

*"Sad thing is...this shit ain't hard. It only takes three steps. One; Locate your target. Two; Kill da motha-fucka...and Three; Bounce, shake the spot, or get ghost. (Points his right finger towards the ground while inspecting his left hand) This shit **here**...a public corner, un-capturable witnesses and a target that's still alive? **Shit!** This is how dumb fucks get caught."*

"I'd watch my mouth if I were you!" Angel replied in an angry tone.

Big Guns pulled the dirty tip of paper from his fingernail and finally looked up. Big Guns smirks, just when he notices Angel has a gun pointing at him. Big Guns thrives on chaos and confrontation. His only reaction was a devilish grin.

(Calm and smug)

*"You are not me Rookie." Big Guns replied as his grin became increasingly more sinister. "You'd better concentrate on killing **him**. (Points in my direction) You should have finished that cop off before turning your gun on me. And if you haven't noticed...your time is running out. Greenhorn!"*

Suddenly something caused Angel to take his eyes off Big Guns for a moment. As he turned and looked towards the sidewalk, he saw what most would call an old Mexican standoff. I was still bleeding and propped up against my car, while two guys stood on the other side of it aiming guns at each other. Hearing what was going on gave me a small sense of relief. Why?

Because now it was possible that I wouldn't be the only one who might die out here tonight. Although I did feel myself getting colder and my heart rate slowing down. Angel still had his gun pointed at Big Guns while the other two had the drop on each other. Big Guns was shaking his head in a disapproving manner as the other two yelled back and forth.

"Put the gun down Man! Darren yelled. "We're s'posed to be on the same side."

"I ain't putting shit down till ya boy does! Same side? We ain't on the same fuckin' side! And don't think I forgot that you had your fuck'en gun to my head in the restaurant! Yeah, you gonna pay for that shit. Ya best believe dat!"

Slim Nate stopped yelling at Darren just long enough to pull another gun from the small of his back and aim it at Angel. Once Slim was comfortable with his aim on both Angel and Darren, he began to yell again.

"Man, I can't wait. As soon as the boss gives the word, It's nighty-night forever for you two Motha-fucka's."

"As soon as I give the word for what?", Sean asked as he walked into the madness and stood next to Big Guns.

Upon seeing Sean, Angel's expression changed. His face displayed a bit of fear as the gun rattled in his hand. Big Guns still had a smirk on his face and Slim Nate had the crazed look of a liquor store robber in his eyes. His head was bouncing back and forth, waiting for Sean to give the OK.

"What's Nate shouting about G and why isn't ***he*** *dead yet?"*

"Well boss, I not sure. We've been waiting for him to kill this dead weight. And... (Nodding towards Angel) somebody's anger for ***us*** *is making it hard for this job to get completed. The rookie has clearly over complicated this shit. That dude should be dead, and we should be gone. Killing a man is not as difficult as he's made it. That's why* ***that*** *motha-fucka is still alive.*

Angel was about to respond but Sean's movement towards my slumped over, rapidly breathing body caused him to stop speaking. Oddly, for a semi-deserted street, you could hear a pin drop. Sean approached cautiously and kneeled beside me. He lifted my head away from my chest and raised it high enough to take a good look at me.

"WHAT THE FUCK! RAY? *Oh Shit! NO...NO, NO! Cousin? Shit! (Turns towards Angel)* ***You*** *shot my cousin!* ***YOU SHOT MY COUSIN!"***

"What? I shot a cop! The cop that I was told to kill." Angel replied as he lowered his gun.

(Sean runs to Angel)

"He ain't no fucking cop! He's my family motha-fucka! Dumb ass!…And I was the Rizzo who robbed you. ***Bitch! [BANG]***

Sean lowered his gun just as quickly as he raised it. Angel's eyes widened as the back of his head exploded. His lifeless body hit the street before chucks of brain matter, hair and skull fragments did. Darren was petrified as he watched. But before he could react... ***[BANG, BANG]*** *Slim Nate smiles as he uses the gun in his left hand to shoot Darren in the chest and the one in his right hand to put one in his head.*

[Just after Darren hits the concrete]

(Exited)

"WHOOO! Did you see dat shit G? Ha! NOW THAT'S HOW YOU KILL A MAN!"

"Damn Slim, that shit was nice. You must have been practicing. You been sneakin' out to the range?"

"Naw, not at the range. I've been shooting at my neighbors Pitt bulls with one of those weekend warrior paint rifles."

As Nate and Big Guns were celebrating the precision of Angel and Darren's deaths, Sean was trying to hold his cousin up. He kept calling Raymond's name. He was trying to keep him alert but noticed he was becoming less and less responsive. When the boys finished their gloating, they made their way towards Sean who was still kneeling next to his cousin.

"G! You and Nate got to get out of here. Ya gotta go before it gets too hot around here."

"Is he really your cousin?"

(With a sad tone in his voice)

"Yeah. He is."

"Is he really a cop?"

(Shaking his head)

"Man... I don't know. (Pauses) Look, you guys gotta go. NOW! Find my father and tell him what's up."

Big Guns and Nate made their way through the last remaining onlookers and disappeared from Sean's sight. I was still partially aware but was beginning to fade in and out of consciousness. Sean was giving me encouragement to stay with him, but he seemed preoccupied with digging through his jacket pockets for something. As Sean searched himself, I could hear sirens in the distance. Sirens that never got any closer. I closed my eyes for what felt like seconds to me and when I reopened them, Sean was talking with some lady. He wasn't digging in his pockets anymore but seemed to be giving this lady instruction. Then things got dark again. This time the seconds felt like minutes. When I opened my eyes again, Sean was gone and through my blurred vision, there was what I thought to be a middle-aged woman staring and shouting questions at me. I was unable to answer her. I think I heard her say that she was staying with me and calling 9-1-1 while the other guy went for help. I was gasping for air. Every breath in sync with my heartbeat. Every heartbeat skipping like one of my dad's old, scratched records. So here I lay, out on the street. Hanging on by the thinnest of threads. And suddenly...I have no more pain. My heartbeat stops, breathing stops, and there's no light. There's nothing...nothing. Just darkness.

CHAPTER SEVENTEEN

Life Before My Eyes

I HAVE A SENSE that I'm awake, but I remain in complete darkness. I'm not sure where I am or even how I got here. I feel as if I'm in limbo. I feel lost and it's hard to explain what I'm feeling. I'm wondering if this is what death is supposed to be like because if it is, then this is not what I expected. But if I were alive... then who would want to live the rest of their life this way?

I don't recall seeing any white light. I wasn't greeted by anyone I could recognize or sadly anyone else for that matter. My Mom or Dad wasn't there welcoming me to a better life. There was nothing. Nothing except a very faint beeping or the sound of muffled voices coming and going. I'm not sure when it happened but I could suddenly hear a voice reaching out to me in the darkness. The voice was familiar, but I never thought for an instant that it sounded the least bit, Angelic. The words I heard were a mixture of condemning anger and nurturing love.

"Boy, what-cha gone and done to ya-self. Lying there just fucked up! I have told ya you reap what ya sow. Boy, don't you worry I'm here now. You're gonna be alright. I hope ya gonna be alright."

I could hear partial portions of concern in her words. Grann would interlace a bit of caring in with a heavier dose of anger. Finding out that I was a cop was obviously a tough blow on the family. Especially finding out under these bizarre circumstances. When Grann spoke to me, she never dwelled on my job. She'd just say, "You're s'posed to be the smart one. It is... what it is. Nobody can change that." Every day she would sit and tell me that if my soul was right, I'll heal. The doctors tell her how they were able to stabilize me but can only do follow up because my healing process will be slow. They won't confirm anything else until I come out of whatever this is that I'm stuck in.

I never heard anyone in the room with Grann other than the doctors or the nurses. Grann normally chose to come alone and only stayed with me for thirty to forty-five minutes every time. I didn't receive many visits from any of my co-workers. Officers never want to be reminded of what could happen to them. This was a common notion with most cops, so Grann would always read me the cards that my co-workers sent the hospital. One day I thought I had heard someone different at my bedside. Hard to make out but I thought it was my aunt Kate sitting with me for a few minutes crying, but I never heard my Uncle Robert or Sean in the room. I was used to my uncle being heartless and showing no emotion but for Sean not to visit wasn't like him. When I was alone... I wondered why Sean hadn't come. The rest of my alone time I spent trying to understand why this happened to me. It's been tough thinking about everything although I'm physically motionless. My mind tries to understand what went down on the street that night. I believe the black outs are giving my body the time it needs to heal. Or perhaps my body and mind are not ready to deal with any of this yet. On the other hand, I think my soul is searching for answers, leaving my physical existence in this world to be determined by what the truth is. Hence my limbo states.

[Days later]

I could now hear Roslyn (the undercover cop posing as my girlfriend) coming into the room. She was slightly more cheerful than the last time she visited. She began by saying that I was looking better today than I have in weeks. She cleared her throat, and then she was silent. No sounds, no movements for several minutes. I began wondering what she might be doing. It wasn't like her to be quiet. I listened. Listened for any movements, noises or words coming from her. And after ten minutes, I heard her faintly say, "May God keep you safe. In your name I pray Lord...amen." Roslyn knew that I never attended church much, so she told me about a year ago that she always kept me in her prayers. "Remember when I told you", Roslyn began, "That someone who burns the candle at both ends like you have, often needs additional spiritual help. That's why I continue to pray for you." She paused, and as Roslyn began to gasp in what sounded like a surprised tone, my eyes began to flutter. Then in one sweeping motion of my eyelids, my eyes were open. The light was painful initially. Blinding and blurry until the black lines creating the details had begun to clear. Once all the color of the world returned, I focused and looked at an Angel leaning over me. She was smiling and calling out for the nurse. "I knew you would make it." She whispered as a nurse came into the room and then quickly left again. It seemed like only moments later that the nurse and a doctor came rushing back into the room. The doctor came around to the right side of the bed, leaned over and flashed a light into my eyes.

"Ma'am I'm going to need you to step outside while we tend to Mr. Kingsley."

"I'll be right outside Raymond. I'll come back in as soon as the doctor is done. (Reaches the door) I'll call your family and give them the good news."

After Roslyn left the room, the doctor began a series of tests. He explained everything he did and why he was doing it. He told me that I would be uncomfortable after he removed the tube from my throat but said he would have to leave the catheter and the IV in. I could barely move. I felt stiff. I'm told that it's a result of lying motionless for a few months. "We're going to take things slow. Start you off on liquids and check your progress. Don't try and speak yet, just blink twice if you understand. (I blink with each eye)

Good, you have a sense of humor. (Taps my good arm) I'm not going to let in any visitors tonight. I'll check your progress in the morning and make a decision after I see you."

I lay motionless. Feeling even more helpless than I did when I was unconscious. I'm too weak to move and can only muster enough strength to whisper one or two words at a time. Two days have passed since I have awakened and not one person from my family has come to see me. Roslyn, like always came to see me again around 2:15pm. The first thing out of her mouth as she came through the door after saying "hello", was her telling me that Bane was ok. She said she's been going by my house and feeding him since my accident happened. She came in and took a seat next to the bed. Normally she's cheerful around me but today she seems like something was bothering her. You could hear it in the tone of her voice when she spoke.

"I need you to listen to me carefully Raymond. I want talk to you about the night you were attacked. Remember you told me that you were ordered to go out there to be back up for that other undercover agent?

(In a painful whisper)

"Yeah? What about it?"

"Don't try to speak Ray. I just want you to listen. I think you were set up. There were no other undercover stings that night. I checked the log and there was nothing for that night. No one in our department even knew you were out there. No one except the commander. And right now, word on the street is that you and Angel were in the middle of a turf war, and it turned bloody. As a matter of fact, the only reason you're not handcuffed to this bed is because you didn't have a gun on you. You had no gunshot residue and no weapon to match ballistics to. With Angel and his crew all dead, it's easy to chalk it up to a drug war."

(Whispering)

"Angel's dead? I asked."

"Only two people died at the scene Ray, Angel and his sidekick Darren.

Ballistics hasn't matched any of the bullets found in Angel or Darren to your gun which was found when they searched your car. Angel actually died from a single gunshot wound to the head and the other guy had one slug in his head and another in his chest. Two guys, two fatal shots, both from separate guns."

"Who got me off the street? How did I get here?"

"A concerned woman sat with you and called it in using your cell phone. Reports say that once she mentioned that you were a police officer the effort to help you intensified."

"How did she know I was a cop?"

"Paramedics say...she was holding your badge when they arrived. (She clears her throat) Ray, the fact that you took part in a phantom operation (clears again) that wasn't even logged or even stranger...the department didn't know about concerns me. Hey, the review board is considering bringing you up on charges. They have the impression that you went off half-cocked and tried to take Angel down by yourself. You're the only witness still alive. So, they're waiting for you to recover or at least for you to get stronger before they de-brief you. They're going to look to you for some of the answers. Hoping you will clear up conflicting testimony from some of the on lookers because there are a few gaps in the depiction of events. Just take what I've said as a warning."

Roslyn stands, leans over and kisses my forehead. As she walks away, she settles into a devilish grin and sarcastically says, "Ok baby. I want you to rest now." Saying so just as one of the nurses pops her head into the room to check quickly hen leaves.

(Almost in a whisper)

"I'm still paying the part of your girlfriend Ray, but I upgraded myself to your fiancé. That's the only way I've been able to get in and see you. (smiles) Thanks for the ring. (laughs) How did you know I'd like it? Doctors are only letting your family or fiancé in to see you right now. (Changing the

tone and volume in her voice) So get some rest Honey, I'll be back after my shift. I love you!"

Roslyn blows me a kiss and giggles as she walks out of the room. I laugh to myself then take a moment to digest what she had told me. I felt like the pieces were starting to come together, but there were still a few things that I needed to know so I could fill in the blanks. I laid back and closed my eyes, trying to take my mind off my injuries. The painkillers were wearing off and I could feel my injuries beginning to throb again. So, for now my mind will be distracted by physical pain until the nurses come with more medicine.

The nurses, I've realized are on a normal two- hour rotation. I don't mean a shift rotation; I'm speaking more about the checking of patient's rooms. They come in, they smile and then they do their jobs. They check the monitors. They change my bandages, and they often change my I-V. A few of them find a way to sound concerned when they ask if I'm feeling any pain or any better. But what's most interesting is no matter how I respond, they smile and then they leave. Always returning in exactly two hours and starts the entire process again.

It's been quiet since the nurses left the room and a bit boring without Roslyn keeping me company. Restless, I settle my head into the pillow and try to lose myself into the game show the nurse left playing on the TV.

"Look there Robert, I told you that boy would make it. Just as strong as his daddy was."

My head rolled slowly towards the door. Grann and Uncle Robert are both here...Together? I was shocked. I mean not that Grann was here, but more so that my uncle was. I tried to sit up but was too weak to lift myself. My speech was still limited to a whisper, so I smiled as I struggled to say "Hello". Grann came in and took the chair next to the bed, while Uncle Robert stayed comfortably leaning in the doorway. Grann reached out and placed her hand onto my arm and smiled. "Welcome back baby." Grann began "You gave us quite a scare. I spoke to your doctor, and he said that you are doing better."

"But he isn't outta the woods yet Ma."

"Well Robert, we've got to be more positive." Grann replied.

I looked at my uncle. I got the feeling that he wasn't the least bit concerned with my recovery. He had that look in his eyes. The one that tells me that he's trying to figure something out. Almost as if he was on the verge of asking me something but wasn't quite ready to do so. He just stood in the doorway staring at me. Grann's hand never left my arm, and she was tapping me as she spoke. The nurse came into the room and interrupted just long enough to take care of her duties. This time was shorter than the last and once the nurse was finished, she smiled at the three of us then headed back to her station just down the hall. Uncle Robert watched the nurse go down the hall, then closed the door to the hospital room and leaned against it.

"Nephew, it's time that we as a family clear a few things up, now that you're feeling better. First thing, your grandmother and I want to know how long you have been lying to us."

"Do we need to do this now Robert? Or can it wait a day or two?" Grann asked.

"This is the reason I came here! So ***now****, right now will be the best time!"*

"Watch your tone we me son!"

"It's obvious that Raymond has been lying to us. Haven't you, Nephew? Lying about where you spend your time. Your job? (Spoken with disgust) We know you are a cop. What I want to know is...how long? How far back does your secret go? Two years? Five? When you first started college?"

I tried to whisper "yes", but they could barely hear me. It sounded like I took a breath. So, I moved my head up and down so he could see me confirm that he was exact and correct about when I started.

"School and the academy at the same time? No wonder you went

missing for a while. (I nod yes) So how long have you been doing this undercover work?"

(Strong whisper)

"About two years now."

"What name did you use on the street?"

"My family nick name Unck."

Grann had pulled her hand away from my arm and made herself as comfortable as she could in that hard hospital chair. Her expression was blank until she heard the questions, then she seemed eagerly interested in the answers.

"Your fellow officers tried to make us believe that you were in the middle of a drug war. In some sort of fight for someone else's territory. (He pauses and moves to the foot of the bed) We knew that was bullshit! But knowing what we know, it didn't explain why you were out there. Not until your cousin helped me put all the pieces together. It was at that moment we realized how much more complicated things had become."

I was wondering what he meant. Complicated for whom? I didn't understand, and he must have seen it on my face. His speech became mono toned. It's the one he used when he had to explain something to Sean and I. Especially when he really didn't want to.

"Angel was your target, wasn't he? (I nod) Well he was ours also. We were beginning to take over his corners. Started jacking his drops, even killed a lot of his crew during the process. Problem was...he thought someone else was doing it. He thought that you were double dipping. You know...buying half his product and then killing his crew for the rest. Sean's crew worked hard on breaking Angel, but Sean made a mistake using your name. Using "Rizzo", unfortunately and unnecessarily confused the entire operation. Life is strange nephew. You sometimes catch a break when you don't expect it. Ours came when we learned that Angel was under surveillance. We chose to exploit that. Which only gave him two choices. One: give up his corners

to us now, or Two: Kill the undercover and pay off his debt for the Intel we provided. (He pauses) It was a good plan. It ***was*** *a good plan. Fortunately, for us, we would have made out either way. (He sighs) I want you to understand me when I tell you this nephew...as slow as it takes for things to finally go well for ya, you damn sure better believe that they'll go to shit twice as fast. Shit on a rocket... you can never be ready for. That's how I felt about what happened to you. I had no idea you were the undercover we sent Angel after. I'm glad your cousin got there when he did. I was reminded of the time you looked out for him in that garage when you guys were teenagers. The tough part is... this all might not have happened if Sean had gotten there on time. The entire situation might have ended differently out on that street if he had. Ya see Nephew, this brief explanation might have cleared up a couple of things for you, but things are never that cut and dry. Life is never that simple."*

Uncle Robert backed away from the edge of the bed, checking his watch and said, "One hour and forty-five minutes." As he moved back towards the door and Grann took a moment to jump in. I was still trying to digest what Uncle Robert had just told me, completely unprepared for what Grann was about to say.

"Boy if you've learned anything from me... I hope it's that things in this life are never simple. Life will always throw you a curve. (I turned to face her) How do you rise to a challenge Raymond, if you do not have a challenge to make you rise? We, (pointing between herself and Uncle Robert) always hoped that you understood how our family operates. Although the way we conduct business has changed over the years, it's how we stay low key about it that keeps us in business. Promises were kept that would keep you semi-sheltered from the family's business. It wasn't what your father wanted. But to join forces with the likes of those folks that we have had to accommodate, bribe, dodge and kill over the years just to stay in business is treasonous to us. Why? Raymond! Why do this to your family? The police have only profited

from our work or made it difficult for us to do what we do. (Shifts in her chair) Although you may actually have done some good for these streets or the community, your crusade for justice hurts ***our*** *business. They may have asked you to take down a few of the city's lower-level dealers...but how soon before they sent you after us. Huh, and what then? The way I see it, you being a cop creates complications for this family. Oh, I've considered the other side of it, to have a body, a voice on the inside to help aid our goals. (Impulsively) It won't work! Too complicated. Complications create conflict and conflict has to be dealt with! To be taken as seriously as life and death. Believe it or not but this isn't the first time your grandmother has had to make life altering decisions. One of the toughest involved your parents."*

I stiffened when she said that. Not knowing what she meant. My face must have been filled with confusion and she reacted to it.

"We never told you how your parents died."

(In a harsh whisper)

"I know my parents were killed! (Uncle Robert lifts his head, surprised by my words) I just don't know why! "

"Well, then it's time that you knew. Thirty years ago, our family was in the middle of a crisis. Your Granddad, God rest his soul, had been dead for at least two years and your uncle and your father had begun to run the business. After he died, I continued my nursing job. Your uncle was taking care of the product and the money. Your Father was the family's muscle. Rival competitors were beginning to make moves against us once your grandfather was gone. They thought that we were weak. Thought they could overtake us. Your dad proved to everyone who tried or thought about trying something that they would risk their lives or the lives of their families if they did. Many people died by your father's hands over the span of some years. He created a reputation of fear for our family throughout this city that made our profits rise. For a while, things were going great. Weren't they Robert? (He moves his head but doesn't look up) We even began to help

more in the community. This helped cover up what we were doing illegally. It was after your father got married and you were born when things began to change. Your Father began to get more involved, seriously involved with rebuilding the community. The downside of helping his community was that he became more reluctant to inflict the fear that we needed to fend off our enemies. Word was getting around that DL Kingsley had gotten soft and our carriers started getting robbed. Something had to be done because we were losing money."

Uncle Robert shook his head in agreement to what Grann was saying but still never raised his head to make eye contact with anyone. He just looked at his watch and said, "One hour", as Grann continued to speak.

"As head of this family and ultimate overseer of all finances, we sat down with your father to discuss how his new movement of kindness was hurting our profits. This was a conversation that didn't end well. He made it clear that he was finished putting fear into this city and would use every resource he had to make it a safer place for his son. He walked away and left us vulnerable to our enemies. Your Grandfather once said that the only way out of this business, this family or our enemies... would be death."

There was a brief silence as Grann asked Uncle Robert to pour her a glass of water as she tried to clear her throat. I lay expressionless and intensely soaked in this small piece of my family's history.

"At this point Raymond our family's financial livelihood was in danger and your father put us there. Something had to be done. Something that would strike fear in our enemies, revitalize our business and shape this community the way we wanted it. I only saw one possible solution. (Touches my arm) I arranged the assassination of your Father."

I was breathless. I sat looking at my grandmother in horrifying shock.

"It had to be public Raymond and it had to happen quickly. The public had to see it as a tragic murder, but our enemies also had to know that our family was behind it. Our enemies had to know that we wouldn't think

twice about killing one of our own to stay profitable. Then the thought of ever crossing this family would die when you father did."

(Angered whisper)

"What about my mother?"

"Now what happened to her was tragic. Her life was spared, and she could have walked away. But when she tried to save a man who was already dead, and she became a liability."

"How could you kill my parents?"

"Thirty minutes."

"Thanks Robert. Honestly Raymond, I had hoped your mom would still be around to take care of you even though I didn't like her. She's the one who put all that pillar of the community shit in your father's head. She could never get with the program like your aunt Kate did. (Pointing towards me) As far as your father is concerned, it wasn't as difficult as you might think. Normally a mother would be shattered if anything happens to her child. Normally. (Breathes heavily) But since DL Kingsley wasn't my son, it didn't bother me at all. He was the bastard son of some slut your grandfather was with a year before he met me. He may have been ***your*** *father, even Robert's brother but he was nothing to me."*

I was furious and couldn't hold back my emotions. Too weak to move and too painful to speak, my anger first manifested with a single tear and then an overwhelming feeling of hatred that I thought impossible to feel for anyone. Especially anyone in my family and now a scowl is the only visual proof of my anger.

"Raymond, the strangest thing is how life has a way of repeating itself. It's ironic but funny how ***you*** *now stand in the way of the profitability of this family. Public interest of this so- called turf war is raising too many questions with the city's government officials. What the papers have reported is the only perception of what happened out there. That will change once anyone hears your side of things, once you're strong enough to tell it. A lot*

of things will come undone if that happens. We have city officials, police captains and undercover cops who can't afford to have any other version told to the public. So, if you die from your injuries, life will go on as normal. The way we need it to go on."

"I can't be a part of this Ma. Not again."

"That's fine Robert, just go and let the boys in."

Uncle Robert raised his head and made eye contact with me. He raised his fist to his heart and pounded it against his chest before he said; "See ya at the morgue Nephew." I felt helpless as he turned, opened the door and walked out. Grann was now standing and reaching into her purse as three guys walked into the room. Two of them I remembered from the street the night I was attacked. The guys I heard called "Big Guns" and "Slim Nate" came walking into the room. Not far behind them was my cousin Sean. My heart collapsed when he came through that door. No one made a sound as they entered. They were all business, like they all knew what had to do be done as they came in. Slim Nate came to one side of the bed and Big Guns came to the other and they both held me down. As if I was strong enough to struggle. Sean grabbed a towel from the bathroom, then came around behind Slim Nate and held the towel over my mouth. Grann found what she was digging for and pulled a syringe out of her purse. She grabbed my I-V and pushed whatever was in the syringe into the tube. Uncle Robert poked his head into the room and said, "Ten minutes." as Grann stepped back from the bed, Big Guns, Slim Nate and Sean let me go. Sean came around the bed and stood next to Grann as Slim Nate and Big Guns left the room. Sean took the syringe from Grann and put it in a paper bag that he pulled from his pocket. My arms were at my sides and my head was becoming hard to hold up. Sean hadn't looked at me from the time he stepped into the hospital room but as he opened the door to leave, he looked at me and whispered, "Sorry Cousin."

(Grann smiles)

"Raymond, people live and die by the choices they make everyday son. Sadly, they also die by circumstances that are totally out of their control. Be fortunate that you will die knowing the truth. Not many have that courtesy. I hope the truth brings you peace. Are you ready? I told you to get ready. To be ready! You never know when your last day on this earth will be. Are you ready Raymond? Then I'll see ya on the other side."

She winked before she stepped out of the room. Her smile was etched into my memory as my breathing slowed. I've felt a lot of emotions in my life, but this feeling of helplessness mixed with nullifying anger was more painful than any injury I have ever been afflicted with. I felt myself slipping away but this time it was painfully silent. The last things I remember as my breathing just about stopped, was how the cruelest people can often be the closest to you and seeing a smiling nurse coming in the room to check up on me. I think it's been about two hours. She asked me how I was feeling today. Then I blacked out.

ACT TWO

CITY UNDER SIEGE

The one thing people cannot escape …is Death.
They can narrowly delay it, but never Escape it.
Death will come for us all, but never the same way.
More importantly (and I'm inflexible about this)
Most of us live our lives unaware that it could come for us at any moment. Doctor's will guess-ti-mate. Our last hours.
But, I don't care what People may tell you...
No one will know the exact day, time or moment
The breath of life will leave any of us.
Whether it comes one night in our sleep,
Violently on a street corner or by someone we call family.
When it's our time...It's our time.
Raymond Kingsley

CHAPTER ONE

Last Day to Be Honored

IT WAS A stormy Thursday afternoon. The rain was falling with an angry contempt, setting the scene for the events happening today. The red and blue lights at the top of the police cars are reflected in the puddles as the drops rapidly fall from the sky. A two-lane processional of squad cars slowly led the black topless hearse up Fortieth Street to Eden's Shepard Baptist church. As the processional approached, the street and stairs in front of the church were lined with Officers from my precinct and other departments from surrounding cities. All wearing their dress blues and white gloves. All… here to honor their fallen brother. Standing together creating an image of solidarity. The police force doesn't like when one of their own is murdered. Doesn't matter if it's by the hand of some dumb ass kid with a gun during a routine traffic stop or by strange circumstances while lying in a hospital bed. Nevertheless, the vast numbers presented by this many cops represents the honor that comes with dawning the uniform.

After the processional passed through the two ladder fire trucks holding our countries flag and came to a stop, six officers carrying umbrellas approached the black and chrome casket at the back of the hearse. Covering it as six other officers lifted it from the hearse. They carefully set it onto a rolling cart before taking a moment to wipe down the handles. Hoping to get a better grip as the rain continued to come down hard. They did their best to keep the coffin dry as every other officer stood at full attention. Saluting as the box climbed the stairs to the doors of the church. Once inside, the pallbearers faced each other, changing their grip, using two hands until the cart could be placed underneath the coffin again. With officers still on each side, the coffin was led down the aisle. The remaining drops of rain cascaded off the uncovered parts of the box as it reached the alter. The church went silent as two of the pallbearers removed the water-soaked American flag from atop the coffin and folded it. Once the flag was formed into a perfect triangle, it was placed into a wood container with a glass top that sat at the head of the coffin. Just before the two that folded the flag took their place next to the others who had split up to stand at attention at the head and foot of the coffin. Once all the officers were at full attention, two attendants from the funeral home quickly walked over to diligently work to get things situated after opening the lid as the Choir began to sing "I know who holds tomorrow". Just before the song's end, every pillow, ruffle and crease were placed perfectly before taking refuse in a corner where they would go unnoticed until the program called for them again.

It's strange. I feel like I'm in a bad dream. I guess the spirit hangs around to see just who and how much the world will miss you. Roslyn sat alone on the left side front pew with a slew of officers sitting in the rows right behind her. My family sat on the right. On the front pew were Grann, Sean and Uncle Robert. Big Guns and Slim Nate took up the entire row just behind them. Nate was fidgety. Nate nervously looked around the church because he has never been around this vast number of cops without them trying to subdue him. Big G on the other hand, was doing what he was there to do. Protect the Kingsley's! Uncle Robert sat closest to the isle, occasionally flipping through messages that came through to his phone. Grann sat to his left. With the regal look of a grandmother who lost someone she cherished so much. Sean was last. Lost in a deep gaze, as if he was battling with conflicting emotions. Grann would occasionally gander across the aisle and politely acknowledge Roslyn with a smile.

"Robert, who is that woman sitting over there?" Grann whispers.

(Still looking at his phone)

"I don't know Ma."

Uncle Robert lifts his head and turns slightly. He raises his hand and motions Big G to lean in closer.

"Yes Boss."

"Who's the J-Lo look-a-like across the way there?"

Before Big G could answer, Slim Nate indiscreetly jumps in.

"I could give a Damn! She's fine as HELL."

Uncle Robert rotates his head to the other side giving Nate a look that said, sit back and shut up and Nate quickly eased back on the pew.

"I don't know Boss", answered Big G. "But I'll look into it."

"Don't bother." Sean leaned in to say. "That's Rizzo's girlfriend."

Uncle Robert nodded and Big G slid back into his seat.

The choir's second song was ending as Pastor William R. Webster stood at the pulpit. His head moves left to right while he scans the people in the church. He grips the sides of the podium and takes a deep breath before he speaks. Pastor Webster talks/preaches with a deep raspy voice, a slight draw, pausing and taking deep breathes in between sentences.

"Days like today... are (short pause) painful. Days like today... are too frequent. (Dramatically look to his right) We are losing our young to violence. To drugs and to wars we shouldn't be fighting. Fights we aren't winning on hostile dessert lands and fights we are losing on our own city's streets. We feel as if we often have had to unnecessarily deal with the loss of someone we love. A grandson. A nephew. A colleague and in many cases a friend. But nonetheless...a loss is a loss. And when you lose someone like this young man, who's future was brightly ahead of him, who gave himself to God, who worked to fix his communi-tay...I myself revisit the question

of what is it ***we*** *are doing wrong. As parents, mentors, and leaders of our communities. What are we doing wrong? There's a generation of kids outside these walls who don't try in school anymore. They want things handed to them. Often taking the easy route. Strong-arming the fruits of someone else's labor. Emulating what they see in the movies. Often using guns to make themselves feel like big shots. Crabs in a barrel. Armed, ignorant and ruthless. Looking for the easiest way to take what they feel the world owes them. It's true...the good often die young. Unnecessarily and I ask...at what cost? (Leans into podium a bit) Days like today...are hard on all of us for different reasons. Days like today...are rainy because an injustice needs to be cleansed from this world. A dirty memory in time sadly set in motion by the death of Detective Raymond Kingsley. Let's take a minute. Would everyone please bow their heads in a moment of prayer?"*

The congregation closed their eyes and lowered their heads as the Pastor began to pray. Sean appeared to be nervous. His reflexes were jumpy. Flinching and opening his eyes every time one of the flashes of the newspaper's cameras would take a picture. Big G continued to scan the church as Slim Nate played with the tithing envelopes and anything else that sat on the back of the pew directly in front of him. He behaved like a kid who was bored and ready to leave. Grann didn't like the small ruckus he was making. She lifted her head slightly, looked over her shoulder at him, gave a nasty look, and then with the middle finger of her right hand directed him to sit back into his seat again. All of this going unnoticed as the Pastor finished praying.

Reverend Webster opened the floor for anyone who wanted to speak. The congregation sat silent. That was until the creaking sound of someone using the pew to stand, broke the silence. Grann came to her feet and with the help of Sean, stood just in front of the casket. The reverend took the microphone from the pulpit and handed it down to Sean, who held it in front of his grandmother. Grann's expression appeared to be solemn as she lightly strokes the coffin with her left hand.

"A day like today is shaded in sorrow and is very, very painful. The loss of any grandchild… under circumstances that we will never come to understand, is heart wrenching. I'm reminded of his father, ***my*** *son, and the pointless way he and his wife also lost their lives. We never want our children to die before we do. That goes for our grandchildren as well. We are all led to believe that the violence in our streets is why my grandson lies before us all. I don't think that's the only reason. I believe a bit of deception plays a part as well. I didn't know that Raymond had joined the police force or was even promoted to detective. These things he kept a secret from us. Sadly, I don't think families talk as much as they should. Deception, mistrust and lies tear more than just families apart. They're destroying communities. I feel... somehow ...that if we, as a family, would have known more of what Raymond was into then we could have protected him somehow. It tears you apart as a guardian when* ***we*** *can't protect the ones we love. I don't know if this could have been avoided. I don't know if I could have provided some kind of comfort for the troubles he may have been hiding. All I know is that I will bury my grandson today. Left with the same unanswerable questions that I was left with when his parents were murdered. What I want to say... is...we must listen to our kids, spouses, or whomever you love. We must not let them leave this earth without letting them know what they meant to us and it hurts much more knowing that I never got to express to my grandson what he meant to this family."*

Grann tapped Sean on his arm, alerting him that she was done speaking. Sean handed the microphone back to Reverend Webster as Grann signaled Uncle Robert to help her back to her seat. Before Grann could sit, Reverend Webster motioned for the ushers to come. They began to move the flowers as two officers's re-draped the casket with another flag and handing the folded one in the box to Roslyn. The ushers shifted the coffin into position as the other officers who were to walk with it, moved to their places. The choir began to sing Eva Pearson's version of

"On My Way Home" as the flag draped box rolled toward the exit to take its last ride.

The rain continued to come down hard. Every drop, creating waves in areas that would puddle or running down the paths that led to the different areas of the cemetery. The processional after arriving slowly came to a stop in front of a small stone structured building with the name "Kingsley" etched across the top of it. While two other stones were bearing the names of Raymond's parents on the outside left and right of the crypt's entrance. The mausoleum was too small to accommodate so many people inside, so a stand was set up 3ft from the entrance for the coffin. A canopy was also set up to protect the immediate family from the rain. The pallbearers moved carefully carrying the coffin to the stand because of the uneven terrain but managed to keep their footing despite the wet ground. The cars that followed the hearse began to empty but Grann opted to stay inside the Limo, while Roslyn, Old Jack, Uncle Robert and Big Gun's took their seats under the canopy in just that order. Roslyn caught a glimpse of Uncle Robert smirking at her as Rev. Webster made his way to the front. The reverend stepped behind the casket, just in front of the officers who placed it there and opened his bible. He started in reading another scripture before asking everyone to bow their heads in a prayer. After the Reverend finishes praying, everyone chanted, "Amen". Rev. Webster extended his arms, inviting Roslyn to come forward. She stood assisted by Old Jack and stepped towards the coffin carrying a single white rose. She closes her eyes and whispers something under her breath before making the sign of the cross as a Catholic would. Roslyn opened her eyes, wipes the tears from her cheek and kisses the rose. When she pulled the rose away from her mouth, you could see the neutral gloss brown outline of her lips against the white pedals. The image she created after laying down the flower, would tug at the patriotic strings of anyone's heart. The pedals came to rest between the white stars on the flag and were a nice contrast against the blue material. The drops of rain pushed their way down the green stem as one of the thorns snagged a thread of one of the red stripes. As her right hand pulled away from the flower, Reverend Webster began to speak.

"We've assembled on this hallowed ground at the final resting place for Raymond Kingsley. Here we place his body but we hold onto his memory and let his spirit ascend to the heavens. Ashes to ashes… and dust to dust. We commit his body back to the earth... from whence it came."

He pauses as a voice rings out over his own. Sean was sitting directly behind his father and asked (loudly), "Why is she the only one who gets to place a flower on the casket?" A woman sitting next to Sean answered, "It's a rite held for immediate family." Big Gun's turns quickly, to face Sean.

"I don't know why it concerns you anyway Playa, you've got somewhere to be in twenty minutes. So don't drag this shit out. Let her set that shit down so we can get this shit over with."

Old Jack, upset and not liking what he heard, spoke up with his loud thundering voice.

"Have some respect for the dead. Consideration for those who are honoring who they have lost. ***Don't be disrespectful!*** *Today is this man's last day to be honored. So put a muzzle on all your uncalled for, impolite, discourteous banter. You'd expect the same if it were someone you loved."*

Big Gun's laughs to himself before asking, "Is this old bastard talking to me? Naw. Can't be! (Turns to Jack) Maybe you should keep the self-righteous commentary to yourself old man, cause I don't want to hear that shit."

Suddenly a 6ft, stout, slightly bearded man stood straight up and took two steps towards Big Guns as he used his cane to balance himself. "I'm not going to ask you again son. This isn't the time or place."

"Rising to your feet and step' en to me is the quickest way to be walking with two of those." Big Guns says as he comes to his feet as well. Sean also stood as Big Guns slid his hands into his pockets and made noises like he was sucking his teeth. While at the same time shifting a toothpick back and

forth in his mouth. His expression turned from a smirk to an annoyed sneer as his eyes locked onto Old Jack.

"If you think I won't fuck you up because were surrounded by cops, then you'd be mistaken. Let's be clear. I won't be disrespected either."

As the voices of the two men elevate, the attention quickly turned away from Roslyn's heart felt moments near the casket. She turned to face the commotion, which led the Reverend to turn as well. The inflection of anger in Big Gun's voice brought about movement of some of the officers, as they began taking steps toward the two men. Old Jack looked around, making a motion with his hands. Waving off any additional help from his fellow officers.

[Turning back to Big Guns]

"I'll do what's needed to keep ***this*** *day from being ruined. I'm warning you son, you're this close to resting in my cross hairs."*

"Motha-Fucka, do I look nervous to you? Ya might want to sit ya old ass down."

"G, let that shit go!" Sean added as he tried to get Big Gun's attention by touching his shoulder. "Come on. This really isn't the time for this."

Big Guns huffs and smirks, but never takes his eyes off of his target. Completely ignoring Sean.

"I think you should listen to your buddy if you want to avoid any trouble. You know...the real problem is that you don't get it. Guys like you...never do. Strutting around like your hot shit. Trying to build a name for yourself in these streets using intimidation, violence and whatever intelligence you can muster. A name that is as easily forgotten as any other low-level, two-bit kid that dies trying to work his way up on those corners. The only difference between you and them… you not only have to contend with your competitors but with any unafraid law-abiding person who will quickly get in your ass. But who also has the time he needs to bring you to justice?"

[With contempt]

"You don't know SHIT old man. You don't shake me. But some words of advice... don't lurk near shadows if you're afraid of the dark. (Points to himself) This monster don' t back down."

In a deeply agitated voice Uncle Robert intervenes. "That's enough! Be quiet and let's go!" Big Gun's shifts his toothpick before raising his hand about chest level and points at Old Jack, Mouthing the words, "Watch your ass Old man." Uncle Robert cuts a nasty look at Big Guns before taking a moment to light his cigar. He takes a couple of deep puffs as he instructs Big Guns with a head nod to take the lead. You could hear the long squealing noise of him sucking his teeth as he cleared a path for Uncle Robert. Sean's head hung low as he stood a faced the coffin. His expression filled with a pain full remorse. Only mere seconds did his eyes meet Roslyn's before he dropped his head even lower. With his eyes now closed, he made a fist with his right hand and pounded his chest twice. "Goodbye cousin." He said with a quiver in his voice just as the gun salute began. He stood, as each gunshot caused him to flinch. Unable to hide his remorse or pain as the sound of the reloading rifles confirmed that his cousin is gone. Sean quickly wipes away his tears before anyone could see them. Suddenly catching eye contact with Roslyn again, he mouths the words, "I'm Sorry" before turning to follow his dad to the car.

CHAPTER TWO

Settling In

THREE CUSTOMERS STAND around inside a local bar watching a 6'1', three-hundred-pound, muscular Samoan man holding a guy up against the counter by the neck. The bar tender threatens to call the police as he picks up a phone. One of the three, appeals to his better judgment. Convincing him that calling wouldn't be a good decision and asked that he be patient. Assuring him that no harm would come to any patrons or the bar. Also ensuring that they'd be finished shortly.

Negotiating with the worried bartender after finding his way behind the bar was Mecca Childs, Meck for short. Meck is a calm, smooth talking businessman who dresses like Russell Simmons. Is just as wealthy and has a way of putting you at ease. As the man in the strong hold struggles to get free, the bartender sets the phone down just before he leans in closer to hear Meck's tip on how to bring more business into the bar. Standing near the Samoan and the guy struggling to get free was Mea, Meck's twin sister. Mea's demeanor is exactly the opposite of her brothers. She is often loud, brash and lacks patience. "I expect you to tell me what I want to know!" Mea shouts while poking at the guy. "Or... I'll have Moo here put more pressure around your Adams apple. Most likely putting a strain on our friendly chat." Mea reached out and pulled up the tee shirt the squirming guy was wearing. Revealing an amateur tattoo that read "punk bitch" across his stomach. Mea smirks before saying, "How cute. Most people try to hide how they really feel about themselves. [Smug] No doubt, your Vernon alright." Mea takes a seat on a bar stool, with her back to the bar, leaning with her arms resting on the brass railing.

"I don't want to have to hurt you. Not so soon, anyway. But honestly, ***that*** *will depend on you... and what you have to say. Right here, right now."*

Vernon pulls at Mountain Moo's fingers and hands. Trying to release the grip around his neck. Moo doesn't flinch as Vernon claws and scratches into Moo's arms. The bar was quiet except for the clinking sounds of the glasses and bottles. Most of the patrons would turn to see what was going on, but actually kept their heads down and stayed out of it. Vernon began to choke after Mountain Moo tightened his grip, just as Mea instructed.

"You're making this harder than it needs to be, Man! You don't have the reputation for being a Bad Ass. So, make this easy for yourself."

Mea motions Mountain Moo to loosen the grip around Vernon's neck. Before sitting him on the barstool. Waiting, she gave him a few moments to get himself together to speak. Mea turns to the bartender, who was still talking to her brother and asks for a small glass of water. Vernon coughs and tries to sooth his neck by rubbing it with one hand. He repeatedly clears his throat and sips the water as Mea begins to question him.

"So, I understand that ***you*** *took over Angel's crew and territories?"*

[Coughs] "Wha...What?"

"After Angel was killed. After Damon was killed. You took over. Right?"

Vernon sips more of his water and blankly turns towards Mea. Mea's posture doesn't change as she raises one eyebrow before turning toward Vernon.

"Let me take a different approach. [Smirking] Let me tell you what I know. It might help things move along here a bit. I know... that your former boss Angel made a mistake shooting someone who he thought robbed him and killed some of his crew. It turns out that he shoots Rob Kingsley's undercover

cop nephew. Only...getting himself killed by the hands of Kingsley's only son. After Angel's death, you moved the operation to the gas station at 7th & Main. Of course, in the absence of true leadership, you quickly assumed the role as [using air quotes] the leader. You weren't met with much resistance from whoever was left from the crew because everyone knows this city is divided. You haven't sat with the council to discuss any new terms yet. Everyone knows there is a mandatory amount of time the council sets aside for grieving and burials. There is no talk of business until that period has passed. I also know... ***You*** *want to present yourself to the council as the area's new leader. [Pauses] Anything I'm saying sound unfamiliar?"*

Vernon barely moves. His mouth was tightly clinched, and his head moved slightly in a disgusted manner. His eyes stayed focused on a neon sign mounted on the wall straight ahead of him. He lowers his chin downward, towards his left shoulder and barely cuts his eyes to look at Mea.

[With contempt]

"What do you want??!"

"Me... nothing Vernon. It's not about what ***I*** *want. Today, to my delight... I'm just a messenger."*

"Then...What?!! What the ***fuck*** *is this about!"*

"Oh Vernon. Don't try to be tough. Your history contradicts it. Look... we need you to be clear on what ***we*** *know. Ideally so that you can be clear with what you'll have to do."*

Mea stopped talking abruptly, to grab a drink that her brother was handing to her. Mountain Moo grunted as he shifted his weight from one leg to another. Vernon started to shift around on the bar stool until Mountain Moo grabbed his shoulder and stopped him from moving.

[Smiling]

"Thanks for the drink big brother."

"Not a problem." Meck replies playfully as he returns to where he was teaching the bar tender how to mix new drinks.

"Where was I?" Mea continues after taking a sip. "Oh Yeah. I was about to tell you [pointing at Vernon] what ***you*** *need to know. As... We... speak, the rest of Angel's crew, your crew, is being eliminated. Eradicated. Delt wit. I really hate for you to find out like this but the last of any breed is usually unaware that they're the last."*

Vernon, although overcome with anger, found himself unable to move. Mountain Moo had one of his massive claws clamped onto his shoulder.

[Mumbling in a bit of pain]

"I know you're not saying they're all dead?"

"Not all of 'em, but that's not important right now."'

Mea motions Mountain Moo to spin Vernon around on the barstool. Meck made his way along the counter and was now standing in front of Vernon. Meck placed what looked like a strip of paper onto the counter, slides it towards Vernon and begins to speak.

"There's life [tapping the paper] in this paper here. Your chance to be reborn. That ticket is a one-way life saver. I know this is all coming at you pretty fast. Believe me when I tell you that every aspect of what's being presented to you has been taken into consideration. Right now, things are a bit vague and you can't see the clear picture. Let me help. [Pours Vernon a shot] Whoever's still alive from your crew has an opportunity to accept the same offer for self-preservation. I am extending you the same courtesy. <u>You</u> will not be making any meetings with the council. Your choices are relocation or death. Either way... it's a fresh start."

Mea rotates on her bar stool and is now facing Vernon.

"The one thing my brother didn't say... and this bares the highest importance... [Whispers] your criminal activities in this city, in this state, are over."

Meck leans onto the counter trying to look into Vernon's eyes.

"So, take the ticket, gather what you own and leave. Go get a new start."

The bar was so quiet you could hear the friction of the paper against the counter as Meck slides the ticket closer to Vernon. Vernon let out a few deep huffs before staring down at the ticket. Mea instructed Mountain Moo with hand signals to fall back.

"None of us are strangers to making decisions." Meck said releasing the ticket as he continued to speak.

"We make thousands of them every day. But there is always a difference with the one's that can change the course of our lives. They feel different. We have to deal with them differently. Our emotions tell us too. And... If you haven't heard this before, I will say it to you now. Don't let emotion decide a life changing moment. Your heart, fucks with you. Your mind knows what's right. It's not often your heart and mind work in tune with each other. Take a descent amount of time to make a good decision."

Meck taps the counter before turning away from Vernon and heads towards the open end of the counter. Meck walks towards his sister who has hopped off the bar stool and was shooing Mountain Moo out the door. Vernon sat with his head down until he senses Meck had passed behind him.

"How will you know what my decision was." Vernon asks.

"By the use or the nonuse of that ticket."

Meck never broke stride as he answered and was gone before another question could be asked. Vernon sat with the ticket below his fingertips. His mind, swimming with questions. Who are they? How did they know how to find me? How do they know so much about the crew? How much of this is truth or bullshit? If they are not from around here, how do they have a working knowledge of the things that's happened? His mind circles back to the idea that this was supposed to be his time. Frustrated, with ticket in hand, he left the stool and walked out of the bar. He stood with his back to the entrance. The sun seemed bright as his eyes adjusted to being back outside. The wind was stronger now than when he first walked in. Vernon's clothes were whipping hard, and the air whistled as it passed his ears. His face wrinkles as he thinks about the offer he was given. "This is my fuck'en time! Ain't nobody chasing me out!" Vernon angrily mumbled as he balls up the ticket and tosses it to the ground. As the wind delays the wrinkled paper from reaching the ground, Vernon curiously looks around as he hears the sound of something different cutting through the wind. That was the last thing he heard before his body is violently thrusted against the building as he's struck with two deadly sniper rounds. The first, hits his chest, heart side. Causing him to hunch and fall backwards. The second enters dead center of his forehead. As Vernon's lifeless body pinballs off the wall and hits the ground, Mea puts the car in gear but not before turning to her brother. "I say kill 'em all and get it over with. We've got to stop wasting money on these damn tickets!"

CHAPTER THREE

A Day in the Bay

City Center, Courtyard, 14th & San Pablo Ave. Oakland Ca.

[Cell phone call]

"I DON'T CARE IF he doesn't understand why Ana! I'm not paying him too! I want you to make it clear to him that we are a task-oriented organization. Him understanding is not a pre-requisite of employment. I need him to finish the job. And... If he can't do that... remind him of the others that we made an example. Remind him that there are only two ways out of this gig now that he's signed on. I don't want him to be the fifth to fall on his sword. He's got skills and is too talented to lose. Just get 'em re-focused. It's always better to retire, than to be retired."

"I'll take care of it when I get back boss. What about the downtown meet with Mr. Kingsley and the council? How do you want to handle that?"

"I've got a few things in the works. I'll let you know what the plans are. Long before the meet comes. Right now, I want you to handle <u>that</u> loose end in the Bay Area first. Fly back when it's done Ana."

(Click)

PROFILE

*Ana Allison Grainger- a 5'7', fair skinned woman with hazel-colored eyes and long hair. Has had a figure like Selma Hyack since she was sixteen. An ex-tomboy, who grew to realize the value of her femininity. Street smart with a master's degree in Psychology. Retired from the Military and a former decorated police SWAT officer. She's Gorgeous, skilled and dangerous. *****

Ana closes her phone and slides the thin device into her left rear pocket. She turns slightly and smiles at a man in a business suit. Who just happens to be sitting on the detailed concrete slab just at the edge of the grass. The businessman signals Ana with two motions. First, instructing her take her time. Second, pointing downward. Showing her that he would be sitting right where he was. Ana's smile as a response is good enough to hold him where he was until she finished speaking with a very large man, Bishop "Tank" McGee. A three-hundred-pound, ex-army demolitions specialist with a monk like calmness. But a big man who could go from Ghandi to Mount St. Helen's within seconds.

Tank stands near Ana gazing at the different architectures of the surrounding buildings. Barely moving his mouth as he spoke. This is so he doesn't give the guy in the suit the impression that they know one another. Tank mumbles, "What do you need Ana?" She discreetly asks him to get the rental car and pull it to the curb along 14th street.

"This is no different than last time Tank. Just time it right. It would be ideal for you to be by [nods] that crosswalk."

As Tank shuffled away, Ana slips a leather glove onto her left hand. The suited man stands with excitement, watching Ana approach. He grins as he focuses onto the sway of her breasts and the graceful shift of her hips as she walks towards him in tight blue jeans and heels. Never noticing her taking something from her jacket pocket and getting it positioned into her gloved hand. The man in the suit, after rising from the concrete, held his arms open awaiting Ana. His jacket hangs like an open curtain as she steps in closely. Seductively wrapping her arms around him while stroking his back with her right hand. Ana sees, from her left, an AC Transit bus ready to pull away from its stop. As the rev of the bus's engine grew louder, she moves her left hand into position. Ana holds a small Derringer handgun tightly in her hand. Careful of it because it has had the barrel cut down two inches. Causing the tip of the 22' caliber bullet to stick out of the narrowed barrel. The suited man rises slightly, feeling something poking into his side. Ana pulls the trigger. It's fortunate that his jacket provided visual cover, and how the shot fired simultaneously with the bus backfiring. The few people in the courtyard reacted to the noise from the bus by ducking and looking around. Not noticing the businessman slump into Ana's arms from the pain. She eases him back into a seated position as she whispers. "If beauty is the last thing you want to see...then I suggest you gaze upon me. If not... take this time to ask God for forgiveness just before look into the light." Ana listened to his painful grunts, expecting that the bullet would be bouncing around and tearing him apart inside. The suited man strangely sat bent over holding his side, grimacing and strangely peering straight ahead. Ana wasted no time providing a cover as she hollers, "FINE! It's over then!" As she walks off, Ana doesn't look back as he painfully calls and reaches out for her. She reaches the crosswalk and Tank pulls up like clockwork. She shuts the car door just as the suited man's body falls to the concrete. Exposing his blood-stained shirt. Now waiting for the signal light to change, Tank pops a chocolate chip cookie into his mouth before looking over his right shoulder.

"Do you think you got 'em? Is he dead?"

"I'm not going to wait to find out Tank. If the bullet doesn't get him, then the patch I put on the back of his shirt will."

"Patch? The size of the Nicotine one's?"

"No. Standard band-aid size."

At that moment Ana pulls what looks like a car alarm remote from her bra. As the others that were enjoying their lunches in the courtyard listen to the shrills of some woman yelling, "OH MY GOD, I THINK HE NEEDS HELP!" Without hesitation Ana presses the button. ***[BOOM]*** *Body parts fly all over the courtyard as the lunch goer's duck. Ana calmly places the remote back into her bra as Tank dumps another cookie into his mouth before pulling away.*

(Chewing on cookies)

"I'd say that answers my question. Effective."

"I'd say. You look hungry Tank. Let's visit Mamma J's for some of the best soul food and eat. We've got more than enough time before our flight leaves."

(Two hours later. In Robert Kingsley's Mid-town Office)

My footsteps were loud. Every step as my feet hit the floor echoed in the hallway. I was out of breath as I burst into my father's office. Robert Kingsley sat with his chair, turned slightly away from the desk, one hand on the arm of the chair and the other cupping his chin.

(Out of breath)

"Dad! Did you hear? Cousin Charles is dead! It's all over the news!"

Turning only his head slightly, Robert looks at his son and softly replies, "I know." As he covers the top half of his face with his hand and starts massaging his temples in a slow circular motion.

(Panicky)

"What are we going to do...dad? You know how important cousin Charles was. Who's going to bleach the whites? Clean the dirty? This is bad!"

With his hand still on his head, Robert peers at his son through his fingers and sighs.

(Still panicky)

"Sooo...what are we going to do?"

Robert leans forward and opens the lower drawer on the right side of his desk. He then raises his left foot onto it as he reclines back into the chair.

(Impulsively)

"We've got to get out there! Ya know? Send someone to Oakland. Send me. We've got to find out what happened. Let's put some new things into motion I know a guy who can help."

Robert mumbles under his breath with a disgusted contempt looking towards his son. "What are we going to do." Pausing as he sits upright in his chair.

"Well...Son... Don't worry about The Bay Area. Big Gun's is already on a plane. He'll find out what I need to know."

Sean looked at his father, his demeanor displaying disappointment. But he thought carefully about his next words as his father searched for a wooden match to light his cigar.

"Do we need that kind of muscle in the Bay? I could've made the trip and figured things out. I have good contacts out there."

"Simply son, our family, our organization must keep a low profile on this. Especially with whatever happened out there. Your 2nd cousin was into some things we cannot be linked too. Besides, I have something else I want you to look into. It's just as important and I need you to move quickly on it."

His directions were explicitly detailed to his son. Presented without the possibility of being misunderstood in regard to what he wanted done. Most importantly... he clarified, no mistakes. He doesn't tolerate mistakes. I felt it in the tone of his voice, the dead look in his eyes and I nodded to assure him that I understood. As I left his office, I was skeptical about his decision to send Big Gun's to Oakland. I know I could find out what happened and probably quicker than Gun's will. I've got great contacts in the Bay area. I couldn't understand why the assignment he gave me was so important. I felt like he was making me prove myself for some reason. But, if that's what he wants, or what Grann wants, then I'll do whatever I have too.

CHAPTER FOUR

One Easy Task?

IT WAS MID-DAY on Wednesday when Slim Nate and Sean pulled in front of his late cousin's house. The block was silent except for the sound of the trees swaying from the November winds. The sun was peeking from behind the clouds, but the gusts of wind were exceptionally strong today. Sean's mind flashes with memories of Raymond as he gazed at his Mustang that still sits in the driveway just behind the fence. The house looked even better than the last time Sean was over here. The house was painted a new color. The concrete in the driveway had been replaced with a decorative stone layout. There were more flowers and accent lighting in the yard. Much more landscaping than he would never expect from Raymond. Appearing too well kept for a home that should be empty. A four-foot chain link fence now protected the front of the yard and driveway. With both the entrance to the walkway and driveway securely locked. Sean sighed with frustration because his right knee has been achy, and he wanted to avoid having to jump this fence.

"If we're going in, we're gonna have to hop it."

"I was hoping to avoid that Slim."

"But cha' can't Sean. The gates are locked. (He steps back and prepares to run) This fence ain't shit! Take one hop and you'll be over it."

Slim Nate took a running start; hit the fence mid-way with his right foot. He grabs the top with his hands and is over it without any effort. Sean's effort to do as Slim did wasn't as enthusiastic. He looked like a gate-hopping beginner as he began to climb. Sticking the toe of his shoe into the links of the fence until he was high enough to throw one leg over without snagging his balls as he pulled the other leg over. Sean's descent to the ground was equally pitiful for anyone who might have been watching. Somehow making it over without ripping his jacket. As he checked to see if he had snagged his coat, Slim Nate was laughing at him.

"Didn't you play basketball? You're telling me you could sky over someone to dunk the ball, but you can't hop a small fence. Shit! That's... some funny shit!"

"Shut the hell up Slim!!"

Nate continued to laugh as Sean made the climb to the front door. He could hear the low thump of music as he reached the top of the stairs. He bobbed his head to what sounded like a Cameo song as Nate ogled over the Mustang.

(Excited)

"This shit is tight."

Sean turned away from the door and looked off the porch to see what he was doing.

"What did you say Slim?"

(Talking louder)

"The car. This motha-fucka is Niice."

"Yeah, it is. Don't touch it!"

"He's right. Don't touch it!"

Slim looks up and around trying to find where the voice we just heard was coming from. Sean was startled after he turned back towards the front door. He had no idea she was standing there. She, Raymond's girlfriend, came outside so quietly. Roslyn stood in front of a half-opened door with her arms crossed and looking slightly annoyed.

"Why are you in my yard?!", she began. "...and what do you want?"

Her arms moved as she squeezed what looked like a remote between her fingers. The music that was playing became quieter as she simultaneously repeated her questions.

(Suddenly smiling, apprehensively)

"Yeah, we hopped over the gate. We didn't know anyone was here."

"Really?! If you thought, there was nobody here...then why ring the doorbell?"

Sean held his hand up to signify that he wanted to surrender.

"Okay. Give me a chance to start over. I came... to talk to you. Can you give me a few minutes?"

Roslyn took a few steps away from the door as her eyes shifted pass Sean and into the yard. Nate plucks at the Mustangs antenna. Causing it to swing back and forth, rapidly. She watches as he rubs his finger across the paint before leaning against the fender.

*"**Hey,** git off <u>my</u> car and leave it alone! You were already told not the touch it!"*

Nate throws his hand through the air. No doubt expressing how he doesn't give a shit about what Roslyn was saying. It took a directional head nod from Sean to move him away from the car. Sean turns towards Roslyn again.

"I'm here to talk to you about my cousin's assets, his estate. Cars, home, etcetera... etcetera... I'm here to give you notice that my family will be immediately taking control of all of his belongings."

"Is that so?" Roslyn answers smugly.

*"We will... obviously give you ample time to find somewhere else to live. Providing enough time for you to move, but we will oversee every item before anything is removed from <u>this</u> property. I know this is sudden and probably difficult. Especially coming into all of this from having nothing, you know. So let me make this as easy as **we** can. My family will give you two weeks*

to leave. Let me be clear, you will be supervised. From this moment until you are out. Look Roz...."

"It's Roslyn! Thank You!"

"Look, um...Roslyn. I know we didn't get a good chance to know each other, (He stares at her ass) but my cuzzo had only good things to say about Cha. Truth is... there's no will. Did you know that? With Raymond having no will there is no way to refute this. Ya can't stop it from happening. ***You*** *don't have a leg to stand on."*

(Soft but direct)

"If you were at all observant, you would know that it wouldn't matter if Ray didn't have a will. This is all I need to prove that this house, the car and all the contents within, is mine. Um...anything that was his...is mine.

Roslyn raises her left hand as the breaking sun causes the diamond on her ring finger to glimmer.

"Legally I don't need much more than this! Although...my marriage certificate is not too shabby to have either.

(Mumbles)

"Rizzo. Married?"

"Yes, he was! My husband. So, all that is his, will remain mine. Will remain, here! So let your family know they will never get one thing that ever belonged to him."

"You can't be serious?"

"Very much so! Okay, so...have the elders look into the laws for how things transfer between spouses after one of them dies. The truth may be difficult to swallow. I suggest they chew on it slowly. It might help it go down better."

Just at that moment Slim Nate walks back over to the car and rests his foot on the bumper. Pulls a marijuana joint from his jacket pocket and prepares to light it. Roslyn, now infuriated, leaves Sean at the front door and walks down to face Slim.

"What is it with you? What don't you get? It's simple...stay away from the car! What about ***that*** *don't you understand?"*

(Cynically laughing)

"I guess I don't take direction well. (Reaches out and grabs her arm) Listen honey! What are you gonna do about it? Huh, What?"

Roslyn devilishly smiles at Slim before putting her fingers to her lips. The result was an ear-piercing whistle.

"...And what the fuck is that supposed to do?" Slim replied with a chuckle.

Sean could hear a low angry growl coming from behind the front door. He had forgotten about Raymond's dog Bane. He darted out from behind the door. Nails clawing the floor on his way out. Sean was incapable of moving as a black fuzzy blur brushed pass his leg. Slim's hand swiftly came away from Roslyn's arm as he looked for a place to run. Bane rapidly barred down on Slim. Sean came down the stairs but kept his distance. With very little space between the front of the car and the gate, Slim didn't have the room he needed to take one hop to get over the gate. Instead, as he grabbed the chain link and tried to pull himself up, Bane locked onto his left calf. Bane aggressively throws his head back and forth in an attempt to tear flesh from Slim's leg. Causing him the fall from the gate.

"Oh Shit! Oow! GET THIS FUCK'EN DOG OFF OF ME! Do something! **SHOOT 'EM! SHOOT 'EM!***"*

Sean looked towards Roslyn as he reached to pull his gun from the small of his back. Immediately stopping as she pulled the hammer back on the 9mm she was pointing at him.

"Don't even think of harming my dog. ***Don't move****!"*

She circled around, causing Sean to move closer to the car. Slim Nate was still yelling as he was being mauled on the other side of it. Holding Sean in her sites as she unlocks the gate near the main walkway. After swinging the gate open, she moves towards the stairs. Roslyn whistles an unfamiliar melody that caused Bane to stop swinging his head but not let go of his grip. With just a clicking noise, Roslyn calls bane to her side. Bane obediently releases Slim before trotting the short distance to Roslyn's side. Slim clutches his leg while randomly shouting from the pain. Sean hesitated to move. Wondering just how disciplined this dog really is. "You could help your friend Sean. Bane's not going to move." Sean was safely able to get into the corner between the car and the gate. Pulling Slim's arm around his shoulder, they moved slowly. Allowing him to hop his way along the fence and out to the car. Sean took an old shirt from the trunk for Slim to wrap his leg with. Roslyn and Bane stood at the open fence. The tilt of her neck combined with the sarcastically smug expression, just reeked of contempt. A dishonoring cockiness Sean's superiors won't be happy to hear about. But realistically, nothing he reports to them about today is going to sit well.

CHAPTER FIVE

It's What I Do

WINDOWS ON THE far wall of the room usher in streams of light along both sides of the Queen-sized bed. Sylvia's moans are soft but intense. Barely able to be heard over the random love songs that were playing in the background. She lies in the middle of the bed, head tilted to her right, mouth seductively open while she rubs her left nipple. Her right-hand rests on her stomach as she concentrates on not clinching and holding her legs open. Sylvia's butter cream thighs quiver as Aprielle wraps her lips around Sylvia's clitoris and maintains a gentle suckling, that makes Sylvia raise her head to have a look. Watching Aprielle's bobbing head movement intensifies the moment for her. Sylvia breathes out slowly with her lips puckered, trying to regulate her increasingly excited state. Aprielle releases her lips hold of her Clit just long enough to lick the juices from Sylvia's inner thigh. Undeniably transferred there from Aprielle's cheek. Sylvia tenses up briefly as the tickle of her tongue hits her spot.

(Panting)

"Oh my God! (Whew) I... I... UHmm, (looking down again at Aprielle) Who... Uhh.. Why can't your brother do that?"

Aprielle responds, looking up at Sylvia and sounding as if she has food in her mouth.

"He doesn't get as much practice as I do."

(Whispering passionately)

"OOH Shit, Girl! Are you this good with your boyfriend?"

Aprielle retracts her tongue and lifts her head.

"Sean? I don't waste this gift on him. I mean, he really hasn't given me good reason too. I ain't doing more with him than I need too. Now! You want to keep asking questions or can I please get to my creamy surprise."

"I'm sorry. Um, yeah... do that Shit!"

Just outside the condo, two men bicker as one works on picking the lock to the front door. One of the men is a bit jittery although they're not at risk of being seen. This condo is on the second floor and takes up the entire level. The nineteen-year-old, kneeling and working on the locks is Charles "Geezy" Logan. Fired from his apprentice job at a local locksmith's and is currently a thief for hire. The second man frustratingly waiting on Geezy is Thomas "Fat Daddy" Thompson. Who is a champion marksman, and owner of, "The Gun Powder Trading Company". He's also a gunsmith, bad gambler and recent gun for hire.

(Nervously looking around)

"What's taking so long with those locks?"

"Relax! I've almost got it. This won't take as long as breaking that five-digit code that let us out on this floor. Shit! Just settle your fat ass down and let me work. (Grunting) Almost... got... It. There! What I tell you? You can't keep a Motha-Fucka like me out. This Is me! I do this shit!"

"I really hope you don't celebrate every time you're successful with something you're s'posed to be good at. Go ahead, dance, gloat and celebrate. Whatever ya do Geezy...do it now. Cause I need fucking silence once we get inside."

Geezy's smile was all but gone as he used his middle finger to direct Fat Daddy to go in. After entering, Fat Daddy tiptoed through each room using tactical precision. While Geezy strolled through, like he was at a flea market. Casually picking shit up along the way. He damn near broke the glass coffee table when he tossed one of the decorative stones from the bookcase. Missing the sofa but nearly hitting the table.

(Whispering Loudly)

"Could ***you*** *possibly make any more noise? (Under his breath) I always get stuck with the fuck'en rookies!"*

"Rookie! Don't get it twisted ya squirmy fat ass. I'm not the one getting his cherry popped. That's Real! So don't worry about what da fuck I'm doing. My part in this shit is done. The rest is on you.

Wit ya scary Bitch ass."

Fat Daddy smiles in such a way that makes Geezy uncomfortable. A smile filled with affection, surprise and admiration. Almost as if he was turned on by the aggression. Geezy's head draws back, giving Fat Daddy a displeasing glare and a shove down the hall. They both continued to walk softly making their way to the room they now hear music coming from.

Sylvia's moans grow louder as the two men approach the open door of the room. Aprielle's head continues to bob with a rhythmic sway as she wraps her arms around Sylvia's thighs. Gently pulling her in closer. Fat Daddy, arriving at the door first, leans against the doorway and begins to take in the show. Sylvia is being tormented with pleasure as the strokes of Aprielle's tongue bring her closer to a climax that she's fighting not to have. Geezy, impulsively darting around Fat Daddy is trying to experience an act he may never see in person again. Frustrated, he pulls Fat Daddy into the hall. Just to the left of the doorway.

(In an agitated whisper)

"Why is your fat ass blocking my view? Huh? Your Gay ass don't need to watch that shit! Move ya ass so a horny Motha-Fucka can learn something. Now ain't the time for a girl-on-girl eclipse. Keep your ***ass*** *on this side of the door and keep quiet."*

Fat Daddy reluctantly stays put. In order to give Geezy a few moments for his peep show. What's surprising is how the women hadn't heard them. Possibly because Aprielle was hitting Sylvia's spot and Sylvia had just broken out into uncontrollable yells of elation. For Geezy, the peep show was brief. Fat Daddy draws his gun and leans into the space of the doorway unoccupied by Geezy. ***[BANG, BANG! BANG, BANG!]*** *He quickly let's off four deadly shots. Aprielle, lost in her enjoyment of vaginal fluids, absorbed two of the shots. The first, entered through her back, heart side. The second went into the back of her head, splitting her forehead open. Splattering blood and tissue fragments all over Sylvia's lower half. With the shots coming in pairs, Sylvia had no time to react herself. The third shot fired hit her on the right side of her chest and left a bigger hole when it exited out her back. Her expression changes from pleasurable torment to life flashing anguish as the fourth slug penetrates the center of her forehead. Quickly blowing out the back of her head and drenching the pillows with blood. Geezy continues to lean onto the right side of the doorway but turns his head with a disgusted expression as he looks toward Fat Daddy.*

(Impulsively springing from the door frame)

*"**DAMN FAT'S**! You couldn't wait until after she had cum?! That would have been some nice shit to watch."*

*"I doubt your virgin ass has ever seen a woman cum. **OOH**, with that in mind... **Yeah**, maybe I was a bit quick on the trigger. My bad."*

*"**Fuck you Fat's!** Ya silk panty-wearing Motha-Fucka! Fuck! You don't get it. Taking a squirting dick in the mouth ain't hardly the same beautiful shit as see' en a lady having an orgasm. (Shakes his head) You don't get it! We could have forced them to rub their pussies together for some double squishy action. OH, HELL MAN, the freaky possibilities are endless. If you had only given it more time. DAMN! I swear you got hate in your heart. Especially to me."*

"You're damn right about that! Ya lonely closet porn Hetero!"

Geezy turns, taking a few steps towards the bed. Studying each woman's curvy attributes while making spanking gestures.

"Do you see these tits Fats? Look at her ass! Damn that's a waste. (Impulsively) You hungry Man? Seeing all this blood, boobies and brains has suddenly given me a craving for a burrito."

"I can eat." Fat's replies.

"I have no doubt about that. (Pauses) I'm play'en wit cha. Let's go before the lunch crowd hits."

[Two Hours Later]

Sean sat at the edge of his girlfriend's sofa, surrounded by the police. His head swinging back and forth, trying to understand and respond to the multitude of questions being thrown at him. With so much so quickly coming at him, Sean's answers were one or two words at the most. He was repeatedly being told to take his time because he was obviously emotionally uneasy and physically jittery. Occasionally Sean would look over his shoulder, hoping to see a better image of his girlfriend. Unfortunately, only catching the flashes from the photographer's cameras. One of the officers broke away from the few who were around Sean and headed out the front door to answer his phone.

(Speaking discretely)

"We're collecting evidence right now. Your son, Mr. Kingsley, is inside answering the detective's questions. Don't worry he'll be released after questioning. There is no reason to detain him. He's just the grieving boyfriend who showed up after officers were already on scene."

Officer Edwards lowers his voice before turning away from a medic who was waiting for the elevator. Pausing to make sure he wasn't being heard by anyone other than Robert Kingsley.

"I'm sorry but I couldn't contain this one. Not like the others. (Listening)

I wasn't first on the scene this time. The place was swarming with the media by the time I got here. The story already ran at six."

Once the medic was on the elevator and the hallway was clear, officer Edwards turned to face the open door of the condo. His voice returned to a normal level as he continued to talk and peer at the buzzing activity still going on inside.

"This clearly was a hit. With all department theories leading to this massacre being related to the other recent unsolved murders around town. (Listening) No! There still aren't any leads for any of those murders either. Well… I can do one of two things. I can hold your son 'til the press leaves or take him out and down the back stairwell through the alley. (Pauses) Uh...sure. I understand. Ok. I'll take care of that. (Listening) Yes, I'll call when I have more to go on."

[Click]

The detective puts his phone away, pulls out a note pad and pen before stepping back into the Condo. "Detective Vickers, I think that's enough questions for Mr. Reynolds. I think were done here. Please, Mr. Reynolds, come with me."

Downtown Colver City

In an abandoned department store parking structure, third level. Ana and Tank lean on a seven series BMW as Meck pays Geezy and Fat Daddy for their completed assignment. Tank, while snacking on a package of Ritz crackers, asks Fat Daddy to stay for a moment as Geezy drives off. Meck walks away to wait with the rest of the crew. Ana begins to chat with Fat Daddy as Tank unwraps Craft cheese singles to eat with his crackers.

"I want to be clear Thomas. The boss likes the work you've done and the bonuses resulting from it. (Tosses front page of the newspaper with Sean's image onto the hood of the car) Actually, the boss has a few more gigs lined

up for you. The problem... or what the boss sees as a problem, are all the questions you've been asking."

"I like details. They drive me. The more I know, the more prepared I can be. That's all. That's why I ask questions."

"Thomas, I've been asked to expound briefly, only briefly, about how this crew works. More importantly...how you should adapt. (Slowly closes and reopens her eyes) We are each given our assignment with all the details needed to get the job done. Nothing more. This, whether we understand it or not, is for our protection. Plausible Deniability. (Nods) If the subtle vagueness is something you can't handle, then we must terminate your employment."

There was a brief uncomfortable silence that was broken up by the sound of Tank gnawing his cheese & crackers. Which oddly made both Ana and Fat Daddy gaze strangely at Tank and laugh.

(Laughing slightly)

"Adjusting will not be a problem, Ana. (Puts his hand up) Please let the boss know, I'm on board. For this pay, I'm around as long as I'm needed."

"That's good to hear Thomas. More work is coming your way. The details will be coming to you in the middle of the week. Mia will drop off your instructions."

Ana nods and Fat Daddy knows that their talk was finished and walks away. Tank holds his hand to his chest, trying to pass the heartburn he was feeling while he waved for the rest of the crew with the other to come over. Mea, as they walked, finishes assuring her brother that the government won't hold his money forever and they should unfreeze his accounts. As they approach Ana and Tank, Mea reminds Meck to be patient, before she addresses Ana.

"So, what's going on? What's our next move?"

Ana signals the group to huddle closer and holds up the newspaper before she begins to speak.

"Everyone has new assignments. Mea's work is the most pivotal at the moment, especially that new job of yours. So, I'll start with her."

[Morning Headline]

Colver City Tribune:
"Kingsley's Linked to Massacre of Lesbian Lovers."

Spaced across the front page, underneath the heading were three photos side by side. A picture of each woman killed and in the center of the two, Sean's mug shot. Followed by a detailed article linking Sean to a lover's triangle that he not only had no idea was going on or was able to be a part of. But it speculated about the women's deaths being related to his family's alleged criminal activity. The paper pulled his prior arrest record and went into full details about it. The writer went as far as to associate Sean with the city's corrupt justice system, judge kickbacks and why his record should never have been sealed. They also added that he couldn't possibly be working for himself or be that well connected. Someone else was clearly pulling the strings. His father was mentioned briefly but only as a respected businessman who clearly must be disappointed with his son. The last few paragraphs of the article declare the writer's resentment with police investigators. Making reference to why they have made no attempts to indicate whom Sean works for or makes strides to eradicate any of the illegal activity.

"Tsk, tsk, tsk. Lord, give me strength! Grann mumbled as she tosses the paper onto the coffee table in front of her. Steadily growing angrier as she chases her morning pills down with a glass of Gin and Orange juice. (Phone rings)

"Did you see this morning's paper Robert? That boy is always caught in the middle of some girl getting killed. Tell me Robert, when is that boy going to get his shit together? (Pauses) Well? Let me be clear. This nonsense can't continue. It's bad for our family. It's bad for business. I don't want to

feel like we're losing ground, control or under scrutiny. Damn cities in a shit spiral and we can't get caught in it. These kinds of articles aren't good for business. It brings unwanted attention. We want to keep our presence for what we do…strong. Okay? We've talked about this before. You know what needs to be done. Son, take care of it!"

[Click]

CHAPTER SIX

Can't Hide Love

[Three weeks after the funeral]

NINE AM MONDAY morning, Roslyn, a little nervous, enters a large conference room in a downtown office building. She approaches a single chair that's set up a few feet in front of a table that is seating a panel of four. Sitting at the end of the table to the right of the brass, was a stenographer who began typing the very moment Roslyn was addressed.

"Good morning, Agent Moreno. Please... have a seat and then we can begin."

As Roslyn takes a seat, she immediately recognizes her lieutenant and his boss (He's the one who initially began to speak) but the other two who sat quietly, jotting down the occasional notes, Roslyn couldn't identify. And uncharacteristic of someone with an official title, the other two never told anyone if they were with the department, Internal affairs or from the FBI.

"This morning, we want to discuss your report. In regard to the events on or around... April one of two thousand and nine. Resulting in the death of a fellow undercover agent. Which also may have jeopardized a separate operation. An operation... that you yourself Agent Moreno were a part of."

Roslyn sits attentively as the others in the room focus intently on to her. Her lieutenant tries to calm her with a quick gesture as her captain continues to speak.

"You stated here in your report that you were supposed to meet with your target, but didn't. You also mentioned receiving an urgent phone call diverting you away from your assignment. Can you go into more details about that for us?"

"It was Saturday, June 11th around 6pm. I had just come from having a celebratory dinner with friends before I stopped by my place to change my clothes. I was in and out quickly although I still had an hour until I was to meet with my target. I was dressed, in character and in need of a Café latte. The call came in just as I was handed my drink. The caller was Daphne Morrison. She was one of three women that Sean Reynolds was dating. I came across her more often than the others. That's because she was the only one, he every brought when he came to visit his cousin, agent Kingsley. Raymond…agent Kingsley encouraged me to befriend her as another possible source of information. Long story short, we exchanged numbers. Now…when I answered the phone, she was amped up, excited, and a bit hysterical. I asked her to slow down. I couldn't make sense of anything she was saying."

Roslyn, if for a moment sheds the straight forward, down to business answers and becomes more animated. The octave of her voice changes as she gets into character and mimics Daphne's voice.

(Begins breathing heavily)

"Oh my God Chica, it's Daph. Shit! Ok…seriously, I just left Sean and he bailed on our date…again. He makes me so FUCKING MAD sometimes. UUGH! So, I'm in the car with him, we're on our way to dinner when he speeds up on this car. I get nervous he's gonna hit something. Cause you know he can't drive. Anyway, as I'm yelling at him, he starts shouting hold on and gets up beside the car. It takes a short time for the guy with the ponytail to understand Sean's gestures. He then impulsively dips into the

parking lot of this liquor store. (Takes a breath) Girl, he gets out of the car and makes two loud ass phone call from the phone booth. Telling each person that the undercover cop will be killed within the hour. Get ready; he'll meet each of them there. (Roslyn returns to her own voice) I asked Daphne to repeat herself so I could be clear on what I had heard. After getting pass her anger about missing out on dinner and being left in that parking lot by Mr. Reynolds. She settled down and went over it again. Apparently, Sean told her that they, and by then she meant his crew, had it set up for one of our under covers to be killed. He also assured that the pony-tailed guy he was gesturing would be the shooter. Shortly after, he apologized before leaving her in the parking lot of Able Liquors. Ms. Morrison continued to rattle on about being left and getting ghetto about how she was going to handle it. At that point I cut her off, hopped in my car and headed for the downtown area Daph mentioned."

Her captain shifts in his chair then asks, "So you knowingly abandoned your assignment."

(With conviction)

"Yes…yes, I did."

"At this point Agent Moreno, what were your intentions?"

"To either warn him or back him up. Depending on what I found upon arriving at the scene. Sir."

One of the two people in the panel that Roslyn didn't recognize was sitting at the left end of the table. This woman was inquisitively looking towards Roslyn before she began scribbling on her note pad. There was a brief silence until Roslyn noticed the panel waiting for her to continue. Just then her lieutenant spoke.

"It says here that you were stopped for speeding on your way to West Texas and Virginia Street."

"Yes, I was."

"Why did you let the officer write you the ticket? Why didn't you just flash your badge and get where you needed to be?"

"I didn't want to complicate the situation with explanations. Although I was concerned about reaching Agent Kingsley…I couldn't blow my cover either. (Softly) …And those minutes at the side of the road, proved to be costly."

"Is that so?"

"Yes Sir! In my opinion."

"All opinions aside, agent…let's just stick to the facts. Only as you remember them, please." Smugly added by the unfamiliar woman at the end of the table.

"The facts…Ooo-kay. (Sighs) At this point I have arrived at the scene and tactically made my way up the street. I hadn't drawn my weapon as I weaved in and out between the parked cars. I didn't want to draw unnecessary attention having my gun at my hip. I had gone unnoticed up to this point but stopped two cars short. Sean Reynolds had begun yelling. His gun barrel was pressed into the chest of former drug dealer Angel Ramirez. Kingsley was on the ground writhing in pain but being shielded by his cousin. Reynolds was shouting, "HE AINT NO COP! THAT'S MY COUSIN!" (Softly coughs) I'll spare you the rest of his expletives. (Takes a sip of water) Now Mr. Reynolds does something completely outside his character. He kills the man at point blank range. In cold blood, no less."

"Is that another of your opinions Ms. Moreno? How can you be certain it is outside his character?"

"I'm sorry, is what my opinion? The fact that I saw Mr. Reynolds kill him… Or whether it is within his nature to kill? Actually, I'm referring to the psyche evaluation in his file. It's not my opinion."

For a moment you only heard the sound of pages turning before Roslyn's captain speaks again.

"Ballistics didn't have a weapon to make a positive match with. Nor did

we have any GSR (Gunshot residue) when we tested Mr. Reynolds. (Taps finger on the table) So, whether he has the ability to kill or has actually killed is still in question. Since you were the only witness to it."

Roslyn took another moment to sip some more water before she continued as the only woman on the panel made eye contact with the quiet man to her left.

"There was a man at the scene known as Slim Nate who killed Angel's buddy seconds after Angel was shot. Mr. Reynolds, unaffected by Slim Nate's actions, immediately tended to Agent Kingsley as the Nate guy and a heavier man celebrated. From my vantage point I couldn't see what Mr. Reynolds was doing with his cousin. Sean was kneeling but I could hear him encouraging Raymond to keep his eyes opened. Within the same breaths, telling the other two to get the hell up out of there. Not surprising how fast they did. Sean was shaking as I approached. Initially he didn't see me. He was talking and I had trouble understanding him. (Mumbles) I couldn't make much sense of it…then."

"I didn't catch that agent Moreno."

"It was nothing Ma'am. Not important to the report. I'll continue. So, Sean hearing me approach, whipped his head around. He was startled at first but seemed more surprised to see me standing behind him. He asked what I was doing here. I didn't answer. Before he knew it, I had shoved him out of the way and took Raymond into my arms. (Her voice became soft with a bit of a quiver) He; Raymond was in bad shape. I could see him zoning in and out. His arm wasn't severed as previously reported. His triceps muscle was hanging and I pulled a bandana from my pocket and tied it up. I tried talking with Raymond but his eyes kept rolling back in his head like I was losing him. I pulled my phone out to dial 911 but before I could, Sean distracted me. He was frantically looking around and yelling something. I realized he was saying that he shouldn't be there. That he couldn't stay there. He kept mumbling the words… "Good, good." He became relieved

that I was there. He told me to take good care of him. He said...I know he's in good hands. Whatever else he said...I couldn't tell you. Who knows? For lack of better words...he hauled ass out of there. He was gone before I could say another word to him. I tried to prop Raymond up while I called it in. I repeated several times that an officer needs assistance and tried to keep him with me until paramedics arrived. By with me, I mean...conscious."

"Actually Agent, I think that is only partially what you meant. (Using air quotes) When you said keeping him with you. I sense a double meaning in your words. Maybe you didn't want to lose him on a more personal level. Isn't that right?" Asks the woman at the end of the table.

(Taken by surprise)

"I'm sorry?"

"Sorry. Don't be sorry Agent."

As she continued to address Roslyn, she leaned forward. Her tone and mannerisms seemed to be less objective, not as neutral but became much more aggressive. But before she could speak, the quiet man to her left touched her forearm as if to let her know he would be taking the lead for now.

"How long have you been in love with him Ms. Moreno? Or...should I say, Mrs. Kingsley?"

I thought I should keep my head up so I wouldn't look like a guilty child but I found myself momentarily looking at my shoes. I was thinking that I had nothing to be ashamed of. Marrying Raymond wasn't something I was trying to hide. Although... coincidentally my superiors didn't know we had wed. I didn't see why it mattered. I wondered where they were going with this line of questioning or how it was even relevant. I lifted my head and immediately noticed the surprised set of expressions my superiors were trying to suppress. I shifted in the direction of the two that I didn't know and without remorse... I answered.

(With Passion)

"I fell in love with Ray. (Unconsciously touches herself) It may have

taken me weeks to realize it. It was sometime after we began the partial partnering of both our operations but deep down, I knew. I was in love."

"Right, in love! Can you tell us how much longer before you both were married?"

"About a month before the incident detailed in the report in front of you."

"Agent, do you think that your actions may have jeopardized your assignment?"

(Without hesitation)

"Not at all."

"How about psychologically? Maybe your newfound infatuation my have affected your judgment? Compromised months, maybe years vested into the investigation you were assigned to."

(Scoffs)

"Infatuation, doesn't come remotely close to my feelings for him. (She smiles) The only judgment I see that's in question… is why we waited. We realized we felt exactly the same about each other but hesitated briefly to act on those feelings. I'm certainly glad that ***we*** *did. As for my assignment, it didn't suffer one bit after marrying Ray. Piss poor intel, in my opinion, is why the case was dragging along then and why it's suffering right now. Psychologically, I'm no different from any other wife who has lost her husband. I'm filled with an almost helpless emptiness and a misguided angry. I suffer from sleepless nights, a helpless denial that I did everything I could & tear-filled questions directed at God. Emotionally that's where I am. (Pauses) When it comes to my job… I'm a dedicated professional and Ray wasn't any different. Falling in love changed nothing for me when it came to my assignment. And…you would be hard pressed to find anyone who would tell you otherwise."*

"I don't think you've satisfied my question Ms Moreno. I want you to tell me, if you think you jeopardized your case."

"If you're asking me to take personal responsibility for the investigation's setbacks, then NO. I understand the department is trying to salvage what they can due to the press coverage but I can't contribute when I'm stuck behind a desk. What happened is unfortunate for the case but traumatic for me. The press is thriving on the cop killed in action by line. Politicians are using every angle to sway public opinion for re-election and now I pound paper all day and silently mourn the love of my life. (Clears her throat) ...And answer isn't satisfying enough, I'm sure the case will find a conclusion whether it was/wasn't compromised or if I'm involved or not. I feel like you want me to take full responsibility for the damage to the case, or justify Marrying Raymond. I'm not sure what you want here."

"Do you have any more to add Agent?"

(Softly)

"You can't hide love. I'm not ashamed to be Agent Roslyn Moreno-Kingsley. That's who I am now. Regardless of the circumstances."

"I meant in reference to the report Agent Moreno...Kingsley."

"No. Nothing more."

The woman at the end conferred with the guy to her left before agreeing they were both done with me...for now. I was excused by my superiors, but not before being told to make myself comfortable at my current desk assignment. I'd most likely be there until further notice. As I stood to leave my thoughts drifted to this; a desk is the death of an action filled career or punishment for what the department deems a mistake. Regardless I will make the most of my new surroundings. It can't make things any worse.

CHAPTER SEVEN

We Meet the Ranks of Power

THE MEET LOCATION with the council, due to the unfamiliarity of this new crew, was agreed upon by using a series of drop points throughout the city. A precautionary measure insisted upon by the heads of the North & West-side crews. It seemed similar to an urban scavenger hunt. Carried out by lower-level thugs from every crew involved. Starting with an untitled page taped to a light post. Then a note slipped into a restaurant menu or even an envelope exchanged between two slow moving cars. These messages would pass back and forth until everyone has agreed on the date and location. So, after weeks of mishandled notes and misguided suggestions, manufactured by oversized egos… the time, date and place for the meet was finally set.

Ana, Meck, Tank and Mountain Moo stand in the center of an abandoned jet hanger in a closed airport five miles outside the city limits. The giant bay doors at each end of the hanger sat open as a light breeze swirls dust around their ankles. Facing the south set of doors as the sun begins to set, they watch three cars approach with their park lights guiding them towards the open bay. The reddish orange glare of the sun settles on the structure as the cars come to a stop just outside the hanger.

The first person out of their car was the controlling council member from the North-side of the city, Donny D Malloy. Donnie grew up on the north side, raised by his mother. She was an illegal alien from Mexico that fell in love and married a local businessman who also happened to be her boss. After his father's death, Donnie took over his father's old military thrift store and now uses it as a front for his illegal activities. Donny D is always followed closely by his right hand and paid muscle. A six foot-four ex-wrestler known only as Tomcat. Also known for sporting tiger striped tattoos on his arms and shoulders. He also wears a distinctive mustache and beard that makes him appear to have jungle predator features.

The next to make his way into the hanger was the West side's council representative, Courtney Blake. A 5 '8', coffee brown Black man with tightly braided cornrows, a neatly trimmed beard and diamond studs in both ears. He's often, maybe always wearing jeans, shirt, a sleeveless sweater and lightly shaded sunglasses. He strolls in with a disturbingly cocky street king confidence wrapped around a paranoid Napoleon complex. He's shadowed by two of his childhood buddies and ex-Kingsley henchman and new parolee, Big Ronnie Ron.

The last and most ominous as he entered, representing the East side and head of the council… Robert Kingsley. He stood beside his car with the smoke from his cigar hitting the air like an industrial smoke stack. He makes sure his brim is tilted low over his brow before he takes a step. Circling behind him was comic thug Slim Nate, street enforcer Big Guns and bringing up the rear, Sean Kingsley Reynolds.

With Ana and her crew standing with their backs toward the north end of the hanger, the other crews positioned themselves into a semi-circle just in front of Ana's crew. Donny stood to the left, Courtney to the right and Robert Kingsley settled directly across from Ana. There were a few moments of respectful nods, one-handed birds flying and wrathful stares exchanged as everyone got familiar with old foes and looked skeptically at new faces. The dirty looks subside as everyone's attentions turn to Mr. Kingsley as he slides his cigar between his fingers and begins to point with it before he spoke.

(Slowly blows smoke into the air)

"Donny. Courtney. Always nice to see other council members."

"I was out of town when I heard the news. Mr. K, my condolences about your nephew."

Mr. Kingsley shrugs his shoulders. His gestures insisting that there's nothing to be concerned about.

"Thanks Donny. I appreciate the concern.

(Quickly shifts his focus) For the new folks standing in front of me, I'm Robert Kingsley. I'm head of this council. The two gentlemen needing to be recognized and standing before you…(points) to my left is Courtney, and Donny D to my right. Unfortunately, the last member of the council is no longer with us."

Donny takes a moment to make the sign of the cross. Closing his eyes before the movements of his hands and head release his prayer towards heaven. He whispers, "Rest in peace Angel." Sean rolls his eyes as his father continues to speak again.

"This meeting took a bit longer to set up. Usually there are individual recommendations made to any member of the council before you can ever meet with this entire council. But different actions, different circumstances have brought us all here. With that said…(pauses) this is what we've come to know. This group of new faces in front of me is not part of Angel's crew. The word is…no one has seen much of any of them lately. This ***is*** *cause for concern. (Puffs his cigar) You there! (Pointing at Meck) Who are you? (Puffs cigar again) Why are you here? What's this about?"*

Meck stands with his arms folded in front of himself, looking annoyingly confused at Mr. Kingsley. Then Meck slowly turns his head and looks at Ana.

[Slowly]

"These aren't difficult questions son. Why are you here?"

Meck turns his eyes away from Mr. Kingsley as Ana touches him on the arm as an indication that she will handle it from here. So…with a raised eyebrow and a soft authoritative tone, Ana responds.

"He doesn't answer because I'm the one you need to be addressing."

*Laughter erupts around the circle. Specifically, from Slim Nate, Big Ronnie Ron, and the two standing with Courtney Blake. "**You Fuck'en kidd'en me? What's this Bullshit?**" Courtney yells with skeptical disrespect. Mr. Kingsley raises his hand in Courtney's direction. Motioning for him to relax for the moment before he stares down Meck and then shifts his eyes back to Ana.*

"In my day it was unheard of for men to talk business or take direction from a woman. (Grumbles of agreement echo around the circle) I mean… unless she was negotiating a price for her sex services. So, for most of the men here… this is a first."

"You damn right it's a first. I've never seen a poodle approach wolves." Courtney bellows.

Ana's eyes seductively rotate around the circle before she flashes a devilish smile.

"Don't let the business suit fool you. I'm not soft and I'm nobodies' pussy. Nobody before you is wearing bobby socks and berets. So, address me with some respect."

*"Whoo…she's feisty! **Fuck You!**" Courtney yells.*

(Puffing his cigar)

*"With all due respect, I'm a flexible man. [Shrugs] Plus, I'm already here so I'll work with what's in front of me. [Clears throat] Let me say this…shortly after Angel's death his crew has slowly disappeared. As well as the cut he owed to the head of this council. Let me make this clear. No one makes any money in this area, in this city without **this** council seeing a piece of it. So, if you're looking to take over Angel's part of the city, then I will be willing to negotiate the terms. Of course…whatever proves to be acceptable for the rest of the council."*

"Mr. Kingsley." Ana begins, "Although I appreciate your thirst for capitalism, your assumption for why we've come here is slightly misunderstood. Let me clarify. (Takes a sec to eyeball Donnie & Courtney) Each of you, by now, has begun to experience a slight but significant loss in profits... whether you'll admit it or not to one another. As well as a reduction of the territories you control. We haven't come here to pay into any antiquated hierarchy of money and power. We don't work this hard to make others wealthy. But...we are serving notice. Right now, what we want... we will take. For example... Angel's territory, which we already control. Now ***let*** *me be clear! We are also unconcerned with any blow- back or retaliation from Siegfried & his white tiger over there, Cooley High or even you... Mr. Kingsley."*

Unseen but heard from a distance someone yells, ***"So bring it!"*** *Donnie D. leans into Tomcat and whispers, "Did you hear that?" Taking a moment to look around as Ana continues.*

"You are all obsolete. Tired cliché's that movie makers portray as inner-city Kingpin's. Your techniques for business are sadly subject to infiltration and disloyalty. You Mr. Kingsley have the most to lose. (Pauses) Open your eyes gentlemen. This is a warning. Prepare yourselves. Every dynasty, no matter how big or small, will eventually fall."

The chatter of cursing reverberated throughout the hanger. Big Gun's found Ana's words disrespectful to Mr. Kingsley and he responded violently. Moving decisively, Big Gun's movements towards Ana were abruptly halted as the momentum of Tank's punch causes him to stumble backward. Ana never flinched and was unfazed. Her eyes were focused squarely on Mr. Kingsley. She never lost eye contact. Mountain Moo and Meck turned in separate directions to insure no one from the other crews were advancing either. Big Gun's regained his balance and returned an equally powerful blow to Tank. At least not before cracking that crazy smile his crew has become accustomed to seeing when he's presented with something he can't respect or someone who provides him with a challenge. The men exchange more punches before Ana points at Moo and says, "End that NOW!!" As Moo separates the men as easily as two squabbling children, Ronnie Ron points directly to Sean and tells him that he will get even with him sooner than he knows. But before the commotion ends Donnie D nudges Tomcat and asks, "You gonna get in on that?" Tomcat shakes his head and replies, "No! I fight for money or for a purpose. Never recklessly."

The sun was gone and the early shade of evening was settling onto the hanger. The shades of darkness or a dark building can make a situation more unsettling. The faces, hands and movements of everyone were becoming harder to make out. Suddenly Meck took a quarter turn away from the group, began waving his right arm in a circular motion over the top of his head. The slamming noise of several levers startled everyone as the bright lights of the hanger smothered the darkness. Revealing a half circle of unhappy expressions. Big Gun's head jerks around the hanger before he backed up and placed himself in front of Mr. Kingsley. Courtney became animated. His every gesture delivered with overt disrespect.

(Moving like a puppet)

"So, dis ***bitch*** *think she swings some fuck'en clout? Huh? You ain't pushing shit round this bitch! You ain't got enough clout to set terms or do what tha fuck you want. Not around here! No more juice than Jr. Kingsley thinks he has."*

"Shut yo' Boys to Men look alike bitch ass up. Unless you want me to send your ass… [Singing] To- the- end-of… the road. [softly] Punk bitch!"

Courtney scoffs at Slim Nate as Mr. Kingsley tries to wield some control with the wave of a hand and the flick of his stogie. Sean nervously chants at his father.

(Nervously)

"Wh…who turned the lights on? (Inquisitively) Ooo-kay. Who turned the lights on? (Intently) Did you hear me? Who turned the lights on? Hold

on dad, I thought everyone around us were the only people around us. I'm mean…I thought we were alone."

"Who said that?" Meck begins to reply cynically. "No one ever assured you that you were. Relax! You're in no more danger now then you were ten minutes ago. With-standing the threats that big boy was yelling directly at you."

Mr. Kingsley emerges from behind his bodyguard dropping his cigar to the ground and stepping on it before glibly speaking at Ana again.

"There's seems to be more going on here than what was intended."

"No argument here Mr. Kingsley. But…whose intentions are you referring too?" Ana asks.

"Whoever's makes this seam less like a meeting and feel more like an ambush."

*"**Ambush?**" Tank hollers out as Ana silences him to listen to Mr. Kingsley.*

"As I was saying…the intentions of others can be obscured into taking any form. Ambush is just one form and from what I've heard already, things seem to be along those lines. Whether it's an unknown number of people secretly turning on lights in a seemingly abandoned hanger or idol warnings unconventionally delivered by the lips of a pretty face. It depends on how you decide to look at it."

"You're right, it's definitely a warning. So, if you find yourselves pushed into a new line of work, (Ana's smile widens slowly) I want you to know who forced you into it."

"You're ballsy. I'll give you that. It's definitely a different approach you've taken. I hope you've thought this through. These streets can be hard on ya. Call me when you're ready to be serious. Ready to discuss terms. Let's go! We've wasted enough time. We're done here."

Mr. Kingsley dips his head, respectfully tipping his hat to Ana before heading to his car. Donny D holds his hand up to his face simulating a telephone as he mouths the words, "Call when you are ready." Not noticing that Tomcat was already at the car. Big Ronnie Ron slowly sizes up Moo as Courtney still talks shit about Ana having no clout. Yelling all the way to his car as his two-knucklehead homies repeated every word.

(Looking on in disgust)

"Sheep!"

"What was that Meck?" Ana asks.

"Sheep. They're like sheep. I don't like sheep. They follow blindly, either by fear or by routine. Shaved or slaughtered because they believe that's their purpose. (Pauses) But…wake one up one day. Make them realize there's something more. Give them a purpose. They may find themselves unwilling to blindly follow but instead, tread their own path."

"Meck I think you're right. Maybe now it's time to separate the sheep from the wolves, the guppies from the sharks. It's time to find out exactly who is capable of leading during a crisis. Time for us to get back to work."

CHAPTER EIGHT

Adjustments

THE NORMAL BUSTLE of waiters bringing food and bust boys cleaning tables weren't a distraction for Ana's occasional Monday morning huddle. Ana stood a short distance from the table, finishing a phone call as the Twins, Meck and Mea sat at the table dressing up their coffee and tea. Mea tips the sugar container over her coffee as she waits for her brother to answer her question.

"Well?" She said impatiently while she rotates the spoon around her coffee cup.

"It's a bit complicated Mia. I'm not sure how to say it. (Sighs deeply) They keep throwing in other stipulations. There's not much I can do. So… I'm patiently but reluctantly going with the flow."

"Are they gonna free up your money or not? Shit, they already got what they needed."

(Smugly)

"According to them…not everything they needed."

"Bullshit! They've got him in custody. His entire operation has been shut down and they have seized all of his cash. They took the house, the cars and all the equipment. What else is there?"

"They don't have the plates, Mia. Your ex-husband is saying that he doesn't have them. That press is junk without the plates."

"Well shit, I never knew where those were. [She winks] And... they've already put us through enough hell trying to get them. Damn! How much longer will they keep this shit up?"

"The Fed's...shit sis, um... maybe until they get what they want. Or... until my lawyer can make some shit happen. Let's hope something happens before I can no longer afford to pay him."

"It's bullshit Meck. This shit they're doing is faulty. They are still fishing for answers. No matter what lies he told the Fed's about you."

"Maybe so. Freezing my accounts was fucked up but if it's what I have to endure to keep us out of prison, then so be it."

"They never had anything that could stick. I made sure my Ex-husband took all of that heat. Locking your accounts is a tactic to squeeze something out of you. (Pauses) They can't break you."

"Damn right about that Mea."

The twins stopped their conversation short as Ana slid into the booth next to Mia. Meck immediately pushes a cup of coffee towards her. Mia simultaneously hands her the container of cream before Ana could even ask for it.

[Sarcastically]

"Damn Bookends. Do you two have signals or does this type of behavior come natural to you both? I'm only joking. Anyway, Thank You both."

Ana takes a moment to prep her coffee, and then gently rotates the cup back and forth between her hands before addressing the twins again.

"Ok gang, our assignments have changed. Mia."

"Uh-hum."

"We need you to get involved a lot deeper with your current assignment than you are already. Get personal. This means you have to be the dolled-up fly-girl a bit longer than you would like. Will that be a problem for you and are you comfortable with lingerie?"

"No problem with any of it. Not at all. It will give me a chance to

perfect my alter ego. Plus, **I** *can be girly without wearing heals. (Winks) Not a problem."*

"Good. Now… (sips her coffee) with some of the other jobs we currently have in play, we need to put a few new pieces in place. Our success depends on it. Most importantly, we need to create some mis-direction. This will be essential and also… your new assignment Meck. (Sips more coffee) I'll have more information for you by this afternoon. We'll go over it then."

Ana pauses as she watches the twins enjoying their breakfast before she takes a couple bites from the Blueberry muffin that Mia ordered when she was away from the table.

"UGH!" Ana grumbles as she takes a napkin and pulls the bite of moldy muffin from her mouth. "Excuse me miss. May I have another one please?" The waitress grimaces and apologizes as she removes the moldy muffin from the table. Ana sips more coffee in an attempt to rid her mouth of the awful taste. Meck offers Ana a slice of bacon or fruit when he realizes the java may not be enough to cleanse her palette.

"Yuck! (Still reacting) Ya know, that happens to me more often than it should. Somehow the bad ones seem to find me. A bit of a gift, I guess. It's been happening since college. Weird, huh?"

Ana turns as the waitress delivers another muffin and apologizes.

"Again, we're sorry about that."

"It's ok, thank you. (Sips again) Um… where was I? Ah, oh…I've got it. Meck, withstanding the details, you must get on top of this quickly. We need your savvy, use that business charm of yours."

(Meck nods)

"I've got you. Subtle and conniving comes second nature to me."

"Hey, don't go at it too hard or too quick. Feel it out. Wait on them to react. Let them draw the conclusions, then run with it. It could get a bit dicey if you're not strategic or careful."

"No worries, Ana. I'll make it happen."

"I'm fully confident in both your and Mia's skills. [Looks around] Let's find the waitress and pay the tab. I've got another meeting in a half hour. Then two more before we [looking at Meck] reconnect late this afternoon. [Nibbles from the muffin] All right yall, thanks for breakfast. I've got to run."

[Two weeks later]

One O'clock on a Thursday afternoon Grann rocked while sitting on her porch swing. The rhythmic sound of the chains grinding over its support hooks kept Grann's motion steady as she rocked. Her eyes were fixated on her great granddaughter, Cee-Jay playing in the yard until she noticed a brief case toting man cautiously approaching. Her face takes on defensive wrinkles as she thought, "Man in a gray suit that plain is only trying to do one of two things. Sell something or poorly sell something. (Crossing her arms) What the hell does ***he*** *want?"*

"Good afternoon, Ma'am. (Pulls a hanker chef to wipe his brow) Excuse me…it's a bit hot out today. Hi, I'm looking for Mrs. Selma Jean Kingsley."

"Now look here, before you say one word, I already have a vacuum. Don't need any washing powder. Don't cook enough to need them plastic containers and I don't need no more security than I can squeeze off with fifteen shots."

"No Ma'am. (Holds left hand to his chest) I'm not here trying to sell you anything."

"If you aint peddling materials, then what's your purpose? Hmm? (Points her finger) What church you come here from? Don't come 'round here with your dull ass suit and slick look, trying to sell me Jesus. I have seen enough pain, suffering, bereavement and bullshit in my days to save my soul three times over. So, save your pre-rehearsed Holy speech. If that's what ya came here for. You can keep the holiness pamphlets in the briefcase. I don't

want 'em. I hope I have covered it all. If I've touched on why you're here... you can turn around and go."

[Chuckles to himself]

"Ma'am I assure you I am not here for any of those reasons. My name is Jason Whitmore. [Extends his hand] I'm a detective working for Alameda County, in the bay area. I'm following up on a few leads on a case involving a Mr. Nicolas Garza. I was hoping I could ask you a few questions."

Grann begins to rock again and looks at Mr. Whitmore with a dead stare. Feeling uncomfortable, he slowly takes away the handshake he tried to extend.

"Questions regarding what exactly? (Looks quickly to her left) No...no little girl, put that down." Grann asks as she continues to swing.

"Ma'am, we are currently trying to establish whether there's any validity in Mr. Garza's statements. That's what led me here. We are trying to talk with possible affiliates of his. I was hoping I could ask you some questions and speak with your grandson Sean Reynolds as well."

"My Grandson? Hard to say where he could be. How he's in and out of town so much. What about him would you need to know?"

"If I can be direct for a moment Mrs. Kingsley, the concern is whether your grandson is or isn't involved with Mr. Garza as he claims. (Hears a faint ringing) In an effort to determine whether Mr. Garza is lying, speaking to Sean would be helpful. (Pulls cell phone from his pocket) I'm sorry Ma'am could you give me just a moment."

Grann continued to sway and watches Mr. Whitmore's demeanor as he spoke. He moved around and nodded his head as he talked. His movements seemed apologetic and reassuring that he'll get done what is expected of him. He lowered his head and sighed deeply as he hung up his phone. Seemingly forgetting where he was for the moment. He spread his thumb and fingers across his forehead to rub his temples until he remembered he was conducting business.

"I'm sorry Mrs. Kingsley."

"Umm-Hmm. Them phones aint nothing but distractions. I tell folks all the time they are nothing but trouble. You might want to consider getting rid of it. You may actually get something done or even seem more professional when dealing with people."

"Again…I'm so sorry Ma'am. If it is at all possible, I will need to call you or come back and talk with you. (Reaches for his pocket) Let me give you one of my cards. (Extends his arm) Please give me a call and let me know when it's most convenient for me to come back and speak with you."

"No need son, keep your card. I don't have much more to say cause I don't know the fella and good luck finding my grandson. I can't help you there either. But let me suggest that wherever you go next… don't bring that phone and you don't wear that suit. I'm hot just looking at you. Alright?"

"That will be fine, Mrs. Kingsley."

"Then alright then."

CHAPTER NINE

It's Not Personal, It's Business

THE BRIGHTNESS AND warmth of the sun ushered in the first of many beautiful summer days. Roslyn was standing in line at her regular morning stop, The Coffee Grind, as her best friend secured a table inside near the window. With two Grande Mocha's in hand, Olivia and Roslyn sipped and dished the dirt as they always do.

"We both know this is one of my favorite places. I also know that you own the restaurant now. Olivia? Why aren't we making and enjoying our coffee… there?"

"First, I never really feel liked making any types of coffee. Second, you know how much I enjoy to people watch Roslyn."

"I thought the reason you dropped out of the academy was because of the pressure. Or was it the other cadets?"

"It was never the pressure Roslyn. I can handle that all day, every day. I'm just partial to relaxing with a good drink and watching people. I was never too excited about apprehending them."

"Well, you're doing what you were meant to do."

"Speaking of doing what we were meant to…have you gone back to work yet?"

"Not any real work. I guess they're giving me time to grieve. Got me uncomfortably behind a desk. I'm unsure what they're waiting on, but I'm

ready to go back. Each time I've asked, my request was denied. They tell me I can't go back undercover. Not right now. I might have been identified at Ray's funeral. The department thinks my cover has been blown. Irregardless that my team had the evidence, finally made the arrests and brought me in with them as part of the process."

"Then what's the problem?"

"A few pictures of me with Raymond made print after his murder. I was acting as his girlfriend as part of his cover and mine. It helped if I was dating someone with his criminal status. So, when it came out that he was a cop, the department accelerated my case to get me out and made the bust before things got compromised."

"How long were you acting as his girlfriend before you two got married? Because I don't remember getting an invitation."

"I fell hard girl. I couldn't fake it anymore. Which made it seem that more convincing. He didn't want any of his family to know so we did it that last run we made to Vegas. I'm sorry I kept it from you."

"Those kinds of secrets come with your line of work. (Catches eye contact) I'm really sorry you lost him."

Roslyn's face turns sorrowful briefly before she smiles and thanks Olivia for the concern. Olivia decides not to let the moment get to heavy as she clears her throat and devilishly smiles at Roslyn.

(Slowly)

"What!"

"You're hiding something Roz; I can feel it. It's time to give up **the** *real dirt. I know you're sitting on something. It's something good, isn't. In-laws? You haven't said much. Girl, stop holding out."*

"Well, all right. You know I always got something good. I got a phone call from Ray's grandmother…"

"Aaww-huh, that must have been nice. How often do you speak with her?"

"Ah...Never! That's what's odd. When we first met, she dismissed me. Seemed annoyed that Raymond brought me to her house. I recall her harshly reminding him not to bring trash from the streets to her door. Cutting her eyes at me as she spoke."

(Surprised)

"NO!!! Ella dijo eso?" {She said that?}

"Amongst other things. That was the only day we have spoken, except of course for the funeral. I made it my practice to distance myself. It worked for Ray. So, I was a bit surprised when she called talking like we were old bingo buddies."

"Que queria?" {What did she want?}

"What does all family want after there's a death in the family??? Su corte." {Their cut}

(Whispered shockingly)

"Noooo!"

"Oh Yeah. She got straight to the point. Began to tell me how she's been the one who's taken care of Raymond all these years. Told me that she bought bonds and opened saving accounts for her son and grandson's. Can you believe that she said I had no reason to chase Ray's cousin off of ***Her*** *family's property? (Rolls her eyes) Yeah! Then her rant continued with a threat. She said let's see if I can chase off the police when she sends them out to remove me. Those were her words exactly."*

"Es grave?" {Is she serious?}

"I get that feeling. (Sips her coffee) Oh wait... there's more. She called me a Ghetto Street serpent who had jammed her fangs into her grandson. (Olivia looks surprised) And...she continues with how she has Ray's Will. Threatening to let the authorities sort it out."

"There's a will??"

"No, not as far as I know Olivia."

"Are you worried that she may produce one?"

"If she does…I'd doubt if it would be real. I know Ray started the process with a Lawyer. We both did…together, but nothing was ever finalized… for either of us. That is why I know she's bluffing. It would clearly be a forgery. You know… She's such a Cunt. (Olivia chokes on her Latte) I purposely came across overtly bitchy as I interrupted her. Jumping in and injecting some truth into a speech that seemed rehearsed and chocked full of lies. I told her that ***MY*** *husband never had a Will. (Softly) It doesn't matter anyway…my name is on the Deed. She can bitch to whomever she wants. I am the only one with the rights to have anyone removed from that property. I told her to do whatever she thinks she has too. But be advised that I will do the same as well. I added that any actions of mine forced against her family is not personal. Not for me anyway. It's business."*

"I like how that sounds Roslyn. Hum… It's not personal…It's business. I like it! How'd she take it?"

"She called me a disrespectful little South of the border Hussie. (Olivia mouths the words: FUCK HER) I've got too much going on right now. Ya know? I don't need this shit. But you know she just continued talking. At this point she started to yell. She spent the next few minutes mumbling obscenities at me. She didn't even seem to be speaking to me directly. Which was strange. Wouldn't even let me respond when I was trying to. So, I eventually hung up on her loud obnoxious ass. (Roslyn shakes her head while rotating her cup) I don't have time for that shit! She is a foul mouthed, mean Ol' Lady. No wonder she's still alive. You know… Evil don't die."

"Girl Ya know, that's right! So, what now?"

"Well…I've only have one thought if she tries anything Olivia… Game on Bitch!"

CHAPTER TEN

Losing Ground

THE MALL WAS unexceptionally crowded for a Thursday evening. The teenagers were hanging out, like they normally do but there's never this much foot traffic on evenings. Not unless it's the holidays. Sean uncharacteristically begins his trek into the mall alone. He slowly walks pass a new furniture store that is exactly where the Old Navy used to be two weeks ago. The aroma of freshly popped popcorn causes him to drift towards a center isle kiosk and buy a bag. He smiled like a child who was handed cotton candy for the first time after being handed the narrow-stripped bag. He ingested a handful of the popcorn before he started walking again. As he savored his snack, he walks pass the expensive but ghetto jewelry store. Who incidentally has two suited, dread locked muscle heads who looked like their feet were hurting from being on them in that entryway all day? They acknowledged Sean with a nod as he passed them but their expressions were similar. Suspicious, just like any police officer that drives by a group of black kids on a corner. He also tried to hurry pass the lady pitching the micro-waveable neck warmers. They always try to put one around your neck even when you're shaking your head and telling her no Thank You. Sean was strolling near the glass barrier that allows him to see the food court just below him and was now heading toward Foot Locker. He slows down because he thinks he hears his name being shouted from somewhere.

(In the distance)

"Aye, Sean. What up? Hey, down here dog. Look down here!"

Sean looks around then moves closer to the glass railing just above the food court and peers over. His eyes follow two Hispanic girls who walk by the cheesy looking but drizzling recycling water fountain before he locks onto Slim Nate. Who happens to be sitting with his arms and legs spread out as wide as he could get them, looking like a slumping letter x, in the power seat. The power seat(s) is at a table that is one or two rows from the restaurants, almost in the middle of the court and facing the glass railing so you can watch all the women walking by. Nate sat alone as Sean came down the escalator. Disrespectfully eyeing and gesturing any woman who passed him, while continuing to shout out at Sean.

"What up Nigga? I thought that was you."

Sean's demeanor was angry. He cut Nate off before he could say another obnoxiously loud word.

"What da fuck is wrong with you Nate? Don't be yelling my name out in public like that. You don't know if a motha- fucka's got enemies roaming around and shit. Don't call attention to me like that and I aint cha nigga. Show me more respect than that."

"Shit Man, you ain't your daddy! Don't nobody know who the fuck you are. You just one of us... Big Time. You're unrecognizable like the rest of us. Stop tripp'en!"

"What the ***fuck*** *is that s' posed to mean Nate?"*

"Nothing. It's nothing man. (Springs up from his seat) Awe shit man; I've got to show you something. Follow me."

Sean walked up the escalator like he was on an airport tram. Trying to catch up with Nate. Nate slows down and waits for Sean near the Ladies Foot Locker. Taking a second to look at some chick who was wearing beige fuzzy boots, hip hugging jeans and a short green tee shirt that exposed her bulging stomach. Nearly covering the word "Sexy" that served as the buckle for her belt.

"That's just some bullshit there. Look at her Sean. What's with the purple headscarf? Bitches look'en like that piss me off. You'd think her girlfriend would tell her, ***that*** *shit…it don't match. But look at* ***her.*** *She's got on a tank top, fucking pajama bottoms and fuzzy ass slippers. Nigga, did she just get out of bed? I don't fuck'en think so. I hate rat packs of fucked up bitches. Them Ho's ain't got a clue. Now, the bitch I want you to see across the way at Victoria's Secret, is the model for how these young ho's should be looking. (Very soft) Come on, you got to see this bitch."*

*Sean and Nate move to the center of the walkway and stopped outside the window of Victoria's Secret. Nate became startled as a woman Walked away from her isle kiosk, stepped up behind him and tried to put something around his neck. Nate dodged her and yelled, "Bitch, I don't want that hot ass shit on me! Back the fuck off. Damn I hate these middle isle Motha-fucka's! Don't they know anything about customer recognition? Look at me. Do I look like I'm gonna buy your shit?" Sean looks strangely at Slim Nate. Not because of his tirade, those are fairly normal. Sean's face was twisted up wondering what business-related things Nate could possibly know anything about. Once Slim Nate stopped cursing at the venders in the immediate area, he came up beside Sean and through his arm around his shoulder. Nate swung his head back and forth as he softly repeated, "Wait for it. Wait for… it." Sean got suckered in and started moving his head left to right in rhythm with Nate's. Neither seeing anything out of the ordinary. Then without warning Slim erupted. "****Bam! Aw Shit! There that bitch is… Look!****"*

"Where you looking Slim?"

"On the right. In the window, dressing the mannequin. You don't see that fine ass bitch rubbing that mannequin's titties?"

"I see her putting a night gown on it. I don't know what you're fuck'en looking at."

"Alright but you do see that apple shaped ass though?"

"Can't miss that. Who is she? Do you know her?"

"Hell naw! I wish! She's already told me twice to fuck off. So now I'm gonna take time out to just stare at her fine ass. (Whispering) Yeah girl, I want to know your secret."

(Sarcastically)

"Smooth. You're smooth."

Sean's focus returned to the shop window as he unintentionally locked eyes with the Hottie behind the glass. He cracked a flattering smirk as she raised a hand and waved in his direction. He smugly excused himself from Nate. Sean moved with a Cooley High confidence. Strolling in his blue jeans, blue argyle sleeveless sweater with his shirt fashionably un-tucked and a pair of bright white un-scuffed tennis shoes. His platinum chain swung like a pendulum around his neck while the stores spot lights glimmered brightly off of his diamond watch and the visibly huge stone hanging from his right ear. Looking like an off hours NBA player, Sean breaches the shops threshold. She welcomes him in with a flirty bat of an eye and a seductive smile. As he walks, he strolls with a giddy cockiness. "Keep an eye out for me Nate." "You betta come back with the digits Nigga." Nate yelled with a bit of jealousy in his voice while creeping slowly closer to the T-Moble kiosk so he could get a better look at her ass again through the glass. While also trying to see if Sean comes away with anything more than just a polite wave. Nate stood with his hands in his pockets and leans towards the window as another woman offering a warm neck pad approaches him.

(Looking to his left)

"Got DAMN! Do you Bitches run in packs? FUCK! No means No!"

Slim Nate found himself drifting towards the front of the store. Trying to see where Sean and the owner of that fine ass he was staring at just moments ago were. While noticing them standing in the middle of the store, he tilted his head and started staring again. He turned his head away quickly when she glanced his way for a moment. With her focus back on Sean he looked towards them again and chuckled to himself as if he had gotten away with something. His expression turned serious for a moment as he scanned the rest of the store. Satisfied that there was no one inside who would bring any harm to Sean, Slim left him and returned to ogling women as he continued walking the mall.

CHAPTER ELEVEN

Dimming the Northern Lights

JUST OUTSIDE DUVERNAY'S, a downtown retail department store, Big Guns & Courtney stand twenty feet behind a popular sidewalk hotdog cart. They are standing at the northeast side of the building in the small parking lot. The two men talk as Big Guns leans against his brandy wine 1979 Impala as Courtney teeters up and over a parking stall tire stop. They talk as Courtney elevates and descends repeatedly with his hands in his pockets.

"So…I hear you're the second most wicked, Motha-fucka in the city now?"

"Always have been Courtney!"

"Naw, I mean…Ya giving out orders now. (Tilts head in a cocky fashion) Not just take'n 'em like you used too Guns. Does Jr. Kingsley know yet?"

Courtney looks up because Guns hadn't responded. He watched him staring at a woman approaching the hot dog cart at the corner.

"I don't think so. I don't know. It doesn't really matter anyway. I'm not about to discuss it. (Watches the woman's hips as she walks away) I'm here Courtney, so what'd you want to talk about?"

"Let me start wit dat sexy ass broad at the air strip. DAMN! I'd try to make her one of my hoes if she wasn't fucking wit my money."

"Women like that…are too classy to fall in with the likes of you or

any of them low budget bitches tattooing your initials on their strung out look'en asses."

"Fuck you, Guns. Dem bitches are making money."

"Believe what you want. Those hoes can barely make your broke ass bail money. But…that bitch at the hanger has two things your bitches will never have…intelligence and looks."

"Like I said, Fuck you! Now, let's talk about her for a minute. I want to know if Kingsley found anything on her yet. If so, what does your crew have planned? Cause, I've been threatened by a few Motha-fucka's in my day and haven't batted a fucking eye. But something bout this Bitch don't feel right. Popp'en up… outta nowhere, try'en to call shots. She aint calling SHIT round here! If there's some kind of plan…then cool, I want to be down. But I aint waiting around for her to come after any of the shit I've built."

Big Guns crossed his arms again as he glares at Courtney. Who began teetering over the concrete tire stop again. He also began mumbling about the hot dogs before turning back to face Big Guns.

"Your thoughts big man?"

"I think you should go get two dogs and settle the fuck down. All that bouncing you're doing is start'en to bug me. (Moves his right hand and rubs his face) To answer your question…we have no info on that woman or her crew."

"Doesn't that shit bother you?"

"No Courtney it doesn't. And honestly, I don't need to know shit about her or her crew. They're all after the same two things… money and power. My job is to make sure we don't lose either. I don't need to know any more than that. I just need to be prepared and so do you."

[Across town in the Northern side of the city]

The clouds moved slowly east as the sun found brief spots to shine through. The open breaks in the clouds allowed the sun to settle above the tennis courts of Mc Govern Park. Donnie steps slightly to his left to warm himself within a small spot of sunlight. Unconcerned of any danger, he stops talking and tilts his head toward the sky to let the sun warm his face. At the same time Tom Cat ensures that the low-level dealer that Donnie is berating doesn't move. Standing behind him with a hand on his shoulder. After about forty seconds, Donnie drops his head and stares at his hostage.

"Tony, is it? Or…is it, Tone? Did you think you'd get away with it? (Donnie's tone turns angry) What, were… you thinking? Is it cause I'm white? (Moves is close) Or…somehow you think I don't know what happens 'round here?'

Donnie stands directly behind Tone, leans in and whispers for just a moment.

"I have my finger on the pulse of anything that beats MY streets. (Yelling) EVERYTHING! What made you think you could peddle your shit on MY turf?"

Tone nervously looks at Tom Cat several times before he answers.

"You…you think these corners are yours. Shit! Word is, your days out here are numbered. Nobody's scared of your Punk Ass! (Voice softens as he nods) Only him!"

Donnie angrily mumbles, "When are these motha-fucka's gonna show some respect?" As his and Tom Cat's attentions shift to the entrance of the tennis court. An overly animated Geezy holds his hands in the air and slowly approaches the three men. "Who the ***fuck…*** *are you?" Donnie yells as Tom Cat takes a more defensive position.*

"Who I actually am, doesn't matter. At this moment I'm just a messenger."

"Can you hear? I said, what the fuck you want?"

"I want to help you D-Bo. (With sincerity) I'm here to help."

Donnie reaches for his weapon and Tom Cat barely flinches as Geezy slides his hands into his pockets. Suddenly interrupting the awkward silence was the sound of a high- pitched whistle cutting through the air. Moving quickly, the sounds of solid projectiles hit Tony's flesh. Moving too fast for anyone to react. [THUMP-THUMP] The first, hitting center mass of his forehead. Splitting open the back of his head and raining blood onto the court. The second entering his chest, heart side as his body falls to the ground. Tom's mouth opens wide with dismay as his eyes follow Tone's body. Panicking, Donnie ducks while bouncing around in half circles trying to triangulate where the shots came from. Tom Cat's movements were slow. His expression was the same as his eyes rotated to the red dot resting in the middle of Donnie's forehead.

(Nervously)

"Ah, don't move brotha. Donnie you've been marked."

"I…I've been…What?"

Donnie realizing what Tom Cat was saying, slowly stopped moving. Geezy pulls a toothpick from his pocket and clinches it between his teeth before mocking the sounds of the bullets hitting Tone. [THUMP-THUMP]

"Man, those shots came right behind each other. Damn! (Pauses for reflection) …And the big fella's right, I wouldn't move."

(Exasperated & nervous)

"Wha…what the fuck is this about? You gonna kill me?"

"Nooo! (Almost laughing) I'm here to help."

"Help! How so? Killing him?"

"The dead dude? Naw, he was just in the way. Consider him a bonus. Damn dude, you look sick. Relax. Aint nobody else dying today. (Points at both Donnie & Tom Cat) Just don't do nothing stupid though."

Donnie stopped cringing long enough to let his anger over take his fear. He looked toward Tom and demanded that he take some action.

"I'm sorry Don, that laser seems to be targeting us both. I can see the light bouncing around. Sorry man, I'm not mov'en."

"Then what the ***fuck*** *do I pay you for?"*

"You pay me to keep you alive. So, if you'd settle down, shut up and listen…we might get through this."

Donnie (making head nods) gestures in hope that Tom would make a move. Only giving up on the heroics when he sees the little red dot center itself on the left side of Tom's chest. Cleary nervous, Donnie's voice wavers as he softly began speaking to Geezy again.

"You said the you're here to help me. I'm curious…how?"

"Shit Man! My bad! Maybe I didn't make myself clear. I ***was*** *sent to help but I didn't mean you."*

"What da fuck does that mean?"

"Relax…shit, I'm gett'en to it. What I have to say comes in two parts. The first part is an offer. The second will shape up into a harsh reality."

"You aint making no sense. Shit! What the fuck you trying to say."

"Well, it's like this… We know the Cat here is on your payroll and the folks I represent mean to change that. (Turns) I'm here to make him an offer. A lucrative offer."

Donnie erupts, yelling and waving his arms wildly at Gezzy.

"You fuck'en kidding me. That's MY guy. You don't talk to MY guy. You talk to me! That kind of shit comes through me. NOT HIM! Who da fu…"?

Donnie takes a step towards Geezy until a bullet whizzed by him and splits open a tennis ball that was sitting on the ground. Donnie quickly steps back as Tom glares in his direction.

"I didn't mean it like that T-Cat."

"Sounded that way to me big man. (Almost singing) Control issues."

"Fuck what he's saying. That's not how I meant it."

"Hear me out T-Cat. Let me talk to ya for a moment while we both ignore Don Nervous for the moment. Ok, the people I represent want to pay you to take a vacation. They will triple what he pays you in a year. Wait… and then double that. When you might ask. Right now! Today! In cash! If

you accept this offer you can collect your money from the guy (Pointing) at the bottom of the hill in the sports coat. He'll also give you the full terms of the agreement. Or... I walk off this court and your fate may be the same as Rig-a-Morty over there."

Tom Cat turns and looks past the grassy area, eyeing a man with a briefcase.

"That's a bullshit offer T-Cat." Donnie yells. "No one's fronting that kinda cash out here."

"We both know Donnie can't match an offer like this. He can't. Oh, I almost forgot to mention that this deal expires in five minutes. It's too late when that brief case walks away."

"How do I know this is on the up and up? How can I be sure that man actually has money in that case?" Tom Cat asks as his focus returns to Geezy.

"The money is real. Let me assure you."

Geezy reaches into his pocket and pulls out a thick rolled up wad of cash. Unfolds it and fans it out so that tom Cat can see that they're all hundreds.

"This was handed to me by the same man just before I came up the hill. All of this...just to ensure my safety. Walking in and out of these courts. So, the way I see it, (places money back into his pocket) if they would pay me this much to deliver a message... why wouldn't that case he's holding have exactly what they say is in it. Anyway, there's only one way to find out."

Geezy side steps, intentionally clearing a path to the gate entrance of the tennis courts. Donnie's face is stoic but his eyes plead to Tom Cat not to move.

"Come on T-Cat, don't do it." Donnie pleads. "I need ya man!"

"It's one hell of a deal. Death or a paid vacation... seems like a no-brainer."

"It's bullshit man. Think about it! Don't do it man."

Without any hesitation Tom takes steps towards the gate.

"Wha…wha…what are you doing?" Donnie yells, holding his hands up in protest. "Ah, come on man! Don't do it."

Tom Cat brazenly passes Donnie without so much as a glance until Donnie pleads, "You can't do this to me man. Don't make this about the money."

(Looks back)

"This isn't personal Donnie. It's always been about the money for me. You knew that. (Almost apologetic) I have to go but I wouldn't move while that laser's still sitting on your chest."

It didn't take long for him to walk off the court and down the hill. Donnie and Geezy look on as Tom Cat is shown the money and then is handed the briefcase. Donnie begins to moan with disgust when Tom gets his instructions as the two men walk away.

Geezy waits for Donnie's personal rant to stop so he could finish his business and leave.

"Sooo…is this how it's going to end? Huh? Bribe my muscle to leave, and then kill me in the open. In broad daylight."

"I told you nobody else was dying today. Have you been listening? I get it, you're worried. Get over it already. Like I said earlier, there's two parts to this message. First, would be the offer and then… some harsh reality. Here's the harshness. (Clears his throat) I want to make sure I say this right. (Pauses) It doesn't benefit anyone and that includes the people who paid me to be here, if you are killed. I'm told it's not actually profitable to take over your territory either. So…you're going to be forced to play a part in an urban experiment."

"Aaah what?"

"Experiment. Yeah, exciting, isn't it? I KNOW! Here's how it will go down. First, they take away the muscle. The protection you've grown comfortable with. You just saw that happen. Easy enough, right. Doing that, will sort of even the playing field around here, so I'm told. Next, with

the cat gone, you'll be forced to fend for yourself. No, no…wait, I meant de-fend yourself and your lively-hood."

"This is some fucked up shit Yo! Who do these fuckers think they are sending you in here? Then trying to intimidate a Motha-fucka. HUH? Now they want to set terms in an area I control. Huh? This is my ***shit 'round here!"***

(Sarcastically)

"They could just KILL YOU. How bout that? Heh? …And you're right. This ***is*** *still Yo shit. They're just making you work harder to keep…Yo shit!"*

"Work…for my own shit? Are you kidding me?"

"Work, fight, keep others from taking it. However, you want to put it. That's the plan. Sooo…work it out, I'm gone."

Geezy pushes his hands and arms away from his chest before making a swiping motion across his neck. Indicating that he was finished. He slowly backs toward the gate to the court. Keeping his focus on Donnie who's standing enraged, waving his arms frantically and yelling to himself. Geezy now feeling a safe distance from Donnie, shakes his head and says to himself," Sink or swim. Shit! That dude is gonna drop like a stone."

CHAPTER TWELVE

Premonition and Punishment

THE AUTUMN EVENING was hot. Even with a window open it was still unbearable to sleep. Sean kicks his leg out from under the covers, hoping the night air would provide some relief. He grunts as he adjusts his head in his pillow and falls deeper asleep. He shifts again and tries to get comfortable. The pattern of his breathing becomes steady as an image begins to appear in his mind. He sees himself walking through a dark hallway. The sound of his footsteps echo off the walls. Raymond's hospital room didn't seem so dark the last time he visited, Sean thought. Raymond also looked more alert than he'd remembered. Grann was still standing at Raymond's bedside as Slim Nate and Big Guns held down his cousin. Keeping him from being able to grab or deflect anything. Sean intensely watches himself, now forcefully muffling his cousin with a towel. Raymond squirmed, he grumbled, and grimaced in pain. With all the injuries that Raymond has endured already, the pain from the man handling quickly began to show on his face. Sean continues to watch himself and the others keeping Raymond subdued so his grandmother could finish with the needle. Although most of the faces in the room were shaded and nearly unrecognizable, Sean's perception wouldn't let him forget who was in the room or what had been done. It was Raymond's image; mannerisms and resistance that were uncannily clear. Sean, in the dream, still watches from the door, seeing how he took part in harming the only person of his family that repeatedly looked after him. Watching shamefully as he gradually removed the towel from over his cousin's mouth. Watching uncomfortably as the weakened fight in Raymond begins to subside. Achingly avoiding eye contact just as the toxin Grann injected into him affects Raymond's motor controls. Now the dream shifts, Sean now focuses more intently on himself, watching as he moves closer to his cousin and whispers, "They're making me do this. I need you to know that. You were always better with this street shit than I was cousin. I'm sorry." Sean rocks nervously in his sleep as the room suddenly goes dark and startles him. It's eerily quiet. All he could hear was the loud reverberating slow whispering of, "I know why!" A single stream of light finds the bed. The light reveals that Raymond is gone. Sean shakes again in his sleep, now that he sees that he's taken his cousin's place and is now the one being restrained. Cringing as he watches a syringe slowly being pulled from his arm. Sean panics in his sleep and in the dream. He struggles to get free. He feels his eyes getting heavy as Grann devilishly winks and waves goodbye to him. His heart rate slows and he could hear Raymond's voice whispering to him, "You're next if you don't get out. You've got to get out!" Sean felt himself slipping away. The room was painfully silent except for the waning self-satisfying chuckle from Grandmother as she passes the nurse coming into the room. The nurse smiles, then Sean blacks out.

Sean awakens hysterical and breathing heavily. It's 3:30 in the morning. "Oh my God. What the fuck!" Sean growls as he sits up in bed. Holding his head in one hand while messaging his temples. His new girlfriend Keisha strokes his back and tells him he's all right. Sean still hasn't caught his breath but slowly works on composing himself. Keisha continues to comfort him as she waits for his breathing to become normal. He takes a few deep breaths and begins to tell her what he could remember about his dream.

"It felt strange. As if my soul was being pulled away from my body against my will. That was one of the sensations. I don't know what dying

feels like but I think that was close. I felt helpless. A total disconnect between body and mind. I was unable to move although I was telling myself too. I was panicky but becoming calm at the same time. (Looks at his arm) Must have been caused by the injection she gave me. I was bursting with a need to escape. The inability to even struggle to get free was excruciating. Even now, I can still hear my grandmother laughing. [Spoken softly] My cousin and I switched places. I could see Raymond's face so clearly, but only his. He was the only one I didn't sense any danger from."

Sean stopped speaking briefly, just long enough to enjoy Keisha's soothing touch. He turns to face her as he stumbles to remember more details from his nightmare.

"My body was lifeless. Um, um…it was unresponsive. It was like all my frantic movements to free myself from the restraints were useless. Damn, but those looks from my grandmother were ominous and bone chilling. The whole thing was creepy."

Keisha continued trying to calm Sean. Rubbing his shoulders and lower back. Repeatedly asking if he was ok.

"Yeah. Um…yeah, I think so. I'm ok. (Rubs his eyes) He said I was next."

"Who said?"

"My cousin. Sounded like a warning. His voice was so clear, so real, as close as you are now."

"Go back to sleep Babe. It's over now. I'm sure that dream won't repeat itself."

(Sarcastically)

"Yeah…sure it won't. I told myself ***that*** *three dreams ago."*

[Six hours later]

Sean arrogantly enters a familiar lair. With his chest out, strutting like a hunter who has bagged his prey. Dangling his new girlfriend, Keisha, like a hard-to-get accessory. A rare prize that he hopes the others wish they had. As they approached the bar, Sean leads her to a seat at the corner end. This way she's facing away from the rest of the crew gathering behind her. Nate, who was standing center of the bar, chugs the rest of his drink before smirking and shaking his head at Sean.

"What! What's the smirk about Nate?"

(Innocently)

"Hanging wit the sexy ass mall chick huh?"

"What's that s'posed to mean?"

"Nothing, young boss man. (Scratches his face) If you don't know… umm, never mind."

Nate sets the glass on the bar and winks at Keisha before turning to join the others. Sean rests his hands onto Keisha's shoulders before hunching and whispering into her ear. "Give me bout fifteen minutes. Order whatever you want." He then motions to the bar tender with a circular rotation of his hand, gesturing for him to set her up. He leans in close enough to kiss her on the cheek before turning towards the rest of the guys. His dad sat at his favorite dimly lit table and used two fingers to call everyone over to him. Without hesitation, everyone moved with a sense of urgency. Finding spots to stand or lean in preparation to listen to the boss, everyone except his son. Sean makes a quick about face and begins talking to his girl again while ordering himself a drink. Big Gun's, standing left of Mr. Kingsley, shakes his head at Sean before beginning to bark directions at him. Sean looks back at Gun's wondering if he had missed a joke, then with a dismissive gesture turns and picks his drink up from the bar. "Hey!" Big Gun's yells, "Get your ASS over here so we can get started!" Sean scoffs, as he becomes agitated with Gun's shouting. Keisha turns slightly on the bar stool, looks at Sean and nods her head towards the guys. Suggesting that it may be time to get over there. Some of the guys turn toward Sean in disbelief waiting on him to move. Sean finally realizes that he is now the center of attention and saunters away from the bar. He breezes by Gun's with a belittling swagger. His every mannerism, as he dragged out getting where he needed to be, was intended to let his girl see that everyone else is beneath him.

"Can you hurry your slow ass up!" Gun's frustratingly shouts.

Sean focuses on his father as he moves to his right.

"What's ***HIS*** *problem Pop? Why's Gun's talking like he's running shit?"*

(Standing just a glance away from Sean)

"That's cause I am running Shit."

(Confused)

"Is this a joke? You fuck'en wit me? (Turns to his father) What' does he mean? He's running shit!"

Sean, growing increasingly agitated, quickly glances over at his girl, who has now turned to face the group. His father clears his throat before lighting his cigar.

"Don't look so surprised son. You haven't sensed that something like this was coming? You don't lead by example. (Puffs) Even the simplest jobs you've been asked to handle, you don't. You carry yourself like you are big shit. You can walk around pretending to be, but you're not. Shit, you're not living up to any other of our expectations either. Strangely enough, Slim has become more reliable with completing jobs…and he's famous for his ability to slack."

(Yells out)

"You gonna do this now! SHIT! I mean…I do my best."

"Your best? Shhhiit!" Big Gun's bellows."

"You putting me on blast like this Pop. Right now?"

Sean nervously looks back towards the bar again. Mr. Kingsley leans forward in his seat and pulls the cigar from his mouth. As he holds it between his fingers, he uses his pinky finger to point at his son.

"Son, this has to be done. Doesn't matter when and since your attention is at the bar, let's start there. First, you know she wasn't s'posed to be brought here. That's part of our rules. I thought I was crystal clear regarding who is

to be in this restaurant during meetings. That's why it's closed to the public while we're here."

"I don't think he gets it boss. (Looking at Sean) It's as if the guidelines don't apply to YOU. Being his son doesn't make you exempt from them. So don't get upset about this shit now. You were man enough to bring her here, deal wit it. Can't bitch up now cause you don't want her to hear this shit."

"Roderick is right son. Lately I've seen you display a healthy disregard for our basic rules. Bringing your Boo Thang here, today, is a perfect example of that. (Puffs) But…poor decisions become the purpose of change. We will also address a few other things that are bad for business."

Mr. Kingsley rises from his chair, taking time to enjoy his cigar. As he inhales and exhales, he makes eye contact with a few of the men sitting and standing around him.

"So here is how we are going to run things moving forward. (Looks at his son) Roderick, from here on out is in the number two slot. I gave it to him because ***you*** *haven't demonstrated that you can handle it son. So, until further notice, everyone including Sean will take all directions from Gun's. I hope that is clear. And…because we have an un-trusted set of ears in the bar, I'll only say this. The way we've done things will be changing round here. We have investments that need protecting. (Taps the table) It's becoming unavoidably hostel out there. There are threats around every corner. Big or small, no threat on our livelihood will be taken lightly. I expect an improved effort from everybody. We will be prepared. This is exactly why I'm making these changes now."*

Sean looks at his father and once again feels like the chastised child who has repeatedly disappointed his dad. You could see that Sean had something he wanted to say to his father but his dad's expression divulged that this might not be the time or place. The room was silent as Mr. Kingsley filled the air with cigar smoke. Everyone looking on waiting for him to say something more but he just nodded his head at Gun's before putting his hand on his son's shoulder. "Let me talk to you son." As Gun's picked up talking to the group, Mr. Kingsley led Sean away from everyone but only halfway towards the bar. His right hand was now wrapped around the Sean, squeezing his son's shoulder while he spoke. In close, his voice was only loud enough for Sean to hear him. Keisha, noticing the separation from the group, swivels on the bar stool and watches the two of them.

"This change **can** *be temporary. But son, that depends on you. Your antics, relationships, poor decisions and general behavior are making it difficult to run this business. Of all the men here, I shouldn't have to explain the damage your lack of focus is causing. I want you to pull it together. I expect a better effort from you… and soon. (Squeezes his son's shoulder) Listen…you haven't learned how to lead. So, you'll have to practice how to follow first. You may not understand, you might not like it, but it's what has to be done. Ok! As your dad, so I'm rooting for you. (Puffs his cigar and point directly at Keisha) First things first…start with that! I'm giving you thirty minutes. Get rid of her, and then get back here. Got it? (Sean nods) Good! Get going."*

CHAPTER THIRTEEN

The Whispers of Change

[Reno Strip club, 12:00pm]
[Club DJ announces with enthusiasm]

"THE FORECAST CALLS for rain. I give you…Alexis. A.K.A…Wet Thunder."

The bright lights create shadows on the stage floor as Alexis makes her ass fluctuate in a clapping motion. Jiggling the curvy mounds of her flesh rhythmically before she descends slowly towards the floor. With her back to the room, she falls into the splits as the men on each side of the stage rage into excited moans while throwing sweaty bills onto the stage. Alexis innocently looks over her right shoulder, holding one finger to her lips while she seductively arches her back and grinds the stage. The music begins to switch back and forth between a track mix of Janet Jackson's, Come back to me, and Mint Condition's Pretty Brown Eyes. Alexis' motions stop briefly as her attention fixates solely on the enormously large man hunched, sitting alone, center stage and just at the end of the catwalk. A small portion of light frames the ominous look in his eyes. He smiles. If you can call raising the left corner of his mouth a smile. This facial occurrence only happens because Alexis spins around and crawls towards him. Sexy, sultry, freaky, focused and sliding through a shower of bills, she reaches for the edge of the stage. With the grace of a ballet dancer, she flips the opposite direction before resting her head and shoulders onto the big man's table. "Got Damn!" "Beautiful!" Two men shouted as she made her descent. She strokes her breasts with one hand while flipping the hair from her face with the other. The hulking figure, smirking before he leans in closer, helps move the hair from her face.

"Hey baby, who's your friend?' She asks as her eyes tell him what direction some guy approached from. Alexis watches as he sinisterly turns only his head to see who was stepping up behind him. She moves away as if their moment had been ruined and returns to entertaining the rest of the crowd. Disappointingly, the sizable man rises and rotates, wondering whom it may be. Behind him stood a 5'6' man wearing a Dick Tracy style hat and trench coat, with his hands in his pockets. He also wore sunglasses with silver lenses that were reflecting the colored lights flickering around the room. He cringes as the sheer size of the man turning around frightens him. His sudden nervous state causes him to stutter.

"Ya…you…ah, Ba- ba- Big Ronnie Ron?"

(With a menacing glare)

"Nicolas Garza? You're late!"

(Surprised)

"You're Samoan? Uh, ok…I thought you were black."

"Does it matter Garza? Cause I thought you were Hispanic…not white. (Pauses) Honestly, I don't give a shit! As long as you do what you're paid to do and say what I tell you to say."

(Hesitantly)

"Uh…O-kay."

The big man signals with just the flip of his hand for Garza to follow. They enter the V.I.P room where he instructs Nicolas to have a seat and then everyone else to leave. Everyone except one of the ladies he caught by the arm.

"Come with me love. Although I've got business to take care of in here, I want you to keep me entertained while I handle it."

Ronnie settles himself into the sofa and sets his eyes on Garza, who's finding it difficult to focus as the stripper begins to dance. Garza's head darts around, signifying in one moment he is too nervous to look and on the other, unable to take his eyes off of her.

"Do I need to go over what you're s'posed to do or do you understand?"

"Ya-yes, I do Big Ron, (pauses, stares then mumbles) Ronnie? But what kind of assurance do I have that you will keep your word. That you'll come through for me."

Garza flinches as the sizable guy loudly slaps the stripper across her ass before pulling her into his lap. She continues to move in an erotic fashion. Seductively leaning her head back to hear what was being whispered to her. She smirks momentarily, and then slowly opens her eyes. Now smiling devilishly, she looks across the room at Garza before beginning to repeat every word being whispered to her.

(Soft & flirtatious)

"Your concerns will not be overlooked Nicolas. But let's call a spade ...a spade. On a personal level, you have the most to gain. Your money laundering charge will cease to exist. (Pauses to readjust her hands from his knees to his thighs) The other charge, it will be reduced so dramatically that you may only get a little probation. But, if ***you're*** *not successful with what you've been asked to do...then I'll be stuck with the fall out. (Singing the first part) So oh...although your concern is warranted, you must understand that any favors promised to you are only contingent on how successful you are for me."*

Garza sits with a confused expression, not sure whom to direct his answer too. Unable to get eye contact with the big man, he lowers his head and directs his answer to the stripper.

"No worries. I know what to do..."

The big man puts up a finger, which causes Garza to pause. With his other hand he slides a roll of money into the opening between her cleavage and her bra. Whispers his gratitude then instructs her to leave the room. After rising from the couch, Garza follows the big man's lead. Garza listens as they both stroll towards the entrance of the room.

"What I need you to do is essential. The Reynolds kid, I'm not so worried about. It's the Kingsley's who must be convinced. It has to be done exactly when and how you were instructed. You do this right…and I promise your problems will go away. (Nudges Garza out the door) I'll be in touch."

[60th and Shattuck Ave. Same day, same time]

A gold 1972 Ford Mustang convertible with wire rims and Vogue tires pulls alongside the curb near the park with its top down and music blaring. Donnie D stands on the sidewalk at the edge of the grass wearing a powder blue sweat suit, white tee shirt, tennis shoes and eating salted cashews from a jar. He's been eagerly awaiting Big Ronnie Ron all morning. Big Ron gradually turns down the Earth Wind & Fire that entertained or annoyed everyone in a half block in every direction before he shut off the engine of his car. Donnie wasted no time; he began talking just as soon as there was no noise drowning him out. Ron sat as comfortably as he could through what seemed to be a rehearsed sales pitch but eventually needed to get out of his car. He stretched his legs before circling around and leaning against his car's passenger side door. Donnie tossed more cashews into his mouth as Ron rested his hands on the top of the door. Not waiting to swallow, Donnie continued his presentation with excited optimism, as Ron's initial expression remained blank. Ron, seeing something out of the corner of his eye, turns his head and looks over his right shoulder. He starts watching a teenager sitting on a fire hydrant across the street. The youngster pops up from his perch as a shaking strung out woman approaches him. He reaches into his pocket then simulates rolling dice with whatever he was clutching tightly in his hand. The kid looks around insuring he was clear to make the deal until he notices Ron looking his direction. Shaking his head, Ron gives the kid an almost unnoticeable motion to leave. Before leaning back onto his car, he watches the kid hurry the other direction up Shattuck and chuckles at the strung-out woman standing briefly at the corner confused at why her meds were heading away from her. Through all of that, Donnie never stopped talking but hesitated briefly as Ron began to chuckle.

(Laughing)

"You want me to do what?"

"Come in and partner this with me Big Ron. You're a natural."

"Come in on what, Malibu's most wanted. (Shaking his head) You can't be serious? Donnie, everybody knows that you don't want a partner... you're looking for muscle."

(Jittery)

"Yeah, you're right. Ok...that's one thing but this gig is right up your alley. This could prove to be profitable for you."

"Profitable...(scoffs) you're barely making any money. Are you blind? The only one who can't see what's happening? How many motha-fucka's you gonna let sell on these corners?"

(Optimistically)

"It's not as bad as it looks. Is it?"

Big Ron points towards the same strung-out women from minutes earlier, who is now buying her drugs from another guy who came from the other direction.

"Man, you should be hitting the panic button. You're losing control out here. I've worked for and been around enough of you guys to recognize the panic in your eyes. This (motioning with his hand) is as manly of a cry for help that I've ever seen. Real talk Donnie, you've said a lot but have failed to say what's most important...at least to me. You haven't dropped a dollar amount. (Pauses) We both know the reason you haven't... Is because you can't. You've got too much invested in those Good Fella's. Trying, I mean

failing to clear your corners. That's why you're offering a guy like me a partnership opportunity. Hoping I can free up some of your money. While at the same time, you're counting on me to clear up these shit heads that are starting to muscle in on your area."

Donnie grabs a fistful of cashews and pops one or two into his mouth as he anxiously looks at Ron.

"Uh…wow, is it that obvious?"

"Not so much as you just being pitifully transparent."

(Nervously offended)

"Come on Big Ron!"

"Sh..it! You've been 'round black folks long enough. (Gestures) I'm just keeping it real. (Laughs) Oh…wait. Did you mean come on cause I've been fucking wit you? Or, as a second attempt to convince me?"

Big Ron awaits an answer, any reaction but Donnie stands motionless.

"Well, it doesn't matter Donnie. Man, you're just wasting your time.

"Wait, hear me out Big Ron. This can be lucrative for you. You come on board we can turn this around. The cash will flow in before you know it."

"Cash aint an issue for me. I got that coming to me without any worry. More importantly…Donnie I aint interested."

"Come on big man, I'm trying to offer you a good opportunity."

(Agitated)

"Oh, like Kingsley did before his bitch ass son sold me out. (Mumbles) I aint forgot about it or close to being done with that shit. (Composes himself) I…don't…need an opportunity. (Huffs) Some advice Donnie, you may have to become more aggressive than these hood rats know you to be. You get your hands dirty, ya might regain control your damn self. And…maybe get some new found respect."

"Get dirty! Seriously?"

"Yeap, that's what I'm saying Mr. Clean."

(Mumbles inquisitively)

"Huh, Get dirty."

[Thursday meeting with Grann]

It's early evening and Robert Kingsley sits down next to his mother on the stairs of her front porch. She has just asked her son to put out the cigar he is puffing on as she clears the smoke away by waving her hand.

"Robert, two days ago you met with all of the boys. How'd that go?"

(Hands his mother an envelope)

"Here's this week's walking around money. (Sighs) Part of it went well but Sean didn't take being demoted pleasantly, especially publicly."

"As I expected! (With disappointment) I know my grandson, what did he do now?"

"He brought some new girl into the bar. Propped her up at the bar during our meeting."

"I know you didn't…"

"No Ma! Nothing important was discussed while she was in there. Sean ***was*** *embarrassed hearing the bad news in front of her though. I had him take her out before we discussed any new business strategies."*

"Good. I don't know when that boy is gonna understand. You hear me? He just has no business sense. I want him to have a taste of what it takes to earn something. Clearly benefiting from the Kingsley name has made things too easy for him. (Taps her son's arm) I want you to start him at the bottom. Don't make him a runner, cause we don't want him to get caught or arrested with anything. So put him on some kind of early morning look out duty or have him run errands. At least until he gets his head screwed on right, toughens up or shows any qualities of leadership. Let's show him that respect is not bestowed on him because he's your son. Let's teach him how to earn it."

"Fine, if that's what you want Ma."

"...And somehow, that boy always cozies up with the wrong women. They always lead to some kind of trouble."

"We may have bigger problems than the numerous women Sean is seen with."

"How so Robert?"

"There's a man in the Bay Area named Garza who's being held on a money laundry charge."

"You know... some guy came around here days ago asking bout that man and Sean."

"Well Ma, ***my*** *sources tell me that during Garza's questioning, he implicated Sean as a contributing part of his money laundering racket."*

"I'm not following you, Robert. How's that possible?"

"Do you remember that strip club in Las Vegas that Sean opened?"

(Disgusted)

"Nothing but self-indulged sinning devils at those doors. A house of whores! I remember telling him to close that alter of tainted flesh."

"Well, he didn't. Now, this Garza has implicated the club. One more problem we may have to handle."

"Have someone look into it so we can protect our interests. I don't want to be any closer to this thing than that. You hear me son? (He nods) We don't want to take any hits on this. We don't know if any implications will find a way back to us, or just Sean. Although, I am curious to see if Sean will come to us with this of if he tries to hide it. It's situations like these that show the measure of a man. But in Sean's case, if he's begun to operate like one."

"I'll get someone to look into it Ma and I will also talk with Sean tonight."

"But not about this Garza stuff!"

"Understood! We'll wait it out."

"Tell my grandson that his take is now being cut in half as punishment

for not doing as he was told. Also keep him busy until we can have this Garza thing looked into."

"While it's on my mind Ma, do I need to get involved with getting into DL's old house?"

"Legally that Spanish harlot is family and rightfully entitled to whatever your nephew left her. (Clears her throat) No Robert! Leave her to me. Removing folks from this family is my specialty. I'll find a way in. I want you to concentrate on keeping our livelihood from being tested, tampered with or more importantly…taken away."

CHAPTER FOURTEEN

The Promise

A THIN SLIGHTLY CURLING vapor ascends from a half-smoked cigar that's clinched between Robert Kingsley's fingers. He sits at his desk, with little or no movement. Seemingly peering out at nothing as if he's in a state of deep thought. His mind drifts to New Year's Eve 1979.

The night air outside of his brother's home is crisp but tolerable as they both step out onto the porch. Briefly escaping the muggy heat from all of the guests inside enjoying DL's yearly party. DL walks towards the first stair, leaning out so he can look up and enjoy the bright glow of the full moon. He descends a few stairs to get a better view just as Robert passes him and stops at the sidewalk.

"You're not leaving, are you Robbie?" DL asks as he approaches his brother.

(Aggravated)

"How many more times do I have to say...STOP calling me that! I hate that name!"

"Sorry little brother. Old habits are hard to break. They're even harder the older we get. (Pauses) Hey... look, I think this is a good opportunity to talk to you. I've had some things on my mind that I need to run by you."

"Wow you're looking really serious. Is this something mom should be a part of?"

"Not this time Rob. This needs to be...just between us."

"Rii...ight, what's up DL?"

Robert turned slightly and moves so he can lean against a nearby-parked car. DL stands in front of his brother with his back to his house. Standing relaxed as his brother leans, with one hand in his pocket and the other ready to emphasize his words.

"I've been thinking a lot about business, family and the kind of legacy I'll leave behind when my number is up."

(Cut his brother off)

"Aw Shit DL, I don't want to hear any morbid, when I die kind of shit."

"Not entirely like that baby Bruh."

"That's good to hear. Cause I was gonna need a drink or a couple of shots first. You know death is something I don't want to talk about." (Lights a cigar)

"I don't want to talk about me dying. I want to ask a big favor from you. In the chance that I do."

Four boys playing in the street distracted Robert. Three of them were wearing baseball gloves while the fourth kid was pulling a tennis ball from a small bucket filled with gasoline. DL stopped speaking for a moment, as he was also curious to see what the kids were doing. The one boy held the dripping tennis ball between his thumb and index finger and yelled, "Here we go!", as he used a lighter to set the ball on fire. That green ball burned with an orange and red glow as he threw it towards one of the other boys. The second boy apprehensively catches it then yells, "It's not really that hot." He then tosses it at the third. Now the ball was giving off a black trail of smoke as the scent of burning rubber drifted in the air. The third kid's eyes widened as he watched that burning orb coming at him. He cringed, becoming terrified and quickly got out of the way.

"What are you doing?" The one kid yelled.

"You're s'posed to catch it!" Another one shouted.

Then the boys began to shout, "GET IT!" Just as the burning ball went bouncing under a couple of parked cars before rolling under and getting wedged in the grate of the corner gutter.

"Aw man", the first kid to get to the ball bellowed. "It went out!"

"No problem. I'll light another one." The kid with the lighter tells the others as he reaches into the bucket again.

"NO, YOU WON'T! Bring me that bucket and give me that lighter!"

A 5'7" shadowy figure stepped out of the darkness into an area lit by the streetlight. He was the father of the first kid and he looked angry. The other kids scatter as the boy hands the bucket to his father.

"What were you thinking? Have you lost your mind? Whose idea was this? Never mind, it couldn't have been anyone but yours. Do you have any idea the damage you could have caused?"

As the father and son walked, his tone was still angry and voice grew louder. His questions were coming too fast for his son to respond as they entered their home. Robert's attention returns back towards DL and says, "Wow. It's crazy what these kids come up with."

"If you remember, we did far worse and we never got caught. (Robert motions in agreement) Far worse."

(Spoken softly)

"Right. (Nodding) Right."

"Let me start over little brother. First, I clearly don't want to talk about my death or anything so morbid. I want to ask you to do me a favor. In case I ever do."

(Inquisitively)

"A favor?"

"More like a promise, Robert."

(Playfully)

"Oh, it's a promise now." (Lights a cigar)

"Ha, Ha! Robert, how bout shutting the hell up so I can tell you what the fuck is on my mind."

Robert gestures for his big brother to get on with it as he exhales a huge puff of smoke.

"Here it is… (Breathes deeply but stays relaxed and calm) In the event that I die, I want you to promise to keep Raymond away from <u>*this*</u> *life we lead. I don't want to be a part of rearing another generation of criminals. I want this to end with me. I want my son to...Um, I don't know…go to college. Maybe open a business. I just don't want him to follow in my footsteps."*

(Slowly exhales smoke)

"That's what you want me to do? You mean…that's all?"

"You don't see this as a big deal Robert? I'm really asking a lot from you. You might want to give it more thought."

"It's done. No more thought, no deeper thought necessary. If that's what you want… I'll handle it."

Robert takes another puff while thinking, "That's some good sounding shit. I should get in on it."

(Impulsively)

"I'm in big brother. I'll take some of that action. That's a good idea. So…why don't you do the same for me."

DL extends his hand and both brothers seal their new pact with a handshake. A faint sound causes DL to turn after hearing his wife calling from the porch. He assures her that he would come back inside soon. But, hesitated to continue his conversation with Robert, waiting for her to step back inside.

"There's one more thing we need to talk about before I head back in Robert."

"Before you start…how's your basement vault looking these days DL?"

DL, looking confused about the question, looks around to make sure the coast is clear before answering.

"My vault is just fine baby brother. Why do you ask? What's going on with yours?"

"Three quarters of it is gone. If I'm not careful it may end up completely empty. Look, here's what I'm getting act…I'm asking if you can float me a loan from yours."

"Didn't we talk about keeping a rainy-day money stash?"

"We did…and I did…but it rained DL."

"Another failed business venture? Or, is it yet another outstanding gambling debt?"

(Frustrated and pointing with the cigar between his fingers)

"Does it matter DL?"

"I guess not, as long as the marker is paid. (Crosses his arms) I can't bail you out this time. I'm locking down any extraneous expenses. Sorry, I can't swing it right now."

"You can't swing it! It's not like you ***not*** *to let me hold something when I need it!"*

"Things are different for me now Robert. I have to think about my family. You should be doing the same. (Expression turns serious) You have to control those money losing bad habits. I can't keep bailing you out. Especially right now."

"Can't…or won't?"

"It's a little of both. It's all a bit complicated. Hey, there's no good time to do what I have to do, but in the spirit of ushering in a new year and starting anew…I thought you should hear this first."

DL found himself staring at the circular red glow of his brother's cigar until the brightness of the full moon captured his attention again.

"I'm done Robert. I'm finished! I can't do this anymore."

"You aren't serious? You can't be! I know you're not DL. (Takes two puffs) Mom's not going be happy to hear any of this."

(DL's eyes return to his brother)

"Whether she does or not, doesn't even matter to me. I'm doing this. I'm doing this for my family, this community and me. I have to be a part of the solution around here. Not the protection for its problems. I've decided to start helping the people around me that can't help themselves. (Pauses) To show faith in the betterment of man…brings elevation of the human spirit."

"You can't just quit DL. Blood in or bleed out. You just can't walk away."

"Watch me baby brotha. It will be easier than you think. Now listen, Vic will take over for me. He's more than capable. He's worked for me long enough to know how we do things. He's reliable and will report directly to you now."

"How soon are you talking about DL?"

(Takes a deep breath)

"Turn around and look at that moon Robert. It's beautiful! Most folks say full moons make people crazy, (Robert points at DL) but I don't. All I see is hope glimmering out of its brightness. It's a chance to start over, to be whole again. Just as the moon cycles…so can we. We don't have to look up and be left with only half or even a quarter slice of ourselves, but be whole. I need to make myself complete again. So…my transformation begins at midnight. This is how I will bring in the New Year."

(Points with his cigar)

"…And your dead set on doing this?"

Robert takes two or three more puffs as his eyebrows fold towards the middle of his face and he studies his brother. Looking at him as if he's a puzzle that's missing a piece.

"Don't worry little brother, things may be different for a while but it will all work out."

"Believe me DL, worrying is the least of my concerns at this point." (Flicks his cigar at the curb)

"What concerns, Ma? I'll take some time next week to sit down with Ma and explain all the details to her. Ok? (Looks towards the house) It's never as bad as it looks and never as bad as you think. Robert I can make this change with minimal disruption and if no one fights me on my decision, the transition can be smooth. But for now, let's get back inside."

"You go on in. (Lights another cigar) Normally I'd follow you, (pauses) but not this time."

Robert watches to image of his brother begin to fade as his focus is returned to the two men who have been talking to him this entire time. Rotating slightly in his chair, with one leg comfortably crossed over the other, Robert rubs his right eye with the lit cigar still between his fingers. Trying to balance his old feelings of disappointment is his brother with his rising sense of contempt with his son. At the same time, entertaining an answer to a question that one of the men has been steadily repeating. Robert sat his cigar at the edge of his desk before closing his eyes again and rubbing the bridge of his nose.

(Spoken slow and angrily)

"Must…I…do…everything? I'm expecting you to handle it Gun's! I don't need to be involved. Wasn't I clear? I thought I was, of course… unless you didn't understand what I was asking of you."

(Spoken softly but confidant)

"I understand."

"For now, Sean works what he's given. No matter how disruptive, unhappy or unhelpful he is. And that will continue… until I say otherwise. There's nothing more to discuss on the subject. Are we clear?"

With the small wave of his hand, the two men left his office. Robert retrieves his cigar from the desks edge as a bit of ash hits the floor. He takes a deep cleansing breath and closes his eyes. Revisiting every disappointing antic that has caused vacillating emotion surrounding if rearing Sean for this business was a mistake. Struggling with the decision of keeping his promise to DL and alienating Raymond, who would have been more of an asset for the family and to the business. More so than his own son who keeps proving that he can't be. Robert's thoughts of Sean's potential or lack of became more fleeting and more frustrating as he tries to quiet his thoughts and enjoy his cigar. He pushes back in his chair, leans to one side and begins massaging his temples before he utters, "Not until I think he's ready. (Softly) …And who knows when that will be."

CHAPTER FIFTEEN

Covert Operation

7:00am Daybreak

Radio response

"THE SUSPECTS NAME is Courtney Blake. The CI (confidential informant) has told us that he leaves his home the same time every morning. Prepare to apprehend him either at the front door or on the porch. We're unsure if he is armed and he is considered to be dangerous. Proceed with caution."

The sirens are kept silent as the squad cars come racing to a stop. With only the lights flashing, the officers exit the cars with their guns drawn. Moving tactically to cover every entrance and exit of 2148 Adeline Way in West Colver. As the team with the battering ram settles into position, the RO knocks, with warrant in hand and waits for anyone to answer the door. He repeats this process two more times with the same non-responsive results. Grabbing his radio, he announces, "First team, prepare to go in." He then takes one step to his left before taking another two backwards. Now kneeling at the left side of the front door and prepared to signal the breach, he began to gesture a silent count to the two men holding the ram. The men holding the ram synchronized their effort, preparing to swing as the count rose with every flip of the kneeling cop's fingers. Suddenly his fingers ball into a fist, quickly causing everyone to hold his or her positions. Then without warning [creaking noise] the front door to the house opens slightly. All movement from every officer was suspended in an effort not to lose the element of surprise. As the door slowly slipped open, a man in his mid-twenties searches himself for something unaware that his door had swung open. Exposing all of the heavily armed men and women on the other side of it. After grabbing at both of his pants pockets, he shakes his head in a motion of personal disappointment as he notices and reaches for a set of keys hanging on a nearby hook. With keys in hand, he turns to face the open doorway. Satisfied that he has everything he needs, he lifts his head. His eyes shuffle back and forth eyeing the onslaught of police waiting to strike. He looks out on the officers with a disconcerting scowl, an expression of unsurprised contempt. The first thing to come to his mind as he looks out was something his grandfather told him.

"The true measure of a man…is in how well he reacts when pressure is unexpected. Training preps you to be ready. Your instincts are only as good as your training. Train yourself for anything, prepare for everything and your instincts will never fail you."

Knowing he couldn't hold them off with just a glare, he reacts the only way he was prepared for. His second thought was, "FUCK!" Just before trying to slam the door and evade by running away down his hall.

(Multiple voices yelling)

"Police Department! Search warrants!"

"Police…put your hands up!"

"You're under arrest!"

The forward motion of the door was brief. It never shut. It was violently forced open as gun drawn cops ran Courtney down. After hearing the yelling officers, Courtney never broke his stride as he tried to get into the kitchen. One officer gets close to him but slips as he reaches out to make the grab. The officer's momentum causes him to stumble to the floor but forces Courtney to hit the doorframe. Slowing him down just enough for another cop to manhandle him to the floor. Every movement was frantic with the officers barking out orders and Courtney bellowing in pain as he was being twisted into a pretzel. A bit groggy from hitting his head on the leg of his kitchen table, he unknowingly began to recite the rights being read to him as he tried to regain focus. Courtney grimaces and complains that the cuffs are too tight but his pleas are ignored and over shadowed by a cop yelling, "Just get 'em out of here."

The bright lights of the local media vans have lit up the surrounding homes. TV cameras focus on the two officers slowly leading Courtney to the back of a patrol car. Hours have passed, as the home was overwrought with official looking people with rubber gloves and masks. Going over every inch of the house to recover evidence. The scene quickly became a circus as a flow of evidence was being carried from the house. Boxes, computers, and safes just seemed to be the normal items removed. But…it was the baker's dozen of under aged girls who were found locked in several rooms erected in the basement that sent the media into a frenzy. The press dubbed him "The marketer of a minor's misery or the Teeny bopper porn pusher". Reports spoke of the condition of the girls as mew information became available. Attention turned to one reporter as she was giving the cue to speak.

"Sources have said that the condition of the girls range from dehydrated, mal-nourished, to even highly drugged. One girl has told reporters that under the impression that this man loved these girls, that they were talked into and some even forced to perform different types of pornography. Starting with live Internet porn but also forced to film sex tapes and even made to complete acts of prostitution. Neighbors spoke of seeing men of all ages entering and leaving the house at all times of the day and night. Police continue to sweep the home for evidence as the homeowner is taken to be

booked on multiple felony counts. All names of the young girls are being checked against missing person reports and runaway lists. This is Amy Chandler, reporting live from West Colver for KTWN, channel two news."

(Five hours later in East Colver)

For Sean it felt like a lazy Saturday although it was Thursday. The clouds continuously traded places with the sun all morning and into the afternoon. This was the third stop today. Every stop made building up to be what Sean sees as an unproductive day. It's been forty-five minutes of just sitting since they arrived. The hazard lights continued to flash on the car that's parked in a narrow alley on 26th Ave. Sean reclines in the driver's seat with the door open, his left leg hanging out of the car and the music blaring as loud as he could handle it. Another one of Kingsley henchmen stands alone behind the car. Leaning on the fence with one foot comfortably propped against it. The henchman keeps watch of the area, as Sean looks through nude photos of old girlfriends on his phone and loses himself in the music. Quickly losing interest, he puts his phone away and decides to get more comfortable, closing his eyes and soaking up some midday sun as it washes over him through the windshield. He bobs his head and taps his fingers against the console. Lost in the music, Sean gets startled when someone knocks loudly against the trunk of the car.

(With disgust)

"What da FUCK you think you're doing? How can you watch the other end of the alley when you're leaned back in the fuck'en seat like that?"

Sean takes a deep breath before he slowly raises his seat and reaches to turn the music down.

"Huh? You say something? I didn't hear you Nate."

"I said…why the fuck aren't you watching the other end of the alley like you were told too? Ya got the music blasting, the hazards on, you're causing unnecessary attention to us. Man…any motha-fucka could just roll

up on us. What you're doing leaves your end of the alley exposed. You can't do this shit!"

"I'm not sweating any of that. I was told to drive, so I'm driving. That's all I plan to do. The rest of that shit is beneath me."

"BENEATH YOU! (Pauses) MOTHA-FUCKA… (catches himself) Ok, look… (pauses again) I'm trying to show you some respect here cause you're the prince in this kingdom but you're fucking up major right now. Driving is just one part of the job you're doing. We know you aint used to this low-level shit but you aint even been fuck'en trying. It's been this way for weeks now, so…FUCK DAT! This shit has to stop. We do what we're s'posed to do cause it keeps us in business. We keep watch cause it keeps the runners safe and keeps us all out of jail. I'm not gonna get caught up because of your lazy ass. Adjust that attitude, Bruh. (Annoyed) Shit, beneath you? The only thing beneath me…is not getting this money. We all have a role to play. Right now, this is yours. So, MAN the fuck up and do what we fuck'en tell you too!"

The moment was uncomfortable as Sean's expression re-enforced that he didn't give a shit. Nate knowing any more talk on the subject would be a waste of time, still managed to rattle off something that he meant to be sarcastic but Sean would take deeper to heart. There was a mutual disappointing or disrespectful glare exchanged before Nate got everyone back in the car. "Let's hit it, we have at least five more stops to make." Nate says as he spins his finger to gesture getting a move on.

(Sarcastically)

"Yessa Boss. I'd be glad… to take you where you want to be. Just point da way Sir."

(Disgusted)

"How bout you just turn the music down a little and stop talking for now."

"If that's what you want Nate."

(Under his breath and shaking his head)

"Damn! It's gonna be a long ass day."

(Two days later)

It was overcast and a bit breezy near the docks on the south side of the city. Sean and Slim Nate were sent to make a big cash pick-up when they were intercepted by Big Guns. He flagged them down exiting the docks just around 7th and Cole. Gun's words were direct as he speaks to Sean and Slim as he rolls down window of his black Escalade.

"Change in plans…Slim I need you to come with me. We got a thing. Sean, you're gonna have to make this cash drop alone."

"Alone! No one makes drops like this with this much cash by themselves. It's always been a two-man play."

"You may not want to hear this, number three…but it's been done before. (Pauses) When the risk is low…and right now the risk is low. I need Slim to handle something else and your father seems to think that you can handle this without supervision. The drop spot is twelve blocks from here. I want to believe you can handle driving twelve blocks."

Sean feels uncomfortable with Gun's words and expression as Slim unlatches his seat belt and gets out of the car. Gun's continues to give direction.

"Make sure you verify that the pick-up guy is really Garza and weigh the case of clean money before you give him the dirty case. You should be in and out of the drop spot within five minutes."

"How do I know the environment is safe from thieves? Shouldn't I have some back up?"

"Do you have your 9mm with you?"

"Yeah."

"Then today… that's all the backup you need. I've seen you kill before, so I'm sure you'll be all right. Once you're done, your dad will be waiting for you."

Slim settles into the Cadillac as Gun's finishes his words with a smirk, a wink and holding up a peace sign as he drives away.

Feeling uneasy about that last look Gun's gave him, Sean took a moment wrestling with weather he should or shouldn't continue this job alone. Thinking a moment about the jobs he's been given; he assures himself that this might be the one that could get him out of the doghouse with his family. "Ok, let's get this thing done." Sean mumbles as he puts his car in gear and heads for the drop spot.

Sean checks his rear-view mirror after making a right turn from Cole Street onto 12th. He notices that police cruisers have blocked the street half a block behind him. Concentrating on seeing the commotion caused him not to see the sirens of the police car that created a blockade in front of him. Sean came to an abrupt stop as a gun-toting officer approaches his car, while another bellows instructions through his car's PA system.

"Driver, turn off your vehicle and put your arms out of the window. (Waits for compliance) Now, take your left arm, keeping the right where it is, remove the keys from the ignition and toss them to the ground. (Sean complies) Now use your left hand to open the car door, and then slowly exit with your hands in the air. (Waits for compliance) Move to the back of the car, stand with legs apart and place your palms flat on the trunk."

The officer who slowly approached with his gun drawn, slid Sean's legs even wider before pulled each arm back one arm at a time and placing them in cuffs. "What is this about?" Sean asked as the officer turned him around and leaned him against his own car. The officer never answered and a man with an ATF vest approached and began searching the car.

(Ten minutes later)

"Maybe you can finally answer my question. Why am I being stopped?" (Smugly)

"As you should know Mr. Reynolds, as a result of your conviction and

parole you can be detained and searched at any time. (Looks at another officer) Please remain Mr. Reynolds into custody for violating his parole."

It wasn't long before Sean found himself handcuffed again inside an interrogation room for hours. He hadn't been formally charged, not allowed to make any calls and they left him with only a glass of water that he couldn't reach because his hands were cuffed behind his back. He has experienced most of their tactics before. If they had anything substantial on him, they would have booked him by now. Then been in there doing the old good cop, bad cop bit. But Sean assumes they don't and that's why no one has come into the room. They know he will ask again what the charge is and when they can't respond legitimately, Sean will insist on being released. So, for now he sits, waits and wonders what their angle with holding him is.

[In another room]

"We don't have much to go on."

"We don't have anything! And the tip about the bag in his trunk was a bust. We can't continue to hold him."

(Clears his throat)

"Well, we have one more shot. Follow me!"

Sean lifted his head as the door to the room opened. Two ATF officers walked in but wouldn't answer any of his questions. One of them took post at the door and the other released one of Sean's hands from the cuffs and then secured the other to the chair. The guy guarding the door began to speak just as the other officer stopped at the center of the table.

(Glaring at Sean)

"You have a phone call."

(Annoyed)

"You haven't answered any of my questions or let me make any calls… but I have a call?"

"Your car is still being processed and we'll have more answers for you once its done. Otherwise…you have a phone call."

(Hesitantly)

"Hello?"

"Hey #3, I need you to report."

"Who is this?" Sean asked although he knew it was Big Gun's.

"You've got people waiting on you. Did you make the switch?"

(Sounding suspicious)

"Who is this? You know this isn't my phone! What do you want with me?"

"Did you or didn't you swap the money? Your father is still waiting for you. What do you want me to tell him?"

"How do you know who I am or where I am?"

"There was thirty-two thousand dollars in that case…Sean. I need to know what I should tell your father."

(Lowers voice slightly and with anger)

"Judas wasn't an accountant and no one will hire one with that name. Freedom has a price and I'm not the Yen for the exchange. If that sounds like gibberish then that's all I have to offer a strange unknown caller."

Sean drops the receiver onto the table then sits back in the chair. You could still faintly hear the caller shouting, "Did you hear me? What are you gonna do about the money? (Trails off) Hello?" One officer looks back at the other at the door who gives confirmation with a nod to end the call. The room became uncomfortably silent as Sean back to being silent and the ATF officer at the door continued with a somewhat unpleased glare.

"Take him back to the holding cell!"

(Confused)

"What? Wait?

The officer in the center of the room shouted as he quickly looks back and forth between Sean and the officer before moving in earshot of his fellow officer.

(Almost whispering)

"Is that it? That can't be it!"

(Also whispering but rapidly)

"We were hoping that phone call would generate probable cause but it didn't. We've been holding him for almost 72 hours and still have nothing! We can only hold him for another three hours. (Eyes still on Sean) So please… (raises his voice) Take him back to the holding cell!"

CHAPTER SIXTEEN

Make It Work

SEAN'S LOFT IS dark, the hour is late and only the light of the TV brightens or darkens the room. After an hour of dozing, Sean finally slips out of consciousness as his chin settles into his chest. He jostles restlessly on his couch, extends his right arm and starts to mumble his daughter's name. Still sound asleep he pleads with his little girl to come back to him. She looks away from her father and towards the open arms of someone standing off in the distance, calling to her as well. Sean continues to call out for her but she slowly and playfully backs away. He calls out even louder, changing from an angry tone so he wouldn't startle her. In the dream as well as on his couch, he shifts again. Then as quick as the blink of an eye, his little girl disappeared and an older young adult image of his daughter stood in front of him, continuing to distance herself as well. Sean advances forward with every step she takes but stops when he feels a hand on his shoulder and a male voice saying, "You won't get her back that easily. You can't fight an enemy you don't recognize until you're stronger. Your enemy isn't always business opposition. Find a way to help yourself first or you will never be able to keep her safe." Sean turns slightly and is startled by the re-appearing image of his cousin Raymond, which causes Sean to awaken violently. His body thrusts forward. He is sweaty, disoriented and trying to catch his breath. Sean looks to each side of himself before he sits up straight. Adjusting his eyes to the light or lack of. He squints and with his vision still blurry, looks in the direction of his girlfriend.

(Frustrated)

"Have you been looking at me the entire time I've been asleep?"

(Sounding annoyed)

"No! I ***was*** *trying to watch* ***this*** *movie but you started moving around and yelling in your sleep. Hmm, those nightmares you've been having must be getting worse. Are you sure you're all right?"*

"I can handle it. (Takes a deep breath then softly whispers) I can handle it."

"I don't know Babe? You've been having them more often now than you were a month ago. At first you would just talk in your sleep but now you are getting physical also. Two nights ago, you rolled over, grabbed my arm and were pulling me. Calling out for Cee-Jay. I don't know, I'm just say'en."

Sean sat with his elbows resting on his legs, taking deep breaths and rubbing his eyes. Keisha sat silently in the chair with her legs tucked underneath her watching as Sean regulated his breathing. Giving him the time, he needed to get calm.

(Takes a deep breath)

"See…I can handle it."

"Ooo…kay? (Dips her head to get eye contact) What about last week? How are you going to handle that?"

"You mean being set up? (Sounding unsure) Shit, I don't know. Things are really confusing right now. I don't know if my dad knows I was picked up or if he played a part in setting me up. (Clinches his fist) I knew something didn't feel right when Gun's drove off. I'm sure glad you got there fast enough to switch those bags. (Softly to himself) I can't believe he actually mentioned an amount."

"What did you say?"

"Nothing. It was nothing."

"Oh, ok…then you're welcome. But don't you think they are all wondering where you are or where the money is?"

"Here's my thought on that Keisha. I was thinking…if I wasn't set up then they'll be looking for the money, and me eventually. But if I was… they'll be expecting me to still be in custody and the money to be lost as evidence. Dad's rule: Stay silent until there's a need to involve a lawyer. You know, I'm pretty sure that back stabbing bitch ass Gun's has told my dad I've been arrested. So, my dad will wait for me to walk through the door or wait to hear from Kyle himself."

"Kyle? Who's Kyle?"

Kyle McKensie. He's our family's lawyer. (Rubs his face with his hand) Ok, so that gives me more time to figure all this shit out."

"Excuse me for saying this Babe, but why waste the effort. Something with this is all fucked up. (Sean turns to face her) Clearly someone wants you out of the way. My questions…why and why now?"

"You're right! This shit definitely doesn't add up. Cause that money drop amount was much larger than it normally is. (Sounding confused) They all get their orders from my dad, especially Gun's. Why would my dad want me out of the way? I've got to get some answers before I have to come face to face with him again."

"I'll ask you again…why? Why confront your dad at all Sean? Ok, they want you out of the way, fine…then take advantage of it."

"Huh, I don't follow."

"I'm saying take advantage of this. You've done nothing but complain about having to take a back seat to that big guy. Telling me about all of the low-level shit jobs they've been having you do. I'm just saying, leave it all behind you. Take this opportunity to become more than they think you can be. You've got the time if they think your still locked up. You've got enough money to live on. Build your own empire. Make it work. Give orders…don't

take them. Prove to your family that you don't need them to be wealthy or to survive."

(Rubs his face again)

"Yeah...yeah! That makes sense. I already have a successful business that my family doesn't know about. I could easily get behind something else. Why should I need to prove anything more to anyone, my dad included? (Smiles) I can make this work. I know what I have to do."

[Sunday morning weeks later]

A single bird soars with its wings fully extended in a bright clear blue sky above a late 1960's convertible Cadillac. Driving alone on a scenic road with the top down. The bird's eye view shows two decorative hats waiving with the light breeze. Protecting the two passengers from the 90-degree sun. Robert Kingsley and his long-time girlfriend Kate, take a relaxed Sunday drive to a secluded mansion just two hours outside of the city. Headed for a rare afternoon lunch with a billionaire recluse. Invitations to this billionaire's home either come by special invite or are financially costly to the person wanting to meet with him. The Cadi turns onto a long winding road with trees that provide temporary seclusion from the sun as the car approaches the elegant metal gate. Kate comments to Robert about how beautiful the estate is as the gate opens. The car comes to a stop as the driveway leads them to the front of the main house. Robert taps Kate before he exits the car and, in an attempt, to seem more of a gentleman than he normally would be, he comes around and opens the door for his wife before reaching into the backseat to retrieve a briefcase. The Kingsley's come around the front of the car and are met by an armed man in butler attire.

(Sounding formal)

"Good afternoon Mr. & Mrs. Kingsley. Welcome to the Tate Estate. (Looking first a Robert) It ***is*** *recommended that all firearms, recording*

devises and cellular phones be placed into the trunk of your car before you may enter the estate."

Robert hands the briefcase to his wife, takes her purse and steps to the back of his car. As he opens the trunk, cameras turn to capture every moment as he sheds himself of weapons and secures everything with the loud slam of a heavy trunk lid.

"Thank you, Mr. Kingsley. Now…I will gladly escort you in once I secure the necessary presidential paperwork you were to bring in the case provided for you."

Robert nods to Kate and she hands the case to the armed butler just as Robert arrives back at her side. At that same moment the front door opens and another armed man comes out, takes the briefcase and steps back inside.

"We appreciate your patience. It will be just a moment as Mr. Tate finishes with his morning appointment."

Robert nods again. Not only acknowledging that he understood but to be sure it is all right to light his cigar. The front door opens again simultaneously with the strike of his match. He quickly clears his vision from the few puffs that he took. Surprised, he pulls the cigar from his mouth as Ana walks out of the house with her purse in hand. Escorted to her seven series BMW by the same guard who stepped out to take in the Kingsley's briefcase. Ana politely nods to Kate as her car door is opened and held for her. She pauses before climbing in and takes a second to look back one more time and devilishly smile at Robert Kingsley. A smile he attempted to deflect with his own spiteful scowl and taking two puffs of his cigar. Ana held her smile just long enough for Kate to look at Robert and kept her eyes on him until the guard closed her car door.

"Thank you for waiting Mr. & Mrs. Kingsley. If you would follow me now, I will take you both to see Mr. Tate."

(Inquisitively)

"What was she doing here? He asked as he fills the air with smoke and watches her drive away.

(Clears throat)

"I'm sorry Mr. Kingsley sir. I am not permitted to discuss any intentions, comments or business of any of Mr. Tate's guests with any of Mr. Tate's guests. The very same discretion will be taken after you've left the estate today as well. So…if you would please (Pauses) I will now take you in."

[Two scenic hours or so later]

Ana's crew gathers at a small reclusive picnic area awaiting her arrival. Mountain Moo towers over a tiny metal grill anchored in the ground. He slyly looks towards the twins, turning multiple Hot Links while he proudly devours one. Meck sits on the top of a nearby table and sips on a Canada Dry and talks discretely to his sister.

(Playfully)

*"What the **hell** are you drinking?"*

"My stomach is upset Mia."

"I thought you'd be feeling great now that the IRS has unfrozen all of your assets. I expected you to be on top of the world."

"I am not overly excited. Not yet. It's my stomach. Probably something I ate last night. It's got me queasy. (Grabs stomach) Anyway, I can't hit the ATM just yet. I have fifteen more days left before I'm financially whole again. Shit my passport hasn't even been cleared yet."

"I'm curious Meck, if neither of us changed our statements, then what happened with my ex-husband to make the Gov'ment release your money?"

"I think it was the change of his original statement. I was told that new evidence was provided that cleared me. Information I'm told that would certainly bury your ex-husband. He changed his original statement in an attempt to keep them from adding on a perjury charge. (Clinches stomach again) Might be too late for that."

Mia's attention drifts momentarily toward Big Moo and his links before turning back to her brother.

"Did I ever say that I was sorry big brother? Sorry that he lied, using your name to get out of trouble and to get back at me. Meck?"

Mia reaches out and touches her brother's hand waiting on a response.

"It's not your fault Mia. I was never angry with you but I'm glad we both won't see any jail time over his bullshit. It will all be over soon. (Smiles) You know your Ex is looking at some serious jail time. (Pokes her) Any regrets Mia?"

"HELL NO! Fuck him! I've been over that shit sticks bullshit a long time ago. (Repeats while chuckling) A long time ago."

Mia grabs at her stomach as it rumbles. Meck looks her over, surprised because he heard it also. He quietly laughs to himself, watching Mia looking longingly over at Big Moo.

"Do you think he's in the mood to share?"

(Still laughing)

"Yeah…uh, I mean NO! Good luck with that. Wow, looks like he just took two down at the same time."

(Impulsive)

"Fuck it! I've got to get me one. I'm going in Meck."

Meck watches his sister spring from the table and continues laughing as she engages in passionate negotiations with Big Moo for a single Hot Link.

The small group never noticed the convertible pull up or their silently driven leader approach them. Tank was the only one who caught a glimpse of Ana and began to gather everyone in a circle. Everyone except Moo and Mia as Ana began to speak.

"I wanted to take some time with everyone so we could share a bit of information with each other. See where we are on most of our assignments. Maybe make some adjustments. But first, let's talk about our progress."

"Progress? Have we actually made any? Seems to me all the players are still playing. Some of the areas are just playing with subs now."

"I don't quite follow you Tank."

(Jumping in)

"What he's saying Ana, (quickly gathers is thoughts) Is…new people have taken over in areas we have been affecting."

"Exactly, thank you Meck. It just doesn't seem like we've made any difference at all Ana."

"Look everyone…we can't judge our progress or effectiveness by the number of people we put into jail. What we're doing is much more complicated than offering plane tickets or taking over drug areas. Good or bad…we're affecting people's lives. Possibly righting some wrongs and ultimately trying to make this city a little less criminally controlled."

Ana is distracted briefly by a small murmuring commotion with Mia and Mountain Moo, which stops when they realize everyone is looking at them.

"I know it seems discouraging but we ***are****, I've been told, making some progress. I thought we would have to decide between eliminating the council members one by one, (Looks around) or letting them gradually knock each other off. The good news is…we don't have to choose. We have found ways to get the enemy more involved. There has been plenty of progress and there is more that can work for our cause. My uncle told me, (Mocking his voice) At this level, it's a thinking man's game. Settle into your position, give your opposition nowhere to run and then be merciless. (Pauses) So…everyone… the important thing to know, (catching eye contact) what we have been doing has many of the people and situations almost exactly how we need them to be. Now it's time to make more adjustments. OK? Good work to this point but we're not finished yet."*

"So, what's next?" Meck asks as he watches his sister wrestle a hot link away from Mountain Moo.

"I will let everyone give reports first before I lay out any new specifics."

CHAPTER SEVENTEEN

Rizzo's Evolution

HE SUDDENLY GRABS his chest with his right hand and clutches what was in his left tightly after the third in a series of bullets punctures his chest. With no time to react the aspiring drug dealer was taken by surprise when his junkie customer took the first gunshot at point blank range. The shots came to quickly. One moment he was reaching into his pocket for the small crack rock, then suddenly short of breath and then dead on his feet. The junkie was halfway to the ground when the second and third shots rang out. With and expression of petrified terror, the dealers body also flops lifelessly to the sidewalk. Sean takes a split second to bask in his work before he plants the gun on the junkie and eases the dealers grip to expose the crack rocks. Satisfied that his staged crime scene was sufficiently set, Sean removes his leather gloves and returned to where he and Donnie D had been talking.

"So, as I was saying Donnie, the new split will be 80/20."

(Shocked)

"Have you lost your Fucking mind? You must be out of your Fucking mind! You just killed in broad daylight. In the open! What the Fuck is wrong with you?"

"I want you to understand that I mean business. I will strike hard and fast. There won't be any hesitation on my part and this neighborhood has to know that there won't be."

(Nervously agitated)

"I'm just say'en... in front of your girlfriend like that? She's right there, (Pauses) in the car Man!"

Sean turns and signals Keisha to roll the car's window down. He picks on her, playing as he asks her to bring it down just a bit more.

"Yeah Babe?" She utters with a sweet tone.

"You saw what I just did, right? Did it bother you?"

"Not at all. What you do at work is what needs to be done. As long as the results of what you do doesn't wake me up at night...I'm aint tripp'en."

She puckers her lips and blows him a kiss before rolling the window back up.

(Shrugs his shoulders)

"She's numb to this shit Donnie. She isn't squeamish about much but she's more so mildly tolerant to violence. Most people are these days. More importantly, only when they aren't affected by it."

"Shit! I mean I never expected that kind of violence from **you**. *I'm just say'en. No disrespect but I believe other motha-fuckas handle that shit for your Pops."*

"I see shit like that every day. This is the type of ruthlessness that I subscribe to Donnie. It's in my blood. I'm just as capable. I pick my moments, (Stretches his neck) as you can see. (Looks around) I want continue talking Donnie but I don't want to do it here. Follow me over to the Tennis courts."

(Anxious)

"I'll walk somewhere else in this park but I will not take one step onto those courts. (Takes a deep breath) Let's head for that bench on the other side."

"It's cool, let's go now. It's about to get crazy over here. We'll be overrun by cops anytime now. I don't want to be around when that happens."

"What about ya girl?"

Sean takes a few steps to signal Keisha. His movements instruct her to circle back as he and Donnie head into the park. The two men casually make their way over the large area of grass and head towards a walking path that is slightly out of the public's view. Sean checks for onlookers before reaching under his shirt into the small of his back to pull out a small compact handgun. He then discretely hands it to Donnie.

"I owe you this. I just hope none of your handprints were on that one I borrowed from you when I killed those two back there."

"Would've been nice if you would have looked at it and then handed it back like you should have. Not just take it, walk away and kill two people with it. Is this one clean?"

(Sean laughs)

"Is it clean? Man, you not as green as people think. Yeah, it's straight. It's brand new."

"How does a guy like you get his hands on a new gun?"

"Let's just say, I know a guy."

Donnie doesn't respond but quickly holsters his new weapon insides his Addidas sweat jacket. His pace also slows as he urges Sean to explain why he arbitrarily chose to kill in ***his*** *neighborhood.*

"I've decided to branch out Donnie and my help can be beneficial to you...to both of us. (Rubs his hands together) Here's my thought. I'll take control; become the feared front man for this area. You'll work with me but must become second in command. Like I said earlier, the take will be 80/20. (Smirks) Ok I'll throw you a bone and I'll do a 70/30 split."

"That's not gonna work for me."

"It's going to have too!"

"Sean, I have never been second to anyone on my corners. You understand...to nobody! I made this side of the city profitable."

"...And you're losing it, right now. It's been months since you've turned any profits. These youngsta's out here don't respect ***you.*** *You've been out here walking around like a broken shell of a criminal. You've lost (snaps*

his fingers) the edge that makes this business work. Face it, if you had what it takes to be successful…you would be. But you're not! If you had to work your way up from nothing to be in control, you would know, wait strike that, understand what was taken from you months ago. (Points discretely across the park) No way you let any of those little motha-fucka's profit on these corners unless they were paying up to you. Look Donnie, I'm offering you a new start. I plan to put money into both our pockets. The only sacrifice you must make is to step out of the way and let me run this shit! (Pauses) If you're willing to do that…then we can keep talking. If not…I'll walk away and let you keep fighting for scraps."

Donnie sighs deeply and fidgets as he scratches at the hair below his bottom lip.

"Ok…shit, I'm listening."

"It's a simple business Donnie. I have three compound elements. It's the plan, the product and unrelenting precision. I have a full proof moneymaking scheme. I know a guy who will provide the product (Donnie mouths the words, you know a guy) and we must be merciless with our efforts to make this money."

"So, what about the others round here try'en to undercut profits?"

"Again, simple. We use Pistols, prevention and personnel. When two or more motha-fucka's die around here… the rest will get the message quickly. They won't even think of trying us. We can knock off two birds with one stone. Whoever is left and willing, can work for us. Their efforts will reflect their compensation. Which in turn will build our profits."

" Well, what about your dad? What about the council? You of all people must be aware that this town has rules. Rules once broken have dire consequences. Something that I am clear on as well and that is why I'm asking."

"Last three Donnie. We have to be aware of pretentiousness, penuriousness and problematic situations."

"What's with you? Did you do time and spend it studying a thesaurus?"

"Don't hate on my vocabulary. I'll deal with my dad when I have too. For now, he'll be fine thinking everything is just the way he wants it. As for the council…(Animated) FUCK THEM greedy bastards! Have any of them reached out to help you? (Donnie shakes his head) Yeah, I didn't think so. So, from now on we're done following those bullshit old ass guidelines. It's time to strike hard, fast and right damn now!"

"Sounds like you've got a handle on most of it. (Squints his eyes)

What is it that you've left out?"

"Perceptive Donnie, here's what I've been thinking about. I know you and I can turn this shit around. The reality is that neither of us will get the respect for doing so. They will never believe we have it in us and that will give us an advantage. Now hear me on this, I'm not trying to compete for anyone's approval, validation or respect. I've realized I can't earn what was never intended for me to have."

"Are you talking about your dad?"

"Amongst others! Profound moment… I've noticed you have to be in the light to cast a shadow. I've been standing in my fathers for years now. So, it's time for me to step up, step out and get into the light myself. Here's how. Together we'll push out the undesirables and hire whoever is hungry to work. We'll create a figurehead although I'll actually be in charge. That way everybody looks up to the boss and our enemies can't pit us against each other."

"You wanna use an alias?"

"Well yeah! I adopted the use of the name "Rizzo" sometime ago but a cop's death and the massive press coverage of it, has discontinued my use of it. I'll have to come up with a new one while we're getting things in order. I'll keep you posted on my new alias."

Donnie quickly stands and whips his head around in two different directions. He expression becomes nervously inquisitive as he concentrates on the noises surrounding him.

"Did you hear that?"

"Hear what Donnie?"

"It sounded like a woman screaming. You sure you didn't hear that? (Sean shakes his head) [Mumbling] Shit! Whatever! (Looks around again) So you were talking about pushing some folks out? Do you have some kind of strategy? An idea when you want to start?"

"It's already underway. I've been casing this area for weeks. (Smiles) I was also fortunate to stumble into a hit man for hire while I was buying my girl a small under the table handgun for her purse. He's the hit man taking care of our pest problem as we speak. That might be some of the noises you say you've been hearing. I expect a few more bodies to be stretched out throughout a four-block radius of us before the hour is up. You may want to lay low when we're done. Are you sure that gun of yours was clean? I hope it was. I'd hate for you to get arrested over some shit you didn't do before we get underway."

"Do I look worried Sean?"

"No, you don't Donnie. That's good. I like the confidence. Build on that. Come tomorrow we are going to hit it hard, fast and in a manner that will surprise a lot of people. Get your game face on and be prepared to embrace the indecency. Here is something my grandmother told me and now I will share it with you. She said there is a difference between inflicting pain upon someone and sitting back as a spectator. The difference…respect is given to the person inflicting the pain and fear is bestowed one the one who ordered it to be done. Figure out what kind of power you want to hold."

Sean slipped both of his hands into his pockets before turning to face Donnie. He removed his smirk and replaced it with an expression more suitable of someone who is consuming control. Donnie immediately recognized the difference as the two of them broke eye contact and Sean began to walk away.

"We'll start tomorrow, Donnie. I expect you to be ready.

CHAPTER EIGHTEEN

Cousin's

ROBERT SITS IN his Cadillac near one of his businesses with Big Guns. He is reading a three-week-old newspaper and talking on the phone. "I'll send three of them over." He emphasizes while flipping to find the second part of the article he was reading. "I understand Ma. I'll make sure. Uh-huh, I know. Yes! Right away." After hanging up from the call he sets his phone on top of the dashboard then tears off a corner of the paper to write an address on it. Robert hands the scrap of paper to Guns before reaching to push is the cars cigarette lighter. Gun's waits for Mr. Kingsley to finish re-folding his newspaper, waits for the lighter to pop back out and waits for his boss to light his cigar. Waiting curiously for the information connected to the scrap of paper.

"Roderick, I need you to handle a couple of things for me and it's important that you are discreet. (Guns nods) First, I need you to grab any three of our guys and have them meet my mother at that address. They will be given instructions from her once they get there."

"Ok boss, I'll grab Slim and two others right awa…"

(Cuts in)

"NO! Not Slim. My mother doesn't have any patience for him. She won't tolerate any of his antics. I don't need that headache. Send someone

else. (Pauses) Speaking of Slim, do you have him working on anything? I don't recall seeing him the last few weeks."

"Last time I spoke with him he had some kind of family shit he was dealing with. But if you want…I'll follow up on where he is and what he's doing."

"Ok. Good. Now, according to the papers there have been a lot of murders on the North side lately. I want you to look into what's going on over there. I'll be out of town for a family reunion. Find out what you can while I'm gone. Check in with Donnie if you can. That area's been quiet for almost a year and now it is suddenly spitting out bodies. I'm a bit curious about what going on over there. Has Donnie gotten himself some new muscle? Is there some type of North side civil war going on? See what you can find out and get back to me as soon as possible."

"Yes Sir!" Gun's responded as opened the car door to get out. "Right away."

[North Carolina one week later]

Two ladies peer out of a kitchen window into a large southern backyard. Watching a small group of men holding beers and shooting the shit around two-barrel BBQ grills.

(With a southern accent)

"Laura, who's that out there with dirty Al, prison Pete, Sam and your husband?"

"Well, excluding my husband…(Pointing) that man there is the only successful criminal standing out there. He's our California cousin, Robert. Most folks just call him RK. The younger ones call him Stogie but he never liked that."

"Successful? How so? What makes him better from the rest of them?"

"Well, he's still stingy as hell. Has not changed one bit since we were small. He never flashy and he is secretive about his money. He rarely talks

about anything personal and even more tight-lipped about business. He never involves any family in his business practices except for brother. (Sips wine) He hides behind a few legitimate businesses but ***we*** *all know you can't make the money that he does legally. (Winks) You know what I'm say'en?"*

In the backyard one of the men laughs and lifts the lid of one of the grills. A huge puff of smoke escapes before the sound of sizzling meat and the sudden flare up of flames captures everyone's attention. Voices raise and fingers point as a healthy debate ensues on who can BBQ the best. Robert lights a cigar and tries to shake off the frustration. He's aggravated as he wonders how many more times, he must endure the same stale argument. So, he decided to cut this shit short.

(Interrupting)

"So, Pete…Al, where are your boys? They were like thirteen the last time I saw them."

"You telling me it's been ten years RK since you've been around the family?"

"Naw, it took that long for you to make parole Pete. RK hasn't been away that long…you have. Have you even seen your son yet?"

"No and I've been out for three days now Al. But his mother sort of promised that he would be coming today. He's s'posed to be with your boy."

"He is. I saw them this morning. They're stopping by some neighborhood street party and should git here late this afternoon."

[Across town]

The music could be heard two blocks away. There were no police insight and both ends of a city street were blocked off with barricades. Three young men, second cousins stand just beyond the barriers and loom over the festivities. Cliff smiles at Jason and Sean tries to discreetly tip his head in an effort to get them to notice two women disappearing into the crowd.

Cliff gives off a low dog growl and then takes off after them. Jason lightly taps Sean on his arm.

"Listen there's something I've got to tell you Sean before we head down the block. This dude we're seeing today (pauses) is a bit unstable. Has been since high school."

"What do you mean? How unstable?"

"Not sure how to put it cousin, but he's off. Depends on the moon, the tide, and effective meds. Shit, I'm not sure. Just keep your eyes open for something weird."

"I don't like surprises J. I thought you said this guy is a good contact?"

"He should be."

"I'll take it on your word J. Let's get to it."

Jason and Sean head in pass the kid's jumpers, the craft booths and caught up with Cliff who was dancing near the DJ's table. Sean folds his arms and stands out of the way as Jason focuses on two women wildly popping their asses as they drop it like it's hot dancing with Cliff. Sean scopes out the area for reasons his southern cousins would never begin to consider. Sean begins to bob his head to the music but studies the position of the tables and the general flow of the people. Sean politely smiles occasionally when he makes eye contact with people walking around him but remains stoic, tentative and attentive. He became distracted as Jason started repeatedly tapping him on the arm.

"Shit! Do you know how annoying that is J? I'm right next to you. Damn, just talk to me!"

"Look alive cousin, it's show time. (Points) our contact is in that house over there. Time to move."

Sean directed Jason to grab Cliff who was reluctant to leave the women he was dancing with. "Bring ya ass! It's time to go!" Jason yells grabbing Cliff's arm. As the three of them cautiously approach the house, Sean slowed the group in order to prep them.

"Normally I would set up a meeting like this in the open without making it accessible to the public not go into an unfamiliar location. If you trust this guy J, then we'll go in but I need you both to be alert."

"We got this. Time, we show you how to we boost bills and fatten pockets, southern style. Cause timid, un-stimulated pussies dry up big cousin…we keep shit wet."

(Sarcastically)

"Wow Cliff, maybe you should try and stay quiet once we're inside. If your gonna say shit like that. (Smirks) What I meant was, load your weapons now but bring attention to yourselves. Let's do it one at a time and conceal each other. We don't want these folks to see us loading weapons."

Jason and Cliff anxiously look at each other. Sean's expression settles on one of disbelief as Cliff flashes the handle of a switch- blade. Jason just shrugs his shoulders when Sean realizes that he has no weapons.

"You've got to be shitting me! How do you come to something like this with nothing? Ok let me stress how important it is for us to be alert in there. Let's be smart. Follow my lead. (Pauses) Hopefully things won't go bad. Don't let anyone get behind you. Get your eyes on the quickest exit in case we need it. If things do go bad, I want to get out, get to safety and then meet up two blocks over."

Sean loads his gun and secures his second clip within reach. Now the three cousins ascend the front stairs of the house. Passing four guys standing and talking on the porch. The front door opens to a small area leading to what looks like the Dining room. The cousins settle two feet in front of a fireplace that sat directly opposite of the living room. Cliff, standing the furthest from Jason and Sean but closest to a door to the left of the fireplace, turn and pushes the door open. As it swung, Cliff peeks into the kitchen. With a pleased expression, he assures the others that the area housed no threats. Sean's eyes, on the other hand, never left the four men watching them from the living room. One man sat alone, dead center of a couch.

Which was the only piece of furniture in the room. Three thugs wearing long braids, oversized baseball caps and un-impressive scowls were standing alongside each other behind the couch. Suddenly the man on the couch began to shout.

(Animated)

"Is that you J-Diesel? Aw shit, you came through! Is that him? Ha, that California money. Well, he don't look like much…but den again, the broke-est looking fuckers got the deepest pockets."

"Yeah, what's up Kernel. This is my cou…"

Sean quickly cuts Jason off and softly says, "No names J." Cliff looks confused and asks, "Cornel? Like an Army Cornel?"

"No Motha-fucka! Like uncooked popcorn! What's it to ya? Bitch ass Nigga?"

After his outburst, Kernel starts moving and jerking like he has some kind of uncontrollable tick. Then he starts to rock.

"I think the motha-fucka has Tourette's."

"Shut up man." Sean says turning to Cliff.

"Hey, I'm just say'en."

Sean gives Cliff a crazy stern look before returning his attention to Kernel.

"Can we get to business Kernel?"

(Slightly annoyed)

"The floor is yours Potna!"

The thugs tense up when Sean reaches to unzip his jacket. But when Kernel throws his arms out to his side like an umpire, they settled down.

"I was told that you are ready for an opportunity to expand your operation."

(Loudly)

"Yep!"

Sean waits for more of a response but Kernel just smiles and starts rocking in his seated position again.

"Can you tell me what you're able to do? Product, pricing?"

Kernel drums the palms of his hand onto his legs before throwing his head wildly left to right. Then without warning he stops moving his head, fixates on Sean and says, "I like what you're saying so far. Keep going. Please, I like how you sound."

"What is this crazy fucker talking about? (Under his breath) Beep beep. Somebody pull up the yellow bus and get that man a helmet." Cliff mumbles.

(Sean's tone changes)

"Keep going with what? You haven't offered one shred of information to inspire me to want to make any deals. I'm here to talk. Tell me something."

Kernel continues to sway but also begins to swing his head again. Then suddenly he sits still, his eyes turn normal and he gives Sean direct eye contact. Almost the same way an Alzheimer patient suddenly becomes lucent.

"Business for me has been growing and I am looking for an opportunity to expand, although I've been hindered by the work of our local drug enforcement agencies. So yes, I am ready to take my business anywhere it can become profitable. You appear to be a serious man so I'll get to the point. I can accommodate any amount you need and crossing state lines isn't a problem for me. I have a couple of trucks. I'll take all the risk on delivery. I expect payment upon arrival. Also, more of side note, if the count is a bit short… don't worry. I'll square it on the next delivery. You'll see, I'm good for it."

The serious look in Kernel's eyes started to fade. It seems with the blink of his eyes, they lost him again. He started shaking his head again in every direction, rocking and mumbling, "I'm good for it. I know I'm good for it. (Now shouting) Yep…I'm good for it! You don't believe me? YOU THINK I'M LYING? YOU CALLING ME A LIAR?"

The three cousins whip their heads around and look at each other in awe as Kernel repeatedly shouts, "I'M NOT A LIAR!"

"This motha-fucka is 51/50 or bat shit crazy!" Cliff shouts.

Sean quickly looking to Cliff says, "You're not helping", before turning back to Kernel.

"I didn't call you a liar. If I had decided to insult you, I would have called you a thief and then put an end to this meeting. How is it on one hand you want to do business with me but on the other, mention how you may intentionally short me? (Pauses) Still expecting to be paid the full asking price. Then you say that you will eventually make good on product that you were on delivering. Because you say I can trust you? (Skeptically) Trust you! You've got to be shitting me rookie! Are you for real? Look, negative actions bring serious consequences in this business. And so far, this isn't a shining moment for you."

"THAT'S FOR DAMN SHURE!" Cliff yells.

"Still not helping cousin!" Jason adds.

Kernel continues to rock but now with a slightly strange but angry look on his face. He struggles to get his hand into a jacket pocket. Sean instinctively reaches for his gun as well just as Kernel pulls a bicycle bell out of his pocket and rings it three times. "What kind of shit is that?" Cliff yells out just before three guys come in from behind them from the kitchen. Sean with his hand inside his jacket looks over his right shoulder shaking his head at Cliff. "I thought the motha-fucka was clear." Cliff utters as he shrugs his shoulders.

Sean again turns back to Kernel. His rocking stops again as his eyes turn cold and his focus to the situation becomes keen and overtly unforgiving.

(Starts softly then builds)

"There you standing the home that we've scared people out of and insult my hospitality! Fine! (Pointing at Sean) You may not have called me a liar but you've seen through my truth. I can respect your mojo. What I don't

like is how he's looking at me. (Pointing at Cliff) With that…is he crazy expression on his face (Still pointing at Cliff) or the smug one on yours. And that my west coast friend, I will not tolerate."

Jason repeatedly taps Sean on the arm and asks, "Was he looking at me or you?" "Does it really matter?" Sean replies as Kernel continues.

"I may not make a deal with you motha-fucka's today but what you won't do is waste my time. (Almost singing) I will be taken seriously or none of you will leave breathing...and that's gangsta!"

Kernel shoves his hand in between the couch cushions just as the thugs behind him also started reaching for their weapons. Sean never waited to see what any of them would pull out. Sean draws his 9mm first and fires four shots. At the same time, Jason turns and kicks one of the guys standing behind him in the balls before wrestling with another for his gun. Cliff pulls out his switch blade but couldn't get it open as he struggles with someone himself. Sean's first shot hit Kernel between his chest and right shoulder. Causing Kernel to topple over and moan. The second shot missed the thug on the left who ducked behind the couch. The other two thugs were both hit with bullets. Thug number two was hit in the neck and the third died instantly. Jason fights to disarm the thug he is wrestling with when suddenly the thug's gun went off. Nearly hitting the one who was peeking over the rear of the couch. The shot startles everybody except Sean. As the thug and Jason pause to look at each other, Sean swiftly slides over and knocks out Jason's assailant using the side of his gun. Cliff manages to get his knife open but cuts himself on the arm as he slides and rotates the blade. It takes three jabs to puncture this guy's flesh before he finally drops. Jason watches Cliff's thug fall while trying to balance as he attempts to hold up the thug Sean just knocked out. Sean spins and stomps the guy rolling around on the floor holding his nuts twice in the head and then looks back at Jason wondering why he's holding that guy. "Let 'em fall J and pick up the gun." Jason retrieves the gun, Cliff wipes his blade using the thug's pants and

Sean stands ready to pull the trigger, covers the living room. Making sure both Kernel and the thug ducking behind the couch didn't make any moves.

"Let's get outta here. J, come take my spot and cover that room. I'm gonna clear the kitchen. When you hear me yell "clear" both of you follow. J, you back out slowly and cover us from behind. You got it?"

"Yeah, go ahead."

Sean enters the kitchen and you could hear the door squeak until it closed. It wasn't long before Sean yelled, "Clear. Let's go!" Cliff follows after hearing Sean as Jason slowly moves. As he backs out, the thug's forehead and eyes rise over the top of the couch. Kernel continues to moan when the thug asks, "Are you alright Kern?"

(Grunting)

"I'm great. (Moans) I really like those guys. We should set up another meeting with them. (Yells) Oh how it burns! I'll never paint again."

Jason catches up with Cliff and Sean just as they were going out of the back door. With no one lurking in the back yard, they made their way down the stairs and alone the side of the house. The cousins moved cautiously. Sean wanted to ensure that the four guys who were on the front stairs when they first entered the house wouldn't ambush them.

"Ok it looks clear. Jason, make sure you conceal that gun before you step out from the side of the house. Hey, don't forget to split up."

Sean composes himself before stepping out and blending in with the people on the street still partying. He weaves his way in the direction he and his cousin's had come from earlier. Cliff and Jason wait like instructed but don't follow Sean's directions about splitting up. They both linger in the open after stepping out. They both stay in front of the house talking to two women at the edge of the sidewalk. Cliff with his gift of gab gets them to smile. Laughter is his icebreaker, so he lays it on thick. Cliff reacts with frustration at Jason who is steadily smacking him on his arm. Jason tries to be discreet with his head nod. Signaling Cliff to look in the direction of the front porch. Cliff never breaks the flow of his conversation but manages to see two of Kernel's henchmen pointing at them. (Sounding like Denzel Washington) "Damn nice to meet you ladies. I have to go right now...but I wish...I had...more time." One of the ladies tells him that he'd better call and he assures her with a wink that he will. He quickly pulls Jason off the curb and uses the crowd to create some distance between them and the thugs. Heading the opposite direction of Sean, Jason keeps looking back to see if the thugs were gaining on them...and they were. The thugs were stumbling and knocking people over. Doing whatever it takes to catch the cousins. Jason and Cliff make it to the opposite set of barriers and turn the corner. Kernel's thugs try to take a shortcut behind a van sitting at the corner. As the first thug came around the front of the van, he never saw the punch that knocked him out. The second thug ducked but got locked into a chokehold. He struggled but had no chance of getting free but he did notice the tiger stripped tattooed arms just before he passed out. Almost in the clear, Jason and Cliff try to look normal as they walked with an accelerated pace. Jason slows as he looks back one more time.

"Come on J! What are you doing?"

"I'm checking our six."

"Man, miss me with the military lingo. You were only in the ROTC one semester and then you quit. And...watching military movies doesn't count."

"Real talk Cliff, I think we're clear. They should've hit that corner by now."

"Who gives a shit J? Man, stop looking for trouble when we're so close to being out of it. Let's just get to the car. I bet Sean is already waiting."

[4pm at the Reunion]

It wasn't long before the yard was full of chairs, tables, family and the aroma of good food. One card table was set up in view of the driveway with an intense game of dominos being played. "King me motha-fucka's!" Prison

Pete yelled out before slamming the last piece in his hand to the table and yelling, "Domino Bitches!"

"King you? Your dumb country ass aint-playing chest." Al says sarcastically.

"Shit Al, the way you mutha-fucka's are getting beat…I should be crowned. (Laughs) So who's washing 'em?"

Robert drops his freshly lit cigar into an ashtray then reaches out to pull the dominos in closer. The sound of them knocking together halted abruptly as they were drowned out by the sound of tires rolling over the gravel as a car pulls through the gate into the front yard. Sam leans back as he could without falling and looks down the side of the house.

(Yelling)

"Who dat is?" Sam shouts receiving no reply.

"Whoever that is can't hear you fool." Pete said laughing.

The elder cousins couldn't see Cliff as he rolled out of the car clutching a handful of fast-food napkins tightly against his open wound. "You wanna put something better on that?" Jason asked as he closes the car door. "A band-aid? A bandage? Man, at least go into the house and clean it."

"Naw. I'll just leave the napkins stuck to it and roll my sleeve down over it. It'll keep till I get me some bar-b-que."

"If you say so. I can smell it from here. The bbq that is, not your arm. Let's go put a dent in it Cliff."

A new domino game was underway as the younger cousin's laughed with each other as they came down the side of the house. The older group at the table started to get louder. "Gimme twenty-five!" Pete shouts as he hops from his seat, slamming the domino onto the table. "Son?" Pete bellows as he looks in Cliff's direction. Cliff, a bit surprised to see his dad, stops as his father approaches him with open arms. As the two men hug it out, Jason casually holds two fingers together and throws out a head nod in his father's direction. Al sarcastically responds with a strange gesture of his own before addressing his son in a serious tone.

"I thought Aaron was supposed to be with the both of you?"

"Yeah, he was. He dropped out at the last minute. Said something bout satisfying some chicken head before this other chick gets there. I knew then he wasn't going with us."

"That's my boy!" (Shaking his head.) "But I swear his dick is going to fall off if he doesn't slow down. Sam casually utters as he places a domino onto the table.

(Impulsively)

"Is that…cousin Stogie?" Cliff yells as he looks in Robert's direction.

Robert quietly says. "Fifteen." After placing his domino and picking up his cigar. He sighs deeply, looking displeasingly at Cliff before he takes a couple of puffs.

"Sorry Robert. I forgot that your hate that name. (Upbeat) How ya been?"

"What happened to your arm?"

"Umm…oh…Well, we got involved in a situation at the block party. Fought with some dudes. Cut myself in the process. No biggie! Probably be worse if Sean hadn't been there."

"Your son made the trip RK?" Sam asks.

"NO! (Turns towards Cliff) Young cousin, you must be mistaken. My son is sitting in a California jail cell. He couldn't have been in North Carolina."

"Actually, Big cousin Smoke Stack, if it weren't for Dean and his new Raymond-ess efforts (Makes the sign of the cross.) I may not have made it out with just this cut. The dude has changed. When things went to shit out there, he didn't hesitate. He got us out. I'm just saying. He is definitely different."

Robert turns to Jason who was nodding proudly in agreement with

Cliff. Turning away from Jason, he pulls the cigar from his mouth, exhales and then takes a sip from his drink.

"If he's here in town, then where is he Jason?" Sam asks.

"We dropped him off at the airport just before we headed over here. He's on his way to Vegas to meet some guy called Memphis Miles. (Pauses) At least I think that's what he said."

Robert's un-amused expression hid the doubt he was feeling about Sean but also created an uncomfortable silence amongst the men. Pete had returned to the table and sat back down. The only sound beside the rest to the family was the noise of the dominos. Robert puffs then slowly blows out the smoke. Cliff who was now standing beside Jason became attentive when Robert turns directly to him.

(Smirking)

"Cousin Smoke Stack?"

Cliff smiles nervously then answers tentatively, "Yeah."

"I can live with that one. (Puffs his cigar) You'd better get that wound clean. (Turns back to the table) That's domino!"

CHAPTER NINETEEN

Lurking Near Shadows

IT'S JUST A few ticks after 11pm. Big Guns has spent the last two hours sitting in a car watching the nightly habits of another potentially usable neighborhood. He drops his head for a moment as he sets his soda back into the consoles cup holder. With his head still down, he hears a tap on his driver's side window. Guns waves his left hand in a dismissive manner then continues to unwrap his beef burrito. The tapping on his window starts again and when he finally decides to look, Guns sees the rubber bottom of a cane pulling away from the window. He takes a bite of his burrito, adjusting while he rolls down the window. Continuing to chew he turns his head and mumbles with attitude, "What?"

"Young man, is everything ok? You've been sitting in front of my house for quite a long time now."

(Sarcastically)

"I'm minding my business sharing some personal time with my Burrito. You might want to mind yours and go back inside."

Guns was just about to roll his window up just as a flashlight started to blind him and the rubber end of a cane was being jammed into his shoulder.

"If you've haven't come from seeing someone or don't have any real business 'round here except with that burrito, then as head of the neighborhood watch, I think you'd better be on your way."

Gun's drops his burrito onto the passenger seat and snatches the cane into the car. The older man stumbles backwards as Guns rapidly exits the car and slaps the flashlight from the old timer's hand.

"Stop fuck'en with me old man and take your nosey ass back to your house!"

The two men square off and size each other up as they get a better look at each other. Gun's snorts and spits onto the ground before he smirks and laughs to himself.

"You're that old ass cop."

"Shadow man." Old Jack expresses with minimal disbelief. "I remember you. Not so scary stuffing your face in a parked car. Last time we met I recall your master tugging your leash and saving your ass. (Stares intently) I know you don't have any business in ***my*** *neighborhood. I think it's time that you leave."*

"I remember we got off on the wrong foot. Yeah, I was stopped before I could break that foot off in ya. (Smiles) But there's no one here to stop me now. (Laughs devilishly) I would usually cut an old motha-fucka a break… but you've got this comin'."

Old Jack turns his leg to provide better balance as Guns charges at him and then shifts his hip and follows through with a punch that knocks Guns back against his car. Guns, not completely to his feet, reaches into the small of his back, pulls his gun and sets it on the hood of his car.

(In a low menacing tone)

"Oh, hell yeah! This is how it should be. I'm going to enjoy this."

Guns smiles. Biting his lower lip as he gets back to his feet and moves his neck in a circular motion until it pops. He smirks again before putting his hands up like a boxer. Making small calculating movements towards old Jack, trying to size him up. Old Jack holds his hands at his side but didn't move as much Guns did. He keeps his eyes on his young target. Swaying, but not so much as a way to keep his balance but more so just to be ready.

Guns side steps, throws a jab and then a couple of combos. Unsuccessful with every punch, Guns wonders how this old man could lift his hands so quickly from his side to block his punches. [Wham] Gun's thoughts were brief as a solid punch struck him across the jaw. Followed by another to his rib cage. Short of breath he lungs at old Jack, who steps back and lets Gun's momentum take him to the ground.

(Derisively)

"So…this is how you like it?"

(Out of breath)

"It aint over yet, motha-fucka!"

Big Guns climbs back to his feet rethinking his strategy as he puts his hands back up. This time it's Jack that sneers and taunts his opponent with a hand gesture. The two men begin to exchange blows and this continues for almost six minutes. Seemingly taking turns in an attempt to see who hits harder. The commotion causes some of the neighbors on that block to look out of their windows or come outside to observe. With a wave of his arm, Jack prevented anyone from getting close or involved. Guns began to concentrate his efforts on Jack's mid-section and arms since he kept them at his side. Hoping it would keep him from being able to defend him-self or weaken him around the middle. But that new strategy was short lived. Jack blocked another of Gun's low punches and then came over the top. With a right hand he caught Guns in his temple. Followed by a left that hit him square on his chin. Gun's body went as stiff as a board but only for a moment. Then he dropped like a stone. Jack laughs to himself as Guns lays passed out on the asphalt. Shaking his head he mutters, "Shadow of the night my ass. These youngsta's have a lot to learn. (Pointing at one of his neighbors) Can you give me a hand with him?"

[Twelve Hours Later]
11:00am

The first initial moments were murky, fuzzy or blurry. The light didn't hurt him as much as the thumping in his head or the throbbing of his other body parts. He moved slowly in order to relieve the strain in his neck by pulling his head from in between the seat and his car's door panel. His eyelids parted slightly as the sound of birds chirping accompanied the morning sun that was being magnified from the passenger window. Big Guns, managing to crack one eye open, realizes he's in his car. His keys and cell phone were next to each other in the open pocket of the car's center console. He grunts, makes a strange face and takes a deep breath. Even with his other eye opening, it was still like looking through a haze. Every move he made revealed a new pain. He tries to re-adjust himself in the drive'rs seat and decides to lean his head back against the headrest. His thoughts beginning to drift to what may have happened to his gun more so than where he actually was. He had no actual concern to how he and his car left from where it was parked last night. His aching flesh encourages Guns to be steady and relax. That was until the sound of his name being called began to drown out the voice in his head hollering, "Ow". His thoughts shifted with annoyance to, "What now?" as he slowly rolls his head to the left in order to focus out of the driver's window. When his eyes settled and formed one image, he saw the wavy headshot of his boss in the passenger seat of his Cadillac. Parked right next to him in the street while looking over and calling at him. Guns rolls down his window.

"Tough night? (Laughs) Couldn't even make it into your house?" (Shakes his head)

Guns turns quickly and looks to his right as much as he could in his condition before turning back towards Robert Kingsley.

"Is that where I am? I'm not even sure how I got here…boss."

"Your phone wasn't on, so I came by. (Winks) Muster up some energy, we need to talk."

Mr. Kingsley instructs his driver to move his Caddy from the middle of the street and park it. Guns took that time to garner the strength to get out of his car. His head was pounding as he got to his feet and closed the car door. He leaned and inched along the side only letting go as he steadied the keys to open the trunk. (Groans) "Got damn, old motha-fucka's got me hurting". The squeaking noise of the trunk lid lifting causes Guns to squint and flinch as if he was hung over. He shakes it off before talking three things from a Styrofoam cooler. A cup, a small bottle of Vodka and a RedBull energy drink. After mixing them both in the cup, Guns finds comfort in his drink as he leans against the rear of the car. He closes his eyes, breathing deeply and rubs his face with one hand. Never noticing that his boss was standing on the sidewalk looking at him.

"You're slipping Roderick, normally you'd never let anyone et this close without putting eyes or hands on them."

(Groggy)

"I'm a bit off my game today."

"What happened? Cause it looks like you got your ASS whupped."

(Sighs, then sips)

"I was checking out that area we'd talked about and ran into that old cop from the funeral."

"Whose funeral?" Robert asks.

"Your nephews. Remember the one you kept me away from getting to at the gravesite."

"Looks like I should have kept you away from him last night. Should this make me worried?"

"NO Boss. (Shakes his head) That old timer has a skill set that took me by surprise. Shit…I lost my focus, I got angry and he got the better of me.

(Sips his drink) I'll leave it at this…lesson learned. I won't let it happen again."

Gun's offers his boss some of what he'd been sipping.

"The best remedy is not to put yourself in a position to need it. No thank you Roderick."

Guns fixes himself another cocktail, closes his trunk and settles once more against the back of his car. He steadies himself again while sipping and stretching his neck. Trying to rid his head of the cobwebs.

(Snaps his fingers)

"Roderick…are you with me? Let me hear what you found out from Donnie. What's going on over there?'

"I caught up with Donnie a few days ago. His demeanor and his attitude were different but he didn't get into a lot of detail about it. But it was strange watching him give orders but even stranger seeing guys show fear when he gave them. After he cleared his crew, he did tell me that he has partnered with some new guy who has cleared out the low-level poachers and put a lot of others to work. Donnie is happy that he's making money again but I get the feeling he is no longer calling the shots. This guy has taken control. (Takes a sip) I waited to say this…apparently Sean initially stepped in to work with Donnie but is also working for this guy now. Donnie said Sean's been out of town the last two weeks running some kind of errands for him."

(In a surprised tone)

"Sean, ***my*** *Sean?"*

"Yeap! So, I looked into it. The guy's name is Stacey Hunter but his crew calls him Stunt. He's new to the area but affiliated with that crew from the airplane hangar."

"That's interesting…go on." (Robert lights a cigar)

"This new dude, Stacey…used to partner with some guy out of Vegas named Garza who cleans his money. Garza is a discreet, highly paid,

well-respected lauder mat. But this Garza got caught up on some Federal charges and may have giving some folks up to get clear of it. That's how I hear it. What was more surprising is unrelated to his money-washing gig, which by the way, continued during the short time he was locked up. (Sips again) Rumor has it that Garza was recently seen in Vegas at Sean's club with Big Ronnie Ron not long ago. The street level dudes say that no one has seen Stacie Hunter except for Donnie and Sean but they'll ride or die for him, like we will for you."

"Who's your source? How credible is the information?"

"Word came to me through my normal channels. This is what I got back. I do not doubt any of it boss. (Sips) Donnie said he wanted to run the change through the council but was aggressively overruled by the new guy and Sean. Neither one seems concerned with speaking with or paying any percentage to the council. But be assured Boss, we're trying to find out what we can on this guy. Sean on the other hand, has not been seen around the city yet. (Pauses) Oh yeah, (Shaking his head) I don't know how true this is…but one of our guys mentioned seeing Slim meeting with Sean. Possibly making some kind of exchange."

"Are we coming up short with product or revenue?"

"No. Everything is adding up."

(Puffs cigar)

"Ok, let me say this, (Looks around) we don't know if someone is getting to our people, planting stories and trying to divide us from within. Nate and Sean talking, isn't an indication of foul play. (Puffs) Here's what I want. Let's take some time to secure our interests and all our incoming cash flow. I want you to make sure our team is doing what we've asked. Any deviation, deal with it swiftly. (Puffs) But handle it more effectively than you did the old timer. (Smirks) We cannot show a weak hand. Take a day or two to get yourself together. I need you sharp and that Vodka isn't helping. (Shakes off ashes) As far as my son is concerned, consider it a family matter. (Holds

*hand to his chest) It is one that **I** will handle personally. Are we clear on that, Roderick?"*

(Quickly and energetically)

"Yes Sir!"

"There are too many things going on in this city that has moved beyond our control. We can't afford to lose our heads. (Softly) Not now! There are too many new threats attempting to undermine us. (Take a long puff) We have plenty to stay focused on. See what else you can find out. Report back to me in a couple days.

[Same Day]
3:50pm

Roslyn was hesitant before she entered her home. The angry sounds of her neighbor carried from across the street. Causing her to turn and look. There was a faded blue Pacific Gas & Electric van with 24-inch rims blocking her neighbor's driveway. She assumes the low deep thump of a bass woofer was rattling the rear license plate because the front of the van didn't have one and it was parked going the wrong direction on the street. Sitting inside of it were two guys with long braids or dreadlocks wearing oversized baseball caps. The passenger was moving nervously in his seat, turning to look in every direction while the driver continued to brush off the old man yelling at him. The old man sternly repeated how this was the third time in three weeks they have parked their auction bought piece of shit across his driveway and have kept him from being able to leave his home. Still pointing at the driver, he threatened to call the police but the disrespectful thug returned his threat with a rude look and the raising of his middle finger. Clearly offended by the gesture, the old man points his index finger angrily as he heads towards his front door. As the driver dumps the contents of a cheap cigar he was gutting onto the sidewalk, he yells, "That's right, fuck off!" to the old man. He now begins to fill the emptied cigar with marijuana as the passenger shouts, "Hurry yo slow ass up Nigga!" as he looks toward the other side of the street. Roslyn hears the neighbor's dog barking just before hearing the rattle of garbage cans being knocked over. Stumbling into her view a third hoodlum appears in the street and heads for the rear of the van. She could see the rear door open and close the driver did not seem to be in a hurry. His head as he concentrated on finishing and lighting his blunt as the third thug climbed into van.

"Where's ya Boy?" The passenger asked looking into the rear of the van.

"I left him!" The third thug answered.

"But I signaled you to get out of there."

"…And I did."

"Did you warn him or did you just leave?"

"I didn't know where he was. I didn't look and I wasn't going to yell out for him. I just got out of there."

"Dumb ass!" Laughed the driver as he choked on his weed.

"Shit! This could be a problem." The passenger says quietly.

"Ya think!" the driver utters as he starts the van.

(Nervously looking toward Roslyn)

"Shit! Let's go! Let's just get out of here."

The van races away from the curb with the music blaring and the odor of marijuana wafting in the air. Something still didn't feel right with Roslyn as she turns and places her key in the door. It was too quiet. Normally she would have to fight her way through Bane to make her way into the house but this time he didn't show up at the door. She notices some flowers and shards of glass lying across the floor as she set her bags down on the couch. Roslyn stands silent a moment, looking around before slowly un-holstering her gun. Moving slowly, she takes a closer look at everything. Seeing that there were a lot of things out of place, she began to check every room. Working her way from the front until she reached the kitchen. There were bathroom cabinets, bedroom dresser drawers left open and picture frames hanging crooked on the walls. Boxes stored in closets were scattered across the floors. Her house was a mess. Although up to this point, she couldn't find anything missing. Roslyn's sigh expressed her frustration, stopping to compose herself before heading towards the kitchen. As she enters, more pieces of glass lead her to a vase that lies beside Bane who's sprawled out on the floor with blood on his head. She softly gasps before cautiously kneeling beside him. There is a brief sense of relief as she touches his side and realizes that he is still breathing. As she rubs his coat, Roslyn hears low tones of whimpering and begins to sooth bane. She looks around her kitchen and notices two things. The frame to the back door has damage showing that it had been pried open and the door to the basement was open although Roslyn knows it should always be closed. Rising to her feet, her eyes dwindle in a curiously intense fashion as she focuses on the slightly open basement door. Better judgment nudged her to secure the back door before doing anything else. With her hands tightly wrapped around the handle of her weapon and with her arms extended she uses the barrel of the gun to pull the door open. She squats at the top of the stairs and sees that the lights were left on. Pointing her weapon and trying to see around corners she knows descending the stairway will take more nerve in this situation. Roslyn takes short breaths to reduce her anxiety with every stair she steps down. She walks softly, cringing every time she makes the wood squeal. The basement was tossed around worse than the other rooms. Plastic storage containers were opened or flipped over. Shelving and even the old wood paneling were pulled away from the walls. Two of the walls were marked with the words "Not here". This bothered Roslyn. Whoever trampled her home wasn't subtle at all. Her mind started swimming with unanswered questions. Now she wondered what it was that the burglars were looking for and who was behind the break in. As Roslyn gets to the bottom of the stairs, she keeps her gun extended. She couldn't believe someone was still here. Surprised that the intruded had not heard her come down the steps, she watches as the intruder rifles through her things. Breathing deeply Roslyn closes one eye to steady her aim before resting her finger on the trigger and slipping the hammer back. She takes two more calming deeps breaths before speaking. Her tone is bubbling with an unforgiving fury as she targets the young man standing in her basement and angrily yells, "Hands where I can see them! DON'T MOVE! (With contempt) What the fuck are you doing in my house?"

CHAPTER TWENTY

Sirens

[Police radio exchange] 6:47pm

[Squelch]

"Possible shooting suspects on Aloe Boulevard. Please advise."

[Squelch]

"Car two-one-five. You are clear for a routine traffic stop. Detain and secure identities of the suspects. Be advised, suspects may be armed. Proceed with caution."

[Squelch]

Fat Daddy gets nervous as Jenk explains the habits of the cops that are trailing them. Jenk sneers, looking into the rear-view mirror as a set of headlights rapidly pulls in closely behind them and then backs off just as fast.

(Still looking into the mirror)

"That's how they do it Fat's, the cops I mean. They're running the plates right now. First, they come in close to see the license plate and after they've called it in, they pace you while they're waiting on a response. Look, see 'em backing off? They'll look to see if there are any outstanding tickets, warrants or any legal reasons to pull us over. But here's what will make you mad, (Checks mirror) when their system comes back with nothing, they will make up some reason to pull us over. (Mumbles) Shit and it's getting dark."

(In disbelief)

"That never happens! They always have a legitimate reason for what they do."

"You can believe that bullshit if you want too. (Tone changes) Don't be so naive! Clearly, you've never been harassed by the thugs in blue. Well, you'll get your first taste of it tonight. (Checks mirror) Cause here he comes."

Jenk looks over his shoulder after hearing the three quick chirps of the police cars siren. He finds a place to pull over as the red lights illuminate his back window.

"Here…we…go. (Sighs) Look Fats; let me say this before he approaches the window. He's probably going to call for back up first unless someone is riding with him. But since you are new to this shit, don't be a smart ass like brother always is. Keep your mouth shut unless they speak to you directly. Even then…try not to say much. Let me handle it."

Even with the blinding light shining on the back of the car, Jenk could see one officer take a power position at the rear of the car as the other approaches the driver's window slowly with his hand on his weapon.

(Taps car door)

"License and registration."

"Is there a problem Officer? Can I ask why you pulled me over?"

"Your license plate light is out. (Takes documents) Sit tight. I'll be back in a moment."

As the officer walks away, Fat Daddy looks at Jenk with an expression filled with both shock and disbelief. (Under his breath) "Seriously, the license plate light." Jenk assures him that he hasn't seen anything yet.

"Aren't you worried Jenk? We have weapons in the car."

"No! Just stay quiet. There's no reason they need to know that. Just let me handle this. You're way too nervous Man. Relax! That reason for stopping us is bullshit. We're clean. They'll have to let us go with nothing more than a fix-it ticket. Chill out… here he comes again."

The officer comes alongside the car again with his hand still perched on his gun. He shifts so that he is not facing Jenk head on but at an angle and then uses his opposite forearm to lean on to the door.

(Authoritatively smug)

"What's going on? Where are you boys coming from tonight?"

"A friend." Jenk quickly answers.

"Is there any weapons or drugs in the car?

"No." Jenk answers confidently and without hesitation.

"Where did you say you were coming from again?"

"A friend."

"Do you mind if we look over the car for anything illegal?"

"Yes…I do mind!"

(Sternly)

"If you're not trying to hide something, you shouldn't have a problem with me and my partner checking the car."

"I'm not obligated to have to prove anything. As a matter of fact, the last time I let someone (air quotes) check my car, they bent and ripped my back seat. They damaged my carpet and threw my stuff all over the car. So…no, I won't willingly let you search my car."

As Jenk spoke, Fat's eyes darted nervously between Jenk and the slightly obscured officer. He wasn't used to hearing someone speak to a cop like Jenk just did. It was at this point Jenk discretely notices Fats initial naive ness quickly shift to a state of outraged annoyance. But still feeling a little out of his element, Fats succumbs to the recommendation to remain quiet.

"I'm sorry Officer but you said that you pulled us over because the license plate light was out. I don't see how that is probable cause to search this car."

Without warning the officer reaches for the volume control on his radio as the crackle of a dispatcher's voice loudly calling out to him. Reaching for the microphone strapped to his shoulder, he responds as Fats shrugs and mouths the words, "What the hell" while curiously turning to look back on the other cop.

"Relax Fats. It's almost over. (Pauses) Or…it's about to get worse. Either way, just sit still." (Winks)

Fats scoffs, expressing more disbelief. The cop pulls away from his radio and returns his attention to Jenk, handing back his license and paperwork. He then lowers his head to have a look at Fat Daddy before speaking in a judgmental tone.

"Ok fellas, looks like you're off the hook. THIS TIME! We're going to send you on your way with a warning. Don't think that little speech of yours worked. If I needed to search this car…I would. (Taps car) So listen close… let's get that light bulb fixed."

He stands and signals the other cop with the twirl of his finger that it was time to saddle back up. Jenk takes a moment, preparing to drive off but waits as Fats erupts in anger.

"WHAT THE FUCK WAS THAT? (Breathes heavily) That didn't have anything to do with any light being out."

"Welcome to my word. This shit happens all the time. They'll use any fucked-up excuse to delay, detain or harass you."

"There are officers that come into my gun shop all the time. They never talk about doing shit like this. Let alone me having to experience it."

"Of course not! In your shop you're a businessman who they can respect. But at night, out here, in a car with a Blackman…(Looks at Fats) you're a criminal by association. They will fuck with your rights, smile and won't give a shit. Real talk."

Jenk starts the car as they watch the cops pull out from behind them, following with an expression of disgust.

"And you're right Fats, pulling us over <u>was</u> bullshit. Who cares why? I mean, since they're letting us go. (Puts car in gear) Now let's get the hell out of here before we get stopped again. You've got to shake this shit off. Take a

couple deep breaths and get your head back in the game. We are still armed to a hilt and have a job to do. (Smiles) It's game time Son! We can work angry...but will we really enjoy it? (Winks) Game on Son!"

[Two hours later]

Random bullets slam into an industrial garbage container as Big Ron and his buddy Eric quickly take cover. [Thump]

(Nervously exited)

"SHIT! Who the hell is shooting at us?"

[Thump, thump]

"How the fuck should I know." Ron replies as he cautiously looks around for the shooter.

"Shit, those bullets are hitting too close. Can you see anybody?"

"No!"

"Do you think it's Sean or maybe that new guy people say he's working for? You did sort of threaten them. So...?"

"I don't fuck'en know! Shit! Shut up a minute and let me think God Dammit! (Exhales) We gotta get out-ta here!"

(Impersonating an Australian and sarcastic)

"That's brilliant Mate...how?

[Thump, thump]

"I'm thinking Dam-mit!"

"Do you think we can move the container? (Grunts) Damn, I think it's too heavy to move Ron. We need help."

"It's just us E. (Looks around) FUCK! Everybody else is gone.

[Thump, thump]

"Eric, we're gonna have to run for it. The car is right over there. You don't wanna get hit so make sure you zigzag. [Ting] Whoa... that one sounded different."

(Grunting)

"Aww shit. Oow! Sh…it, my side is burning."

"Are you bleeding E? Can you move?"

(Still grunting)

"There's no blood Ron. Maybe I got lucky." He replies while looking at the hole near him on the can.

"The next time they fire, be ready. We're going!"

The two men were motionless, listening for their opportunity to run for the car. The warehouse area became eerily quiet until Eric lost his balance and fell onto the garbage container. The thud triggered three staggered gunshots. When the third ricocheted off the top of the container, the dash for the car began. "Go, GO!" Ron yelled as he abandoned the zigzag pattern and just ran as fast as he could. The bullets whizzed pass them both like the sound of angry bees. Ron stumbles, feeling a sting as he reaches first for his shoulder and then for his abdomen. Eric reaches the car first, jumping into the driver's seat before stretching over to push open the passenger door. Ron could barely get the door shut as Eric smokes the tires trying to get traction to the rear of his Corvette. [Bang, bang] [Crash] The rear window shatters and a taillight lens falls out as two bullets hit the rear of the car. With his foot heavily on the gas pedal, Eric puts distance between whoever's shooting and themselves.

[9:35pm]

(Tire screeching in the distance)

Mia leans on an ambulance outside of a gas station mini-mart chatting up the driver as she waits for her twin brother to finish pumping the gas. Just as the driver leans in closer to puts the moves on her, they quickly swing their heads towards the street. (Hearing loud screeching tires) Meck lets go of the pump handle and moves to the end of his car just in time to see a Corvette sliding recklessly through the intersection. The Vette, making a left turn in front of the gas station almost hits the car in the lane next to it before swinging completely in the opposite direction and nearly missing the curb of the center island.

"Wow, I bet you see that Corvette sooner than you think." Mia tells the ambulance driver as she taps him on the chest with her finger.

"Come on now, let's be positive."

(As she walks away)

"Can't you see it? That's too much car for that guy. (Scoffs) Positive? (Smiles) Don't sound so naïve. It makes you look like a rookie. (Laughs) That car is going to repaint the scenery. (Waves goodbye) You'll see."

[Inside the Corvette]

Both men groan as Eric tries to control the car with one arm while clutching his side with the other. Ron leans his shoulder against the door panel in an attempt to apply pressure to one of his wounds. His short breaths reveal pain as he pulls napkins form the glove box and jams them into his ribcage attempting to slow down the bleeding on the other. Eric begins to slump in the driver's seat as the car veers back and forth across the road. Nearly missing an oncoming car.

(Yelling)

"HEY! Keep your shit together. (Frantically) Hey…HEY!"

Eric tries to pull himself upright in his seat. He coughs and spits blood across the steering wheel. He struggles to keep his left eye open while also trying to keep the car in the middle of the three blurry roads that he sees. He coughs again before wheezing with conviction, "Shit! Ron, I'm ok." At that moment Eric's head slumps into his chest and his hand drops form the steering wheel. Pulling it and the car to the left. Launching them across the opposite side of the road. The jeering change of direction causes Ron to look up, grab the steering wheel and try to straighten the car. But Ron's impulsive yank only kept them from t-boning a parked car. Instead, they slammed into the quarter panel of an old Buick. The fiberglass fender of the Corvette exploded on impact, shooting red chunks into the air before pushing the Buick against the curb and forcing the car across a driveway. Ron was yelling, "HIT THE BRAKES!", as they went head on into an Oak tree. [CRASH] The sound of the impact was described as distinctively and disturbingly louder than the claps of a southern lightning storm. The front of the car imploded like a bug on a windshield. At impact Eric levitated over his seat before his head was thrown into the windshield. As the front-end crumbles around the tree, the steering wheel crushes his legs between the seat. Momentum flings him backward and his head shatters the side glass. Leaving a bloody mess as he collapses on top of the center console. Ron, at the point of impact instinctively pulls his legs in closer to his body and uses his arms to brace himself. His head bumps the roof of the car before momentum thrusts him forward. Forcing him to slam into the dashboard because the airbags of this chopped together car didn't work. Ron sees a bright white light as his head and upper body are whipped violently back into the seat. Ron fights blacking out as the sound of the crash wakens the surrounding neighbors. Ron lifts his head slowly. Dazed, he uses any remaining strength to get the door open. Still holding the wound at his side, he rolls out of the car and hits the ground. Someone yells, "Stay down. Help is on the way." Using every ounce of strength, he gets to his feet. With his head ringing and his vision blurring, he staggers across someone's lawn and passes out. Dropping only after seeing the hazy image of a lady pointing and yelling into a cell phone. Big Ron lye's motionless as an old timer in his robe and slippers stands watch over the area. Shivering a little bit, he pulls one hand from his robe pocket to wave one arm as he signals the fire truck coming his direction. The fire truck rolls in quietly. No sirens, just the bright lights rotating atop the truck. First on the scene four firemen came off that rig and immediately pulled medical equipment and split up to provide first aid and secure what appeared to be a gruesome scene.

The sirens that were blaring now as they got closer were from an ambulance coming up the street. The EMT'S moved swiftly to pull a gurney and supplies form the truck. One EMT stops for a moment and looks towards the mangled wreck. "Tell me that's not the car from earlier tonight." His partner smirks as he begins moving towards the wreckage. "Looks like it is. The bright side…if there is any, (Pauses) you won't have to wait to pay on that bet. Come on, let's get to work."

[Mid-Afternoon two days later]

Four police cars barrel threw red lights and intersections in hot pursuit of a speeding car. The sirens echoed for blocks as traffic moved aside to make room for the reckless convoy. Uncertain and paranoid, Slim Nate pulls over. Nervously preparing for the worst as the police cruisers go rushing by him. The waning wails of the sirens were now being drowned out by the loud impression of sirens coming from the sidewalk. Nate looks to his right and sees big Guns with his hand hovering near his mouth, trying to project the sounds.

(Yelling)

"Yo! I know you heard that! You're looking right at me. Pull your ass over! We need to talk."

Acknowledging Gun's request with a head nod, Nate moves his car. Taking the first open space he could find up the street. Gun's approaches the car and begins talking at Nate just as soon as his car door opens.

(Lightly rubbing an orange)

"Where the hell have you been Slim? Last I heard you were taking care of some family business. No one's spoken to or heard from you since. The Boss wants me to find out what the hell is up. Good thing I saw you."

"Is this how it's going to be Gun's? Huh? No hello? No, how's the bitches dawg? Nothing…? (Sincere) Shit, it's good to see you too…Killa."

Nate comes out of the street to the sidewalk as Gun's stands near a garbage can and begins to peel the orange he had been softening. Nate leans one the back end of his car and starts talking as he watches Gun's barbaric peeling technique.

"I quit Dawg. I'm and independent now. I work for myself."

(Eating)

"Doing What?"

"Uh...well, a little collection. Some gun work. It's hard to dial it in for you. Each job has different needs. It's whatever Dawg, as long as the pay is right. I found a come up to start doing high dollar freelance jobs."

(Annoyed)

"So, if you aren't with us, then which of our enemies are you working with? Seems like a fucked-up way to show your loyalty. Just up and disappear like that. I'm just say'en."

(Chuckling)

"Loyalty? Are you kidding me? What's that? Why should I expect any to come my way? It certainly wasn't shown to his own son. Fuck, what I saw done to Sean was fucked up! I mean, I do agree he could be green at times but you don't bust him down to street level. You killed any respect or credibility he had. Just to teach a lesson? That amongst other shit was fucked up. (Chuckles again) Loyalty? Yeah right!"

"Oh, I see. So, you're partnering up with Sean and this new mystery Motha-fucka now? It sounds like your allegiance has changed."

"Damn! Those small ass ears on that big add head must make it hard to hear huh? I'm...an...independent! You know...solo bolo."

Big Guns softly repeats Nate's last words before shoving another orange slice into his mouth. Nate makes himself more comfortable against before speaking again.

"Look man, I've got nothing but respect for the boss and his Fam for putting money in my pockets. But there are lucrative opportunities out here. Word has it a lot of motha-fucka's are striking out on their own. Shit and

on their own terms. I like the sound of that. The time is right! Folks are out to get theirs so I'm gonna get out there and get mine."

(Angry)

"So that's how you want to part ways? Do business? Just disappear with no explanation? What…you just planned to throw up a peace sign at our old crew like this shit you're doing is Ok? You don't leave a job like that!"

(Aggravated)

"I aint been punching no motha- fucking clock! What the fuck you want…a two weeks' notice? That's ridiculous! I've seen bitches die for far less stupid shit for this crew than just wanting out. (Pauses) Tell me when there was any regard for losing them. There wasn't and I learned there would never be. Especially if you base it on how RK treated his nephew's death. Nigga's are easy to replace. Those were your words. (Twists his lips) So what rank must I reach before I become indispensable or untouchable? Every day on these streets is kill or be killed with the type of shit we do. I would rather worry about the enemy in front of me than the guy fighting in the foxhole next to me. Sometimes the only person you can rely on is yourself. So, with dat said…it's time for me, to do…for me."

"I hear ya, but I don't want to see you become an enemy to us Slim."

Nate rises and heads back around to his driver's door and opens it. He looks across the roof of the car at Big Gun's and hold up a very confident peace sign. Making sure that it was seen before replying, "I've got to run Dawg but hear me when I say this…we go way back so I'm not actually worried about that. (Smiles) Don't treat me like one and…I won't turn on ya! (Taps the top of the car) That's real talk!"

CHAPTER TWENTY-ONE

Restless

[3:25am]

(Car door closes)

"Thanks for meeting me, Ana."

"Where is he now Mia?"

"Asleep, (sighs) finally."

"Do we need to do this somewhere else?"

"No, we're fine. He'll be down for the rest of the night."

"Good. That's good. (Concerned) Are you all right Mia? You seem a little shaken."

"I don't know how much longer I can do this Ana. These nights with him are steadily getting worse."

"What do you mean…exactly?"

"It starts with the bad dreams he's been having. I'm fairly confident the hearing the sound of his cousin's voice is subconsciously having a strange affect on him. He's been talking extensively in his sleep and now seems to be physically acting out parts of these dreams."

"He hasn't hurt you? Has he?"

"I don't give him the chance. I've resisted fucking him up. You know how I am Ana. Truth is…I get clear of him when he's acting out but I get

in close again when I put on the concerned girlfriend act. Also…I don't want to blow my cover because I had to violently beat the shit out of him for putting his hands near me. (Scoffs) You know I won't put up with any bullshit. (Breaths deeply) He's been having narrated conversations as he sleeps. Then he wakes up in an accelerated state of panic."

Ana takes a moment to turn her engine over and crank the heater up. Mia puts her forehead against the passenger window and looks up at the building.

"How much of what he rambles can you remember Mia?"

"Quite a bit. But he usually fills in the blanks."

"I guess that's helpful."

"Not always! We spend hours trying to make sense of his dreams. It's like a puzzle…and you know how I hate puzzles."

(Laughing)

"Yeah, ***you*** *might not but your cover, Keisha, she seems to love them. (Winks)*

"Which is why it takes all night. He's struggling to connect to dots. Trying to synchronize what he can remember with whatever I might have heard. Oh…and he repeatedly goes over it until it makes sense or until his anxiety level lowers enough for him to get back to sleep."

"Can you give me any examples?"

"Okay, so two weeks ago as he talked in his sleep, he began to change his voice and flopped around in bed. He told me that the dream began with his Father and Grandmother sitting on her porch talking about him. As they spoke, he could see everything he was doing. You know, as if they were narrating. He said his actions were always opposite of their opinions. Here's how it went:

"Sorry I'm late Ma. (Pointing) Who's the guy in the suit walking away as I drove up?" Robert Kingsley asks.

"A lawyer." Grann answers rocking on her porch swing. "I needed some legal advice. Sadly, he gave me nothing but bad news."

"Well, I hate to be the barer of more bad news Ma but I have to tell you about your grandson."

(Sternly)

"Don't light that cigar, Robert! (Watches him put it away) Now, what could he have possibly done? I thought we had him out of the way?"

"The Police didn't have enough to hold him like we had hoped. That was something we didn't find out as fast as we should have and the money that we planted was never recovered."

(Lips clinched tightly and uttered slowly)

"Umm Hmm."

"I was at the card table at the reunion when the younger cousins told me Sean had come to town for business and never showed at the reunion. They were vague about what they were up too but they did say that he left and headed for Vegas."

(Exhaling)

"…Ahh not that den of whores again. I'm tired of that boy not listening."

"Not exactly the club this time Ma. They told me he went to meet with a potential supplier. Ok, so word has gotten around that he's working for someone else."

"Are these just rumors Robert? Sean has often proven himself to be a flake."

"I've been learning that there is a lot of truth to it."

"I've always thought him to be weak. We will have to deal with him before he becomes and embarrassment or a threat. The first being the most likely (clears throat) so don't let him ruin this families name."

Mia went on telling Ana that at this point of the dream, he would just keep repeating, "Embarrassment…he's no threat." Repeating it until his mumbles turned silent or he began spewing only partial dialogue again. Mia takes a moment to look up at the apartment window before she continues. Stopping briefly only because she thought she saw a light come on. "What's wrong Mia?" Ana asks. "Oh…nothing." She replied pulling her head away from the car window. "It was nothing."

"What happened last week? I'm only assuming that these dreams are a regular occurrence now."

Mia picks up where she left off and began to talk about Tuesday morning around 1:30am.

"Ana, Sean starts talking in his sleep again but this time he jumps up out of bed suddenly and starts walking around the room. While still asleep, he looks to be holding a conversation with his new alias, Stacey Hunter. That went like this:

"Do you understand that our future depends on them believing that "I" exist?"

"Yeah Stacey, I know how important it is!"

"There can be no confusion. Both of the Rizzo's are dead and I will not be mistaken for or thought to be an impersonation of either of them."

"That will not be a problem, Stacey. Word about you has already hit the streets."

"Good…and from now on I prefer, Hunt. I want you and Donnie to call me Hunt."

Mia continues, telling Ana how freaky it was listening to how effortlessly Sean's voice changes between his and Stacey's when the roles change. She mentions that Stacey's voice is the deeper between the two and far more ominous. Mia went on to say that she was even more surprised at what was being said.

"That was good work you and that Slim looking kid that you suggested did with those two trying to get away in that Corvette. Although the one we wanted dead is still alive, he'll soon learn that he can't threaten ***us*** *and not expect consequences."*

"Yeah, but there are others Hunt that need to be shown as well."

"Oh…we'll get to whomever we need to when the time is right. (Twitches) For now, there is a lot to do. You know… loose ends we need to tie up before our coming out event. But…first we must decipher our allies from our enemies. If we stay sharp, we'll spot the lies, the liars or anyone who wishes to do us harm. That includes family. (Clears throat) But for now, let's start with getting some rest."

Mia pauses dramatically to ensure Ana knew that it was at that moment (using her hands) Sean dropped to the floor alongside the bed and was sound asleep.

"Did you talk to him about that dream Mia?"

"No! I asked him the next morning if he'd remembered anything from last night. He told me "NO" and seemed more concerned about how he got on the floor with a blanket over him. I just told him that he rolled out of bed and hit the floor. Since I couldn't wake him, I left him there and covered him up. (Checks window again) What's interesting to me Ana, is that he never remembers any of the dreams or conversations involving his alter ego. Which brings me too tonight.

(Exited)

"Yes! Tell me about tonight. I'm curious about what's got you ready to leave your post."

"It started when he jumped out of bed and grabbed the corner lamp. He threw his arm around it as if he had it in a choke hold. His right hand, shaped like a gun was pressed up against the lampshade. You could see an aggressive desperation in his eyes. Taking small steps as if he was making sure no one was creeping up behind him. I got up but moved slowly. I was unsure if he was really asleep or having some kind of episode. As soon as I got out of bed, he yelled and told me not to move. I was like…fuck! Cause this time Ana, he didn't appear to be sleep walking. It seemed like he was experiencing this shit. He looked me straight in my eyes and called me Roslyn. Then

quickly shifted his eyes nervously to his left, making references as if his father was standing nearby. Sean started to randomly yell, instructing no one to move. I stopped and planted my ass at the far end of the bed. I found myself trying to talk over him at times. Hoping to snap him out of it. Well, it wasn't working. He stood, pointing at me, still shouting and shifting that lamp around like a life was in his hands. Without effort, Sean's voice gets deeper. Which led me to believe that his alter ego just surfaced. Sean's eyes, his expression, both turned cold and emotionless when the change happened. It was as if his demeanor would flip flop from an uneasy nervous wreck to a calculating and brash aggressor. (Sighs) It was unsettling but I will circle back to some of the rest of this shit later and it will make more sense when I do. I'm just bypassing some of his talking for now. (Pauses) As I was saying, suddenly his voice went deep and he said, "This is for the best. It has to be done." Using his hand, he motioned like he squeezed a trigger and then let the lamp fall to the floor. Then he quickly held both hands together, pointing his make shift gun to his left. I couldn't make out what he was mumbling before he leaned up against the wall, closed his eyes and began to snore. I stayed where I was and softly called out to him until he woke. (Twists lips) Man, it didn't take long for him to start freaking out about how he got against the wall."

"Was he able to talk about this dream?"

"Shit Yeah! (Takes a deep breath) He didn't wait. He rubbed his eyes first then jumped right in. He said his dream started as he stood amongst the charred ruins of his cousin's house. The smoke lingered around him floating like a fog while a few of the remaining embers still glowed red and gave off a bit of heat. His mannerisms were twitchy and made him appear nervous. You could see the tension of the moment as his muscles pulsate. With his left arm, he clutches tightly in almost a choking manner and he uses his right hand to squeeze the handle of his 9mm as he presses the barrel closely against the temple of his captive. Sean tightens his grip

around his grandmother's neck before gritting his teeth and asking her to stop squirming. She did Justas she heard her grandson pull back on guns hammer. Sean told me he looked to his left, warning his father not to take another step. Once he was sure his dad wasn't moving, he turned back to shout at Roslyn. He started apologizing. He tries to re-assure her that he had nothing to do with her house burning to the ground. He arrived just in time to find his grandmother supervising two thugs digging through the rubble. How he got there was one of those dream mysteries. It was like there was a flash of light and BOOM he was there. (Shake her head) He startled them and suddenly…guns were drawn. Outnumbered, he quickly grabbed his grandmother before seeing his cousin Raymond appear, gun down the two thugs and then vanish before his eyes. When Roslyn asked why he was there, Sean told her that his life is in danger and he was instructed by someone close to him to take the fight to them. Next thing he knows…he appears in the yard. Ana, I'm sorry if it seems like I'm all over the place but that's how Sean was telling it. (Check out the window again) Sean says he looks at his dad before his voice changes and his eyes go cold. Okay so somewhere in here his dad was calling him a thief, a liar and a coward. Telling him that he doesn't have the conviction to take his ideas or actions to any level of success. Robert Kingsley lit a cigar, casually told him to let her go and waited for Sean to punk out and release his mother. Instead, Sean tilts his head, gives his dad a creepy look while speaking softly to his grandmother. The distinct change in his voice generated a fear in her never seen before by his father. Sean nestled the barrel into her skin and asked her if she was ready. (Ana's eyes widen) He wanted to know if everything was, more so if anything was right with her soul because she would only have mere seconds to be sure. (Mia gets quieter) With his mouth close to her ear, he softly says, "Old lady, there are no atheists in Heaven and no remorse for a content sinner. I will be overjoyed to help you meet your maker. (Mia whispers, I'm imitating Sean.) He whispered, "I know now that this is my purpose. I have accepted what I have to do. (Ana is frozen with anxiousness.) Starting with you grandma, I have to reset the balance."

(Shouts)

"Mia, he didn't! That's crazy."

"No doubt! (Sighs) But remember Ana, I'm watching him choke the corner lamp while he's acting this out in his sleep. I wouldn't take my eyes off him. His gun was 3ft away on the nightstand…loaded. My instincts were kicking in Ana but I fought them off to keep ***this*** *girlfriend shit up. So anyway, he whispers… let's set things right and then pulls the trigger. (Ana's eyes widen again) The bullet pierces her skull. Shooting fragments out of the other side of her head. Sean steps back and lets her lifeless body plunge into the ashes around them. He immediately aims his weapon before his father could raise his. Don't move dad Sean said he shouted just as his cousin appears behind his father. Yeah Unck, don't move. Is what Raymond said before he disappeared again. Roslyn stood facing her in-laws with her gun drawn. She rotates slowly, trying to line them up in case she needed to hit them both with two quick shots. Sean said she sarcastically shouted, WHAT NOW HERO! That's when he woke up. Breathing heavily, squinting, standing in the corner of the room with a broken lamp at his feet and ready to ask twenty questions."*

(Exhausted)

"Damn!" Ana says softly, shaking her head.

"I'm no doctor Ana but he seems to be moving towards a mental state that only a professional should handle."

"Mia, can you stay with it just a little longer? We…are…so…close."

(Mia takes a deep breath filled with frustration.)

"I can't promise that I won't hurt him. I can't do another night like tonight."

(Smiles)

"I need you to fight those instincts of yours Mia. At least until we have what we want."

[Mid-day a week later]

(Grann and Robert talk in her front yard)

"Ma, we need to talk about Sean."

"Well, there's not much left to say Robert… I think he has to die.

ACT THREE

SHADOWS & SECRETS

Life's unpredictable) *Dressed for a smile*

[Same day and 10 blocks away when young Raymond and Sean entered that rundown garage for a pickup.]

My mother assured me that if I believed hard enough that I could fly. I could hold out my arms and feel the wind surround and lift me. The warm breeze of life supporting me as I soar like a bird or float aimlessly like an autumn leaf that signals a change is coming. The soft sound in her voice reassured me that if I believed, I could be rewarded with whatever my heart desired. I would only have to reach out and it would be there for the taking. (Softly) So, I listened and I learned to believe.

I was probably too young to notice how up and down my mother really was. Maybe I was too naive or too blind to see it. What I did remember was that she seemed tired…a lot. Making me promises that she would barely keep and often in exchange for me to stop pestering her.

It was late one afternoon; I'd been trying to wake her for hours. Mom was calling out as she slept and had been shivering a little each time, I went in to wake her. I was hungry but I knew if I let her rest, she would take care of me when she got up. She always came through.

Hours later my mom had finally got up. I could hear her stumbling around in her room. I sat quietly playing as she yelled, "I know your hungry baby. Mommy's gonna fix that. (Impulsively) I'll get you a treat too! (Voice trailing off) I know you like treats." When she emerged from her room, she physically didn't look like herself. Her hair was undone but nothing time with a comb couldn't fix. She had on a blouse (un-tucked) with blue cotton sweatpants. She slipped on her rain boots and put on her oversized coat. Mom took time to make sure my hair was brushed and my ponytails weren't frizzy. Mom dressed me with one of her favorite dresses, my white leggings and shoes. She pulled my heavy, warm coat from the closet, put me in it and we were on our way to eat. We headed down the street two blocks to Anne's Coffee shop. We ordered lunch and mom told stories of when she was a little girl and how she would come here with her mother. A few folks would stop to tell me how pretty I looked and my mother took a moment to dole out the gratitude. I was spell bound by her stories. She had a way of making you feel a part of them. We laughed, we smiled, and I felt like I was the most important thing in her world. I'll never forget ***that*** *lunch. It was great! As we walked out the café with my hand in hers, she asked, "So baby…are you ready for your treat?" I shook my head yes because what kid wouldn't want one. But she'll never know that I enjoyed the time she spent with me, talked with me and played with me more than any candy she could give me.*

[Three more blocks away from home]

I remember we skipped. Yes, we were skipping down the street as we got close to the store. Mom led me to the edge of the sidewalk just behind a fire hydrant. She put her hands on my shoulders and looked directly into my eyes. "I want you to stay here until I come back. Be a good girl and don't move! Okay! (I nodded) Ok baby, I'll be right back." I stood with my arms at my side eagerly awaiting her return. It was a short time after mom had gone in that an older lady stopped and asked me if I was lost. If I was ok and tried to grab my hand so we could go and find someone responsible for me. I avoided her grasp and pointed at the store. My mom had just come out…she was smiling, walking with one hand in her coat pocket and the other holding a chocolate bar. "See baby, I told you I'd get it for you." Mom took two steps towards me as the door to the store violently swung open and shattered the glass. Mom was looking at me as the "BOOM" from a shot gun blast sent nearby people ducking for cover. The old lady reached out to grab me but couldn't because I'd taken a few steps toward my mother and was just out of her reach. A second shot rang out as the force of the buckshots took her of her feet, shortly before falling.

(Shrieking)

"MOMMY…"

A big man tackled the guy with the gun. I hurried to my mother as her blood coated the sidewalk and my leggings when I kneeled beside her. My mouth quivered as I called out to her but I knew by the look in her eyes that she was already gone. I continued to scream out for her and it took every ounce of my strength not to let anyone pull me away from her. But some battles you may be too small or just not physically strong enough to win. I now stood off to the side, tears in my eyes and blood on my clothes. But I wasn't sad…I was angry! I listened to this killer give an explanation for his actions but I didn't understand what he was saying and no one would explain it to me. They just kept asking me short questions until my aunt Jackie showed up. As one cop said, to collect me. I watched my mother go into a bag but never saw handcuffs go on that man. I looked in his direction and any humanity, love or compassion left my eyes. I tried to burn a hole through his flesh as if my eyes were capable of it. His actions today put holes in my happiness and he took from me the one person who provided it.

As I grew, not much made me happy. Nothing settled me like my mother's smile. But if something happened to give me joy, I was hard pressed to let anyone take it away from me and most times joy was short lived. I found comfort in my misery. Shit, the damage was done. Not even the truth of that day could fix my pain. I couldn't see it as a child, her shaking, the odd behavior and the drug use. Maybe that's why it took her so long to come out of her room. She didn't want her baby to see her until that ***hit*** *she'd taken could make her well again. I did hear much, much later that she had pistol-whipped the clerk of that store. Robbed the cash register and picked up my candy bar on the way out. I took that candy out of her hand and wouldn't let it go. I can't begin to tell you how many times I closed my eyes and yelled, "Fuck the treat, I'd rather have you Mom!"*

I was also too young to understand what was right or wrong about her actions. I can say that watching her die in front of me had a profound affect on me. Especially when I heard phrases like, Only the strong survive, Kill or be killed, an eye for an eye and it is what you make of it. Those phrases are angering and ridiculous to me.

*As I've grown, the death of my mother has made me cold, bitter and driven me to never rely on the promises of others. To count only on myself in order to have more than what I need. And come by what I need using the best means I can find to do so. Mom told me that if I believed hard enough…I could fly. What she didn't say…is that there are a lot of gun toting hunters out there gunning for birds like me. So, if I fly, I've decided to be the hunter not the prey. I decided to be educated but street smart and to be kind when necessary but ruthless without guilt. My mother also taught me that if I wanted anything bad enough, I could just reach out and take whatever my heart desired. I know now…**that** statement is not always the truth. But right or wrong, legal or not…I have to find a better way. I know her spirit guides me every day. Whatever I do, I do to honor Evelyn Sullivan. My name is Maya.*

CHAPTER ONE

Grave Intentions

[Mid-afternoon November 2nd]

THE RAIN IS unrelenting. Raymond's mausoleum looks morbid in the rain-soaked gray color of day. Roslyn and Old Jack walk up a small pathway to meet with the cemetery's administrator. As Roslyn gets closer, she sees the door that secures the tomb pulled from its frame, damaged and lying on the ground.

"How could anyone desecrate someone's place of rest?" Old Jack mutters as they approached.

Hearing the tail end of Jack's comment, a well-dressed man clutching a leather-bound notebook responds while holding out his hand to greet them.

"We were wondering the same thing and let me assure you both; we have every intention to find out. (Pauses) Good afternoon Mrs. Moreno-Kingsley. We here at Kingdom Paradise Cemetery cannot express enough remorse for such vandalism and depredation. Our staff is working directly with local law enforcement to return the remains of your husband to you and repair his place of rest as promptly as we can. We are also implementing new security measures for the cemetery. We don't yet know if this was an isolated incident and we want to be sure something this tragic will never happen again. We will take new measures to ensure that it will not."

"Do you have any idea of when or how this happened?"

"Yes, we do ma'am. Our security cameras show three darkly dressed individuals out front around 1:45am. Two of the three men scaled the fence and disappeared into the cemetery. The last one, tampered with the lock on the front gate until he was able to get it open. That same man then drove a small flatbed truck onto the property."

Jack steps aside to have a look at the damaged mausoleum door and then quickly gives his opinion.

"Looks like they used a battery powered saw, cut the door at the hinges and then tossed it aside Roslyn."

"Ma'am the security footage also shows a fuzzy image of the truck exiting the property with what looked like a casket, covered and strapped to it. There are no alarms on the gates so our workers didn't discover the damage until they made their morning rounds."

Roslyn, standing almost statuesque, moves her head slightly, examining the outside condition of the mausoleum.

(With concern)

"Ma'am, are you alright?"

(Responding quickly)

"Yes, I'm fine, just processing! (Closes her umbrella) I want to take a look inside, if I may."

"Indeed, you may ma'am. There ***is*** *something that you may want to see."*

The other umbrellas began to close in a syncopated sequence before Roslyn, Jack and the cemetery manager step inside out of the rain. Roslyn gasps looking at the damage done to the detailed concrete housing that encapsulated her husband's casket. The lid or cap that was hand chiseled with the image of the Kingsley's crest had been recklessly tossed aside and now sat on its edge in front of the enclosure. Every side of the enclosure met with some type of damage, specifically the corners. This was possibly done so that the casket could be lifted out. There were orange Mexican marigolds and pictures of Raymond all over the floor. Around the base of the crypt were decorated skulls made of sugar, sugar cane, candies and candles. The faint scent of incense was still in the air. Stepping closer, Roslyn focuses all her attention on the rear wall and at the words that were boldly painted on the stones across the chiseled cross. She begins to read but louder than she realizes.

"Absent is the flesh,

Therefore, the spirit is free...to be renewed

El, que no descansa...vive

"Ma'am, May I ask what the last parts of those words say?"

Roslyn steps closer with her eyes still on the wall, taking one hand and gently swiping it along the damaged part of the concrete enclosure. She never turns to look at anyone else. She just takes a deep breath before exhaling slowly. Remaining focused on the wall as she exhales again nervously before responding.

(Intensely)

"It says, he who isn't at rest...lives!"

An uncomfortable silence fell amongst everyone as Roslyn pulls out her cell phone and takes a few pictures. Jack taps the manager on the arm and they step back out into the rain, leaving Roslyn alone to take this all in. Moments later she steps out of the crypt, ducking under Jack's umbrella and re-engages with the cemetery's manager.

"I can be reached any time of day if you receive any new information. (Sighs) And once all the evidence... that's if there's any, is collected...let me know what the cost of repairing the mausoleum will be."

"Ma'am this is an above normal situation and we are prepared to cover the repairs at this time. Here is my card again if you have any further questions or concerns... don't hesitate."

The rain becomes heavy again as Old Jack and Roslyn descend the small path back to his car.

"Any ideas to what that message meant?" Jack asks.

Roslyn stops walking and just stares off into the distance. Jack turns towards her, hoping she would turn as well and look in his direction but she didn't. Lost in the gray rain-soaked curtain falling in front of her, she took a deep breath before vocalizing her thoughts.

"I was thinking about that moment when the son of Christ's tomb was opened and the only thing there was his shroud and an angel. His words, his prophecy and our faith had been strengthened for all who believed. (Scratches herself behind the ear) But what am I to believe after reading those words? Written and left by thieves most likely. This isn't the second coming. This seems like a senseless act, monstrous and cruel for me and to Raymond's memory. I immediately felt a spooky, unsettling rush in the pit of my stomach. Why were the last of those words written in Spanish? (Looks at Jack) That seems to solidify to me that it was purposefully personal. Why it was left there isn't what concerns me."

"There seems to be something else on your mind Roslyn. May I ask what it is?"

"Yes, you're right, there is. Today is November 2nd. It's All Souls Day. In my coulter it's the continued celebration of the Day of the dead. Families go to cemeteries to be with the souls of the departed. To encourage visits by our lost loved ones in the hopes that they will hear our prayers. (She holds one hand out and catches the rain) Why today of all days? (Turns towards Jack) Honestly, I'm more interested with why someone would do this and who wanted that message delivered."

[Same day, mid-afternoon at Grann's]

"Now what took you so long to get out here to see me?"

(Apprehensively)

"I've been out of town Grann."

"Seems to me... you've been avoiding your family grandson."

"Not at all! (Quickly) I've been busy. I've just been busy."

"Uh-huh! Remember now, I want you to keep some truth when you speak to me Sean. We will get into what you've been busy with later on but for now, follow me. I want to show you something."

Grann leads Sean around the back of her house alongside of what looks like the remains of an old rotted wood garage that's collapsing in on an old pick-up truck. After climbing three rotted small wood steps, Grann opened a door on the right rear side of the structure. After stepping in, she moves just enough for Sean to step in and close the door. There wasn't much left of this garage to step around in. There was only enough room for a cot and two top loading freezers that sat side by side. Sean stood; looking a bit skeptical about his surroundings for a moment until he noticed Grann removing a master lock from a false wall that swung open to expose another opening just at the end of the second freezer. The opening revealed a stairway that led them underground at least one story.

"I asked you to come with me so we can discuss your focus or the lack thereof that you seem to have with your family and our business. Most important, for me, would be the business that supports this family. You seem to be drifting away from what's important. (Takes a deep breath) I brought you down here because this is where I come when I feel like I'm losing site of things. (Clears throat) Like you seem to be."

Sean looks at Grann as she fumbles around looking for the other light switch.

"Have you gotten yourself a vault yet Grandson?"

"Ahh…no! No, I haven't."

"Well, you should. Your dad, your uncle and I all have one. Every item stored in them is specific to the vault's owner. It's great for when you need to stash some things away. You definitely need one, especially from all them gals you seem to run through. You may find it to be a lifesaver. (Finds switch) Let me show you mine."

Grann flips the light switch and lights along the corridor came on one after the other like on a runway, illuminating the pathway. The lights begin to highlight the shapes of people that appear to be leaning out from the corridor walls.

(Proudly)

"I call this the Hall of Souls. Seeing these fallen enemies often reminds me of what's most important."

"And what's that?"

"You'll see soon enough."

Grann quickly heads down the hall to the center of her vault while Sean walks and looks around slowly. Studying what she considers to be artwork. Eye-bawling each slab leaning out from the walls. Every representation was life-like, full-sized figures of people. People she considered to be her enemies. They were eerie replicas, keepsakes of folks who were just in her way. Each figure had a plate with a name and a year of entombment. One date went as far back as 1943. But every plaque had some personal meaning for her. The first plaque Sean saw read; Rival. Another read; crooked detective then cowardly Mayor. And others were even something verbally negative about family. Almost at the end of the walkway Sean stopped in front of a hulking figure of his uncle DL and his Aunt Rachael. Sean looks down at his uncle's plaque that read; Misguided Do-gooder, his death ended the sabotage. Then he looks over at his aunt's plate that read; Loving wife, a tragic miss-opportunity. Sean suddenly felt an unsettling feeling rising in his gut, causing the hairs to stand up on the back of his neck. He suddenly felt cold as he slowly and apprehensively turned to look behind himself. He reaches out and touches the rubber representation of his cousin Raymond. His plaque was written with only a one-word inscription; B-E-T-R-A-Y-E-R. Sean looks at his cousin with a mixture of confusion and agitation. Confused as to how his grandmother got the likenesses of all these people but agitated about so many family members being considered enemies. He feels anger as he recalls that phone call in the interrogation room. He mouths the words, "Who is fooled by the mask of betrayal? The family or our enemies? Or is it the fool who continues to believe the lie but knows better? And is it too late to tell the difference. I hope not. I'm so sorry cousin."

(Grann yells from the center of her vault)

"Always room for more on that wall! Now come, come and step in here Sean. I'm not getting any younger or warmer in here waiting on you."

Sean takes a moment to ease the anger from his face before catching up to his grandmother. He looks around the area, noticing a sizable combination safe surrounded by a scattered number of smaller sized fireproof safes, brass items and a few other things he could care less about. Grann re-captures his attention by snapping her fingers.

"I want you to listen to what I'm saying here Sean. Everything you do out there (gesturing) needs to go un-noticed. You will have to make choices. Decisions grandson, that will alter the lives of those in your way and choices that should hopefully better your life. You will need to be financially ready for a rainy day or even a fresh start if the need arises. This life we lead is unpredictable. This is why everything you put away in your vault will prove useful. But let me be clear, everything you save should be undetectable to even the closest person to you. To be safe let's just say…undetectable to everybody until the day you are laid to rest. Your dad calls his vault "Hooker's swallow". I'm not amused although he thinks it's humorous. I don't understand the fascination both you and your father have with those vile satanic panty droppers. I guess that's why you've held on to that whorehouse you own. (Clears throat) Anyway, his vault, your father's, it's his place for riches, keepsakes and secrets. Mine however, reminds me of a family legacy and everything it takes to keep a legacy intact."

Sean rotates his neck, attempting to hold his frustration at bay. Unknowingly his movements appear like a child who was ready to pull away and go anywhere else. But his movements were actually more like he's having an inner struggle with a stronger personality that's fighting him for control. Grann holds her fingers to her eyes and clears her throat.

"I need you here grandson. (Snaps her fingers) Don't go all A-D-D on me. You never had that shit so don't take it on now. I wanted you to see all of this for one reason. I want you to see that building a nest egg or financially securing your future will take time to do. Everything you can and don't see took my effort, good fortune and time to store in here. Any basic good versus evil scenario should tell us that those who oppose your ideals would hinder you from reaching your goals. It's the people on those walls out there that remind me of that. Enemies should never deter, interfere or delay you from reaching your goals, especially financially. I've spent decades trying to make a better way for my family and those people in that hall could ***never*** *keep me from doing that. (Looks at Sean) Don't let anyone keep you from doing what is necessary for the one's you love. (Sean nods) Your father tells me he hasn't seen much of you. I know that you told me you've been busy but I'm concerned that your priorities for the continuing prosperity of this family has become somewhat poorly managed. I'm concerned that the disciplinary actions that were intended to make you a better leader may have caused you to act out. Making you even susceptible to making more poor choices and frankly it has to stop. (Sean scowls briefly) You can't lead in this family if you can't work within the structure that shapes our success. (Sean's eyes grow cold) Are you angry? Trust me the resentment will give you more focus. I don't think you're ready to lead. You still lack discipline. Corinthians chapter thirteen verse one says, When I was a child, I spoke like a child, I thought like a child, I reasoned like a child. When I became a man, I gave up childish ways. I want you to take that to heart. It's time to grow up. The things you do away from this family must stop. It hurts our reputation and profitability. Secrets strip away at the foundation of what makes this family what it is and what it must continue to be. Trust is the key. Grandson, my parents taught me that lies, threats and betrayal must be dealt with swiftly*

(raises her voice) and **MUST BE UPROOTED.** *How else can you ever be successful?"*

As Grann moves towards her trophy hall, the voice in Sean's head reminds him that everything they're hearing is bullshit and reinforces that the decisions made for financial independence were right. Grann, now pointing at her human ornaments, continued speaking although not noticing that Sean wasn't listening.

"There comes a point in our lives when we have to decide what's important to us and then immediately dedicate our every effort to that thing. But more often than we'd like to admit, there are obligations placed on us and we re-direct our efforts to handle what is expected of us. You grandson…are no different! (Sean re-engages) You may not see it but you're approaching ***that*** *same type of crossroads. And…you will also have to decide what is most important to you."*

Sean follows his grandmother out of her vault, taking a glance at Raymond one last time as they headed back to the middle of her yard. Sean follows his grandmother as she moves towards her porch and to her rocking chair. His face and mannerisms exuding shame, disappointment and a suppressed animosity. She gets comfortable before glaring at her grandson.

"I can see something is bothering you. Whatever it is, you'd better chew it up and swallow it. You're an adult now and will have to make difficult choices. I want you to think about what's best for you. But before you do anything unwise, do what's best for ***this*** *family. As you've seen earlier, poor decisions can have grave circumstances. (Clears her throat) You've got a good head on your shoulders so I'm confident you'll do what's right. And by right, I mean what's right for this family"*

Sean takes a deep breath, with his eyes still projecting a non-verbal expression of disrespect as he nods to Grann before turning to head for his car. Who knew that a flight of stairs and the flick of a light switch could finally change how he feels about his grandmother. How it gives him insight about her character and may even have caused him to lose respect for her. Even make him more suspicious of her intentions. As he waved goodbye to his grandmother and walked away, he thought to himself how the whispers of the dead are now truer than he wanted to believe.

(As she rocks, she yells)

"Oh, and one last thing before you go. Call your father! He's waiting to hear from you!"

CHAPTER TWO

Jekyll into Hyde

FOR WEEKS DONNIE and Sean have spent days full of violence, deception and misdirection. Working to build Stacey's no nonsense, no pity and no mercy reputation. The acts committed in order to make people believe that "Stacey Hunter" is real and has also transformed how the community perceives Sean and Donnie. Any attempt to muscle in on their North side business is dealt with swiftly and harshly. The violence has made the unseen Stacey Hunter an urban legend. He has become someone to fear but at the same time a sought-after employer. Even without any physical evidence that he exists. Every day as agreed Donnie handles the street level jobs and assignments while Sean relays the orders from the boss. Donnie, knowing that Stacey Hunter is just another alias of Sean's, often plays along when the "boss" drives up to have a word. Donnie is doing whatever it takes to keep the sham believable and the cash coming in. Donnie has become willing to overlook and even put up with most of Sean's odd behavior.

The new business duo is sitting on the bench where they first forged their partnership when a familiar face strolls up.

"Slim."

(Nods respectfully)

"Donnie."

"Nate, what's up folks? What it do?"

"It ain't nothing Sean. Just dropped by to holla for a second."

"Arr..ight, What up?"

"Ran into Gun's a couple days ago."

(Indifferent)

"Ah-huh!"

"Asked me to give you a message if I ran into you. (Sounding disgusted) I told him I ain't no messenger pigeon. Hire a service if you want something delivered. I told him to meet my price for my services or walk away because your dad don't get any free favors from me. Even if your dad sent him ask'en. Anyway…seems like your pops wants to talk wit you."

Sean's expression changes and his voice briefly dropped two octaves. Slim and Donnie looked at each other strangely when it happened.

"Why would I want to do that Slim? (Clears throat) Is he hoping for a touching father/son moment? (Looks like he's thinking and mumbles) What's the angle here?"

"Gun's said your dad mentioned forks and dirt. Said you would understand. He wants to hook up at the end of the week."

"Yeah, I get it. Slim, tell 'em I'll be there."

"Ah HELL naw! Send one of Stacey Hunter's minions if you have too. Cause I know your cheap ass (Smiles) ain't pay'en no one to deliver messages."

After laughing at Slim, Sean seemed normal again as he nodded and assured Slim he'd take care of it. Slim bounces a peace sign off his chest, makes some altered saluting gesture with his pinky finger before he turns and walks off. Donnie pulls a Kit-Kat from a bag sitting next to him on the bench and starts to unwrap it.

(Biting off a piece)

"Are you worried about meeting with your old man?"

"No! I've been expecting it after talking to my grandmother. I'll just

have to go and get it over with. (Flinches as if he yelled, "FUCK" in his head) Let me go find J-Will so he can tell them I'll be there."

[Later that week]

A bird's eye view sees a convertible Cadillac cruising the 312 highway on a seventy-degree day. Driving west, the mid-day sun glimmers from every piece of chrome on Robert Kingsley's classic. With his trademark cigar secure in his mouth and one hand pivoting the steering wheel, he reaches to turn the radio up.

[Dj talking]

"This is the afternoon drive. I'm Kevin Kyle, serving ya Soul, R&B, Hip-Hop, Classic Rap, Jazz and a little of who knows what in between. Punch'en a clock every day, all afternoon for you. It's just part of my charm. So, here's a jam that should take you across any Bay and into Oakland. Here's Tower of Power with; "You're still a young man". On 103.8, KXLG. Extra-large radio. Giving you the largest doses of the best music."

Coming the opposite direction in his silver Range Rover Sport, riding on twenty-two-inch rims with dark tinted windows and leaning against the door panel is Robert's only son...Sean. Who seems to be carrying quite a chip on his shoulder. He's driving just above the speed limit with his windows slightly lowered. He sipping on a mixture of Red Bull and Vodka that he has in a sports bottle while playing Ice Cube's "No Vaseline" loud enough to vibrate his rear license plate. Something moved him to leave earlier than he usually would so he could be sure there wouldn't be any traps or surprises waiting for him. Sean, listening to his GPS, takes the Kauckenbaugh east exit and circles all the areas nearby that someone could hide in. Driving slowly, he scans these areas before heading to the place they're to meet.

They agreed to meet out front of this old decaying diner called "Fork in the Road". What's left of it is sitting on a patch of dirt, on a nearly abandoned frontage road. More recognizable was a 30ft rusty metal fork that leans slightly in the ground just out at the edge of the road. As if God had dropped it tines down and it jammed itself into the earth. But as far as the diner was concerned it had seen better days. Not much was left of the structure. The right rear corner of the foundation had rotted away, causing the building to lean. A small section of the roof became dry rotted and was collapsing onto the front counter. Ivy was draped from the imploded part of the roof to the floor and was now overtaking what was left of the counter. Weeds sprouted up through the planks of the short wooden porch and consumed the entire entryway.

Sean abruptly comes to a stop out front and stirs up a cloud of dust as he slides the trucks shifter into park. Disappointingly he looked out over the hood as a thick layer of dirt settled on his newly washed S.U.V. He settles back against the seat and looks around. Repeatedly checking his mirrors and his blind spots. Preparing to disrupt an ambush if it were necessary. He quickly chambers a round into his Glock and sets the safety before holstering his gun in the small of his back. Sean now takes more precautions because recent events have made him more cautious. Regardless of whom he would be meeting with.

Sean steps out of his truck, pops the crick in his neck and walks to his rear door. He takes a slow 360-degree assessment of the area. Hoping to reassure himself that he is alone… still. Satisfied that no creatures are stirring, he lowers the tailgate and takes a seat. In the distance he could hear a car coming up the road. Not hard to do in a forgotten and uninhabited area. The noise from the tires pounding an old asphalt road is unmistakable. Loose gravel enters the treads of the tires, some rocks are quickly projected anywhere, while others rotate and smash against what's on the ground again. This distinct down-home sound is rarely heard in the city so it immediately gets Sean's attention. As his father pulls in behind his truck, Sean crosses his arms and gets comfortable. Robert takes a moment to put the top up before stepping out of his car. But as he did, he wasted no time getting after Sean.

(Approaching Sean)

"You, son, haven't been reporting to Roderick and it's been a while since you have. There's been a lot of talk about where you've been and what you've been doing. (Takes a Puff of his cigar) But we'll get to that soon enough. (Smiles briefly) Your grandmother hopes you took her talk to heart."

(Dry)

"I heard her out."

"Oh, you did, did you? Why am I having trouble believing that? At the very least I hope you learned something. (Pauses) What am I saying? You know what…never mind. (Impulsively) You on the run or something? Been hearing a lot of things and no one has seen you. I shouldn't have to track you down to speak with you. What's been going on?"

(Drops from his tailgate and kicks at the dirt)

"Just been busy dad, that's all."

"Busy huh? Busy enough to come out to Carolina? Your cousins tell me you were out there on some kind of business."

"That's right! I hit town for a bit. Handled some business then bounced."

"Tell me why?"

"There's no need to do that."

"No need?"

"No. None at all! (Gets eye contact) Is that why you wanted to see me?"

"Not exactly. I wanted to talk to you about responsibility, loyalty and leadership. (Gestures) Whatever you've been doing, I mean… wasting time with, is keeping you from your responsibilities to your family and our business. Your poor decision making and lack of interest in what you're

supposed to be doing isn't building any confidence around your ability to lead." (Sean cuts in)

"My actions or feelings clearly didn't matter when you gave Guns my spot and embarrassed me by demoting me to a low level nobody. If you were trying to make a point, I heard you loud and clear. (Swipes away smoke) You think I can't lead but you haven't given me much of an opportunity too. Ya know, my old basketball coach used to say, led by example. I haven't seen much of one from you when it comes to me. There have been no forms of mentoring. You handle me like I'm some unavoidable disappointment."

(Puffs and exhales smoke slowly)

"I'll do what I must do, if it will make you a stronger person and if ever…a better leader. Even if I have to strip your ego to nothing in order for you to understand the steps, the time or the experience needed to keep you from being weak. I'm trying to fix you son. (Puffs) I wouldn't use the word disappointment… you're more like a spoiled kid with money who has no clue about how it's earned or who may die to keep it in your pockets. You're not ready for the type of sacrifice needed to keep, as ya'll say, your pockets fat. (Puffs) Here's a good tip for ***you*** *son. I'll keep it simple. (With the cigar in his mouth) You work at success, not just step into it."*

Sean sighs slowly and deeply. He feels the sense of inadequacy washing over him. It happens quite often when he's around his dad. Sean closes his eyes and rotates his neck in small circles trying to release some of his sudden tension, if at all possible.

(Sounding frustrated)

"Fix me! Well, you certainly accomplished that dad!"

"Listen to you. That's what I mean. You take every little thing so personal. You can't in this line of work. I see so much of your mother in you. And…those traits will get you killed out here. (Pauses) Good thing I'm here to help with that. I want you to get back to work. Talk to Roderick,

for now you'll still take direction from him. (Puffs) Let's get you back to the only thing that's important right now, the family business."

Sean crosses on leg over the other, clutching the truck with both hands before leaning his head as far back as he could. He begins to make low short resonating tones before clearing his throat and forcing out a non-disrespectful response.

(With animosity)

"I'm afraid dad, that that isn't in my best interest!"

"Oh, it isn't? Does this have anything to do with this guy I hear you're working for?"

(Body tenses)

"Absolutely nothing to do with it. This is about ***my*** *opportunity to do things my way and make a shit load of money in the process."*

"And how do you intend to do that? You're taking orders from an outsider. I assume you're not even getting an even third of the take. Let's hope Donnie doesn't pull in more than you. Is this your idea of personal advancement? You're walking yourself to a crossroads son (Flicks ashes) and you'd better be sure about the direction you take. The decision you make can be life changing or life ending. (Quickly spoken) There's no threat with what was just said. Look, you are going to either demonstrate a revitalized loyalty to your family or suffer a fate similar to the others who decided to choose poorly."

Sean crosses his arms and closes his eyes again. He takes two abrupt short breaths before taking a long deep one and then he exhales slowly. His father looks away. Waiting for what he considers as Sean's theatrics to stop. He was filled with a flood of emotion and had finally reached a boiling point that cracked his psyche. Sean's eyes fluttered and then opened slowly with a wicked disposition. Something was now different about his expression, his mannerisms and his demeanor. His father didn't see it. It was gradually happening right in front of Roberts eyes and he would never know in those moment Sean's eyes were closed, he was losing his son. The more Robert rambled on; the more dominant Stacey became. In the blink of an eye some might say that when he opened his eyes, Sean was gone. Now his eyes hurled daggers of disrespect, his expression exuding contempt and the tone of his voice was deeper than Sean had ever spoken.

(With contempt)

"I finally get to see ***THE*** *man others aspire to be. Others…but not me! Why do I feel like I've been in this exact moment before? (Sucks teeth) Remind me again (looks around) why we're out here talking?"*

Stacey loudly sucks on his teeth. Pulls a toothpick from his pocket, puts it in his mouth and occasionally pulls it out to bolster his contemptuous expression. Robert takes his cigar from his mouth and gives his son a displeasing glare.

"Boy, I swear you're scatter brained most days. This is exactly what bothers me about you. You're never in the moment when it calls for you to be. Pay attention! (Pauses) This has always been about ***your*** *loyalty to this family and whether or not you can take the direction given to you. So you can first, contribute to the financial advancement of our family. Second, prove you have what it takes to lead someday. Right now, I don't think you do and I'm unsure if you ever will. But…baby steps son…until you stop performing like one."*

(Sarcastically)

"You make it sound so…um, inviting. However, I will decide what to do? I almost feel like I don't want to miss out on sustaining an empire that I have to prove myself to lead. Maybe there isn't anything better out there for me. (Scoffs) But I'm sure I'll find something, Pops!"

(Exhaling smoke)

"From where I'm standing the choices should be obvious. I want to hear you say you're ready to do what's right. Ready to get back to business?"

"For You? I…won't…do…that! I don't need to. And from now on, will never have to!"

(Chuckles)

"Still like doing things the hard way. (Softly) Damn!"

Stacey reaches into his pocket and pulls out an old business card. He folds it and starts to clean his fingernails.

"Not the hard way. From now on…the only way that's acceptable. Mine!"

"Right now, son I'm not sure if you're being stubborn, stupid, and selfish or downright ass backwards with any or all of your decisions lately. (Puffs) I expected better from you."

Stacey continues to look at Robert with a mild discontent. With his head tilted, lips twisted and eyes full of malice. He sucks his teeth a couple of times before responding.

"Son? You really don't know anything about me? I'm not surprised! (Shifts toothpick) I'm not who I appear to be and your opinion of me is only going to get worse. I don't expect you to understand or even care about anything I'm involved in. Truthfully, it doesn't matter to me if you do. I'm done with that old life Pops. Get on board…or get run over."

"Now you see, that's where you are wrong and clearly you need a reminder. Even if you decided to continue the foolish financial venture with Donnie, you should've also reminded each other that there is a protocol. That's right, a hierarchy that must be followed. (Mannerisms change) Word has it that profits are growing on the North-side. If that is true, then a percentage has to be paid to the counsel and let me tell you that no one has seen a dime from Donnie since the Cat left the yard. That's when his revenue dried up. Tough break back then but now, what's due…must be paid."

(Authoritatively)

"Donnie's not running the North-Side anymore. I have no intention to give away anything I earn to anyone either."

"That's not your decision is it son? You're working for some mystery man. (Pauses) He'll have to come to some arrangement as soon as you explain how things work around here. I'm expecting you to take care of that."

(Scoffs loudly)

"Don't hold your breath Pops. Your message was already received and rejected just as quickly as it was relayed. So, hear me closely, (voice deepens) I'm not worried about threats, consequences or much else at this point. You are not on my payroll and I'm not paying anything so you can feel like you are."

Stacey flicks the paper he was using to clean his nails to the ground. He pulls his keys from his pocket, presses a button on the faub to start his truck and closes the tailgate.

"Things are how I want them to be Pops. You might want to check on your own operation. People close to you aren't who you think they are. Tighten up your shit! (Without looking back) I'm gone. I've got other things to do."

Stacey snidely looks back and throws up a peace sign to Robert, sneering devilishly as he gets into the truck.

"I didn't say we were done here!"

"You didn't have too Pops. I know when I've had enough. I've got more important shit to do at the moment. I'm out!"

Robert stands looking disconcerted watching as his son circles the fork, still glaring disrespectfully as he drives away. Robert expels his cigar butt from the tip of his fingers with an intense velocity. He watches as the Range rover disappears from his view and thinks to himself as he lights another cigar.

(Shaking his head)

"Always the hard way. That boy is going to force a conclusion that I won't be able to stop or live with."

CHAPTER THREE

Make them believe

[New York. Manhattan Apartment, 8:30pm Two weeks ago.]

SLIM NATE SIGNALS with a nod of his head that he is ready. He squeezes the handle of his gun tightly as he raises his leg and kicks open the door to apartment B307. Slim and his cohort burst in violently as they startle the man sitting on his couch. Nate yells, "Grab his Bitch ass!" as the big dude hurdles the couch and smashes the apartment's owner into his coffee table. Then lifts him to his feet quickly and puts him into a light sleeper hold.

(Groaning)

"What the fuck! Let me go! What is this shit?"

Slim Nate comes around the couch, shamefully looking at the man as he struggles to get free.

"Can you keep him quiet? At least until... (Pauses and nods) you know." Nate asks.

A thirty-five-inch tiger striped arm flexes and tightens around this man's neck, causing him to choke and stop moving altogether. Nate slips his gun into the holster inside his jacket before speaking again.

"Thanks Tom Cat. Shit! You've made me a believer. I guess that

wrestling shit is real. No disrespect. (Pauses) Oh, you can ease up a bit. I've got a few questions for him."

Slim tries to get eye contact.

"Dude, I know you can hear me. Just nod if you find it hard to speak. Are you…Garza? (He nods yes) Do you have any idea why we are here?"

Garza tries to speak but struggles under the restraint.

"Tom Cat, can you ease up a little more?"

The vein in Tom Cat's bicep becomes less prominent as his muscles begin to relax. Garza gasps as if he had just come from under water. Then softly answers, "No."

"Two and a half weeks ago you were in Vegas at a strip club. You were given 72 hours to come up with Sean's money…and you didn't. He also told you not to make him come and find you…didn't he? (Pokes him in the chest) So what do ya know? (Gestures) Poof! Here we are."

(Nervously)

"I did try to contact him and couldn't get any response. (Curiously) He sent you after me? (Impulsively) I have his money! You can take it now!"

"Oh, we intend to take a lot more that that! (Smiles) See now, you are what some might say… are a day late and a dollar short. Sean, as strange as it may seem, is no longer in control. Which has made Stacey's expectations of outstanding debts a major priority? ***We*** *are here only to bring you back to him."*

(Still nervous and pointing)

"I don't know a Stacey. I haven't done business with him. But Sean's money is ***right*** *there. You can just take it and leave."*

"It's not that simple Mr. Garza and I'm not going to complicate the issue talking to you about things I'm not aware of. Any missing details can be discussed with Stacey or Sean if he emerges."

Garza continues to struggle and repeatedly calls out to be released. Slim Nate signals Tom Cat by holding out his fist, turning it and squeezing tightly. Tom Cat in turn applies pressure to Garza's neck until his body goes limp.

"Just lay him on the couch for now Tom Cat until I come back with the bag and the knock out syringe. Make sure he doesn't wake up too quickly. (Stops at the door) Can you also break that TV stand apart? I think he was pointing to it when he was talking about the money. I'll be right back."

Nate heads out of the apartment, drawing no attention to himself but hurries back. He gives Garza a shot of something that will keep him unconscious for a lengthy period of time. With Tom Cat's help they lay out a body bag and stuff Garza and all the money they could find into it. "Here, put this on." Nate shouts as he throws Tom Cat a paramedic's shirt. As he gets buttoned up, Nate checks the hallway to make sure it's clear.

"What's out there?" Tom asks.

"Nothing. I mean no one. Which is exactly what I want to see. We don't want anyone knowing what apartment we come out of. (Pauses) Ready? (Winks) Cool! Let's go!"

Each of them grabs an end of the bag and lay it on a cart that Nate had sitting near the elevator. Virtually undetected they get Garza into a van and take a short drive to Westchester Airport. Once they reach the hanger, they secure the unconscious cargo onto a small aircraft.

"What now?" Tom Cat asks.

"Well, I'm afraid it's the end of the road on this job for you. (Hands him a roll of cash) I'll get him to Stacey so I can get paid as well. Stacey said he'd be in touch if he needs you."

The two shake hands before Tom Cat gets into the van and drives away. Slim Nate administers another dose of whatever is in that syringe and then hides it when the pilot asks him to get strapped in. He acknowledges the pilot, discreetly zips the bag closed and asks for an ETA as he takes his seat.

[Grassy farmland, Sacramento, Ca. 3:20am
Unadvisedly Longer than 72 hours]

(One week ago)

The light of a flame brightens the darkness slightly but struggles to stay lit in the brisk morning air. The flame dances along the visco fuse, snapping and popping until it ignites the first clump of dry hay. Fighting against the air, the flames struggle to spread. Coasting along the bottom of the 8ft x 11ft wooden structure until the flames eventually consume the entire gasoline-soaked floor before scorching and climbing the walls. Long air holes that were cut into the floor allow smoke to consume the inside of the structure. But with nowhere for the smoke to escape, it gets thicker as the snapping flames begin to blaze. The soft murmur of coughs cannot be heard over the crackle of the burning hay. A groggy, half dazed man tries to lift his head but finds it difficult as he struggles to breath. He finds himself immobilized after jerking and tugging at his restraints to get free. The force of the heat and the thickness of the smoke causes him to squint at first. Then turn his head as the sound of his choking synchronizes with the echoing movement of the chains that keep him from escaping. The thick black smoke tumbles in circles above his head in the small space below the roof and fills his lungs every time he coughs and tries to call out for help. Suddenly there was a loud pop before the flames consumed the entire structure. His attempts to find air, to get free and the hope of surviving fades as his consciousness does.

The heat from the flames burn hotter than a high school bonfire but rage like an exploding tanker truck as the billows of black smoke fill the morning air. The scent of cooking flesh is too much for one of the two men to handle as they watch the shack roast. He begins to heave and then throws up on the farms grassy field. The other man looks at him as he bends over and is yakking his guts up. He slowly backs away from the heat, still looking at the man who is hunched over and begins to yell.

"Fuck'en pansy! Like you've never been to a fuck'en bar-b-que! So... because you don't smell charcoal, you getting sick? Stand your hunch'en ass up and stop killing that grass! You're s'posed to be roasting marshmallows when a fire burns like that. Not coughing up corn!"

He scoffs and shakes his head as he watches him stand up and wipe his mouth.

(Sarcastically)

"You good yet? (The other nods) Cool! Let's go before that smoke starts to call somebody. (Still shaking his head) Good thing I've got some water in the car. You can rinse with it. Make sure you do it before you get in. There's no way you're riding with me with your breath smelling like...Yak. Now hurry up, we have to start setting up for the next guy."

[Mia's place currently]

Ana makes herself comfortable in the apartment Mia made home when they first got into town. She tries to sit comfortably in one of the two chairs that are in Mia's empty living room. Ana peers at an ol' west picture of Mia and her twin brother that's hanging on the wall while she waits on Mia to come out of the kitchen.

(Loudly)

"Hey Ana, do you want ice?'

"Yes!"

"Wait! Damn, I don't have any. My trays are empty."

"That's ok. Just put it in a glass."

"Is the bottle, ok? I don't have any dishes."

(Laughing)

"Yes, that's fine."

Mia comes from her kitchen with two bottles of Cola in her hands and sets them down on the one speaker that's turned on its side between the two chairs before she sits down.

"Thank you, Mia. I thought you were going to fix this place up?"

"Eh…I was, but I've been away more than I've been here. So, I have never actually gotten around to it."

Ana takes a sip of her drink and sets her bottle back onto the speaker. She crosses her legs and tries to get comfortable in the rolling style office chair she's sitting in.

"So, Mia, you sounded a bit excited when you called. Since you've made me wait, I'm expecting somewhat of a juicy story. Don't keep me waiting. What's up?'

(Eyebrow rises)

"That thing with Kingsley's son is over. It's done. Sean kicked me out. I mean he kicked Keisha out."

"What?"

"I mean Stacey kicked me out."

"When did that happen, Mia?"

"About two days ago."

(Inquisitively)

"So, it manifested? The alter ego? I thought that was only happening when he slept."

"Well, it seems he's become a Day Walker! (Laughs)

"That's fascinating. You've got my attention."

(Mia sips her drink)

"He came home a little after one in the afternoon. I knew right off something wasn't right and it had nothing to do with the two women that walked in with him. My first indication was with the way he moved. The second was that toothpick sticking out of his mouth and finally, that brash confidence that seemingly erased his normally half-witted bravado. He appeared quicker, sharper and unaffected by my sarcastic replies. He took them in stride and was now very direct with what he said. (Chuckles) Like I said, he came through the door with two skanky bitches on his arm. Now I

know that he has many that work for him but he's never brought any home. It bothered me, how he slowly moved that toothpick from one side of his mouth to the other. I was sitting on the chair in the living room watching TV. He began annoyingly clearing his throat before he looked over at me. Looking at me as if I'm some long-lost stalker who surprisingly climbed a fire escape just before popping up at the worst opportune time. He turns my direction and says with contempt, what the fuck are you doing here? I looked at him and said, uh…dumb ass, I live here. (Points at herself) Uh, I'm the girlfriend. That shouldn't be hard to remember… short bus. (Mia smirks) Then I asked about the skank bookends he came home with. Without hesitation he replies, (Mocking the low voice) bullshit! Stacey Hunter aint got any live-ins and once again… who da fuck are you? He then said, look here, whoever you are, you need to raise up, get your shit and go! (Mia sips her drink again) Can you believe that shit?"

"That's unlike him Mia."

(Quickly)

"I know, that's so…unlike ***Sean****. But Stacey looked at me with this partly confused but mostly annoyed expression and said, seriously… who the fuck, are you? My place is only a pleasure pass through for my women. I've always lived alone. It keeps things uncomplicated. I only do… uncomplicated. Looking at you, you're not even my type. I like my women tom-boyishly feminine with a slight authority complex. You don't look like you fit the bill."*

(Laughs)

"So, the alter ego likes the woman you normally are Mia? Not Keisha, the fake girlfriend you've been masquerading to be for Sean. That's a bit funny."

"Ha-ha-ha. I was gonna flip the script, pull my gun from under the pillow and bust a cap in his chauvinist sounding ass. You know, see if that hot lead would make his blood boil for me then! (Scoffs) But before I could

answer or move, he started telling the skanks to wait at the dining room table. I took that moment he distracted himself to slide my gun back under the pillow. He then returned his attention to me and the next thing he said was with a charisma Sean just doesn't possess. He took his jacket off, laid it over the top of the couch before coming around the other side and sitting down as close to me as he could get. He stretched out and crossed one leg over the other along the outer left side of the coffee table. Although he removed the toothpick and set it atop a coaster in front of himself, he still sucked his teeth as he spoke. I looked directly into his eyes and I saw something different. He was confident, he was charming, he was direct, and he was…"

(Simultaneously)

"Everything Sean is not!"

"Right! Egg-xactly Ana! You get it! (Chuckles) So he cracks a smile and says, let's slow down a minute. I know this is coming at you a bit fast but understand it's turning my head a bit also. I can see by how comfortable you seem to be in that chair that you're not a crazy squatter. You both, the chair and you, look so cozy together. What I'm having trouble with or maybe it's more of a memory lapse, is that I don't recall having a live-in girlfriend when I woke up this morning. (Pauses) But strangely I seem to recognize you from a dream. Look, there's no way around it, I'm gonna be the bad guy here and I'm proudly ok with that. (Pauses) I'm sure you're terrific. I'm sure somebody somewhere can't get enough of you but my truth in all of this is that I have absolutely no memory of you. Nor of you and I in any intimate fashion. That's fucked up…I know but (Gestures) Stacey Hunter doesn't embellish the truth. So, whatever ***you*** *thought we had couldn't have been real. Even looking at you now, I feel nothing."*

"No! WOW, are you kidding?"

"Wait Ana, he turns and says, do you have somewhere to go? He waits for me to respond, then sighs and says...that's great. I'll give you a couple of hours to collect what you need and make a new start of it. Ok great!

You've been really good about this. Thanks for not making this difficult. (Mia reaches for her drink) Girl, he taps my knee, gets up and mumbles, good talk."

"Mia, did you make that last part up? I mean, who talks like that?"

"No, that really happened. He actually said it. Just before he popped up from the couch, called for the skank squad and asked me to give back any and all keys before he walked out the door. Ana, if he had been someone I actually cared about, I swear I would have been this close to punching him in the neck."

(Laughing)

"I'm sure you would have done more than that."

"Hey, who knew when you gave me this assignment that things would get so strange. I didn't know sub-consciously hearing his cousin's voice would trigger all of that. I knew when he started flipping out that I wouldn't be staying around him much longer. Could you imagine? I wanted to hurt him as he spoke. I'm better off not being there."

"I didn't expect anything to be festering inside him like that either. We only wanted you to keep tabs on him. Try to slip in some subliminal messages and intensify the issues between him and his dad. No one could have foreseen a split personality lying dormant in him. (Eyebrow rises) This new development ought to make things more interesting."

"Interesting? You've hit that right on the head. I'm just saying Ana, and hear me when I say…he's wasting no time settling into the other personality. There are stories being told about (Uses air quotes) Stacey's vicious nature. And he's leaving no doubt that there is ***no*** *more Sean between those ears. He's got street thugs waiting in line to work for him but scared to death because they do."*

"Mia, honestly how is he doing that?"

"With money and intimidation. Many say some of the things he does is brutal. How folks know he's behind the torturing or the murders with

no trace of evidence pointing to him is worth figuring out. Sean was smart but not as clever as Stacey seem to be. But he is making believers out of a lot of people. They physically stare Sean in the face but follow a completely different man. (Sips drink) Stacey Hunter."

"I'm just not understanding some of this Mia. What makes them suddenly so afraid?"

"Did you hear what happened at the abandoned farm about 30 miles outside of Sacramento? (Ana shakes her head) It was all over the news a couple weeks ago."

[Flashback] Local broadcast two weeks ago

"An unidentified mans charred remains were found today on a farm just outside of Sacramento. The body had been chained and suspended in the air as a small wooden structure burned and collapsed around him. Authorities have not yet identified the victim but an investigation is currently underway." [End flashback]

"I heard about it, Mia but how does anyone know that he was behind it?"

"Apparently the up chucker that was with him is trying to build his own street cred by telling folks that he was there."

"Interesting developments Mia but I want to circle back to something you said. Fire escapes? That reference seemed a bit personal."

"Well, I will admit that I've climbed a few, all in an effort to gaze for the truth. Then I release my emotions by beating the shit out of 'em for lying. (Laughs) I've done my share."

"But getting back to Sean, this is still out of character for him."

"Maybe for Sean but not for Stacey. (Pauses) Ana, people are saying that the examples that he is making of people who cross him are creatively brutal. This has become his calling card and no one in that area wants to see that side of Stacey."

"What about Mr. Kingsley? How has he reacted to the change in his son?'

"I'm hearing that he is firm in his belief that Sean isn't capable of these horrific things and believes they're creative lies that are keeping people from challenging Sean or Donnie."

"Yea, well…he won't believe anything until he hears it from the only person, he trusts other than his mother and I'm sure he's trying to set up another meeting anytime now."

"…And who is that, Ana?"

"East Street Bill!"

CHAPTER FOUR

Clues and Crime scenes

[Bonfire site]

ROSLYN FLASHES HER badge before crossing the caution tape and making her way up the grass to the crime scene. The stench of gas and burnt flesh still fills the air as the forensic team diligently searches and collects evidence around the blackened, mummy-like cadaver as it hovers in the mid-day air. Suspended and swaying by chains that have been secured to four individual anchored metal posts. As she stands in awe of such a brutal death, Roslyn stares off into space, focused on a series of memories involving her and her husband. The old images fade as she looks toward the African-American man standing and studying the crime scene. Still unaware of Roslyn's presence, she softly clears her throat in order to get his attention.

"Hey! Is that Roslyn Moreno? As I live and breathe. It is."

"Well, I used to be. Look at you! J. Everett Bailey. It has been a while but it's good to see you again. And it's Moreno-Kingsley now."

"It's always good to see a familiar face. It's been a few years since we both left the Bay area for new jobs. (Pauses) You look great."

"From you, I'll take that. (Smiles) Thank you! I know ***you*** *never hand out many compliments. (Survey's area) This looks pretty gruesome. You may*

have your work cut out for you. If you don't mind me being nosey, what happened here?"

(Walks to her)

"This is a variation of an old torture technique called the hangman. I read a case file on it three years ago. This victim was restrained with chains around the wrists, ankles, and then secured to beams concreted into the ground. In the older case, the murderer built a bonfire around the body but could never get it hot enough to do much more than char the captive's flesh. The fire eventually burned the ropes from the posts and to the murderer's dismay gave the victim a fighting chance to escape. The file referenced two additional similar cases. It was notated that the murderer may have been working out the bugs. Evidence showed some slight evolution to the supplies and the technique used. Some of the others were killed before the fires scorched their bodies. But that serial murderer was eventually caught before his fourth victim was harmed. (Clears throat) The file references the only guy convicted for the crimes. Who only went by Slicky Bo. He is currently doing time for at least the last hangman attempt. But this scene, although similar, is far more advanced in its execution. Clearly done by a copycat but feels like a retaliation scenario to me"

"What gives you that impression?"

"We have found trace elements of gasoline-soaked hay in the surrounding area and some other substance we'll send to have tested. Also, satellite imaging showed nothing here a few days ago but suddenly a wooden structure appears according to locals (Points) or at least what's left of it. As you can see, the metal posts were anchored into the ground and metal flooring welded to the posts before what's left of the wooden shack was built around it all. The holes you see, those were pre-cut into the flooring to provide air to help the fire breath. But we've found no evidence of a chimney so there was nowhere for the smoke to escape. The flames did get hot enough to bring the structure down but didn't reach temperatures hot

enough to cremate the victim. See how the chains are secured to the posts and the victim secured to the chains? That ensures the flames wouldn't set the victim free. This fire did get really hot, so we are going to send samples to the lab to determine the accelerant used. There was something more than just gasoline used to bring this thing down. We also believe that the victim died from smoke inhalation long before the burning structure fell to ashes around him. So, although we have found traces of singed flesh against the chains, he may have died long before feeling his flesh roasting could have ever affected him. But to answer your question, only a sick bastard would do something like this to a total stranger. In these parts…this seems personal."

"Have you identified the victim yet?"

"Not yet. Coroners will compare his dental work with the records data base once they start the autopsy."

"I'd guess the murderer intended for the victim to be helpless looking at the awkward way the body is strung up."

"Yeah, I'd say so. To have the torso and the legs twisted in opposite directions of each other like that, pretty much assures the difficulty of getting free. I'd say this wasn't the least bit random."

"It most often never is when you start to look into it, Bailey."

"You have a good eye for this Roslyn. You should have joined me on the C.S.I team."

"I've always enjoyed the cloak and dagger aspect of the job at bit more Bailey. Out in the field trying to prevent the crimes. As opposed to piecing it together once there is a corpse to identify. Don't get me wrong, I respect what you do here."

(Inquisitively)

"So…what brings you to Sacramento from Colver city to find me out at a crime scene Ms. Roslyn?"

"Well for starters, a leave of absence. Specifically…a need for your eye

for details Bailey. It's a fresh pair of eyes that I need. I feel like I've missed something."

Roslyn pulls an envelope from her purse and shows him a few photos from her husband's gravesite. But also gave him a quick summary of all the events that weren't flashed across the news channels.

"Let me just add that I'm sorry to hear about your husband."

Roslyn gracefully nods as Bailey flips through the pictures. He looks closely at one photo more than the others. Roslyn seemed surprised that it wasn't the one taken of the tomb but the still framed surveillance picture of the truck as it left the yard.

(Pointing at the truck)

"Bailey, we couldn't get any of the numbers from the license plate."

"That's not what I'm focused on. I see there is some sort of old business logo on the door of that old truck. You may want to enhance that photo and see what you can make out. You may be able to trace it that way. (Sifting) Also, I've noticed something odd on this other picture. (Points) Do you see it?"

"Not sure we're looking at the same thing."

"There's more to see besides the obvious destruction. There seems to be a bigger mystery surrounding your late husband. (Shaking his head) The visual evidence that I'm looking at doesn't add up. You will have to look harder at a few things."

"What exactly do you see that I don't? What are you looking at?"

"Right here, in this picture of the outside of the crypt. (Points) That looks like a ground's keeper in the top right corner. There, slightly obscured in the background. See how he's standing? From the area he is standing in the cemetery, he appears to be pointing in two directions like the arms on a clock."

"I didn't notice that before."

"He definitely looks to be pointing at the top of the crypt. It's hard to

make out but it also looks as if he is pointing to the head stone near him as well."

"Have you seen anything like this Bailey?"

"Honestly, I've seen much worse but this does border on the creepy side. Is someone trying to tell you something?"

"It would appear that way. There was a message spray painted inside the crypt. (Flips photos) See it here? Now I wonder if there's something painted on top of it."

"It's worth a look. (Rubs his chin) I know this is a bit off topic, but do you still have that huge dog?"

"Bane? Yep! Sure do!"

"Then it would seem that you have a mystery to solve Velma. (Laughs slightly) You'd better grab steroid Scoobie and see what's on top of that crypt."

"You were always good at keeping things light. (Nods) But you're right. Looks like I will need to make a couple of calls. Maybe even cash in a favor or two in order to follow this up."

Roslyn thanks Bailey and lets him get back to his active crime scene. She walks away thinking about her next moves and the possibility of new possibilities that may lead her to find her husband. She leaves the farm and quickly looks for a place to eat, rest, send some photos and make a few phones calls."

(Three hours later)

The sky remained dark as it rained heavily most of the morning. A few droplets would randomly fall from the sky as a reminder that the storm hadn't passed yet. Old Jack stands just outside of Raymond's crypt while his nephew carefully pulls his leg over the ladder as he gets on top of it.

[Phone ringing]

"Hello? [Radio playing in the background] (Frantically) Wait, wait…

hold on! I dropped my earpiece. SHIT! (Faintly) All…most…YES! Hello? Hello?"

"Are you there, Roslyn?"

"Yes. I can hear you now."

"I'm sorry for the delay Roslyn. It took longer than I thought to coordinate with the cemeteries ground keepers but we're ready now."

"No worries Jack. I've just been eating up road heading back. What did you find?"

"Hold on for a moment. I'm going to give the phone to my nephew who's on top of the crypt right now. Just a second…"

Jack settles himself and tosses his phone. They both look at each other and physically celebrate after the successful catch.

"Hi, Mrs. Kingsley. Yes, there is definitely something up here."

"What do you see?"

"I'm looking at two proverbs. The first reads:

Where there is love, there is life; Mahatma Gandhi.

And the second says… Follow the truth and the journey may bring you peace. Accept the reality and you may experience more than you ever expected; M. Rashid."

Roslyn asks Jack's nephew Jacob to re-read the second proverb but just a bit slower this time. He takes his time and annunciates to make the words clear. As he finishes, Roslyn is silent on the opposite end.

"Mrs. Kingsley, before I hand the phone back, I need to tell you that these proverbs have not been spray painted onto the surface up here. (Pauses) They have been chiseled into the stonework. And looking at the deterioration of the stones, they've been here as long as the crypt has."

Roslyn hears fumbling as she looks for her interstate turn off before Jack begins to speak again.

"It's Jack again. We took pictures so you won't have to make that climb."

"So did you have enough time to see if it was actually a headstone that other arm was pointing too?"

"I was just getting to that. Studying the perspective of the photo, the closest headstone is for a man named Joseph Hartley. Born 1928, died 1979. I don't know what you can make of that but that's the best that we've got."

"I will definitely look into it. Can you also send me the picture of the headstone?"

"Sure can. Well, I'll have my nephew send everything to you. I'm not any good with those phones and that texting."

"Thank you for the help, Jack and please relay my gratitude to your nephew."

"You're welcome. Call me if you need me. I'm always ready to help."

Roslyn touches the side of her earpiece and hangs up the call. As the low volume of music plays in the background the night sky begins to darken as she sets her cruise control. She begins to meditate on the words read from the top of the crypt and ponders on what her next move will be when she returns to Colver.

CHAPTER FIVE

East Street Bill

TWO MEN BEGIN to chat comfortably in the home of William Charles Tate. Known to Mayor's and respectable businessmen as Bill Tate but made a name for himself on the streets once as East Street Bill. Bill stands mixing a drink at his bar while graciously letting Robert Kingsley smoke a cigar out on his veranda. He listens intensely to Robert as he pours the contents of his mixing cup into a tall glass. He lifts his head up briefly in order to look at Robert who is putting on an air of over confidence as he sits with his legs crossed, his cigar clinched between his fingers and brashly speaking a bit out of turn.

"You've had quite an interesting career up to now. I find it quite impressive. It's a shame we never got together on any profitable endeavors. No one would even suspect how you've gotten where you are. (Chuckles) I remember some of the early days. A street thug becomes a college grad, then a small business owner. In time you become a district council member, a city official then counsel to three Mayors and all before you skillfully become a high paid consultant and millionaire. Quite a resume and all the while you're behind the scenes. Providing information to both sides of this community and making a mint while you consult from your comfortable home just outside of the city. That's impressive for a kid once known as East Street Bill. (Laughs) I remember your days out there hustling and how

respected you were. You were destined to be a street legend. I remember when you gave it up to pursue something more legitimate and now people working on both sides of the law deeply respect you. Impressively that's both sides of the community, criminals and city hierarchy. We wait impatiently, willing to give you any riches you require for the things that you know. That's quite an accomplishment for a street kid. It's an impressive niche you've carved out for yourself."

Bill smiles insidiously before walking away from his bar and taking a seat across from Robert. He sets his drink on the small table next to himself and removes all emotion from his face as he turns his attention back to his guest.

"I recall that you also had an opportunity to go legit but passed on your chance because of family restraints, as it were. A concept I believe your brother embraced prior to his untimely death. Different paths, different choices but we're both where we're supposed to be. (Smiles) But I assure you Mr. Kingsley, the walk down memory lane may make you feel like you possibly understand the man you have paid to see today but let me assure you that my business, political history and professional connections are already public knowledge. But that old street history that we share will get you no more favor with me if that is your intentions. So, let's start like we did the last time you were here and have you taken a minute to tell me what exactly you need to know."

Robert's moment of feeling intelligently superior or equal ended quickly as an awkward silence befalls the room and Bill waits for him to speak rather than puff on that cigar.

(Exhales smoke)

"Ah yes…let me get to it. (Nervously) Time is money, right? (Humbly) I have some concerns that I need to get my head around."

"I'm going to ask you to be expedient and more specific. Time is not a luxury you have an excess amount of Mr. Kingsley."

"Ok, well…I have been hearing rumors about my son and the violent nature of a guy he's working for. His name is Stacey Hunter. I'm wondering what's been said about him. What you may have heard. What you might know."

"About your son or Stacey Hunter?"

"The Hunter guy obviously. I know all I need to about my son."

"Is that so Mr. Kingsley? (Casually sips his drink) Your son… ***is*** *Stacey Hunter."*

(Choking)

"Wha…wha…what! That's impossible."

Bill stands, picks up his drink, moves to the edge of his veranda and looks out at the view before turning to face Robert again.

"Not impossible Mr. Kingsley. But in your eyes…improbable."

"In ***my*** *eyes? You don't say." Robert said before raising an eyebrow and putting his cigar back into his mouth. (Puffs)*

"I've heard the rumors but didn't believe any of them. I'd believe my son having an inexperienced tepidness maybe but that type of violent behavior is just not in my son."

(Pivot's)

"Apparently, it most certainly is! Somehow you can't see such ruthlessness in your son but it's definitely in the dominant personality that has emerged and is now in control of him. Many have said that there are no longer any traits, behaviors or vocal responses when your son is addressed. In short, Sean is gone and Stacey Hunter is in full control. And…he's proving to be a dangerous, manipulative, soulless, up and coming force of nature. For Stacey there are no traditions and no rules and no loyalty to either. His only focus will be an unchallenged monopoly of anything he pursues."

"Are you sure no one's gotten to my son? Somehow, he might be putting on an act? Laziness better describes his character."

"Those questions, I don't have answers for. This doesn't appear to be an

event to place blame or point fingers Mr. Kingsley. Right now, your son is leading a crew who believes he ***is*** *Stacey Hunter and they are aching to be as violent as he's willing to be."*

(Mumbling and shaking his head)

"Shh…iiit! What is it with this fucking kid? (Expressing every syllable) Got to be fuck'en kidding me! (Puffs and exhales slowly) Why does that boy continue to disappoint me? He bails on himself and this family. Fuhk'en amazing!"

"I want to remind you not to overlook that. Along with this transformation, your son invites new threats but rehashes an old one as well. (Paces) It's an old wound, one that has been festering for some time now. (Sips his drink) I'd advise caution surrounding any old threat(s). It is anger, fear and desperation that intensifies the possibility of retaliation. Therefore, the probability of unexpected attacks that often results in collateral damage."

"I've got more important things to concern myself with than the enemies my son has made and what they may or may not do?"

"That is your prerogative Mr. Kingsley. (Turns to the view from the veranda) Have you heard that your former employee, the ex-muscle of now imprisoned Courtney Blake and new leader of the Westside has been hospitalized?"

(Unconcerned)

"Ronnie? (Displays a dismissive attitude with the wave of the hand holding the cigar) What about him?"

"Ambushed by a barrage of gunfire just outside one of his chop shops. He tried ducking for cover before fleeing at unsafe speeds. Narrowly escaping the carnage that left him nearly unconscious after his dying buddy imploded the car into an unforgiving oak tree. Ronnie's road to his current state was supposedly sanctioned and partially carried out by Stacey Hunter, your son. But the recovering Ronnie believes, somebody decided to get to him before he got to them. But he still believes without proof, it all to be orchestrated

by your son. (Pauses) If it was Stacey, Sean or whoever he believes himself to be, with Ronnie surviving, there will be some form of retaliation. No matter who he believes is at fault."

Bill turns, waiting for a comment or reaction from Robert. But when he just sat there puffing his cigar, Bill continued to talk.

"He woke up in the I.C.U about a week ago and remained silent for the most part. I'm speaking about Ronnie. He lay there and hadn't uttered a word until he could talk with someone he trusted. I'm told he was brief as he gasped to get the words out. His directions were explicit about one thing. Kill Sean Reynolds. It has been Ronnie's cousin who has been asking questions everywhere he can about Sean's whereabouts. It has even been said that he did so with your son standing right in front of him. Having never actually seen your son, he believed he was talking to Stacey Hunter."

"I'm having difficulty Bill with the notion that my son could be behind any of this. So, what exactly are you trying to tell me?"

"Due to the situation caused by your son or Stacey Hunter, I'm saying that sooner or later blood will spill. Whether it's after Ronnie's cousin finds out Stacey is actually Sean or if Stacey recognizes that a threat to Sean is a physical threat to himself. It's kill or be killed for Ronnie as he lays in that hospital and he's looking to be made whole until he feels justified or he loses his own life. Mr. Kingsley, I'm advising that you don't get caught in the crossfire. Whether you feel an obligation to protect your son or not."

(Puffs and exhales)

"Did you mean Stacey?"

"I'm referring to them both, if it's easier for you to grasp. They may share the same body but they are separate in consciousness. Different in how they handle things and right now your son lies dormant."

"I understand! My son is going through some strange shit! I'll have to find a way to handle that. But when it comes to business and the streets, it's the same old shit. (Puffs) It is still a revenge driven, cutthroat, remorseless

opportunity for the weakest to fall to his enemy. I have no intention of engaging or being toppled by aggressive inexperience."

Bill captures Robert's attention as he softly taps his watch as an indication that this session is close to an end.

"Mr. Kingsley, there are some fast-developing dangers out there to a long-time business man like yourself. First, this wasn't made public knowledge but your old buddy judge Sheppard died last week and your favorite police chief decided to retire. So, you will no longer have police or city officials looking the other way for you. This city is now full of new blood and they're all young and eager to make names for themselves. Also, on an earlier note, don't take the actions of the aggressively inexperienced too lightly, even if it's your son."

"No need to warn me, I'm not very worried about my son even if he's acting like someone else. (Stands) My last trip here was a reminder that there are a few arrogant, unseasoned, opportunists vying for my demise. (Puffs) I've gotten where I am by knowing who or what are the real dangers to my businesses and me. I appreciate your advice. It doesn't come cheap. I even value it, but I can't throw out a lifetime of instinct worrying about anyone I don't consider to be on my level. I've witnessed, been a part of and have dealt with far worse than I anticipate with these young folk. That's including my son. Thank you for your time." (Stands and starts heading for the exit)

CHAPTER SIX

Bedside Bounty

[Continuous loud knocking]

BLOOD BEGINS TO spread across the elastic bandage that covered Ronnie's wound. He groans frustratingly as he pulls his red tipped fingers away from his torso. "Fucking stitches tore again." He mumbles as he pushes himself from the edge of his bed to get to his feet. Every step he took toward the chair in the corner was short, wobbly and cautious. With his injuries still healing from his accident, Ronnie needed to re-dress his bandage, wrap his right leg with a brace and use the cane that is leaning against the wall to help him get around.

The heavy knocking at his front door gradually turned to banging. Ronnie's anger at the loud banging was just as prevalent as his frustration with his mobility and pace to reach the door. Standing shirtless in military print pajama pants, he silences the pounding when he opens the door. Ronnie angrily glares at his two cousins as he uses the cane and the door to stabilize his balance.

"Why the FUCK are you banging at my door so hard for Charles?"

(Playfully)

"You scared? Are you hiding? Are you a curtain peeker? Huh? Why did it take your slow ass this long to get here? Huh, hop-a -long?"

"Just bring your ignant ass in here! (Shifts weight) Kelly, did you get my pain medication?"

"Yeah, I've got it right here."

Kelly, the less playful of the two cousin's hands Ronnie a bag stuffed with marijuana and an additional bag of special cookies that you're told to only eat half of each one at a time because of its potency.

"A full one will get you **too** *high. Your bout with paranoia can't handle that." Kelley added.*

"We'll see. I might just be what I need." (Closes front door)

"Trust me on this Ron, it's not. Just eat half and don't smoke a joint before you do. Half a cookie will give you a six or seven hour high but you'll peak at the three-hour mark. So don't overdo it."

Ronnie begins to move from the door as Kelly sits on the couch and Charles gets comfortable on the opposite arm of it.

"Got damn you're moving slow! Is this going to take all day? Are you going to tell us why we're here or is your mouth moving as slowly as you are?"

"Can you just fuck'en sit there a shut the fuck up for a minute? I need to put on a shirt before I come back in here and sit down. Oh, and I don't need to hear any shit about how long it takes."

[Ten minutes later]

Ronnie enters his living room and sits in his chair. He takes a second to open the bag of cookies, snaps off a half and devours it before he begins to speak.

(Vehemently)

"There's something I need you to handle for me Charles. I'm going to send you after somebody and I want them hurt badly. But if I had my way, dead would be better."

"Aww Ronnie, come on! I'm no stick-up kid. No trigger man or even any good with guns. I'm a car guy. I'm a driver."

"And it's those skills that I'm asking you to use."

"You lost me Ron."

"Look, everyone around here knows you can drive your ass off. (Charles nods) I know you're good behind the wheel and that's what I need."

Charles, still motionless and confused, gestures to Ronnie to help him understand.

"I need you to find someone and once you do, use your car to cripple them. Making it look like an accident. But remember this, discretion is the key."

"So, you want me to hit the streets and pull off some stunt man shit. In whatever shitty road conditions, I come upon."

"Yep!"

"Normally I'd say this is some dumb ass shit. But fuck it, I need a challenge. I'm in. Who's the target?"

"Sean Kingsley! (Taps his cane against the floor) That pampered, golden spooned, jail house snitch! I know he was the one that put that hit out on me. I'm sure of it."

"How can you be sure? How do you know it wasn't that preppy sweater wearing child porn king? You did ruin whatever little cash flow he had left by taking control of his beloved Westside territory."

Ronnie closes his eyes briefly and laughs to himself as he rubs his hand across his scalp.

"I have no doubt that this is a fucking certainty since I regained consciousness Charles. The only reason his preppy ass emerges from his cell is because he's paying me to have my people protect him while he's inside. Shit, he is not going to mess that up. But Sean, yeah…he and I still have unfinished business. If I were he, I'd be thinking…how I can get him before he gets me. He may have won the first round, but I intend to finish it."

"So, what exactly are you asking for Ron? Are you just expecting Charles to drive around until he finds him and then run him down?"

"No Kelly. That will get someone arrested. This has to look like an accident. Feel like an accident. It has to seem like an unfortunate set of random circumstances. (Taps floor again) Can you make that possible Charles?"

"I'd have to set the car up in advance. I have something I can put into the fender that will blow the tire remotely. I can have it ready to go in a day. I just need something that won't trace back to us if the car is impounded. But if things go the way, I hope… I'll just pop, slide, make contact and then keep going."

"I didn't understand one bit of that car lingo. Just get it done as quickly as possible. Sean's been hanging out with Malibu's most wanted over on the North side. I'd swing by there first."

(Laughing)

"He does look like 'em." Charles shouted.

"Well, all jokes aside, a good friend died next to me in that accident. It's about time that pussy Sean Kingsley gives his life for a life."

CHAPTER SEVEN

Misfortune is Lady Luck

THE ECHO FROM the "POP" was loud enough for people to mistake it for a gunshot. So loud it sent most of the downtown pedestrians ducking for cover while the others looked for the source of the noise. The screeching of tires got louder as the small car with the big rims careened out of control. Its front rim dug deeply into the pavement after the rubber band thin tire shredded into flapping projectile strips.

There happened to be four people standing at the corner of Broadway & 14th. That included Big Guns and Robert Kingsley as the out-of-control car barreled towards them. Robert, thinking he wasn't in danger didn't move. The two strangers standing to his right hurryingly dived, looking for safety behind a traffic control box. Instinctively Big Guns grabbed for Robert's arm and attempted to pull him out of the way but lost his grip as the backend of the car knocked Robert away from him. There were gasps and screams as his body was thrown eight or ten feet before he landed onto the sidewalk. He slammed rigidly into ground. His head hit even harder as he lay on the concrete with his arms suspended in the air slightly above his torso. Guns stood in shock, wondering how the car had just narrowly missed him. Gun's first instinct was to pull out his gun and fire into the car, but he quickly decided that it was more important to make sure his boss wasn't dead.

Big Guns wasn't the first one to Robert's side. There was a woman who was yelling that she is a doctor, while simultaneously instructing people closest to her to give them more room. Big Guns settled into his bodyguard roll, moving people and providing whatever amount of room was needed. It wasn't long before the doctor called for him to relinquish his post and be more useful securing Mr. Kingsley's head. Guns looked down into the vacant eyes of his boss. There was no immediate sign of awareness, just an empty vessel lying on the sidewalk. Guns had seen the same soulless gaze in many of the dudes he had taken pleasure of knocking unconscious. He shifted his attention to the doctor who had two fingers firmly on Kingsley's wrist. She was looking at her watch as Kingsley's arms began to fall to his sides. The doctor would look up from time to time as she worked on retrieving her patient's vitals. She wasn't confident about Mr. Kingsley's current state and her expression regarding his condition would normally be reassuring for most people but Big Guns works, intimidates and survives in a business full of deception. Therefore, he recognizes that his boss's health is more serious than the doctor wants him to realize. She broke the awkwardness by asking personal medical questions, none of which Guns had answers for. She pressed him for a response.

[Sirens in the distance]

"I don't know. He's my boss, not my best friend. Your guess is as good as mine."

She began to mumble something about head trauma as she flashed a small light across Mr. Kingsley's eyes. She sighed deeply before mouthing the words, "Thank goodness" as two EMT's emerged through the crowd. "We'll take it from here." One of the paramedics said to Guns after tapping him on the shoulder. Big Guns stood, moves to the side and became a bystander as the doctor gave instructions to the EMT's. They secured his neck, strapped him to a board and prepared Mr. Kingsley to be moved.

[24 Hours later in Southern California]

(Phone rings)

Maya moves, shifting the man that was lying atop of her as she reaches underneath the left pillow of the hotel bed for her cell phone.

"You're seriously going to answer that right now?"

(Sarcastically)

"Uh…yeah! You're not giving me any reason not too at the moment. I'm not feeling you inside me. I'm not feeling stimulated yet. So… I'm gonna take this call and give you time to move (motions with her finger) ***this*** *in a direction that ends with sexual satisfaction. Don't you want to live up to what you were bragging about? If not…you can just get up now, get out and not worry about ever hooking up with me again. (Emphatically stares before she speaks again) Your call!"*

(Agitated)

"Answer your phone. I'm going to the bathroom 'til you're done."

Maya chuckles as the man in the tank top and ankle high socks shuffles off to the bathroom. Mumbling, "What the HELL are you trying to do to me?" as he looks down at his dick. She flips open the phone to answer the call.

"Hello!"

"I hope this isn't a bad time?"

"Not at all, G-ma Kingsley. (Lips twisted) I was just trying to break a sweat doing this new work out but so far, it's just been weak and disappointing."

"I don't know why y'all young folk bother. I don't know if you're getting healthier or just working yourselves faster to a grave. (Gets quiet) Never mind that, something terrible has happened and I need you here. There's a lot to do and I need someone I can rely on."

"Ok G-ma, when?"

"Make it soon, alright! Make it soon. I wouldn't ask you to come if it wasn't important."

"Yes Ma'am. See you soon." [Hangs up]

(From the Bathroom)

"What kind of name is G-ma?

"Ya know. I'd be less worried about what I call my Godmother if I were you and concentrate on not being so limp. (Door opens) I hope that flapping noise I heard coming from in there has you ready to perform better this time because you're off to a bad start. I don't want to get my hopes up and you can't deliver. (Stares his direction) If not, let's just quit now. I have a flight to catch."

[22 hours later]

Maya rented a car and spent a few hours driving around the city before finding her way to Grann's house. It has been more than a decade since she's seen Mrs. Selma-Jean Kingsley and Maya can't recall any time ever visiting her home. She drifts into her memories as she drives, recalling a moment of her childhood. She was a little girl when she first encountered Grann. Pulling away from this old woman and wrapping her arms around the blood-soaked corpse of her dead mother on the day that she died. Maya ponders on how this woman that she met on the most traumatic day of her life, would drop by often to check on her. How she would also provide financial care packages whenever Maya's aunt needed it. So, when Grann calls for any reason, Maya never hesitates to show gratitude to the woman who taught her the most about financial independence, self-awareness, confidence, and social defiance.

After finding Grann's home, Maya stood at Grann's door with the posture of a debutant. Very much the lady her mother began teaching her how to be. Standing five foot seven, and curvy. Her skin is a coffee crème complexion. And she sees the world through heart-breaking brown eyes, especially when the light hits them just right. But her mother's DNA is only one part of Maya's characteristics. She was introduced to the gritty, pity-less, no nonsense realities that have shaped her into one of the most respected women is Southern California. By the very woman whose door she stands in front of.

[Maya knocks]

(Faint yelling)

"Who's that at my door? It's late! You ought to know better!

[Door opens]

(Softly yelling)

"G-Ma, it's only 5 o'clock."

"Young lady…that's late enough for me. (Smirks) Well now, look how beautiful you are. But I see danger in your eyes and that may be helpful. Yes, helpful indeed."

"For what…exactly?"

"Come in and we'll talk about it."

Grann welcomed her in and escorted Maya to her sitting room. As she entered, she thought to herself that her mentor's home was exactly how she imagined it would be. There was a scent of aroma candles that barely masked that old person, musty home smell. Every room Maya could see had antique furniture that sat on dark hardwood floors. The chair she sat in even creaked. There were pictures on the walls but none of them were of any family. The only photos with people in them were of her wedding and one of a young lady in a nurse's outfit that Maya just assumed was Grann. The lights in the house were dim. Grann would turn lights on and off as she made her way through her home.

Maya waited for her Godmother to get settled as the strong scent of Vanilla and Jasmine wafted from the candles burning in each corner of the room. After clearing her throat, Grann smirks and sits down before turning her attention to Maya.

"There was an unexpected accident that has left a void in the leadership of my family's businesses which may cause problems with personnel and profitability. I'm asking you to take charge for me. My son is still unconscious, and I need someone sharp and savvy to take the helm."

"You really want me to do this G-Ma? I thought you had a grandson? Wouldn't he be better suited to step in?"

"Yes love, I do have a grandson. No, he is not someone I would choose to rely on, even if he hadn't turned his back on this family. (Tips her head) But you my dear…are the right person at this family's time of need. Now listen, this is important. The men that work for this family are loyal, but loyal to my son. Generally, most men find it problematic taking orders from a woman. But I believe that won't be a problem for you. (Intensely) I expect you to get control and keep it. You've been taught exactly how to do that. (Maya nods) You're smart; you're cunning and capable of unforgiving ruthlessness. They will see quickly why you've been put in charge."

"I'll try to make you proud G-ma."

"I know that you will, but I need you to break a few motha-fucka's. That's the aggressiveness I want from you. Get out there and show the strength of this family. I want you to help restore the profitability of this family until my son can return or the right successor proves they're worthy to do so. (Maya smiles briefly) I'm going to the hospital to check on Robert tomorrow. While I'm there I will set up a time next week for you to get acquainted with the fellas. I will make the arrangements for one o'clock at Cantelli's restaurant."

"Yes Ma'am, but I need to know who the key employees are before I meet with them. Um, respectfully ma'am, you're not going to handcuff me on this job, are you? What I mean to say…you're not going to restrict or control the way I work."

"Not at all Love. (Rubs her right knee) I want you to operate in whatever way you see fit. Just do what I ask and things will be fine."

Maya turns her attention away from one of the candles when she notices how quiet the room had become. Grann had stopped talking and was gazing at the black and white picture of herself as a young nurse."

"What is it G-ma?" Maya asks.

Grann drops her head and sways slightly as if she is sifting through memories. She is also smirking as if she had just come to peace with something.

"It's nothing child. Just thinking how you can spend your entire youthful years scratching, clawing, fighting to get everything you want and then spend your golden years trying to hold on to it. Savageness is restless."

(Sighs)

"Is that what I have to look forward too?"

(Clears her throat)

"The fight never stops. The only comfort in ***that*** *struggle will be a good plan for keeping what you have earned and find ways to outsmart the ones trying to take it. (Breaths deeply) Now then, after you get my son's zombies under your control, I want you to go after a man my grandson abandoned his family to work for… and I want you to destroy him. This guy amongst others is threatening the comfortable nest egg we've built for ourselves and it's a threat that won't be taken lightly."*

"Who is he?"

"I'm not sure love. He's been nothing but trouble every time I've heard his name. I don't want this man finding his fortunes on our sidewalks. A penny left on the ground is a penny in someone else's pocket. (Raises her eyebrow) Success accompanied with profits eventually leads to expansion. I want you to shut down those aspirations. I'm not big on change and lately there have been several disruptions to our way of life. If there has to be change 'round here, we will remain at the forefront of it. Like we always have."

"Yes ma'am. I will find out who he is, where he is and shut his operation down. Including anyone aligning themselves with him."

"Good. That's what I want. Maybe then the protocol grandson will see the error of his ways and turn back to his family. Especially once there is nowhere or no one else to turn too."

"I don't know what your grandson looks like. How will I know who he is?"

"He and this white boy, they hang out in this park in the North side of the city. Sniff out the salt and pepper figures of inexperience and he won't be hard to find. (Gestures) Do your best to convince him that with his father incapacitated, his duty ***should*** *be to* ***his*** *family. (Shakes her head) His mindset these days are only on self-preservation. That boy is hardheaded and even mindless at times, but he may need to shoulder the responsibility of this family's future. God forbid his father doesn't recover. (Sighs) But first things first love, let's get you to work."*

CHAPTER EIGHT

For whom the bell tolls

THERE IS A soft chime that echo's every time anyone walks into Cantelli's restaurant. In lieu of a quickly scheduled meeting, the owner prepares to open for his lunch crowd. Maya sits at a table just out of site of the front door and has a pleasant chat with him. When the bell rings, she asks if it had ever become an annoyance over the years. Smiling at Maya from the table he was dressing, he told her that the bell is an old and necessary business practice for his family.

"It's like an…ah…uh…early warning system. My papa always told me that you want to see what or who is coming. (Points) That bell is a reminder to look up or look around. There could be family, to your delight, walking in. Or…the inevitability of someone is facing an enemy. (As he moves to another table) That bell has saved lives and averted many tragedies. I've seen enough bloodshed over the years. Have been remodeled more times than a person is business should be. That bell may give someone the few seconds they need to get out of harm's way. (Lowers his head) It has for me."

"Personally?"

"Are you asking if someone came through those doors after me?"

"I'm sorry. I don't mean to pry."

"No. No one after me. (Smiles) It seems someone can always be caught during dinner. Therefore, you can find yourself in the middle of something

meant for someone else. (Pauses) Papa always said; business, revenge, payback, a vendetta, call it what you want to but that rage always derives from something personal. It's always the people closest to you that you don't see coming. Expect the worst from them."

Maya waited, anticipating that Paulie was going to say something more but he just smiled briefly, repeatedly nodded his head and went back to preparing the tables. She thanks him for the words of wisdom just as the bell began to ring a few times.

Big Guns inhales before pulling the blunt from his mouth. He exhales slowly as a slew of guys funnel around him into the restaurant. His body language suggests that he was unhappy about being summoned there. With a scowl, Guns slowly looks around. Trying to catch a glimpse of who might have been the one that called them there. Big Guns looks farther into the restaurant and caught direct eye contact with the owner. Paulie's expression was less than pleasant. Staring with a scowl of his own until Guns understood the purpose of his unfriendly gaze.

"Jackson! Come here man. (Waits) Take my cigar outside and put it out."

The bell chimed and Jackson stepped out. Paulie nodded respectfully and continued working on his preparation of the tables.

[Bell rings again]

"Who is it that we're s'posed to meet? Jackson asks Guns who is still scanning the restaurant.

"Not sure. I was just given a time and a location. The rest would be explained once we got here. That's the entire message from Mrs. Kingsley."

(Loudly)

"It's absolutely no surprise to me why the profits provided by this group and the Kingsley family finances are in trouble. Amongst other problems, punctuality doesn't appear to be important. I wonder if the unconscious

Mr. Kingsley would accept the team being more than an hour late. Cause it's unacceptable as far as I'm concerned."

Big Guns and the crew turn around to find Maya who is now standing center of the restaurant with her arms and her hands behind her back. She begins to slowly move toward the group of men.

"So, you're the one?" Gun asks.

(Inquisitively)

"She's the one?" Jackson repeats. "Fuck! Really?"

"This aint the time J, I'm gonna need you to shut that down right now." Gun's frustratingly says to Jackson.

Maya faces the group and waits for the interaction between the two to end before officially addressing everyone.

"I'm Maya Sullivan and I've been brought here to run this crew and to repair the financial problems until Mr. Kingsley gets healthy or heaven forbid a worthy replacement becomes necessary."

[Incoherent mumbling fills the room]

"So, from this moment forward you all will take your direction from me. There is no hierarchy here. Everyone works for me from this moment on."

The mumbling quiets down before everyone looks towards Guns who is initially standing with both hands in his pockets and a threatening smirk on his face. That is before his eyes deaden. He takes one hand out of his pocket and begins to pull at the hairs below his bottom lip. The moment of silence seemed to be endless and uncomfortable but Guns eventually clears his throat and speaks.

(With contempt)

"So, you've summoned us, someone completely unfamiliar to anyone here and tell us that you're in charge now. Mrs. Kingsley may have asked me to be here and I did that out of respect for her but I only take orders from her son. He made me second in command. So, until I hear from him…I'm in charge of this group."

"I know these transitions can be difficult, Roderick, is it? (Smiles devilishly) But I will have no problem helping any one of you through it or to understand why it has to be this way. (Pauses) Let me begin with this."

Maya's left-hand swings from behind her back. [Gun fires]

The motion of firing a single shot was faster than anyone had expected. A single bullet hits Jackson center of his heart and he drops dead. Standing next to Guns, Jackson's lifeless body falls to the floor and immediately startles the rest of the crew.

"I've spent the last couple of days watching all of you, your movements and your habits. That dude was openly stealing money and product from the family. (Looks at Guns) I'm not sure how you missed that? (Smiles again) But be assured, I didn't. (Slowly averts her eyes) Moving forward gentlemen…it will not be tolerated."

Big Gun's tone as he laughed was deep like Barry White's but slow, methodical, rhythmic and bordering on psychotic. He continued to laugh as he looked down at Jackson. Before slowly returning his loathsome gaze to Maya as if he was unfazed by her marksmanship. He continued to stare at her waiting to see if she would buckle under his physical intimidation but when she didn't, he tried to intimidate through his tone.

"If you hadn't killed 'em, I would have eventually. I'm not easily impressed. I don't think you're going to kill everyone that gets out of line or takes a little extra out of the pot? We have other ways of dealing with such problems. If you take that stance with everybody, there will be no one to lead. Not saying this group is willing to be led by you."

"Like most, you use fear to get folks to follow you, Roderick. Fear doesn't offer genuine loyalty…only respect does. So once these gentlemen have nothing to fear…especially from YOU, then they will follow the one of us they can respect. I'm not here to threaten anyone. My responsibility is getting things in order until Mr. Kingsley can do it himself. No one is asking you to be submissive here. Only to follow me until the boss returns. If you find

that you can't do that and would rather get in the way, then you will give me no choice but to go through you. Rid this crew of the obstacle. That way I can do what was asked of me. And let me warn you, Roderick...I don't need to get physical with you or use a gun to earn their respect. I... am not afraid of you. (Returns her arms behind her back) So, what's it going to be?"

"Get on board or get out of the way huh? Is that the deal? Is that the threat? Huh? If I don't...then what?"

"No threats, no coercion. This is just how it will be. With you or without you."

Big Guns sniff's a couple of times, then wipes at his nose, crosses his arms and laughs again as his bites down on his lower lip.

"Then all of this is a waste of time. Lady it will take more than words to get me to step out of the way."

The rest of the crew begins to cheer Guns on as he stood basking in his cockiness and nodding at Maya as if to say...what now. Maya stretches her neck briefly before looking at and speaking directly to Big Guns.

"Roderick Thomas Rodgers. (Dramatically pauses) Arrested by the Feds for drug and gun trafficking across state lines four years ago. Released six months later after agreeing to become an informant for them. (Smirks) If everyone here thinks he's been spending every Thursday at an undisclosed McDonald's visiting with his daughter all these years, then you'd be mistaken. Roderick ***has*** *no children and has been slipping information to the Feds in a little room inside a dental office two miles out of the city. Maybe if you'd pushed Mr. Kingsley clear of that car just as hard as you've been pushing information, I might not be here right now and the crew might have never known the truth about you. (Winks) But let me prove to you that I can be fair. I'll give you the chance, right now, to clear your conscious. I'll give you an opportunity to tell everyone that it isn't true."*

The eyes of the crew are inundated with disbelief and disappointment as they began to turn toward Big Guns. There are now cracks showing in his demeanor and his embarrassed expression is not helping anyone believe that what they have heard… isn't true. Maya looks directly at Guns who instinctively averted his attention to any movements from the guys. Big Guns surveys the room, tries to clear the lump in his throat but never responded to the opportunity to dispel anything she said. Maya holsters her weapon in the small of her back and crosses her arms as she waits.

"You must be outta ya fucking mind. I have nothing but respect for Mr. Kingsley. I'd take a bullet for that man!"

"So, you'd take a slug for him but won't hesitate to sell him out to the Feds in order to stay out of prison?"

"Chalk that up to the game. You're loyal to others until you're forced to choose self-preservation. I'm no different."

*"Maybe the next thing you tell any Feds is that your cover is blown. Makes me wonder how much you may have given them already. Lucky for you…**I'm** not here to deal with that problem and **I** wasn't asked too. (Smiles) So Roderick, I'm curious. Right now, in this moment, will it take anything more than my words for you to step away? (Pauses) You deserve a few moments. It's only fair that I give them to you. Right fellas?"*

All the rowdy rants throughout the room were now in support of Maya. Amazing how quickly loyalties can shift she thought. It's exactly what she was expecting and with the waving motion of her hands, she was able to get them to quiet down.

"Your silence says more than you know. But any information that you have given doesn't affect the job I was brought here to do. So… you're not my enemy. But… from this moment forward you will have no affiliation with or any business associated with the Kingsley's. (Motions the crew) No one here will make any moves against you."

(In a deep tone)

"I'm not worried about any of these motha-fucka's. Never will be!"

"That display of machismo seems self-serving and at this point…

unnecessary. I believe we are done here. You are free to turn and leave. I will alert Mr. Kingsley of your decision to make a living elsewhere."

Big Gun's posture remains indifferent as he preps and lights a blunt. His expression was now mean and wrathful, as his eyes never wandered from Maya. He begins backing slowly to the door with an insolent swagger, taking deep puffs from his blunt that he lit as he does. The bell rings as he opens the door and turns with a sly look to Maya.

"You should have killed me! This bad decision may come back and hurt you."

"Roderick, I'm not as worried as you should be."

Big Guns let the door close behind him as he takes a few steps away heading to his right. He inhales again on his blunt and stares angrily through the glass. Holding the blunt in one hand and flipping everyone off with the other. He puckers his lips and slowly exhales. As the smoke fills the air around his face, his head turns slightly to what sounded like a pop. His eyes widen as the force of a bullet thrusts him into the glass just before a second renders him lifeless. Two big guys grabbed Big Guns before his body could hit the sidewalk as the remaining members of Maya's new crew stood in awe. The big men quickly threw Guns into the backseat of a car that sat at the curb, came inside and grabbed Jason's body as well, all before speeding away.

"That did not just happen?" One member of the crew yelled out.

(Under her breath)

"That slim guy, (nods) worth the money."

Maya turns and gathers the attention of the group. Giving what she felt was enough time to digest what had happened.

"Where I come from, we deal with problems swiftly and decisively. That's why that was handled quickly, cleanly and as quietly as possible. We owed it to Mr. Cantelli not to bring unwanted attention to his place of business. (Motions with the wave of her hand) Let's all go into the bigger

dining area where there is a table set up for us to have lunch. During that time, I will lay out what is expected of us and what will not be tolerated. Remember these words gentlemen; Loyalty, money and morality. Only one of those things is something we can loosely hold on too. Don't choose the wrong one!"

CHAPTER NINE

Urgent care

ROSLYN SHUFFLES THROUGH the photos sent by Old Jack's nephew as she sits in one of the conference rooms of Ellis Hampton hospital in downtown Colver. She talks on the phone to a friend from her department. Recapping what they spoke about a week ago as she waits to have a consultation with one of the doctors.

"The only pertinent thing I found on your head stone guy was that he actually had two death certificates. (Pauses) The first…came about sixteen years earlier than the second."

"How can that be Denise?"

"What I found while researching his medical records is that he had some kind of condition that made him appear to be dead although he actually wasn't. Examiners debated paralysis and Lazarus syndrome but could never definitively say what actually happened to him. Three days after being pronounced dead, the strangest thing happened. The coroner reported that he heard knocking coming from one of the freezer drawers."

"Are you kidding me? That's creepy!"

"Right! Just thinking about being in that room with that happening freaks me out. Anyway, the report says they heard faint yelling and that's what prompted them to open the drawer and unzip the bag. While shivering and stuttering, he slowly tried to sit up before asking what had happened.

The morgue sent him to a local hospital without hesitation. Surprisingly they gave this man a clean bill of health. He then lived another sixteen years after that without incident before unquestionably dying the second time."

"Unquestionably? I assume they took the time to verify his second passing Denise?"

"Authorities took a routine approach. His body was recovered in a field after his friend's small plane crashed. His cause of death was recorded as blunt force trauma to the head."

"Let me circle back to his first death. I find it hard to believe that he just blacked out with no other prier symptoms."

"He was tested for anything out of the ordinary in his system with the techniques and tools available at the time. I looked deeper into his family's records but didn't find much."

"Any surviving relatives that I can track down? (Watches someone approaching the door) Denise you may have to speak quickly; I see the doctor coming now."

"I'm still looking into that Roslyn. I'll let you know when I have something. Let me ask you something, what information are you hoping to get from this doctor?"

"He is supposed to be an expert on these types of strange medical occurrences and it was his father who treated Joseph Hartley when he arrived from the morgue."

"Ok, I can't wait to hear how that goes. But until then, let me just say that some of us miss you around here. We hope you find peace during this unfortunate situation. We're here to lift your spirits when you need it the most. If you need anything, call anytime."

"Thank you, Denise. That is appreciated. I'll have to call you back in a few hours. (Door opens) Hello doctor, thank you for taking the time to see me."

[5th floor ICU. Same day, same hospital]

Kate stops stroking Robert's face and tries to settle her restless granddaughter who's getting a disapproving look from Grann. With nothing to keep their attention, kids begin to act up in hospitals. Cee-Jay stops resisting after she was given a piece of candy and was told to sit still. Satisfied that Cee-Jay would now be settled for a while, Kate cups Robert's warm motionless hand, takes a deep breath and speaks directly to Grann. Explaining softly to Grann what the doctor said when he came to the room yesterday.

"The doctor told me that the swelling in his head is going down... (Clears her throat) and that is a good thing. The rest will be up to him as his body and mind come out of the trauma from the accident. (Rubs his hand) He's strong. I have no worries. I know he'll come out of it any day now."

Grann flashes an apathetic smile before nodding up and down. Kate turns to the corner of the room and keeps her tone gentle. Maya, who's leaning against the windowsill, becomes attentive when Kate addresses her.

"Have you found my son yet? I understand that is one of the few reasons that you have joined us."

Maya who is softly bouncing against the sill unnoticeably glances towards Grann for approval before responding to Kate.

"I have some feelers out but nothing solid has come back yet. I have also reached out to some contacts in Reno. They will drop by your son's club and see if he is there or has been there. But locally, any sight of him has been minimal to zero. (Nods) That is all that I can tell you at this point."

Grann, leaving no break after Maya's response, offers up other unconventional places in the city to look for him. As she talks, a nurse comes into the room and tends to Robert.

"Let us worry about Sean, Kate. You have enough to worry about with my son and your granddaughter."

Grann's begins to speak slowly. Suddenly keeping a closer eye on what the nurse was doing and clearly bothered by her actions.

(Agitated)

"What in the blue blazes are you doing over there? (Points) Yes...you!"

"I'm just following the doctor's instructions ma'am. I'm not really sure what you're asking."

"My son has already been given anti-seizure meds. You all have been pumping him full of them for the last few days and his swelling has been coming down. Now, it looks to me like you're preparing to change to coma inducing medications. Is that what you're doing?"

"Yes, ma'am that is what the doctor has called for."

(Loudly)

"There is no way I'm going to allow that! Stop what you're doing, step away from my son and get that doctor in here! (Mumbles) Someone must be outta their ever-loving mind! Not today! Uh-uh...not up in here!"

The room fell quiet except for a few displeasing mumbles from Grann as she returned to speaking to Kate about her son. The hostility was all but gone from her voice when everyone heard the quick rap of a courtesy knock just before the supervising nurse came in to speak with Kate as well. The nurse seemed to be directing her attention directly to Kate. She was interrupted immediately as Grann took offense to being overlooked. The nurse then overtly gestures to satisfy her that everyone is being included as she explains that the request to speak with the doctor will be relayed as soon as he comes out of another consultation and begins to make rounds.

(Dismissively)

"Access... to a doctor's care...when in need MY ass. Fucking health care commercials! Toilets, lawyers, politicians and health care...(Scoffs) all full of shit! (Looks at the nurse) I suppose we'll have to wait! WON'T WE? (Points) Until then...do not send another soft sole comfort caregiver in here

for any reason. I'm here and I will take care of all things medical until I speak with the doctor."

Shaking her head, Kate mouths an apology as the supervising nurse walks out hoping to avoid further aggravated confrontation. Grann begins to glare into the hallway, noticing someone standing in the doorway as the nurse walks out. Kate looks towards the door and immediately recognizes the business dressed woman as her mind flashes momentarily to East Street Bill's driveway.

"Your Face…I remember your face." Kate utters. "He spoke about you. But I'm not sure what business you would have here with Robert."

"I assure you…no business, no agenda. I'm just stopping by as a show of support. Not to pay my respects. I wouldn't want anyone's injuries to be that dire. I am just in the hospital checking on a friend and heard Mr. Kingsley was here as well."

Kate's eyes remained on Ana until recognizing her sincerity. Only then did Kate nod and thank her for the sentiment. Grann on the other hand remembered her son's interpretation of each encounter with Ana and wasn't as moved or pleasant.

"You're the one! I see it now, how some folks may underestimate you. My son has told me all about you. You're a cinnamon fleshed devil. I can see the evil seeping through your ora. I'm not fooled. The devil takes on many forms. Good church folk know the devil is always busy. (Smiles) Did you step back into the realm just to prove that? (Shakes her head) I'm not sure why this day has been filled with so many annoyances."

Ana smiles politely as Grann aggressively points a withered church fan in her direction.

"I'm sorry you feel that way ma'am. Professional differences aside, isn't the basic humanity or health of any man more important? Everything isn't about secrets, lies and undermining your enemies at every turn or even at all cost."

"Honey, if you don't believe that it should be...you're in the wrong business. Devils aren't delusional!"

"...And that's my cue. Time to get some air." Kate blurted nervously as she gets up, takes Cee-Jay from her seat and leads her out of the hospital room. Stopping briefly, but only to politely speak to Ana before passing her by.

"Thank you for the concern if you were being sincere. I need all the good will I can get."

"I can see why you would and yes, I was sincere. Good luck to you both."

Ana softly touches Kate on her arm before returning her attention to Grann who was now gesturing with her fan that Ana could leave as well. Maya tips her head respectfully when she catches eye contact with Ana. Grann just twists her lips and continues to shoo with her fan until Ana is no longer visible.

"Maya dear I want you to hear this clearly and I pray Robert hears this as well. (Fans herself) The lesson here is not to buy into the bullshit of that woman's imagined concern. There is always an advantage to be gained. You hear me? She comes in here to find an edge but hides her truth by saying she's "paying respect". Showing concern for a man she knows nothing about, that behaivor is tactical. The devil before me is full of lies and I rebuke her false sentimentality. (Looks at Maya) I'm not sure what she is after. But I'll bet diamonds to dog shit it's not a random act of kindness."

Maya shakes her head and laughs to herself as Grann gets up to check her son's equipment and vitals.

"Do you see it Maya? What she did? It was very smart. It's a convenient opportunity to keep tabs on your enemy. (Speaks softly) Yeah...that's very smart. Maya, she hears about the accident, then wonders if there's an advantage to be gained. How well is her enemy? Hmm...well, let's find a reason to drop in. So, she could see for herself. She found a reason, whether it was real or fake. She'll just say it's a friend or family member. Hmm...

who's going to check? Actually, who really gives a shit about her reasons? Can't fool me! She moves just as boldly as a thief in broad daylight. Strolling in here to find out as much as she could. (Grann sits down) It doesn't take long to catch on or question her real motives. Keep your emotions in check Maya and look for the truth. Your enemies don't always hide in the shadows. Some are bold enough to show you that they are a force to be reckoned with. You can't let someone walk up and slap you across the mouth. Show them why you must be respected."

"Do you want me to look into why she came and what's she's doing?"

"Don't waste any time on that Maya. Some people my dear deserve the concern. Others will never be a threat and she hardly (Chuckles) scratches a nerve. You'll instinctively know who to keep an eye on. Forget about her, we have bigger fish to fry."

Both ladies suddenly look up.

"Mrs. Kingsley, hello I'm Dr. Stewart. I'm here to speak with you about the direction of your son's care."

"Proves my point, doesn't he Maya dear? You have work to tend to. Now go…go and find my grandson. (Turns back to the doctor as Maya exits) Hi, thanks for stopping in. Are you ready to discuss bad decisions in patient care? As a retired nurse I can give you multiple examples where good nursing has saved doctors like you from having your mal-practice insurance ravaged. (Voice softens) No threat, we're both here to save lives. Now, let's talk about what is and isn't appropriate with my son's care."

CHAPTER TEN

Blackouts

THE SOUNDS OF muffled music could be heard thumping outside of the strip club's office door. Sean rolls his head as his eyes open slowly. He tries to shake off the haze as he realizes where he is. He sighs frustratingly as he raises his left hand to rub his head but stops midway in the motion when he realizes he's holding a half-filled glass of Cranberry & Vodka in the other. "How did I get to Vegas?" He thought as the door to his office opened. One of his waitresses enters and is nervously asking him if he is ok. She hurriedly sets a drink that he doesn't remember asking for on the edge of his desk and begins to back out of the room before he could answer. Sean calls out to her, pleading for her not to leave but the frightened waitress makes no eye contact and hurries out of the office.

(Waning)

"Wait! Don't leave." Sean calls out as he grows quiet.

Before the door could close, the club's manager settles the waitress down with a light touch before she steps across the threshold into the doorway. Claire, a five-foot six busty blond pushes the door open before crossing her arms and staring directly at Sean. She disappointingly looks at him as he sits with a rolled-up ski mask atop his head, clear safety goggles over his eyes and visible signs of ash and smoke residue around his nose.

(Emotionally spent)

"Claire, can you tell me how I got here?"

"Sure. (Takes a deep breath) You staggered through the front door all clumsy and rudely stumbled passed our paying customers. Profusely smelling like burnt timber. You then came to your office, sat down with what was expressed to me as a deranged look on your face. You then continued to press your call button demanding several drinks. The girls immediately came to get me because you were frightening them with odd behavior and offensive comments. (Eyebrow rises) Where did you get the fireman's jacket? I always thought they were flame resistant? Anyway, this is the third time you've shown up under strange circumstances. It's the second time you've sat at your desk heaving psychotically before asking several of us hours later how you happened to get here. (Sighs) What's going on with you? Some of the girls may quit if you don't stop with the bi-polar behavior. Let me just say, and hopefully I'm not over stepping my bounds here, but you pay me to manager this club. Not make sense of or explain any of your eccentric behavior. I'm here to keep the patrons coming through the door, girls on the stage and our profit margins in the black."

(Softly)

"Let me explain. This usually happens in the middle of the night. I black out. No memory of anything lately. (Whispers to himself) What… is…going…on with me?"

"Well boss, whatever it is, it's not my place to ask. But it is becoming disruptive to business. (Smiles politely) So if you're feeling alright, I'll leave you alone and get back to the day to day."

Claire closes the door as Sean engulfs the rest of the drink he was still clutching in his right hand. In a frustrating motion Sean rubs the ski mask from his head, tosses the safety glasses across the desk and removed the smoke-tinged jacket tossing it into the corner to his right. He picks up another drink and finishes it quickly. Impulsively he picks up the phone at his desk, hammers on the buttons and dials a familiar number.

"Come on, come on." He chants impatiently waiting for his girlfriend to answer.

Mia and her brother are relaxing in his apartment when one of her two cell phones starts ringing. After checking who was calling, she hesitates on whether she should answer or not. Meck smiles snidely after making kissy gestures and doing an impression of Keisha before telling her to answer it. Mia sets the phone as is, ringing on the arm of the sofa before she stands in the middle of the room still deliberating. Meck breezes by her and hits the accept button forcing her to answer it. Mia mouths the words, "Damn I hate you sometimes." Before loudly answering "Hello?"

"Hey it's me! I'm in Reno."

(With attitude)

"What the fuck, do you want?"

"Keisha, do you remember when I woke up in the alley around the corner from our place?"

(Assertively)

"You mean your place! Are you kidding?"

"Do you remember when I was in that alley standing over this guy? He was unconscious, my knuckles were bloody, and he was beaten to a pulp and I didn't know how I got there. (Breathes heavily) Well, it's happened again."

(Annoyed)

"And… what do you want from me?"

"Well, I need you to help me make sense of it. You are the only one who can."

"I don't know about that. Ya know, I don't have time for your delusional personality swings Sean. Find a head- shrinker if you want help."

"Wait… WHAT! Why not?"

"You dumped me remember? You told me to get my things and get out. Like I was some sorta low budget gold digging dope dealer groupie! You seemed very sure of yourself at the time. It was clear to me that you didn't

want me. So don't think that now I'm willing to answer to your medically psychotic tragedy."

"Keisha, it seems to be happening more often. I don't know what to do. I need someone to talk to. I need some advice."

"SEEK HELP, like I said earlier! Then go see you father."

"See my dad for what? There is nothing I want to say or hear from him."

"I didn't say talk to him. I said go see him. Haven't you heard? Your dad is in the hospital."

"Why?"

"He was hit by a car."

"What…when?"

"Not sure but it's the word that's spreading around right now. I thought I owed you at least that much to let you know. But…I can't help you otherwise Sean. I won't."

"I wasn't asking about my dad. I meant, when did I break up with you? I don't remember doing that. I need your help. I'm losing myself."

(Angrily)

"Well, you've lost me too! You really need to get your shit together. (Pauses) You looked at me, you ended it and you were a dick about it! Telling me now that you don't remember doing any of it only makes you a psychotic asshole in my book! I can't continue to do this with you right now. I've gotta go." [Click]

"Keisha…Keisha! (Pounds fist on his desk) FUCK!"

Frustrated, Sean dials Donnie whose phone is going to voice mail. He closes his eyes and takes in deep breaths with both elbows on the desk and his hands rubbing his face. He reaches for his intercom button and asks Claire to come back to his office. As he waits, he closes his eyes again and attempts to recall any of his last movements before waking in his office. With his thumb and forefinger at the bridge of his nose, Sean shakes his head as he draws a blank. Claire enters, closing the door behind her before standing with her arms crossed again. As Sean continues to rub the bridge of his nose, he invites her to come over and have a seat.

"No thank you, boss, I'm fine right here."

"Are you afraid to get close to me Claire?"

"Your behavior these past couple of visits has been an unpredictable masquerade of uncharacteristic and antagonistic disharmony…but no I'm not afraid."

"Ok good. But you mentioned earlier that this was the third time I've shown up like this. What exactly did you mean?"

"First, you had Donnie call to say that you wouldn't be around because you were dealing with family issues. Then he asks me to extend courtesy to some guy that I've never met and you've never spoke of. Someone I was told would look over things until you could return. (Shifts) Then you come through the door walking and talking like some kind of Alfa asshole barking orders at everyone. You were even physically inappropriate with one of the girls. Yeah, um…who quit by the way. (Points) You show up, retreat to this office, suck down anywhere from five to ten mixed drinks before becoming a complete shithead to the girls and passing out or disappearing all together."

"Where did I come from? Was I dressed like this each time? Did I give any indication to what I had been doing?"

"You've got to slow down. (Sighs) No one here can tell you what you've been up to. And believe me, the way you've been acting, we'd just rather avoid you."

"Is that why folks are keeping a distance from me?"

"Basically, yes. You come in, you drink heavily and then you go through some kind of verbal debate with yourself before passing out. But I will tell you… that every time you've shown up like this you've reeked of charred wood or ash from a burning building. And…with that said, I need to show you something."

Claire walks across the room picks up a remote from the edge of his desk and turns on the 55-inch TV mounted on the wall to the left of the desk. She switches through the channels finding the local news and then she turns up the volume.

[Voice of Anchorman]

"A gruesome scene today at a local auto shop has authorities baffled and horrified. The body of a man was found who had been missing from a hospital in Colver. Nurses say the man came for a therapy follow up before disappearing. His body was found in the burning auto shop today in a tub filled with cooking oil. The tub had been rigged to electricity causing the body to burn before eventually setting the building on fire. Authorities are not releasing any information about the death due to the graphic nature of the crime. The fire department found the body of Ronald Woodson shortly after entering the structure. The victim's body was bound, gagged and found, for lack of better words, found frying in an electrically rigged vat. Fire officials and forensic teams are on the scene gathering clues that may lead to a suspect in Mr. Woodson's death. Fireman, Trent Dilford was also found unconscious at the rear of the building with part of his uniform missing. Authorities are asking for any information the public can provide to aid with this case. More of this story to come at our live at six broadcast."

Claire abruptly cuts the TV off and quickly set the remote onto the desk. Sean sat quietly and reached for another drink and chugs it. "Why did I need to see that?" He asks after wiping his mouth with the back of his hand.

(Calmly intense)

"That jacket you had on earlier and have now thrown into the corner… any idea whose name is on it?"

Sean tries to compose himself, shaking his head as Claire walks over and lifts the jacket from the floor. She straightens it before holding it up for him to see.

"This is why I'm concerned Sean. You can clearly see this jacket belongs

to that fireman the news spoke about. And I bet you have no idea how it ended up on your back. You ever wonder whether anyone could identify you leaving that area or has seen you wearing it coming into the club."

"These people only see lights, ice and tits. Not much you can see with how dark we keep it out there."

"I apologize if I seem to be panicky boss."

"Claire, the objective right now is not to be."

"My suggestion Sean is that you quickly dispose of this coat before it jeopardizes the profitability of your club. We don't need people storming in here looking for answers."

"Look Claire, I know there are unexplainable things going on with me right now. I'm having a hard time getting a handle on it. I'm stressing and I need answers. I know I've got some shit to work out."

"Look Sean, I have enough of my own shit to worry about. I have a boyfriend that may be strung out and emotionally wrapped around his ex-wife's finger. I have a seventeen-year-old daughter who thinks that working for you or me is her destiny just because her ass is bigger than her IQ. Also, pile on everyone else's shit around here and it becomes more than anyone wants to deal with."

"Just bear with me, can ya do that? Hold this business together until this weird shit with me passes. (Points) And don't worry I'll get rid of the jacket."

"This isn't about worrying. It's about honesty, integrity and a moral sense of what's proper. I have a business degree Sean, not the questionable morality of an unethical lawyer. A lot could be at risk here if things blow up on you. I'm not comfortable unless I am prepared."

(Optimistically)

"Everything (touches desk with his fingers) here will be fine."

Claire's expression wasn't completely reaffirming as she drops the fireman's jacket. But she nodded to show that she was on board.

"Oh, before I forget…there has been some woman in the club the last

couple days asking for you. She's no one that I recognize so I told her you haven't been here and not sure when you would be."

"Any idea what she wants?"

"No. She didn't say and I didn't ask."

"Do I still have a car in the parking lot?

"No but you have that old work truck. The keys are in the right top drawer of your desk."

"Ok. Have someone bring me some coffee. I'll try to get myself together and then I'll leave out of the rear exit and head back home for a while."

Claire nods and tells him, "Right away." She looks back at him before she shuts the office door. Leaving him alone, frustrated and contemplating his next move.

CHAPTER ELEVEN

Pursuing the Heir

[North Colver, 1:20pm]

MAYA REMOVES HER sweat suit jacket and ties it around her waist before adjusting her breasts and tossing a piece of gum into her mouth. She pulls a black beanie from her pocket, puts it on and fixes whatever hair is sticking out as attractively as possible. She assumes a provocative urban pose and begins smacking her lips and chewing loudly. Deciding to position herself as bait, she waits outside of a popular Bar-b-que joint at the edge of the sidewalk instead of causing a stir inside.

Donnie stands inside to the left of the counter waiting for his order. He turns slightly and discreetly to eye a woman who walked in and stood in line. That's when he spotted Maya out of the corner of his eye. He smirks devilishly after noticing her smiling. He leans back a bit to get a better look at her through the window. Her expression and mannerisms were coy and inviting. Her movements were enough to keep Donnie peeking.

[Woman suddenly speaks loudly]

"Sir! Excuse me Sir! Your order is ready. Sir here's your order."

"Oh…right. Um, thank you."

Donnie smiles politely before tapping the counter three times and mouthing the words "Thank You" one more time. Heading out of the door he tries to gather as much swagger as a ghetto raised white dude could. He tries to channel Denzel from any movie where he walked towards someone. Donnie's confidence is high as he steps out into ***his*** *neighborhood. Maya on the other hand was trying to decide how to play it. She wonders if she should act ghetto because her Intel tells her he's attracted to that type of woman or maybe save the charade and just deal with this straight up. Hurriedly she decides not to put on airs for their first meet and just be the no-nonsense woman she was taught to be. So, she removes the gum, puts her jacket back on and covers the girls (her breasts) before Donnie steps up.*

"Nah see, the other way was working better for you. A better person than me said you should never cover the sexy. Trust...you got dat working. (Smugly) Hey, I'm Donnie."

(Sassy with attitude)

"I know who you are."

Donnie's feeling of coming away with a new love interest melts away as he tries to figure out who she is and how she knows him.

"I'm looking for Sean and I hear you know how I can find him."

"Are you a friend of his? (Scoffs) Ya can't be. You must be an angry girlfriend, a baby mama or an over eager new chick that can't take no for an answer? (Laughs) Forgive me, I'm just trying to pin the tail on that nice looking ass. Be patient tho, it may take me awhile to figure it out."

"Why should I be any of those? Why can't I just have a business interest in him?"

"It isn't normal for a beautiful woman like you to lure me over here and then ask about Sean. Gotta say...I'm fuck'en disappointed over here."

"I'm sure you're no stranger to it. And by that, I mean, women and disappointment. (Clears her throat) I'm not exactly a woman with a lot of patience and I have a task to complete so...where is Sean Reynolds?"

"You don't think I'm just gonna give my boy up to the first skirt that

strolls up and asks for him? Who are you anyway? Huh, it aint never that easy. Check with his family if you really need him."

"I'm ***with*** *his family jack ass. Who do you think told me about you? Oh…I get it. You don't know where he is either. I can see it in your eyes. Shit, I didn't want to believe that you would be as useless as I was told you might be. It's ironic how the truth hits you. I was also told you needed help running this side of the city. So, I'm not surprised. Do you at least know where your boss is?"*

(Reluctantly)

"And that would be?"

"Oh, you know who I mean…the man paying just enough to keep you from updating that bad baby blue sweat suit. By the looks of ya, he's taking all the profits. Does that ring any bells? Close your eyes and focus on an image if it'll help. (Stares annoyingly) My boys tell me his name is Stacey Hunter."

"Ya boys huh? Look, I don't know where either one of them are. It's not my turn to watch them. (Smirks) Sounds more to me like the big dog is looking for his pup. And the one thing I do not do, is roll over for the big dog. I do not answer too or provide answers for Mr. Kingsley. You'll have to find another yard to hunt in. I'm out."

Donnie twists his lips, sniffs his bag of Bar-B-Que and throws a peace sign up above his head before walking off. Maya cuts her eyes as she watches him walk away.

(Under her breath)

"Another yard…"

[Two weeks later]
[Oakland, California 2:00pm]

"No Grann, I haven't found Sean yet but I'm looking at the guy he's s'posed to be working for. --- I'm in East Oakland. --- No ma'am he looks

to be alone. --- There are a lot of people around so I'll approach when he's off to himself. ---Yes, I'll get back as soon as I'm done here. ---Yes ma'am, I understand. No worries...I won't." [Ends call]

Maya accepts a sticky cup of freshly squeezed lemonade from a vender as she hangs up her phone but turns her head quickly so that she wouldn't lose track of her target. She watches Stacey Hunter move through the crowd, making his way to the stage just in front of the police sub-station at one corner of Eastmont Mall. The parking lot between the mall, McDonalds and the police station was set up for the second annual Neighborhoods for Hope festival. The parking lot is lined with health, art, jewelry and food venders. There were also comedians, musicians, preachers and politicians all taking the stage to inspire togetherness in the community for a better Oakland.

Maya watches him closely as she herself shuffles through the crowd to keep up with him. He didn't seem to be the way he had been described to her by Kingsley's crew. He was smiling, shaking hands and chatting up some very influential people. She found his mannerisms to be odd. He moved too freely to be carrying a weapon. There were no bulges in his shirt and he wasn't hiding a gun in the small of his back. He appeared to be weaponless but she'll move cautiously in case he isn't. Maya sipped on her drink, reminding herself that this isn't the person she watched in Colver for two days waiting to run into Sean. This man is acting calmly. Not at all intimidating as he was on those corners with his crew. This guy is hob-knobbing. Walking tall and rubbing shoulders. Strolling through this festival acting like a man that's with his people and for the people. Maya watches but is not as easily swayed as most of the folks he's interacting with. She continued to sip on her lemonade wondering how to get close enough to grab his attention and get a location for Sean out of him.

A popular local band takes the stage and the crowd rushes as close as possible to enjoy the music. Not fond of the music, Stacey casually walks toward the sidewalk and stares into his phone. Maya takes this opportunity to lightly brush up against him and by doing so started a dialogue.

"Oh, I'm sorry, I didn't see you. (Whispers into his phone) Let me get back to you. (Turns) Don't I know you? You look familiar."

"Maybe you just think you do." Maya responds coyly.

"I'm confident that I do. I've always been good with recognizing faces and/or (Looks her up and down) figures. (Snaps his fingers before tapping his forehead) I'm sure it'll come to me. (Smirks) yeah, I remember. It appears your good looks don't hinder you from leading the Kingsley's crew. I hear you're a killer and won't easily back down. Not too bad of a leader either. Damn shame! The fact that you lead young horny men must make objectification hard to deal with. I'd bet even tougher for you to keep a relationship. Shit, I'm having a tough time not ogling you right now."

"That's a very sexist remark. Let me return the gesture by saying…you must have to beat the insecure woman with daddy issues away with a stick. It must be tough to be a sex magnet for hood rats. (Smiles devilishly) You clearly seem to be intimidated by strong women."

"Honestly, I just balance myself between one and or the other. If the pussy is wet, tight and won't kill me, I'm flexible either way."

(Sarcastically)

"That's so noble of you."

"It was…wasn't it?"

(Impulsively)

"Let me stop wasting time. I'm looking for Sean Reynolds. I know he works for you. Can you tell me where to find 'em?"

"How do you know him? (Squints) Do you know him? I'm not in the habit of giving his location to random women. It's… not what I do. So, I don't know what to tell you. He's not easily accessible these days. Your guess is as good as mine."

"You've got to know more than that. Where did you see 'em last? When was the last time you spoke? (Pauses) I think you're holding out on me."

"He'll emerge as the need arises. (Taps nose with his finger) Your concerns shouldn't be whether I'm holding out on you but if your crew has what it takes to outlast me."

"And what exactly is that supposed to mean?"

"You're captain of the Titanic. You're managing that team that always loses to the Globetrotters. The Kingsley's and your crew are a dying species. It won't be long before it's all over."

"You're either trying to divert my attention from Sean or that was an overt threat."

"Not a threat but my words are unapologetically delivered with certainty. Just like the U.S. mail. Treat my words like a promise from someone you trust. I'm about actions…not words. That's how I get down. (Points) I'm wondering why they sent you after Sean. I know for a fact he doesn't want anything to do with his family or their business. So, you're wasting your time if you're on a leadership rescue mission. (Scoffs) It doesn't matter anyway; the Kingsley's won't have much business once I expand."

"You are quite the cocky son-of-a-bitch! You make a lot of assumptions. Don't you think that this passive aggressive stance you've taken makes what you say any less of a threat. I would rather hear from Sean himself about what he is willing or not willing to do. As opposed to you telling me what you think he wants."

"Ok then, like I said, he'll pop up when he's ready. (Smugly) Would you like me to pass on a message?"

"As helpful as you've been, I wouldn't want you to waste the effort. Thanks, but no thanks! (Shakes her head) I see I'm just wasting my time here with you."

"I'm sorry you feel that way street goddess. I was actually enjoying myself

here. (Pauses) It's sad that we all didn't get what we were after. (Winks) But I can live with that."

"I'm sure you can."

Stacey tried to sound heartfelt when he told Maya to enjoy the rest of the festival. For Maya, his smile wasn't as annoying as the dismissive motion to stare back into his phone actually was. She turns to walk away while calling him several versions of "asshole" in her head. Her thoughts also drifted to what Grann's reaction would be with what she had to report. Grann takes bad news the same way a troubled drunk sitting at the end of a bar would take a free drink; straight with no chaser. Grann would say, "Don't know why folks bother to hide anything. Given enough time and everyone will know the bride is pregnant." And adding insult to injury, with Sean still M-I-A, any threat like the one just posed by Stacey will not be taken lightly. Regardless, Maya would have to make her way back and update Grann. While bracing for new directions that will most likely be unpleasantly relayed and hostile in nature.

CHAPTER TWELVE

Breadcrumbs

THERE WAS A moment when Roslyn thought about skipping her lunch with Denise. She felt tired, frustrated and short of options. She's been chasing a ghost for months now and still hasn't gotten any concrete answers. She toiled with what she knew and has lost sleep wondering where each clue she's discovered would lead her.

Roslyn sits quietly at her dining room table with her eyes closed, rubbing Bane's head between his ears. Breathing steadily & rhythmically, she thinks about everything she knows up to this point. How this all started with her husband's missing coffin, the words left in and on Raymond's crypt and the haunting photo of someone pointing at a head stone. But loudest of all were the words from the doctor she had interviewed.

Dr. McManus Jr. opened up an old file his father had on Joseph Hartley. It outlined every test that could be run during that era after he was brought in panicky from the morgue. Other than having signs of a heart murmur, there wasn't any physical evidence else that could have caused Hartley's unexplained deathly condition. This information didn't help Roslyn to make any connection with this man and Raymond. Nor how it could help locating his remains. She sat, her mind riddled, eyes still closed, tired and having trouble connecting the dots.

[Doorbell buzzes]

Roslyn rises from her chair and tells Bane to lie down before she heads to answer the door. She has been expecting Denise and was hoping she might bring good news. (Door opens)

"Wow woman, you look tired. Have you been getting any rest?"

"No, not very much. Come on in Denise."

Denise enters Roslyn's home but freezes just before taking a seat on the couch. Her eyes widened and were locked onto Bane who was still lying down but raised his head in a curious manner. Denise, who was unresponsive to Roslyn, began to shake.

"Denise…Denise, look at me. He won't hurt you. Bane is well trained. He won't move until I tell 'em to."

(Skeptically)

"Eh heh."

Roslyn gave Bane a series of commands to prove just how obedient he is. The last one called for him to lie down again.

"Ya see? (Warmly) Have a seat. (Breaths deeply) It's good to see you, Denise."

"How are you holding up Roslyn? You look so…tired."

"Not well at all. I can't stop the images of the past few months from flashing repeatedly through my mind. Day or night, they won't stop. (Sighs) Maybe I'm looking at everything too closely."

"You could be and it seems to be taking its toll."

"I feel like I'm missing something. I know I can't force the answers but I feel that I have been."

"You've been going hard at this with minimal support. And it does look like it is taking a toll on you. Maybe getting back to work can ease some of your anxiety. You are due to return to work soon. Aren't you?"

"In a couple of weeks, I think. But I would like to put this all behind me before I do. (Spoken softly) Clear mind, healed soul…that's the peace I'm looking for. I'm just afraid I'm never going to find him."

"I might be able to help you with that."

"How so?"

"Well, I followed up on the logo from the truck in the photo. I was able to get the owners name and business address."

"That's good news."

"I thought I would take you out there but right now I think getting some rest is more important for you."

"I'm fine. You've given me my second wind. Let me grab a few things and we can go."

Roslyn gets up but turns to look at Bane before going into her bed room. (Pointing) "Don't move. Understood, don't move." Bane groans and lowers his head again. Roslyn winks at Denise and then hurries so they can go.

The ladies take Denise's car forty-four miles to a small town called Apostasy. Roslyn slept most of the way. That was until Denise nudged her just before exiting the off ramp to this small town. This quiet community couldn't have been any bigger than thirteen square blocks. Within the first four blocks there was a building in such bad condition that the only way to help it would be to finish knocking it down. Roslyn thought she saw a sign that read "City Hall" hanging from it. The ladies were puzzled on how most of the buildings seem industrial. As they looked around there were no signs of any schools or churches. There were stop signs but no street lights. The concrete was collapsing on the sidewalks but there were no painted crosswalks. The names on the street signs were fading and the streets were hauntingly empty. No signs of homeless or drunks sleeping on bus stops, not even a cop slowly patrolling the streets.

"Something here doesn't feel right. Did you bring your gun Roslyn?"

"I'm on leave Denise. Did you bring yours?"

"I work on a desk. You know I don't carry."

The two ladies turn briefly towards each other bump fists and chant simultaneously, "Bad assess who kick assess, no weapons needed." They both laugh and say, "Girl...you're so crazy.", as they pull up next to a gated parking lot.

At first glance it just looked like a fenced off parking lot. As they scanned the area, they saw three adjacent buildings. One marked "storage", another marked "repairs" and the last was too far for Roslyn to make out. This lot just like the town looked desolate and abandoned. There was a swarm of pigeons flying in circles before splitting up with some landing on a roof and the others touching down on the asphalt and bumping into each other around the tire of the only truck in the lot. There was an elderly man moving slowly, taking small step towards the truck and kicking at the birds along the way. The ladies hurried out of the car in order to get the guy's attention before he could get into the truck.

(Loudly)

"Hello! Excuse me sir. Hi!"

Denise stops yelling briefly as the man turns and looks their way.

"Yes, hi...I was the one who called you the other day. I'm glad we caught you."

The ladies move inside the fence as Denise continued to speak.

"You're late. I was just about to leave. I suppose you're that police gal that called me?"

"Yes... hi. We're with the Colver city police department and we were hoping to ask a couple questions that may help with our investigation."

"Such pretty ladies to be cops, the best I've seen lately. Do you have any identification? (Roslyn shows her badge) Questions huh? Fire away."

"Sir, we are following leads on a missing person's case. There was a truck pictured at our crime scene that we believe belongs to a trucking company that you own. Does this truck look familiar? Is this your logo?"

Roslyn pulls out two photos for the man to look at. One picture was taken from the cemetery's video cameras and the other that was cropped onto the logo. He took the photos; hands shaking and flips one over the other before handing them back.

"That's Bessie there in the first picture. (Gazes off briefly) Yeah that truck was one of my most reliable trucks. It never broke down. You could always count on that truck, just as much as counting on the sun to come up in the morning. (Clears throat) I don't own any of them anymore. Sold 'em. Yep, sold Bessie and a bunch of other trucks like her a little more than a year ago."

"Was the business still lucrative? What made you sell?" Denise asked.

"The business crashed over ten years ago and the trucks were just sitting on the lot. Damn city started coming up with ways to fine me. I think they were trying to squeeze me out of my property. So, I brought everything up to their codes and decided to sell what I wasn't using. Needed the space, ya see. There's still money to be made even with an empty lot."

"Sir, can you remember who you sold those trucks too?" Roslyn asked.

"A politician, I think. With all the people around him, he looked important. He's not from around here but people seem to know who he is. (Digs in his wallet) I think I still have his card here somewhere. Yes, here it is…William Tate was his name."

Denise quickly eyes Roslyn whose movements made her appear to have recognized the name. She then cues Denise to wrap this up.

"Thank you so much sir. That is very helpful. We thank you for taking the time with us."

The old man waves his hand in the air and starts to move for his truck. Roslyn and Denise walk out of the fence back to the car.

"I saw your reaction Roz. Do you know that man?"

"I don't know him personally but I know who he is. But if there's any man that will have the answers that I'm looking for, it will be East Street Bill."

CHAPTER THIRTEEN

Finding the shroud

-Follow the truth and the journey may bring you peace. Accept the reality and you may experience more than you ever expected. M. Rashid-

[Easter Sunday]

ROSLYN ENTERS THE large entryway of East Street Bill's home marveling at its beauty. She takes a deep breath as she soaks in the intricate details of the marble and glass until a husky voice redirects her attention.

"Hello Mrs. Kingsley, welcome to my home."

"Thank you for seeing me on such short notice Mr. Tate. I'm sorry if I'm imposing on you during this Easter Sunday."

"No imposition at all. Personally, I'm more of a spiritual man than a religious one. Finding eggs isn't always what it's cracked up to be, not even for the kids. I like to reflect on the true meaning of the day. With that said… I will be glad to help you however I can."

Bill invites Roslyn in with a motion of his hand and begins to walk her in the direction of his sitting room. Without hesitation she dives right in with her questions.

"I have learned that your reputation for advising and providing spot

on information is irrefutable. This is why I'm seeking your counsel with recovering my husband. (He smiles) If I may, I would like to start by asking you about an old trucking company and the trucks that you acquired a year ago."

"Yes, Doug Bradley's old company. I bought his fleet to help my niece with a business project she had gotten involved with."

"Well sir, one of those trucks with its faded logo was spotted leaving a cemetery with my husband's casket strapped to the back of it. (Pauses) I'm wondering if you can provide any information that will help me recover his remains."

"I have answers that will help you but I must finish with another client first. Forgive me, I must ask that you give me a few moments to finish with them first. (Gestures) If you would please wait for me in this room, I'll be back with you in a bit."

Bill smiles gracefully before turning to walk down the hall. Roslyn cautiously enters a room that has a few people comfortably waiting as well. As she enters, she nods a "hello" to whomever she made eye contact with. There was soft soothing music playing but the room and the people in it were oddly quiet Roslyn thought. Roslyn found a seat and noticed the others in the room casually looking at each other, giving her the feeling that they all knew something that she didn't. As promised, Bill didn't take long to return. He took a seat across from her but tapped the arm of her seat before he began to speak.

"This is a rare occasion. It is not often when I cannot provide all the answers or details that someone is looking for when they come to my home. The answers that you seek are more complicated and I may need to defer to one or more of the people in this room to help fill in the blanks."

Roslyn takes a moment to look around the room wondering to herself who here could possibly help her before returning her attention to Bill.

"To paint a broader picture for you Mrs. Kingsley, I will ask my niece Ana to begin." (Motions to Ana)

"Hi, I'm Ana. I'm part of the local D.E.A. Tasked with the assignment to investigate the drug trade in Colver and when possible, take down the Kingsley crime family. The others you see here are a part of my team. That's Tank & the twins, Mia and Meck. I have been a part of this case for the past three years. Tracking the Kingsley's, their employees, the other crews and everyone's drug involvement within this city. Following Robert Kingsley's son Sean is how we became familiar with you and your husband."

"Were you aware that Raymond and I were both on undercover assignments?" Roslyn asks.

"We became aware of you both the night your husband was attacked by Angel and his crew. We discovered who you both really were and the assignments you both had after your husband was admitted to the hospital. A colleague & I were sent to debrief your husband and ask for his assistance. When we arrived on his hospital floor he had gone into cardiac arrest. That was right after seeing his grandmother, uncle and crew down in the lobby. The doctor's worked quickly but it did take a little time to stabilize him"

(Shocked)

"Stabilized him? What do you mean… ***stabilized him!*** *When I arrived they told me that Raymond had died. (Solemnly) They let me see him very briefly before taking his body away."*

Ana sees pain in Roslyn's expression and continues with a forethoughtful temperament.

"We acted swiftly. We put your husband into protective custody, moved him to an I.C.U and then restricted any information to his family and reporters. 48 hours later doctors told us and only us that we were able to speak with him. (Abruptly) He immediately asked about you, when he came to. (Pauses) He was weak and communicating with him went slowly. We were finally able to exchange information after a few hours and get his

consent to help us with our investigation. We immediately put information out about his death. Then we set up the funeral and his grave site. It's been old fashioned police work from that point and on. We've managed to put our people in key places to gather evidence and take down crews when possible. Raymond has been a great asset to this investigation. But as of late, we've run into a few problems."

Roslyn ascends from her seat and gazes at East Street Bill before turning back to Ana.

(Nervously)

"Did I hear you correctly? Are you saying that Raymond is alive?"

With a reverence, Ana smiles as Roslyn notices that she was no longer looking at her but passed her. Roslyn rotates gradually just as a familiar voice answer from the entrance of the room.

(Smiling lovingly)

"Alive...yes, I am!"

Overwhelmed with a rush of emotions an inaudible sound comes from Roslyn before she side steps the chair. And with the grace of a long jumper, runs and jumps into Raymond's arms. Despite knowing that they were being watched, their embrace was sensual and intimate as they become reacquainted with each other.

"I'm sorry it had to be done this way. It was wrong to withhold the truth from you. Also putting you through the funeral and leaving you to deal with my family afterwards. I can't imagine the strength you had to muster up until now. Sorry I put you through this sweetheart."

"I...I...felt alone and lost. I am not ashamed to say that I considered grief counseling. Losing you was horrifying enough but to have your remains taken was difficult for my mind and emotions."

Raymond takes his bride by the hand and walks her to the front of the fireplace which puts them center stage to everyone else. He looks her in the eye and begins to rub one of her hands as he softly speaks.

"After I woke, I needed to deal with the fact that my grandmother not only killed my dad but tried to kill me. The doctors told me that whatever was injected into my I.V. slowly put me into cardiac arrest. My heart stopped and I flat lined. They were able to counter that drug and revive me. If not, that funeral would have been real. (Taps her hand) Before Ana and her team came to speak with me, I was devastated by the betrayal of my family. Then I was presented with an opportunity that was mutually beneficial to us both, her team and I. My death had to seem real to the rest of my family. We couldn't jeopardize the investigation at that stage by telling you the truth. (Pauses) After knowing that I was no longer a threat to my family and clear to make moves, I asked the D.E.A to let me provide clues so that you could learn that I was alive."

"Was the damage to the mausoleum, the casket on the truck, the spray paint on the wall and the two quotes etched into the stone work all clues to get the ball rolling?" Roslyn asks.

Ana clears her throat before taking a step forward as she intervenes to answer Roslyn.

"No, not initially. We were monitoring the gravesite based on old rumors that Raymond's grandmother was rumored to grave dig her enemies' plots. Some say either to destroy the remains as added revenge or by asking ransom for their return. Of course, none of that was ever proven. We just monitored as a precaution."

"I figured she might do that as leverage to get you to sign over my parent's house to her. That way she could access my dad's vault but we'll discuss that later."

"Actually Ray, after what's happened at the house, it makes sense now."

"One of the sensors we put in the mausoleum was triggered and we caught a group of young men just after they had removed the coffin and was carting it down to the ground keeper's shack. We used that opportunity to put some clues in place and as you've said...get the ball rolling."

"I needed you to know I was safe Roz. This proves to me that I was right. I knew you were a good detective."

Roslyn looks lovingly into Raymond's eyes and softly recites, "Follow the truth and the journey may bring you peace." Raymond squeezes her hand and responds, "…And where there's love…there is life. (Kisses her) I love you."

The room is silent as they ease out of their embrace. East Street Bill settles into his seat as the reunited couple share a moment. He looks at his niece and asks, "Ana, you started to mention running into problems. What kind of problems?"

"As you know we sent Mia in undercover to become his girlfriend as a way to stay close to Sean. But within a short period of time Uncle William his mind, his emotions and his personality began to split."

"How can that be?" Raymond asks with concern.

"I'm no doctor but his behavior could have been a by-product of his grief for you. Or…even his guilt. What's most important to know is that this 2nd personality is far more aggressive, sadistic and uncharacteristically violet. We believe he enjoys the hands-on retaliation more than your cousin ever would. This change in him was sudden and unexpected. And according to my sources, your cousin's opposing dominate personality is now in complete control."

"So, what happens next? This can't be the end of it?" Roslyn asks.

"That's being discussed as we speak. The initial investigation and dismantling of the crews in Colver was going to plan but Sean's psychosis splitting was something no one saw coming. This dominant personality of Stacey Hunter has revived the drug trade on the north side of the city. He is now threatening expansion and maybe gearing up for far worse."

"Roz, for me, this has become more than stopping the crime reign of my family or vindication for what they've done to me. I must find a way to save Sean…even if it's from himself."

"How exactly are you going to do that Ray?"

"I don't know."

Suddenly East Street Bill stands and speaks.

"Awaken my son, for many will settle comfortably with who they hate to be. Never seeking to nurture or accept who they really are. It's this absurdity and lack of self-awareness that causes us to lose ourselves. Naively believing we are something or someone other than who we should excel to be."

"Uncle William, may I ask who you were just quoting?"

"Yes, you can ask. It's a quote from author/poet M. Rashid. (Looks towards Raymond & Roslyn) I'm glad that the two of you still have each other. Hold on to it. This journey will only get worse and you'll need each other to get through it. It's the second chances that some of us aren't always granted or are lucky to get. Isn't that right young lady? (Looking at Mia before he winks at his niece) Now if you'll excuse me, I must attend to some other matters. Good day to you all."

CHAPTER FOURTEEN

A Cleansing Fire

IT'S THREE IN the morning and a small mouse shuffles along the inside garage doors of Robert Kingsley's auto shop slowly working its way to a garbage can that's spilling over in the corner. The mouse stops midway between doors to curiously sniff around the moving arms of a clock. As one of the hands strikes the mouse's whiskers, it runs nervously towards the center of the shop and settles quickly around the crumbs of an Oreo cookie. There was an incredible explosive "BOOM" that flooded the auto shop with roaring hot flames. It didn't take long for anything that could burn to ignite and as the heat grew the loose used tires started burning. The rubber air hoses started to hiss just before they each popped from the heat. The Breakers in the electrical panel next to the air compressor were melting as sparks randomly exploded out of the panel. And as the heat intensifies, the gas tanks of three cars erupted and the entire shop was engulfed in unapproachable, uncontrollable red-hot flames. The light from the blaze illuminated the night sky as the smoke from the flames clouded the air. The sirens were faint but audible during the early quiet of the morning. But just as the first fire engine pulls up to the scene, a second device hidden in the bushes at the opposite end from the garage doors exploded.

[KA-BOOM!]

The force of the explosion shatters the windows of a two door Honda that a man parked on the street next to the shop was living in. This new heat source was making it difficult for the fire fighters to reach the hydrant and the homeless man on that corner.

The smell of burning oil and rubber now floods the air as sheets of water shower the thick smoke in an attempt to blanket the flames. One of the fire fighters began pumping water from the truck as another struggled through the heat to pull the man in the Honda out of harm's way. The heat was intense and the fire continued to rage. Colver electric company was called in and instructed to shut off the transformer on this block in order to hinder electrical explosions. As the flames grew even higher, a one-ton air conditioning machine and two exhaust fans fell through the compromised roof. That's when a second set of fire trucks were called in to help douse the flames from the backside of the auto shop. After a few hours of fighting, the fire fighters were just keeping the flames from spreading to neighboring businesses. They fought this fire all night and as the sun began to rise, there wasn't much to do but stand, let the flames burn themselves out and watch the auto shop eventually collapse on itself.

[6am-ish across town]

A thin ray of light breaks the darkness of an alley on 11th Ave. The vagrant sitting beside the dumpster finds the small warmth of light refreshing as he takes sips from a collection of near empty beer bottles that he'd gathered. He sat and leaned comfortably against the back wall of a bar knowing that this morning he would not be bothered. This was the only day of the week the manager of the bar would come in after 11am. This reassured that the vagrant could sit awhile longer without being threatened to move on. With a widening ray of sun on his face and his choice of near empty bottles to drink from, he leans his head back and savors the warm malt in his mouth. That was until he felt like someone had harshly shoved him. After choking on the liquid briefly he turns just as one of those spinning vents from the roof hits the ground close to him. He could now smell smoke and stumbled to his feet. He slid a couple of bottles into his weathered jacket pocket and staggers to the front of the building to investigate.

[Six minutes earlier]

The morning light is still braking and small coffee shop across the street from the bar called "I'll grind It" was already open for their patrons. A customer stands at the counter gazing at the steam as an employee makes a cappuccino for another who's sitting at one of the tables working on a computer. Tina, the 5ft "2" cashier greets the man at her counter with her gorgeous smile.

"Good morning, sir, welcome to I'll grind it, what can we get for you this morning?"

He returns the smile but doesn't respond. He becomes distracted by the sound of the front door opening as a regular customer walks out singing with his daily hot chocolate and scone. As this man with the cup marked "Fred" turns left to walk to his car, the bar directly across the street explodes. [Ka-boom] The force of the blast knocks Fred to the ground and shatters the coffee shops windows and door glass inward all over the floor. Tina stood behind the counter with her eyes bulged and mouth open in awe as her customer squats instinctively to protect himself. Fred, who managed to salvage his hot chocolate, came to his feet and turned to see what knocked him over. At first glance Fred sees a vagrant with a beer bottle in his hand, standing close to the flames attempting to warm himself from the heat. Tina comes from behind the counter and steps outside to check on Fred. They both stood silent watching the flames raging from the windows and scorching the outer walls of the bar. Large billows of smoke filled the air as the rising flames threatened to jump to the buildings on either side of the bar. "Has anyone called the fire department?" Tina asks her co-worker Jeff as he steps out of the coffee shop to join them.

"I just did. (Shakes his head) But it may take a while before anyone gets here."

"Why do you say that?" Fred asks as Jeff hands him a new scone.

"The news this morning reported that the fire department had two different fire stations fighting another blaze on the other side of the city. The firemen that are normally around the corner are one of those crews. So, who is left to send across the street?"

Fred responded by hunching his shoulders before softly thanking them both for the replacement scone. And before turning to leave, he shook his head again in disgust as the vagrant across the street sat against the hydrant and hurled empty bottles at the burning building.

"That's just sad." Tina said solemnly.

"No Tina, what that bum is doing is just pathetic."

"No, I don't mean him Jeff. I meant how someone's livelihood is burning to the ground and there's no one around to save it."

"Our tax dollars at work. That's why I don't pay taxes. (Shrugs) Look at it this way…we are out of harm's way and we're at a safe distance. Let's just concentrate on cleaning up before any more of our customers come in. (Opens the front door) Why don't you give the owner a call. Tell them about the windows and I'll start picking up the glass."

"Ok Jeff, (smiles) I'm on it."

As they both reenter the coffee shop, they turned as they heard someone shouting from across the street.

"Hey Coffee people, you got some spare marsh mellows?"

[Hours later]

****BREAKING NEWS****

"This is a Channel 8 special news report. We interrupt your regular programming for this special news report. Firefighters have been battling

two different three alarm fires through the early morning well into the afternoon. These images are coming to you live from our channel 8 traffic helicopters. Preliminary reports speculate that the blaze from the auto shop and Gentleman's bar may be the work of an arsonist. With each fire still endangering neighboring businesses. (Puts a finger to his earpiece) This just in…a janitorial supply warehouse in downtown Colver has exploded and is currently engulfed in flames. Authorities have asked for help from neighboring cities to assist in putting these fires out. This being due to the Colver city fire departments depleted personnel already battling to bring the first two fires under control. We will bring you more on each horrific blaze with our eight Am broadcast. This has been David Dunn, channel 8 news."

Grann turns away from the hospitals TV and looks at her son. She touches his arm and strokes it softly.

"Well now son, it might be best that you're not awake to see what I just watched. It appears we're gonna have to show someone that they're fucking with the wrong family. And the consequences should be lethal." (Smirks)

Grann finishes her rubbing motion of Robert's arm with two soft taps before drifting into a short gaze out of the window. She closes her eyes briefly and smiles. After opening her eyes, she lifts her Bible from her lap. As she places the Bible into her satchel size of a purse she mumbles, "For what happens next, the good word cannot be accessible or present for." Looking straight ahead now she perches her lips and begins to make sounds with her mouth as if she was savoring something she may have been chewing on.

"Maya my child, here's what I want. We cannot afford to look vulnerable. If someone is attacking Robert personally, it won't take long before they try to hit us professionally. Find out what you can. Fortify our people and verify who's behind this before we hit back. We will not budge, bend or be bullied into breaking. If this man you've mentioned is actually carrying out these acts against us, then we must verify his involvement and swiftly mount his head on my wall."

"And what about finding your grandson?"

"Your concerns currently are my family's financial welfare. I need you on the front lines of that. My grandson will find his way, even if he has to stumble shamelessly back. (Coughs) But right now there are so many more important things to deal with. My faith is in you to lead. You know what I want…let's get it done."

[7pm, same night. Kingsley stash house]

The sun was nearly down as two men approach a second-floor apartment door dressed in what almost looks like police riot gear. The distinguishing differences between the two were their physical size and choice of weapons they carried. One of the two men silently takes cover between the apartment's window and the door. He holds a sawed-off shotgun low around his legs and softly leans against the wall as his thinner partner raises his leg to kick the door in. The heavier man cautions the other to wait after hearing voices inside getting louder.

[Inside the apartment]

(Agitated)

"FUCK! Can you turn it to something ***I*** *want to watch? I don't give a SHIT about burning buildings."*

(Solemnly)

"I used to work at that auto shop. Damn, a three-alarm fire and now it's a fuck'en parking lot. Damn!"

(Angrily)

"Who gives a shit Justin? Turn it to the game!"

"Damn Jason, don't you know that both of those places belong to Robert Kingsley?"

"What you don't understand Justin is, I don't give a shit! Kingsley's paying me to run ***this*** *spot. I'm only concerned about these last two re-ups we have tonight and fucking my girl afterward. (He slaps his woman's ass*

as she heads for the restroom.) And since I'm in charge, I'm telling you to turn the fucking channel to the game!"

Justin's expression as he switched the channel looked more like a pitied disappointment. More so because of Jason's lack of awareness than his need to prove his manliness in front of his woman.

Just outside the door, the heavier man gives the other the cue to kick in the door with a silent count down. (Moving his fingers) "One… two… three." With his right leg in the air, he aims to the right of the loose door handle. With one swift kick, the weak wood around the lock shatters and the door violently crashes inward. Startled by the intrusion and the site of weapons, Justin and Jason throw their hands in the air quickly as the man with the shotgun shouts, "Git your fuck'en hands up and don't think about moving!" The other of the two assailants pulled out his left-handed 9mm and pushed the woman in the kitchen to the couch before yanking the other from the bathroom and pulling her into the room with the others.

"Listen up! Now that I have your weapons, I want everyone away from the door and standing near the TV. I don't want everyone moving at the same time. Ladies first and I want you both on the right side of the TV. Move now and move slowly. If you do what I ask, no harm will come to the ladies."

The two ladies begin to shuffle as Justin scoffs loudly and shakes his head. He notices Jason moving along with the women. Justin mumbles, "Bitch ass", under his breath as the man with the shotgun sets the barrel heart side of Jason's chest.

"Were you unclear when I said ladies only?"

(Nervously)

"I'm going to stand with whomever you said no harm would come to even if I have to bitch up for it to happen."

"Bitch up huh? (With disgust) Well, if that's your choice. (Points) Drop

your pants around your ankles and tie your shirt in a knot in the front. (Shakes his head watching him do it) That's a got damn shame!"

(Ladies yelling simultaneously)

"DAMN RIGHT IT IS!"

As the man with the shotgun pulls back from Jason and keeps everyone from moving, his partner turns over the other rooms. He starts filling as many bags as possible with drugs and money. Then tossing the bags one by one into the room where his buddy was waiting and everyone else was nervously standing. Justin clears his throat and in an unthreatening manner gets the attention of the guy with the shotgun.

"Aren't you afraid someone else might show up any minute? You're not even watching the door."

(Laughs)

"I'm not concerned about anyone else. We've got that covered. (Looks directly at Justin) I want you to stay quiet now. If you can, you'll get through this."

At that moment the other man kicks a bag into the main room while carrying two out on his shoulders. "Is that everything?" the man with the shotgun asks."

"Yeah, that's everything. Let's get out of here."

The shotgun guy looks back and forth between the two ladies before resting his eyes on the one standing behind Jason. "You heard em Nicole, let's get out of here." Jason begins to curse, confused as his lover steps out from behind him and picks up two of the four bags from the floor. But just as the words "dirty bitch" leaves Jason's mouth, he's hit in the head with the butt of the shotgun and collapses to the floor. "Shut yo dumb ass up!" The man with the shotgun mumbles as he rolls Jason over with his foot to see if he is really out cold. Satisfied that he was, he takes a couple steps back before slowly kneeling as Nicole helps pull the last two bags over his shoulders and adjusts them as he stands. Justin looks over at his lady before looking down at Jason with a frustrated anger that's ready to erupt inside of him. The bigger of the two men saddles his shotgun across his arm to show he's not being threatening.

"Look kid, I can see that out of the two of you you're the only one with any real heart. Some advice…get away from his bitch ass before he gets you killed. If you want to work for a real mutha-fucka, come down to the North-side Park and holla at Donnie. It won't be long before the entire Kingsley shit is shut down. Stacey Hunter plans to make sure of that."

He shifts the shotgun to a firing position as the other two exit the apartment. As he backs out of the door himself, he shouts, "Make sure you come to the park." Those words echoed in the complex. It was the sudden silence that assured Justin that the threat was gone. With even more animosity he looks a Jason sprawled out on the floor before taking his girls hand and saying, "Let's go. I've got to report this but I'm going to drop you off before I do."

(Concerned)

"What about him?" She asks.

(Shrugs his shoulders)

"What about him? Fuck 'em, let's go!"

CHAPTER FIFTEEN

The Plan(s)

[3:30pm, Ana's loft, downtown Colver]

"I'VE ASKED YOU all here because the powers that be want us to put a stop to what's beginning to happen in this city. Now they want us to take the fight the different dealers. Situations are escalating and becoming too violent to sit back and let these folks take each other out. We've received word that Sean or Stacey Hunter is robbing the Kingsley's drug spots, bars and street corners at an alarming rate. (Pauses) Although there is no direct evidence that these crimes are being committed by Stacey Hunter, the body count is becoming too high not to take action."

"Well Ana, what are they expecting us to do?" Mia asks.

"Stacey Hunter is a shadow. He can't be easily drawn out. But we have to find a way. Word on the street is he prides himself to be ***the*** *modern-day Nino Brown. He's masterminding a trail of crime, carnage, assault and big money with his hands on all the profits. Regrettably, none of the criminal activity is able to be traced back to him. If we swooped in to make arrests, we could definitely get Donnie with what we have on him already but anything to tie in Stacey Hunter would be circumstantial."*

"I want to be clear; it seems like you are looking for a big score by taking down Stacey Hunter. But they don't seem to be concerned about Sean."

"Raymond, the powers that be aren't concerned with deciphering anyone's mental or criminal state. They will not differentiate. They just don't care. Clean streets and changing the public's perception is what they expect our goal to be. They will sort it out after we have people in custody. (Looks around the room) But we have something in the plus column. The good people who outrank me don't know Sean **is** *Stacey Hunter. They believe this is a turf war between the two. (Waits for grumbling to stop) Our new task is to learn who these new players for the Kingsley are, to get close to Stacey Hunter and secure some hard evidence in order to arrest and convict."*

"And how do they want us to do that?" Mia asks.

"How indeed?" Meck responds sarcastically.

"We are to infiltrate. I've given it some thought, it's possible. We can use the missing money plates Mia recovered. We'll use them as bait."

(Surprised)

"I thought those plates were gone? You had them all along Mia? Why didn't you say something?"

"Sorry big bro. The less you knew, the faster they'd declare your innocence from that mess with my ex-husband and free up your accounts. That's the way dad had the plan set up. So, take that up with him. (Points a wiggling finger) Technically I don't have them. Ana does."

"Uncle Will, your dad… was right. It benefitted us all to hold on to them. And a lot of heat will come down on **me** *if the powers that be knew I had them. So, let's keep a hush on that until it becomes relevant or necessary for that to matter."*

"What's our play here? Is my dad playing a part or is he letting us handle it all?" Meck asks.

"We've been giving it some thought. We'll need Meck to head up this one. We don't want to jog Sean's memory with anyone he may remember. In Mia's case, both Sean and Stacey would recognize Keisha. Raymond, you and Roslyn are a no brainer. So that just leaves Meck to infiltrate. At

this point we want to avoid a personality shake up. Everyone sitting here understands that any and all evidence could get stuck with Sean. Especially if we can't prove the existence of Stacey Hunter and compile what we need against him alone."

"Sean may not be emotionally ready to be thrown into the physical consequences Stacey has created."

"I think you're right Raymond. I agree we'll have to find a way to save your cousin. Let's you and I put our heads together on that, especially if he has awareness of Stacey Hunter's antics."

"So, what are you proposing Ana?"

"Mia...I want to exploit man's second primal need. In my opinion: Power is the first. Which drives man's primal need to consume everything."

(Overly excited)

"OHH, OHH...let me guess the second. (Yells) Here it is...surr-vey says! Ding! The sixth deadly sin...greed!"

[Playful applause]

"Yes Mia, greed is correct. (Laughs briefly) Meck, I want to use the plates to appeal to Stacey Hunter's greed and get close to him. Let's come up with a plan and I want you to work with Tank on this one. Even I may have to get a little dirty on this one. Our best bet is to start with Donnie and find a way to use him to pull in Stacey."

"How soon should I hit the streets? Meck asks.

"They, the power that be, would like it to be like yesterday. But I don't want anything put into motion until we know how to approach it in and out."

"Copy that!" Meck says softly after pulling a toothpick from his mouth.

"The end game is simple everyone and that's not the problem. We've removed bigger players to make city streets safer more often than we've gotten credit for. At the heart of it, it's always the same basic plan. Shut down as much drug activity as possible with convictable arrests. (Looks around

the room) It's how we get there with positive results for everyone that is the unknown variable. There's a lot at stake and this may not be personal for everyone here. So…no idea is a bad idea at this point. (Rubs her hands together) Let's talk it out. Let's make a plan."

[Daybreak, two days after the apartment robbery]

The doors to Sacred Heart church open promptly at 6am for their parishioners. The dark morning sky disappears as the emerging light on the horizon accentuates the cross a top the front of the church roof. Shadows darken the stone work and the beautiful stained-glass windows but with the light of day looming, this house of God transforms.

Initially the church feels cold when parishioners first step in. Candles illuminate the alter as the soft organ playing of Father Keith invites prayer and reflection. Maya is greeted by Mont senior O' Brian before she dips her finger into the small bowl and touches her forehead to begin the sign of the cross. She makes her way to the second to last pew on the left-side of the church. As Maya sits, she lowers her head and silently begins to pray.

"Oh father, be with me. Forgive me for bringing such vile business into your house. This is the only place I feel at peace or where I feel safe. Surround me with your grace as I continue to work outside my comfort zone. Although I'm in charge, I'm used to working alone. I don't know who to trust and there are new enemies lurking. I ask for the wisdom to see Judas before he or she can do me harm. The devil is busy and I need strength to overtake my enemies or keep them at bay. (Pauses) Hail Mary, full of grace, the Lord…"

Whispering voices echo in the rear of the church and break Maya's concentration. She stops her prayer but never lifts her head as she listens intently.

(Voices echoing)

"Good morning. Peace be unto you."

"Uh, (Clears throat) Um… good morning."

"How can we, (Gestures) in the house of the savior...be of help? Confession? Silent prayer?"

"Well, um...it's father, right?"

"Yes."

"I'm looking for a friend. (Impulsively) Oh, there she is."

This Catholic man of Christ waves in hand in the air and makes the sign of the cross. "Then go my son." He began. "Go with God." Justin bows to the priest before stepping into the sanctuary. He looks up at the detailed wood work and high ceilings of the sanctuary in awe. He takes small steps, taking in the beautiful imagery of the confessional booths, the stained-glass windows and the stoutness of the organ pipes. Maya's head remained down but before Justin could acknowledge her, she was asking him to take a seat.

"Tell me about the other night." Maya said softly with her eyes closed.

(In a loud whisper)

"Two men came in. And a woman that was there with Jason, she helped with the robbery. They took bags of our product and money. With that shotgun pointed at me it felt like they were there for a long time but they were in and out in 30 minutes. One of the guy's bashed Jason in the head and then offered me a job. Told me to go down to the North-side Park and talk to Donnie."

[Organ music stops]

"Here's what I want you to do. Visit all of the work houses and bring me a report of what's left in each one. (Lifts her head) I've promoted you. The word is already out. Carry yourself accordingly. Some of them may not agree with my decision but show them that you are worthy of the title, the respect and being the direct connection to me. (Looks at him) I need to know how much profit and product remains in each location. Meet me right here around 5pm with the results. (Clears her throat) This is an audition for my trust. My fuse is short and my patience is even shorter. You understand?"

"Yes, I do. But one thing, (Hesitantly) I don't want to offend you. What do you want me to call you?"

"Remind everyone they can call me Sully. That's it for now. I'll see you at five."

Justin stands and quickly heads for the exit. Maya also stands but stops in the middle of the isle and stares solemnly at Jesus on the cross above the altar.

"Are you alright Miss? You seem troubled." Father Keith asked as he prepared for mass.

"Father, I'm wondering how I can fend off an enemy that I can't see coming. How do I fight a battle that isn't mine but I'm obligated to lead? (Lowers her head) And…how can I heal the pains of my past when every choice I make leads to more pain and uncertainty."

"You walk by faith. Let go of your sins and pain. The son of God has already sacrificed on the cross for your sins. Lay your burdens at his feet and lean on your faith."

"Footsteps in the sand father?"

"It goes deeper than just letting God carry you. Your strength will come from letting him…in. Walking with him and becoming strong enough in Christ so you won't need to be carried. Find your strength."

"Thank you, Father. Your words are a comfort."

Maya tips her head with respect before walking towards the exit. She walks out into the morning light of day and recites this part of the 23rd Psalm, her way.

"Yea though I walk through the valley of the shadow of death…I will fear no evil. For thou art with me! (Stops at the top of the stairs and looks into the sky) Give me strength Lord, for what will come. For the evil that's expected for me to do and for the folks who are intended to be on the receiving end."

[1pm North-side Park]

Donnie stands on the grass about ten feet from his favorite bench. He stands impatiently in his baggy baby blue sweat suit with his knock off timberland's waiting for one of his regular workers to approach him. He pulls off his fishing style hat from his head and runs his fingers through his hair as he gestures for this guy to hurry up.

"Damn you're slow. What's up? Huh? What are you trying to hand me?" Donnie asks in a frustrated tone.

"It's an old flip phone. It was given to me by Stacey to give to you. He said he'd call soon."

[Phone rings]

"Yo, what up dog? Why the burner?"

"Precautions Donnie…just taking precautions. (Impulsive) Look man, I need you to keep an eye on the day-to-day shit. This Kingsley war is about to bust wide open. It might get messy. I've got to bury these fuckers while we've got the advantage. Once it's done, I will expand into their areas. Take this town with a force no one is ready for. But I need you to handle the normal shit while I handle finishing them off. That's all right now. The less you know the better it will be…for now. I'll send another phone in several days. Alright hermano…that's the plan."

[5pm Sacred Heart church]

As the sun set, its reddish hue looked beautiful in the sky as the light touched the top of the church. Justin completely overlooks it as he climbs the steps to enter the church. The sanctuary is quiet as more candles are being lit. Justin apprehensively makes his way along the right-side to the first confessional booth. He felt out of place as he made his way down the aisle. It seems strange that no one was paying any attention to him. He thought… who doesn't see a young black man wearing all black with white tennis shoes, a watch bigger than his wrist and a glistening diamond incrusted cross that has no thought of repenting strolling through the sanctuary.

The mahogany-stained detailed confessional booth had chiseled crosses, two red curtains and a door in the middle that was centered between two round, tall columns. Justin was instructed to knock softly twice before slipping into the curtain on his right. Instead, he silently called out, "Sully, Sully." There was a pause before a response came. "Step in and have a seat." Although he was suspicious, he did as he was told. He cautiously took a seat as a voice projected through the wooden meshed window.

"Let's hear what 'cha got."

"Are you sure about doing this ***here****?" Justin asks.*

"Don't worry about your surroundings. We are safe here. You and I are the only two that know about this church. (Pauses) I would like it to stay that way. So…tell me what you found out."

(Sighs)

"I'll make it easy. Every spot that we do business out of was hit on the same night, at or around the same time. Our product and money are gone! Looks like we'll have to start from scratch."

"Were there casualties? Was anyone hurt? Why were you the only one to report initially?"

"Half of our shopkeepers were killed trying to protect the business. The others decided to lay low until there was someone trustworthy to report too."

"Were they afraid also?"

"To report? Some of them…yes. Others, not so much. It was a matter of who do you trust. Stacey Hunter implored six different women to get close to and under some of our shopkeepers. They extracted information before betraying them and walking away with the robbers. That's what I've heard."

"Can anyone identify any of the women?"

"Yes."

"Something this coordinated had to take some time to set up. And long before I came on the scene."

Maya musically taps the inside wall of the confessional as she collects her thoughts. Justin peeks out of the curtain to assure himself that they weren't being watched.

"Here's what I want you to do,"

Maya's voice becomes softer and Justin inches closer to the mesh in order to hear her detailed instructions. Her details were specific and she carefully explained them for fifteen to twenty minutes. Taking moments in between to ask him, "Are you with me?" Justin would nod his head and make noises to assure her that he was getting it all.

"I want a three-week time frame for the completion and reveal. Ok?"

"Got it!"

"If any of our people are too squeamish to carry this out, I need to know right away. I know a couple of free lancers that I could pull in if needed. (Pauses) Are you with me?"

"Yes, I'm with you and my instructions are clear except for one thing. Am I getting my hands dirty on this?"

You may need too Justin, in order to inspire leadership. If no one feels the need to question your leadership abilities…then just lead them."

"Ok Sully, I've got it."

"Then we're done here. (Taps wall again) Go with God. But if you can't…go with your gut! Intuition is a powerful ally."

CHAPTER SIXTEEN

The Bait

DONNIE WAS SET to be our first target. We figured he was our best shot to possibly draw out Stacey Hunter. The team came up with several ideas but there were flaws when discussed with real situational details. We needed to get Donnie alone but that wasn't the problem. We could always deploy any slutty chick to accomplish that. The problem as we saw it was piquing his interest once we did. So, Ana asked me to step up and be Keisha again. That's easy enough. Keeping Stacey Hunter from seeing my alter ego until we get the hook into Donnie will be the challenge. Donnie also has to be separated from Stacey Hunter and that shouldn't be an issue because Stacey doesn't show his face too often. But Donnie has to be away from that park. We can't make him nervous so the working plan is from me to get his attention and my brother Meck to hold it. We have a small amount of intel to work with, the other details of our plan is still a bit sketchy but we live for this kind of uncertainty and pressure. Ready or not, we go in 24 hours.

[28 hours later. June 21st, Oakland Ca.]

Keisha sits in on workshop A of the Cannabis business summit & expo. It's 7:30am and she listens to the change is California's laws regarding medical marijuana. Its standing room only in one of the large conference rooms but Keisha manages to keep a loose eye on Donnie and how intently he is paying attention. He took notes as the orator explains how the legal number of plants you can raise has changed. Keisha went unnoticed as planned until the orator opened the question-and-answer period.

(Pointing)

"Yes, you ma'am, there is the middle row."

"I'm wondering if there has been any change in the Federal government's position on legalization or could our indoor grows and warehouses still be raided? Resulting with the possibility of facing prosecution regardless of the state laws."

"That's a good question. (Pauses) You can still be raided. All of your crops can be confiscated and destroyed. The Feds may or may not take your equipment. So, keep your receipts. Here's what may happen. You will be arrested if you are there. If not, a warrant will be put out for you. Be as prepared as possible. Most doctors have access to a lawyer that is specific to their situation. So, if your lawyer's good, you could be released within 24 hours. If your paperwork is in order, you could get your equipment back or be reimbursed for it. But your crops will be a total loss. (Scans the room) Make sure you have a copy of your license on one wall in every room that has product in it. Make sure you stay within your city's guidelines. The city of Alameda will let you raise 12 trees and Oakland would let you raise up to 72. I will speak later on how that will be changing. If you stay under the limit the Feds will hand the case back over to the city and you may get back to business a bit faster."

Keisha purposefully diverted her eyes as Donnie and a few others turning around to see who had asked the question. She continued to act aloof as the speaker continued to answer. Donnie looked surprised to see someone from his city sitting in on this seminar and randomly turned attempting to get eye contact with her. Another ten minutes passes and the orator checks his watch before ending the morning seminar. Keisha quickly makes her way out of the conference room with the rest of the crowd. She heads towards the lobby and suddenly feels a light touch on her shoulder. She turns to engage a smirking Donnie.

"You're Keisha, right? You used to date Sean."

"You're right, I used too."

"What happened with that?"

(Sassy)

"Like you don't know. It's hard to stay with someone who suddenly doesn't recognize you. (Raises an eyebrow) Personality conflicts, (Points) that's your boy! He ended it…and I'm good with that. Ya know what's strange? I wasn't expecting to see anyone from home."

"I had no idea, of all people, you were into this."

(Sarcastically)

"Ya didn't huh? I wasn't advertising."

Keisha turns to walk away but senses Donnie is still walking behind her.

"Oh, you're following me huh. (Laughs) So…this is what we're doing now. You just decided to come with?"

"You don't mind if I hang with you until after the lunch break? Good company in an unfamiliar city is all."

Keisha nods as they both exit the hotel and her gesture lets Donnie see that she was ok with his company. They both head towards the city center while Donnie continues to talk.

"I had no idea you would be here for this seminar or even interested in this semi-legal marijuana business."

"I can say the same for you Donnie. So, you're trying to go legal huh?"

"Maybe. I'm considering it."

"Yeah ok, phff, if you say so. I know you're considering taking advantage of making money legitimately. Capitalizing on a growing industry that fits your skill set without prosecution from local law enforcement. I think this is a great opportunity to plant roots in a new place. Me, in a new city and you in another aspect of the drug game."

"I could use a change of pace."

"I thought you already had a good thing going? Why the sudden interest in this now?"

Before Donnie answers he holds the door open as they walk into a local Togo's, order and sit down.

"To follow up on your question, I like the upside of supplying marketable plants for multiple dispensary locations. It's smart business. A business I don't have to share. Unless of course you're going to start up in Colver"

"You don't have to worry about me starting up in Colver Donnie. I've already got started here in the bay area. These seminars are helping me to know the difference between the Federal and state laws. But I'm also getting the insight to protect the business and myself."

(Surprised)

"You've already got started?"

"Yeah, I have three thousand square foot in a small warehouse in Berkeley and my second crop is almost ready to harvest."

"I'm going to need to pick your brain on the smaller important details I will need to get started."

(Grabs a potato chip)

"That won't be a problem. The seeds, lamps, electrical layouts, ventilation and other equipment are very important. But not as important as having the money to get started."

"What do you mean?"

"The startup costs will be expensive initially. Just to set up a 1000 square foot space will cost you at least ten thousand dollars."

"Really, that much!"

"Yes, and an additional ten grand for every additional one thousand square foot you use to expand. Believe me, it's worth it. (Bites her sandwich) What are you hoping to sell from your first crop?"

"I want to get as much as I can out of my first crop. I want to sell the leaves and the kef."

"So that you know, they now sell tables that help screen the kef as you handle the plants. I would take a look into it at the innovation's booth after your next seminar. (Lowers her voice) I hope what I say next won't be offensive to you but I have to say it. (Pauses) I hope you lose the baggy sweat suits when you enter each dispensary to sell product. You should want to go unnoticed, especially to thieves and cops. It will get tiring having to pull out credentials and explaining why you're carrying so many products and not get arrested. I would suggest a more business casual attire when you make your visits."

"No offense taken but I'll consider it."

It suddenly gets quiet at the table as they both chew on their sandwiches. Keisha looks over the lists of afternoon courses as Donnie takes a potato chip down the wrong tube and clears his throat.

[Coughs repeatedly]

"Did you say you were working with three thousand square feet?"

"Yep."

"How could you expand so fast? Where did you get that kind of money so fast?"

(Impulsively)

"Grab the rest of your chips and I'll explain on our way back to the hotel."

Keisha waits for a few people to walk around them, leaving them side by side on the sidewalk before beginning to speak again.

"I was given the warehouse space after my favorite uncle died. A year later I had the notion to do this but didn't have the cash. I met a guy who was discretely perfecting his ability to counterfeit. I gave him two thousand dollars and he gave me ten grand in counterfeit hundred-dollar bills. As long as no one put them under a black light they would pass a visual and

pen test. He's that good! I used the initial ten I bought from him to get myself started then expanded when my profits started rolling in. (Stops walking) He has mentioned testing in other markets. I could put you in touch with him if you'd like."

(Smiles devilishly)

"Ten thousand in untraceable counterfeit bills, yeah, I'm wit dat! That could definitely remedy my financial instability. Hell yes! Put me in touch."

Keisha unbuttons the top of her blouse as Donnie makes no attempt to avert his eyes. She reaches into her bra, pulls out a business card and hands it to him. The card was black with black lettering that could only be seen if you tilted the card and the light hit it just right. With the card between his thumb and forefinger, he moved the card until he could read, M. Melvin Murray; artist. Then he flipped the card and saw, "Life awakens on the proper canvas."

"Make sure you tell 'em "Keesh" gave you the card. It should ease his suspicion if he knows you got the number from me. If you don't, he won't do business with you at all."

Donnie nods as he flips the card between his fingers before it disappears.

"Clever trick. Good luck with your afternoon seminar…and word of advice, have patience. He is a bit peculiar about his work. Don't trip! Have your money, show a little interest and you'll have what you want before you know it."

Keisha smiles before bouncing two of her fingers off her forehead. Her piss-poor salute was an attempt to quickly say goodbye before disappearing into the crowd. Donnie throws up a head nod before turning to look for the Innovation gallery.

[Kinko's San Jose, Ca]

It had been 24 hours since the conversation with Keisha. Donnie seemed excited that this black business card would lead to needed cash and eventually a new cash cow opportunity for him. It took him twenty more minutes than he expected but he found the small track mall copy store he was looking for.

The repetitive rotations of machine's pushing paper were almost louder than the clerk who greeted Donnie from a distance as he walked through the door.

"Hello sir, welcome to Kinko's. How may I help you?"

"Uh, well, I'm looking for M. Melvin Murray."

"Oh, you want three M. Let me get him for you. (Looking at another customer) Sir! You have to turn that over if you want to copy that. (Faintly) Hey Mel, someone's here to see you."

Meck shouts, "Thank you. Be right there", from the back room before taking a deep cleansing breath as he settles into his character. He re-ties his apron as he exits the back room and adjusts one of the printers before approaching Donnie. A 5'11', pigeon toed, business casual, Ivy League polished, glasses wearing, well put together black man strolls up to a sweat suit toting Donnie.

(In a British Cockney accent)

"How can I help you?"

Donnie doesn't speak. He flips the black business card given to him between his fingers before he holds it out for Mel to see.

*"A preferred customer, aye? Not many are privy to one of those. How did you happen to come by **that**?"*

"It was "Keesh" who passed it to me. She told me how you may be able to help me."

"And how's that?"

Donnie begins flipping the card again until he made it disappear and then he smirks.

"Find a president that carries some weight and then replicate the dead. I hear you're good with cloning wafer Clinton's."

"Ah, I see it. Wafer Clinton's as opposed to saying thin Bills. A bit of a

stretch. But still clever. (Invitingly waves a hand) Come on back, let's talk about it."

As Donnie crosses the threshold coming into the back, a loud tone bellows from somewhere in the room. Melvin casually informs Donnie that he triggered a metal detector and inquired if he was carrying a weapon. Which Donnie admitted that he is.

The back room was a maze of sturdy-built shelving, boxes filled with toner, multiple rows of colored paper, binders, and any other supplies needed to bind books or make charts. As you get passed the racks of supplies towards the back of the room was an old-style printing press, a silk-screening table, a computer, printer and a couple small buckets full of old bingo tokens. Melvin pulls out a chair that he offers to Donnie who gracefully declines with a hand gesture.

"So, ***this*** *is where the magic happens?" Donnie quips.*

"Not always. It actually doesn't matter where it happens, just as long as my hands are steady, the supplies are plentiful and the conditions are optimal to drive every step towards completion."

"Exactly how does this work?"

"You're not asking about the details of how I work are you?"

"Oh no, not at all. I meant, what should I expect. How do I get what I'm looking for?"

"It's simple. Good money for bad. I give you ten thousand in counterfeit bills and you give me three thousand. Once I've received payment you can wait nearby for 48 hours and I'll put the cash in your hand or I'll Fed-Ex Kinko's paper goods where ever you want me to deliver it."

"Keisha told me she paid $2000.00."

"She did and it's what I asked her for. That was when the bills were untested. She assumed the risk for my artistry. I know the bills will pass a simple glance of the eye and the mark from a pen if tested. That is why I increased the price. (Smiles derisively) If you'd like to try your luck with

my prototype black light bills, then I'll let you have those Clinton's for the afore mentioned two thousand."

"I'll take the proven counterfeits. We can talk about the black light prototypes after you have perfected and tested them. I need to hit the ground running. I have no time to help you test but I would like to do some business."

Donnie begins to shuffle but stops moving when he sees the apprehensive posture of Melvin.

"I want to reach for my money, nothing else. Is that, ok?"

After an approving head nod Donnie reaches into his left pants pocket and pulls out a roll of money wrapped in a rubber band. He confidently hands that roll to Melvin.

"There's three thousand in that roll but I have more." Donnie now reaches into his other pocket and pulls out another wad of money. He carefully counts another three thousand and holds it out towards Melvin.

"Can you give me twenty thousand tested bills within the same timeframe?"

"Twenty thousand in forty-eight hours? (Rubs his face) It is a shorter time frame than I'm accustomed too. (Chuckles) But I can make it happen."

"Man, that's awesome. I will wait in the area during the next 48."

Donnie is all smiles as Melvin takes the rest of the money and hands him an all-white business card in return. Donnie moves the card under the florescent lighting and reveals an address and a time for delivery.

"You will be met by a very large friend of mine Donnie when you arrive to pick up your order. Don't be alarmed. He won't speak and he will not cause you any harm. Please do not shoot him. He will verify who you are by retrieving the white card that I just gave you. He will also make a call to assure me that you have received what you've paid for. After that, he will quietly walk away. (Donnie nods) I wish you luck with whatever you're doing and I want to take the time to thank you for your business."

"I like your style M. Melvin Murray. I like your style."

CHAPTER SEVENTEEN

Retaliation

THIS IS A news story with a bullet and by tomorrow will be on every news affiliate across the country. The images of this crime scene are strange. Not your typical car accident, stabbing or shooting. It's that TV drama stuff that you watch on an hour episode but don't believe actually happens in real life. After the initial local broadcasts, the images were being held back from the public due to the graphic details. But for those who caught Colver's first broadcast, witnessed something that most common folk aren't prepared to see.

The yellow caution tape and barricades closed off four city streets that led towards the crime scene. Police cruisers, crime scene vans and traffic SUVs' all lined the streets as the CPD'S helicopters hovered above and were trying to force news copters to clear the area. Investigators were already processing and cataloging evidence as local TV broadcasted aerial images for their special news reports. These aerial images were the closest any affiliate could get to the scene before their helicopters were pushed out of the perimeter.

Every crime scene tells a story. Stories that unfold and reveal its plot as the details in the evidence come to light. Be it a rouge hair or a speck of blood spatter. Often the location itself tells us whether it is a crime of passion, a murder of convenience or a precursor for others to follow its style. There is usually a compiled group of things that provides answers to this simple question…why. But today, even the experienced investigators were having a head scratching time with this crime scene. This was a first for most of the crew working the scene so the attention to the details and an observed effort not to destroy evidence was very crucial.

At first glance the investigators were looking at five men of different ages, heights and nationalities standing on a sidewalk in front of a chain link fence. There was actually a thin green screen strapped to the fence shielding the renovation of the buildings behind it. It was the perfect backdrop for evidence they hoped to find looking at the men. The ground was damp even as the sun came up and the light drizzles of rain tapered off. The investigators huddle briefly, working out a plan to protect the scene and collect evidence without keeping the coroner waiting around all day before he could move the bodies. Five men, all dead but positioned in five different recognizable homeboy-esq poses. Every pose explained on yellow tags found hanging somewhere on each body. It was decided that photos would be taken of each man initially before anyone could step onto the sidewalk to take closer looks. Investigators after an hour were finally cleared to approach the first body. They found the first tag hanging around the victim's neck.

[The Holding up the wall pose]

-This is reminiscent of people waiting at a bus stop or hanging out on the side of a liquor store. You lean against the wall with your arms crossed, one leg bent at the knee with that foot firmly pressed against the wall. The longer you lean, the more often you switch to the opposite leg. -

The lead investigator stepped aside as a medical examiner pulled out a micro-cassette tape to record what he sees but instructed one other person to take notes as well.

"Twenty-sixth of August, it's 7:35am, we begin a preliminary examination of the first corpse placed on downtown street. Let's verify for the record how this position the deceased was placed in was achieved. First

subject has been propped against the fence with his right leg straight to the ground and his left bent at the knee. His neck and ankles have been cleverly fastened to the chain link fence with clear tie straps, causing visible bruising. Bungee cords were pulled through the belt loops of the pants and hooked to the fence as well to help stabilize the body. His arms have been crossed below the chest and held in position with sharpened lengths of eraser less pencils that have been pushed into the flesh. Subject has an IPod placed into his left hand with a cable running up to his right ear only. The head is held up by two metal stems jammed beneath the skin between the chin and the clavicle. The metal used appears to be pieces of filed screwdrivers without the handles. An oversized baseball cap has been positioned on the head, pulled low over the brow in order to cover the eyes. (Pauses) Currently there are no visual signs for the cause of death. A deeper exam is warranted once we get the subject onto a table."

The photographer takes a few detailed pics of the first body and the medical examiner finds the yellow tag in the top pocket of the second victim.

[The jailhouse pose]

-This is one of a few that shares the name. This particular pose is used in many photos sent to wives, side pieces, homeboy's and families from prison yards across this nation. How do you execute? It's simple. Squat down low with each arm resting on your legs or one arm bent with a hand resting around the mouth. The latter of the two was chosen for this criminal. -

"This subject was placed in a squatting position and stabilized on a base that has a rod that spans from its base up to a vest that has been put around the subject's torso. Much like a mannequin would. The arms have been strapped to the legs, with the strapping hidden in the clothing by using long Velcro strips. The left arm has been bent at the elbow and it looks as if super glue was applied to affix the left hand to the chin. The right hand hangs off the leg just in front of the knee. To give the appearance that the

body weight is resting on the balls of the feet, four-inch angled wedges were nailed through the shoes into the feet. A similar oversized baseball hat was used again to cover the eyes. Side note…I don't even want to imagine how the lips and cheeks were held with that expression before rigor mortis set in." [Camera's flash]

A couple of the examiners stood looking confused as well at the expression hidden below the baseball cap as the medical examiner pulled the third card from the back pocket of the next body.

[The, I see Ya!]

-This position is highly effective at sporting events, concerts, state fairs, picnic's or anywhere there is a vast distance between you and somebody that sees you. Normally you'd like to acknowledge the person(s) without having to shout amongst a big crowd or push your way towards them. What do you do? Most people stand with their feet shoulder width apart and hold one arm out (your choice) almost parallel to the ground and points at them. Your other hand is held closely near the chest with two fingers giving the "peace sign". Its hello and goodbye wrapped in two gestures while making minimal effort or contact. -

"This subject is also being supported by the fence. Straps were placed following the rotator cuffs under the arm pits and then secured to the chain link with tie straps and bungee cords. This was continued with the waist and the ankles. To make this subject point, three of his fingers were glued to the palm. The thumb is also glued to the one finger that was set to point. A modified yard stick was used under the shirt as support for the arm and finger. A metal rod was pushed into the body just at the belt line with the other end secured to the yard stick keeping the arm upright. The opposite arm appears to have Velcro that's pulling away from the abdomen. A slew of Popsicle sticks was used on the hand to make a peace sign. Multiple sharp

objects were placed in the flesh to provide a natural looking tilt of the head. A black hoodie was used instead of a hat for this subject." [cameras flash]

A question was asked among the badges working the scene. A question regarding the similarities of the bodies except for their positions and whether there was a need to continue or just begin removing the dead from the street. As someone grabbed the next the card the medical examiner answered.

"As repetitive as this may be, we not only have to secure as much evidence of this crime scene as possible but also gather medical findings here at the site before the shards of metal or the contraptions used to hold these bodies in place are removed or post mortem bruising begins to contradict what the crime scene has to offer. (Looks over glasses) So re-engage your interest and let's move to the next body."

[The so whatcha wanna do Mutha-Fucka]

-This pose when used with someone real, real meaning a no-nonsense person of action. A person who will want to beat you with no remorse or leave you exposed to gunfire. Often when a situation exceeds the use of words and quickly escalates into a physical confrontation, someone often says, "So...whatcha wanna do?" Mutha-fucka, adds some flavor. Ask Samuel Jackson if this is unclear. Those words are often followed with more cussing and taunting until someone enters the others personal space. The aggressor usually has their arms out wide, palms up and feet staggered just in case they need to put power behind a punch. -

"The positioning of this man is similar to two of the others that are standing. Except this man's left foot is mounted to a stand with a rod secured into the calf. This is because the feet had to be staggered slightly. A rig was also placed allowing them to lie in a natural looking open position. There is also something sharp used at the back of the neck and pushed into the shoulders to keep the head in a position where the chin is tilted upward. There are big framed woman's glasses covering the eyes. A 9mm handgun is

jammed down the front of the pants. Let's see if we're lucky enough to get prints off of that." [Camera's flash]

The last card was sticking out of the shoe on the last body. The title of the pose was spelled out on the concrete next to the body with multiple colors of sidewalk chalk that began to run due to the drizzle.

[The stop and frisk]

-This unfortunate position usually begins innocently in the eyes of law enforcement but normally starts with something they will never admit to…profiling. Some people believe that the victims of police harassment bring this unnecessary treatment on themselves. This is not always true. Although visually ridiculous, pants hanging off their ass or wearing a down jacket zipped up in 80-degree weather isn't always probable cause. The biggest problem…perception <u>is not</u> reality and people often assume that it is. With that said, there isn't always cause for the stops that often lead to a civilian being unjustly detained or worse. Shocked, sprayed, beaten, shot or murdered. In a perfect world police would have a solid reason for escalation other than an ego infected complex or prejudice. To be fair, if the public would follow reasonable police direction, then maybe everyone goes home alive. But these days you can shift a toothpick in your mouth and a cop will fear for his/her life and just might shoot you with a predisposition to kill rather than incapacitate. It's the wild wild west out here and justice always seems to lean towards the boys in blue. Not even the best video evidence can convict a rouge cop.-

"Wow, not sure how I feel about that. But let's press on. (Pauses) The last victim is laid out stomach down on the sidewalk. The hands have been handcuffed behind the back and the feet have been zipped tied together. There are signs of robe burns around the neck. There are three bullet holes through his back and one that shattered the side of the head across the sidewalk. Dreadlocks are covering what's left of the face. A wallet is hanging

halfway out of the right rear pocket of his sagging pants with a blood-soaked beanie lying next to the body. The words, "Embrace a life; don't take one" are silk screened on the back of this man's tee shirt."

[Camera's flash]

The lead medical examiner stands after looking over the last body and shakes his head in disgust. A deep voice causes the few standing around the body to turn. They began to listen as the melodious tone of his voice and words drew them all in.

"Overlooking the commentary of police violence, first glance of this crime scene would make most contemplate approaching a true nodus or a horrific statement regarding inner city violence. If we take a closer look at what we could reveal, it may tell use much more than what we initially see. These men weren't just put on display. This goes deeper, maybe a score to settle. I get the sense that these murders are motivated by revenge. The poses, the names and words painted on the walls tell us of this cities failure to end criminal drug activity. What we see here may seem sadistic and sick, maybe even un-nerving but to do something like this takes patience & fore thought. We have a responsibility to identify them, criminals or not."

"Sir, if I may…take a look at the right side of the fence where the statement was spray painted."

Everyone turns, focuses and reads the words before the one investigator speaks again.

-Who's to blame? Who's helping?

Stopping t**h**reats City wide **un**til **the**y'**r**e gone!

It's a good start…You're welcome Colver

Now connect the dots-

"I think whoever is responsible is trying to point us in a direction by challenging us. They said connect the dots, so it's like a puzzle."

"A puzzle? How do you mean?" The brass with the deep voice asked.

"If we look at the words, you can see certain letters are underlined and some bolder than the others. As a man who likes puzzles, I believe there's something more within the message. If we take the underlined letters and the bold ones and put them together, they spell "Stacey Hunter".

"Do you think you may be reaching a bit?"

"No, not at all sir. Why else would they accentuate those specific letters? Why not just paint each of those men's nicknames and corners they've worked if not to give a hint of whom they were working for. We can confirm with the drug enforcement division if they have any information on any of them."

"It's worth a follow up. Identify who these men are. Find out who this Stacey Hunter is and if he does exist. We've been picking bodies up all over this city the last two weeks. There is clearly a war or power struggle going on that the narcotics department should look into with an expedient sense of urgency. We have to close this case quickly. We need answers and we need them fast. This will be in the national spot light by the end of the day and this city cannot afford the bad press. Get it done."

CHAPTER EIGHTEEN

The Sisters

[Ana's loft, Downtown Colver]

RAYMOND STANDS AT Ana's living room window with his hands behind his back gazing out at the city's skyline. CNN plays softly on the TV describing the gruesome scene of downtown Colver's flesh statues. Engaged in a conversation with his wife and Ana, Raymond finds comfort in the night sky before choosing his next words.

"This seems like it's getting out of hand Ana."

"I think we just need to trust the process Love."

"The process Roslyn, I don't think it's as simple as that. But if the process consisted of these crews taking each other out, then things are right on schedule. Stacey Hunter is everything that my cousin isn't and who ever hit his crew has become vicious front-page news. This can only get worse which will add a degree of difficulty to the original end game."

"Do you still have site on what that is? You're a cop so you know how the details of cases change and not always in a way that will help us."

"Ana my family doesn't need to know I'm alive in order to be arrested for their crimes against me or otherwise. The only family I'm concerned about is the lovely woman sitting on your sofa. (Turns back to the window) The only other one that I'm concerned with didn't recognize me when I

brushed passed him in Oakland a few months back. (Softly) So how do I save Sean? I hope we can find the best way to intervene before more people die. I feel like we are losing our part in this or it's being departmentalized. When do we step in Ana?"

"We start by trying to figure out what your cousin as Stacey Hunter will do next."

"I've been giving that some thought. I think Stacey is accessing Sean's memories. How else would he have known where all the Kingsley stash houses were and when to hit them?"

"That's an interesting thought Love."

Raymond perches his lips, raises an eyebrow and nods as he looks at the ladies' images in the glass. Ana crosses her legs and prompts him to continue.

"Do you see some type of pattern?"

"Just greed Roslyn. And if he subconsciously knows where to hit them, them being my family and its crew, then why wouldn't he."

"Why wouldn't he what?" Roslyn asks.

"Go after his father's vault. He's been teased with it our entire childhood. (Mocks his uncle) It will be yours someday if you grow to deserve it. Listen close enough and I may slip you the location. (Pauses) Sean's been hearing stuff like that his entire life. So why not hit it while my uncle is laid up unconscious."

"Does he know where it is? I mean, did he before the personality split?" Ana asks.

"I don't think so. The devil was in the details of all the stories we heard as children or overheard as teenagers. It wasn't until last night that I think I figured it out. So, I doubt that he knows."

(Impulsively)

"So, he may break into his father's house like your grandmother had some thugs break into ours." Roslyn adds.

"What?"

"We'll have to catch up on that and some other things later but at least now I know what they were looking for and that it's not down there."

"Oh, it's down there and hiding in plain sight."

"Really!"

"Yep, but we'll catch up on that later. But if I'm right, he won't find anything in ***his*** *father's basement."*

"Why not Raymond?"

"That house is my aunt's domain and she wouldn't allow any room to exist in her home that she couldn't enter. So, I know it is not there. But I believe the reasons go deeper than that."

(Smiles)

"How so star gazer?" (Ana laughs)

"I think it goes back to my three aunts; Kate, Cassie and Cora. I overheard my grandmother telling this story to someone while she was on the phone. My grandmother called my aunts the profit and loss gals or the sisters for short and she was disappointed with my uncle Robert because he let them get in the way of the family's business."

"The Sister's huh, that's nicer than anything that she has ever called me my love."

"I'm sure it is Roz. (Solemnly) I was told that my Uncle Robert met my Aunt's Kate and Cassie at the same time but appealed to the both of them in very different ways. Kate became equivocally infatuated and she and my uncle fell hard in love with each other. Cassie on the other hand was already aware of Robert's city-wide reputation for making money and giving others an opportunity to do so working for him. So, when he offered Cassie a job, she jumped right into doing anything that he asked. But Robert would quickly learn that if her pay didn't match the risk then don't bother approaching her. He also learned that there was no job beneath her. Robert frequently tested Cassie's limits. She was unafraid and prepared to take any risk. Well, as long as the payment rewarded her for it. As Cassie made more

money with my uncle, Kate became more committed, loyal and in love with him. With two parts of his life flourishing for him and my dad protecting everybody, they say Robert began to take bigger risks as well. But we have to balance the good with the bad and Robert's crutch for a long time was his gambling. I overheard my grandmother talking and she would say that he would lose more often than she cared to remember. Some of those risks he took knowing whatever Cassie would often bring in could cover his debts. Eventually he got in so deep that he would have to start borrowing in order to keep up with payment."

"Were your parents still alive when his debt got out of control?" Ana asks.

"I think they were. Just before my dad decided to become a model citizen my uncle asked my dad to bail him out of a jam but my dad told him that he couldn't and explained why. That led to Robert trying to squeeze more profits from everyone so that he could skim off the top to pay his bookies. Not long after that my parents died. My father's death changed the dynamics of the family's business. My uncle could no longer hide his skimming and was forced to find other ways to get clear of his debt. Still head over heels in love, Kate turned a blind eye when Robert began to pimp woman on the side. He couldn't keep her unaware of it so he did everything he could to reassure that no one would come between them and that he'd keep work away from home. Even that became difficult when he began to whore out Cassie and then went after the youngest sister Cora. Cora was enticed by the big money Cassie was bringing home but wouldn't sell her body to earn it. Cora declined the few awkward attempts Robert made trying to persuade her. Cassie broadened her perspective to the upper-class clientele. That was until one of the city officials she was hosting became overly demanding and physical. This led to Cassie killing him. The reports show the incident as an accidental death. It's been said that she wrestled the gun away from him and she blew the back of his head out. It's also said that my uncle paid some

folks off to get the accidental death put on the final reports. The details were a bit sketchy though. Cassie was wearing gloves with no gunshot residue on them and the city official was the only one with prints on the gun."

"Didn't Cassie die that night also?"

Raymond turns away from the window and looks at Roslyn.

"Her body was found on the stairs at the entrance of the city official's home. The medical examiner's reports show that she died from an overdose. Another detail that was also left out of the report was that the home was robbed and cleaned out of anything of value. Paintings and two safes that were said to hold bonds and a shit load of cash. Unrelated or not, when the smoke cleared, the official's opponent won the election and my uncle was suddenly able to clear his gambling debts. (Ana and Roslyn groan) Ya see, Cora believes that the entire thing was a set up to rob the official who grew wealthy on kickbacks and bribes. My uncle paying into that fortune quite a bit himself. Cora also believes that Cassie was never really whoring and that Robert sacrificed her and may have injected her with the drug that killed her in order to stage the crime scene. Ultimately her suspicions couldn't be validated so Cassie's death could never be solved. Police don't often look into the deaths of overdosed call girls. It all was quickly swept under the carpet. Cora explicitly didn't want anything to do with Robert and eventually Kate. Specifically, as her big sister's loyalties remained with her man."

"Ok Raymond, you mentioned earlier that you believed Stacy Hunter will go after your uncle's vault. How does any of these stories relate?" Ana curiously asked.

"Sean has always believed that his father's vault was a physical room somewhere outside the house. (Sniffs) His mother wouldn't allow any physical evidence of the family business in her home. So, Sean thinks it may be in of his father's businesses. I don't believe that to be true."

"You don't!" The ladies say at the same time.

"One of the other things that came between Kate and Cora after

Cassie's death was the burial arrangements. Cora wanted her big sis and herself to take care of laying Cassie to rest but Kate kept deflecting Cora and justifying letting Robert handle everything because he was paying for it. My grandmother respects Kate because she never leaves Robert's side, even at the expense of her own family. Cassie was laid to rest and entombed in a mausoleum hall, not in the ground. She was given no church or graveside service. I heard Grann tell my uncle that they needed more people to bring in big money for them like that Kimber Kelly he had cremated."

"You lost me my love. Who is Kimber Kelly?"

"Kimber Kelly was the name of the call girl who reportedly overdosed in the city official's home. I've been told that Cassie used that name while working with my uncle. That name was also placed in the mausoleum not too far from Cassie's. (Sighs deeply) I believe he cremated Cassie and that her ashes were placed nearby. I think he filled the coffin with all the money and valuables from the robbery then avoided any ceremony so no one could look into that casket. And once the name plates were put in place, with Cassie's name with the urn and Kimber's name marking the riches, no one would be the wiser to the location of his vault. (The room falls silent) That's my theory at least. But I do believe it will be a considerable target for Stacey Hunter. He's hit everything else."

Raymond turns back to the window and gazes at the skyline again. Ana holds an oversized tea cup between her hands and turns it slowly while softly speaking to Roslyn.

"We will have to check into your husband's theory. I'm going to ask you to do that if you can. I will check with the twins and see where we are with Donnie. (Takes a sip) My superiors have aligned there thinking with the local police department. They all agree there are too many bodies popping up with little or no answers. Our leads are fading so it's becoming increasingly difficult to end this. They want results and they want them soon. Let's get a warrant to exhume the casket of Cassie Reynolds. I want to know what's

in that casket. But let's also see if we can find a way for Stacey Hunter to show himself. (Sips her tea) Any other thoughts Mr. Kingsley?"

"Yes. Whoever is running the day to day while my uncle is in the hospital may just force Mr. Hunter's hand. This act of violence against his crew is cold, calculated, vicious and intended to squeeze him from multiple angles. He'll have to respond. We'll have to find a way to intercede before the body count grows."

CHAPTER NINETEEN

Tou che' Bitch

IT'S BEEN A few days after the flesh statues were found and Stacey Hunter sits on his couch watching TV and awaiting calls from Donnie and other members from his crew. It's late in the afternoon and he finishes a slice of pizza and the first of three cranberry & Vodka's he has lined up on his coffee table. Laid out on the couch next to him were several schematics from Robert Kingsley's businesses and fire department uniform with an investigator ID pinned to it. He was taking a break from looking for structural anomalies that he may have to look into when his doorbell rang.

[Opens door]

"Hello. Stacey Hunter?"

"Yes."

"Sign here please."

"Have a good day."

The courier retrieves his pen before handing Stacey a thin cardboard like envelope before turning to head for his truck. Stacey tears the strip from the package as he steps back inside and shuts the door. He pulls out a clear CD cover that has a sticky note on it that says, "Watch me".

"I hope this isn't that bootleg porno that Donnie was telling me about. I'd have to add more cups to that table if it's anything like he described."

Stacey Hunter sits at the edge of the couch as the picture on the video comes into focus. The fuzziness clears showing the front of an abandoned truck distribution center. The only letters left on the pylon sign read "E.A.R.S distribution and Outlet". There was a trailer out front that was riddled with bullet holes and had a homeless man peeking out from the back of it. The camera shook as the person carrying it began to walk. At the far-right end of the front of the building (the length of five houses) was a gated entrance. The pathway along this side led to the rear of the building and was covered with weeds. The end of this walkway leads to stairs for the rear loading dock that has train tracks just beyond it. The rear dock was just as long as the one in front. The train tracks were overrun with weeds and brush that had grown as high as the dock itself. The camera turns suddenly to a cracked set of concrete steps that led up to the dock. The walls and rusted roll-up doors were completely covered with graphitized artwork. The camera jitters again facing the concrete before slowly rising to show a pair of bloodied white tennis shoes, ankles bound by black duct tape and a dirty oversized baby blue sweat suit. As the camera continued to pan upward, you could see a white tee shirt spotted with blood and a man's arms were up over his head. His wrists were bound with rope and hung from a hook that was attached to one of the overhead beams. The camera now focuses in on the beaten, bruised and swollen face of Donnie who hangs like a huge catch being weighed on a fishing dock. "What the Fuck!" Stacey shouted as he reaches for one of the drinks in front of him. There had been no commentary up to this point, just sounds made as the person filming moved. But just shortly after showing Donnie's face, a woman began to speak.

"In case you've been under a rock the past few days and have wondered why your crew hasn't checked in, let me get you caught up."

As Maya speaks, photos of the downtown statues are held in front of the lens and slowly rotated until the last one was shown. Then she continues to talk.

"These are images from the other night. I'm sure you're also wondering

why there has been little or no response from your crew. I'll get to that in a minute. Well as you can see, here hangs what's left of Donnie. He ***may*** *survive. He still has a small window if medical help can get to him within the hour. So, if I were you, I'd try to figure out where he is…and fast. As far as the rest of your crew is concerned, well, they didn't fare as well as Donnie."*

The camera turns to the right of Donnie and reveals five others. Spaced out and hanging alongside of him. Each man swaying like a broken chime in the wind. If you're standing on the railroad tracks and looking up at the wall or roll-up doors just behind each man, there was a 3ft wide back drop painted white with a characterized image showing how each man died. Stacey freezes the video in order to look at these images. The first shows how the velocity of bullets invades this man's chest cavity and thrusts him from his feet. The next shows a dark figure standing behind someone as his throat gets sliced. The last visible image shows a man strapped to a target as arrows penetrate his chest. He presses play on the remote and the video shows an open roll-up door at the opposite end of the dock from where Donnie was hanging. Maya continues to speak.

"There is no commentary needed for what you're about to see. But it will answer the question of the whereabouts of the rest of your crew."

There wasn't much light as the camera moved inside. Two sky lights provided angled rays of daylight that couldn't illuminate the entire space. The camera begins to pan from right to left. The first clear image was of a work bench with a varied number of tools, a vice, an angle grinder and a gas-powered generator. There were also rolls of duct tape, a couple boxes of unsharpened pencils and a small pile of screw driver handles. But Stacey could only make out the items by pausing the footage. As the images begin to shift again, the light shined brightest on fifteen men laid out on the floor. Three rows with five bodies in each. Every man dead but laid out in the clothes they died in. Laid out on the cold concrete positioned as if they had been put into a coffin. Whatever drugs or weapons that were on them, neatly placed on the right side of their bodies. The camera moved fast enough to count fifteen souls but not slow enough to identify anyone. The image begins to shake again as the inside view of the open roll-up door gets closer. It moves toward the daylight, out the door, down the nearby stairs, across the railroad tracks and through a gap in the fence. It wasn't until the camera swung from an empty lot of an old furniture store back to the six men dangling from that rear dock that Maya begins to speak again for the last bit of footage.

"I needed you to see the caliber of person whom you decided to FUCK with. You damaged our business by robbing our stash houses and killing anyone who'd get in your way. So, I decided to do you one better and eliminate your entire revenue stream. As you can see, I left no stone unturned. That's everyone from your smallest street dealer all the way up the food chain to the men who take orders from you and Donnie. (Laughs) Leaving only ***you and Donnie****. That's in case you can get to him in time. (Gets quiet) On second thought...I've decided to help you with that. Why? Because I want to show you that I'm not a complete monster. And why should Donnie continue to suffer because of your poor decision process. I want you to turn to your local news and see how I helped."*

[Video stops]

Stacey sits in silence for only moments before cycling through the inputs to find a local news channel and picking up another drink.

"This is Aubrey Easton with a four o'clock news brief. (Turns up volume) Police are canvassing a local abandoned warehouse after receiving complaints of a bad odor coming from the area. Twenty men of various ages were found dead. Authorities will not allow any images to come from inside the crime scene. Investigators believe this scene may be the work shop for the flesh statues left on the downtown city streets just days ago. Paramedics

were rushed to the scene to work on the only surviving man of the ordeal. Investigators are eager to question him just as soon as doctors will allow."

Stacey mutes the TV, guzzles his drink and slides back into his couch. He holds a glass in on hand and rubs his face in frustration with his left. He stares straight ahead, begins to shake his head and only utters, "Tou che' Bitch!"

CHAPTER TWENTY

Incitement

IT HAS BEEN a couple of days since Robert Kingsley suddenly awakened from his head trauma. The hospital has restricted visitors except for Kate until a series of testing had been completed. After receiving good results from the Glascow coma scale, his intracranial pressure monitoring and an MRI, he was told his health was much better but he'd be held for further observation.

Robert had just pushed his lunch tray away from himself when Grann and Maya walked into the room. Grann took the chair next to the bed and Maya stood at the foot of it.

"So, Ma, what have I missed?" Robert asks as he nods respectfully to Maya.

"Glad you're back with us son. I thought we may have lost you. It's good you made it. You know, I won't be around much longer so I need you to step in and take control of this mess as soon as you're up and around."

"Mess! What mess? What happened?"

"Your son is missing. Were engaged in a turf war and our business is less than promising or profitable. I need these things to be set right. (Taps his arm) You look confused. We'll slow it down. Maya, my love, will you give us the details."

"Yes Ma'am. I would first like to say how I am glad you are up and around. Your leadership is very much needed with all that's been going on."

"I'm sorry but who are you? (Turns) Ma, who is she?"

"Maya is like family son. She has been handling the day to day since your accident."

Robert sits silent for a moment and you could see the apprehensiveness in his expression but he motioned with a hand gesture for Maya to continue.

"There is nothing pleasing with what you're about to hear. Let me just say...it's all bad news. Three events have happened that affect you both professionally and personally. First, there were three major fires that burned two of your legitimate businesses to the ground."

"Which businesses are we talking about?"

"It was your bar, the auto shop and the janitorial supply." Maya says softly.

"Arson is what the preliminary report shows. Investigators mentioned evidence of some kind of explosive devises but that's all they would tell me. It's still an active investigation and they will only speak with the legal owner."

Robert looks at his mother in disbelief after she'd finished speaking. He adjusts himself in the bed and asks, "When did this happen?"

"About a month ago. Sir, each fire started within hours of the next. Two of the three structures were reduced to rubble. Each blaze making newspapers and network news."

Robert sighs and then rubs the back of his neck.

"The next number of events involves the family's business. Which is in shambles at the moment?"

"How so?"

"There was a bit of resistance after Grann set up a meeting with the crew. I was asked to instruct them that I would be in charge until we found Sean or until you were able to step back in. But due to his egotistical

resistance and unmoral behavior to the family, we had to put Big Guns down."

"You killed Roderick! Was that necessary?"

"Your mom was willing to overlook the fact that he was informing to the Feds."

(Whispers despondently)

"The Feds. When was he doing that?"

"When he was visiting with the child he actually didn't have."

(Soft and disgusted)

"God damn lies!"

Robert shakes his head but stops when Grann taps his arm and starts speaking.

"He wasn't actually giving them anything that would be of concern. I just wanted to keep an eye on him. At least until his actions proved otherwise."

"But Grann's instructions to me were, if Roderick will not comply with the new chain of command, then play it safe. He should be eliminated immediately. (Pauses) He gave me no choice so I put him down."

"Roderick was a good leader. Even better muscle when you needed it. I wonder what info he could've been giving to them?"

"I'm looking into that son."

"The next thing Mr. Kingsley, every one of our stash houses was robbed, simultaneously. We lost a lot of money, all of our product and several men who tried to protect our assets. Business at the moment has been crippled."

"Was it that new crew behind it? They have been the cause of a few unwanted situations city wide."

"Are you talking about that fancy looking heifer that stopped by here and called herself checking in on you?" Grann asks.

"Kate told me about that and yes I am Mom."

"I looked her up. Her name is Ana Allison Grainger. She has no arrest

record but has been implicated for a lot of shit in multiple cities. Her crew has overrun, ran out and taken out dangerous crews where ever they have decided to go. Leaving small cells behind that remain loyal to them even if they move on. (Mumbles and pounds her fist against her chest) Respect!"

(Impulsively angry)

"Do you need a moment? Cause it looks like your nipples are hard. You might want to get her wet before you nestle between her inner thighs and try to wet bump her pussy with yours. If not…let's get on with it."

(Intensely)

"Let me make this perfectly clear to you! I'm not into women. Never will be! I'm into men with moderately stable self- esteems who've chosen to worship me. In case you were wondering. (Scoffs) But I don't have to have a hard on for her to respect what she does or how she does it. Some opposition deserves respect even if you are opposed to what they do or their very existence."

"That's pretty good! I see why you put her in charge ma."

"Incidentally, her crew wasn't involved with the robbery. It was orchestrated by Stacey Hunter and his people.

Robert starts to choke on the water he was drinking.

(Still coughing)

"Are you sure?"

"One-hundred percent. Do you know who he is?"

"I've heard of him. He was brought to my attention a while ago but I didn't see 'em as a threat. Why would he act out against us now?"

"Maybe he's trying to expand his territory. He's taken over Donnie's area completely. Donnie is reporting to him. So was your son until he disappeared. One of our guys told me personally that the man that robbed our spot on 9th Ave offered him the opportunity to come work with them. In short, to answer your question, I'm not sure why. But his actions

forced a reaction. So, we responded. I set plans in motion to respond with unemotional absolution but with unimaginable brutality."

"Was that your handy work I watched on the news the other day?"

"I thought you gave up on your artwork sweetheart? Nice work." Grann added.

"Thank you. It may have been a little over the top but I wanted to send a strong message."

"I thought that was Donnie being rolled on a gurney passed this room." Robert thinks to himself. "Let me tell you what should come with a message like the one you sent. Expect drastic and desperate forms of retaliation. (Clears throat) It's one thing to hurt a man's business. It's an entirely different to leave him feeling desperate. It can make even the most docile man or son dangerous. Even unpredictable."

"Did you say…son?"

"I'm just speaking in general. Here's the point I'm making. If you push any person into desperation, paint anyone into a corner, give them nothing to lose; I don't care if you are a man, woman, girl or boy, they can become a powder keg. Maya…it's Maya right?"

"Yes, sir it is."

"You will want to see your enemy self-implode rather than explode near you."

Robert raises an eyebrow and with that gesture asked if she understood. Maya just gracefully nodded.

"I would like to give you some advice if you're open to it. First, I would tell you to keep an eye out for retaliation. If he's savvy, he'll hit quickly. Next, gather whomever you can and rebuild our revenue stream. (Starts writing on some paper) Go to this address. It's a restaurant that not many know that I own. Ask to speak to the manager and only the manager. Tell Nick that Mr. Kingsley has bugs in the flour and he'll get you what you need to get our business going again. I'll follow up on that in a couple of days."

"Any advice in case I run into Stacey Hunter? Because two well placed bullets can end this entire thing."

"You don't have to kill him. You've got him beaten; now you have to break him. You can do that without ending his life."

"That's not what I taught you! Are you going soft on my Robert?"

"No Ma, but I do have a newfound respect for life and that also extends pass my own."

Just at that moment Kate bursts into the room almost out of breath. Her words were rushing from her mouth too fast for anyone to understand. Confused by everyone's lack of concern, Kate's eyes appeal to anyone as she awaits someone to acknowledge her."

"I didn't catch any of what you just said Kate. Can you repeat what you said?"

Robert watches Kate take two cleansing deep breaths which helps her slow her heart rate. But her voice still shrieked when she began to speak.

"Why do the police want to exhume my sister's body?"

"What the fuck!" Robert shouts as he leans forward off the mattress.

(Almost hysterical)

"I was like…what! What for?! Then they said that they were working a cold case and wanted permission to re-examine her body. I was like… uh NO! Absolutely not! (Takes a deep breath) Robert I won't have this! Understand? I've lost Cassie and I've lost Cora because of Cassie's death. I will not relive any of this! (Lowers her voice) Something must be done. There has to someone you can call to keep that from happening. I don't want my sister's remains disturbed."

(Calmly)

"Kate you're right. I don't want ***that*** *either. Right now, I need you to breathe. I'm not going to let that happen. Again*

For me Kate…breathe. That's good. I'll call a couple of my last contacts and get an injunction or something. Don't get worked up, I'll take care of it."

"And that's my cue. I don't want any part of this conversation. I'll leave it for the both of you to figure out."

Grann taps Robert's arm before standing as quickly as she could. She looks over at Maya, and tells her, "It's time to go", as she points towards the door.

"Ma, you said earlier that you won't be around much longer. What did you mean by that?"

"Don't get worked up. Tomorrow is not promised to us. I meant anything can happen. We won't live forever. I'm not trying to worry you but I'm reminding you that you need to be ready. Be ready to get out of that bed and work with Maya to fix our financial problems. Be ready if I happen to go away and ready to get your own house in order if that's what life calls you to do. (Taps the foot of the bed as she goes by) You're looking better. Keep it up so they will send you home."

"I think I'll walk out with your mother Robert."

"You're going also Kate?"

"Yes love. I have to pick up Cee-Jay in thirty minutes. I might as well get a jump on the traffic."

Kate steps to Robert and softly takes his face into her hands before kissing him like she would never see him again. She begins to pull away but leans in and kissed him again. When she pulls back into his sightline she whispers, "I love you."

(Just as soft)

"Love you too."

"I'll come back in the morning. I'm told they may release you tomorrow so I'll bring you something comfortable to wear. (Blows another kiss) See you in the morning."

[Three hours later]

Robert's hospital room is dark except for the light of the TV changing brightness in between commercials and a small glimmer coming in from the hall. He lay back comfortably watching a ball game until he noticed a shadow blocking the light in the doorway. Robert turns on a light over the bed and rotates his head towards the door when he thought he heard someone say, "We only have thirty."

"Who's that standing there? Step into the light."

"I'm comfortable where I am. My voice should be all you need."

"Nathaniel, Nate, Slim, is that you?"

"Yes... it... is."

"It's been some time. What brings you here? Concern for your fellow man? Pity? Or maybe strong desires to be sarcastic? (Clears throat) Because I know it isn't loyalty."

"I'm sorry Mr. Kingsley, but it's none of the above."

"Then why are you here? I know you're a freelance for hire now, are you working? Are you here to finish what a car couldn't do?"

(Quietly)

"Twenty-five."

"What'd you say?"

"Oh, nothing you should be concerned about. I'm on a short time table and won't be bothering you much longer. But to answer your question...I'm not here to kill you. As a matter of fact, I don't even have a weapon on me. (Impulsively) And what would I have to gain from that? Trust me; no one wants the media coverage or the heat that would come from bumping you off."

"That news is comforting but you haven't said why you are here."

"Twenty."

"Excuse me. I need to get by you." A nurse says to Slim as she slips by

him to get into the room. "I don't mean to interrupt but I need to administer this medicine into your IV."

The nurse pulls a tray table close and puts a syringe down as she asks for his arm so she could make the injection. As she slips the needle into the tube already placed in his arm, she stops abruptly as Robert interrupts her with a question.

"What exactly are you giving me?"

"This is dexamethasone. This is helping to bring the swelling down for your cerebral edema. If it makes you comfortable, I'll show you on your chart where your doctor has prescribed it."

"No need. You can go ahead."

The nurse gives him the injection, checks his vitals and tells him to hit the call button if he needs anything before walking out. Robert now smiles slyly as he turns to face Slim again.

"I get it. I know what you're doing. You were here when we did the countdown on my nephew. I get the sense that you're trying to recreate that moment. I see you've got your timing wrong. I'm sure you didn't expect for that nurse to come so soon. She clearly interrupted something. So Slim, if you're not here to kill me then why are you in my doorway?"

"I'm out on a collection job tonight and I have less than fifteen minutes left to get to work."

"And what possibly could you be collecting here in the hospital or standing in my doorway? Collection implies containment, capture and delivery to someone for a cause or payment."

"Mr. Kingsley, I'm here for you."

"For me? How do you expect to do that?"

"I plan to wait until the conditions are right and proceed with delivery."

"You sound absurd."

Robert squints and rubs his eyes as Slim suddenly starts to get blurry. He immediately presses his call button for the nurse.

"You're not thinking clearly Slim. With a nurse coming back to the room how do you expect to take me anywhere?"

"Me? I'm going walk away from your room like any other unsuspected visitor and go to my car. After you pass out, and you will pass out, the nurses will be sure to bring you wherever I've asked them too. I'm sure you can feel the effect of the drug by now. You are looking a little woozy. Five! I think that's all you have until you black out."

The nurse comes back into the room and Mr. Kingsley tries to speak but he is now slurring his words. He tries to focus as the nurse begins to talk to Slim.

"What do you want me to do?"

"After he is out, put him in some clothes (kicks a bag into the room), put him in a wheel chair and bring him down to the patient drop off area. I'll be there waiting to pick up my dad as far as anyone else is concerned."

"Nathaniel, I am a little concerned about the back lash from this."

"No worries. Your last shift here is tonight, right? You're leaving for your new job tomorrow. I hate to see you leave but I'd appreciate the help before you do. Look at this as a well-paid opportunity for a new start. Here's my friend Tonja now to help you. She'll walk away once you've brought him to me. Make it appear that you both are colleges and it should be a piece of cake. I'm heading to the car."

Looking at Mr. Kingsley, Slim smiles before lowering his head and taking a final look at him as his eye lids get heavier. "Easy peesy, payment on delivery." Slim says boastfully as he winks and positions his fingers like a gun and pulls the trigger. The real nurse looks at Tonja and says, "Let's get to work." Robert Kingsley blacks out.

CHAPTER TWENTY-ONE

Several missing moments

ROSLYN AND RAYMOND sit at a back table inside of a coffee shop that he would often meet her at while he was working undercover. They have coffee, tea, and scones while speaking discreetly about what led to the charade of his death and why it was necessary to advance the case against Raymond's family. Raymond would repeatedly apologize for putting her through it all but also verbalized an uncertainty on how he could save his cousin.

"Ray, the day of your funeral I watched someone walking away from the burial site. Everything within me was assuring me that you were alive. So, I told myself you couldn't be dead. It couldn't be true until I looked you over before the casket was closed. During that moment, watching that person walk away from the burial site, I felt something."

"It's clear to me my love that the heart doesn't lie. It ***was*** *me cautiously leaving the burial site. It was also me that you captured in that photo pointing at the head stones. I wanted you to know I was alive but for the safety of the case, any moves I made had to be done in secrecy."*

Roslyn strokes his hand before reaching up and softly touches his face. She gazes at her husband lovingly and chokes up a little when she speaks.

"Now that I can hold you again, speak with you, gaze into those eyes,

(Sighs) I'm relieved it was a farce. I must say it was challenging but now I can appreciate the breadcrumbs."

Roslyn smiles before she reaches across the table and eats a piece of his scone. He laughs to himself as she leaves hers untouched.

"You are my world, Ray. Eres el amor de mi vida. I knew it shortly after we started working together. I been given an opportunity that many wives would be desperate to have. I intend to make the most of it. I love you!"

Raymond sets his tea to the side; he tells her that he loves her also and then kisses his wife passionately. Solidifying the emotion that is expressed when you are given a second chance with your soul mate.

"Umm…that was better than the scone."

(Playful)

"It should be."

(She winks)

"Si mi amor, you're damned right it was."

"If public indecency wasn't a crime, I'd have you on this table right now Roz."

"You'd better stop toying with me love. You're going to get all you can handle when we get back to the room. You'd better hydrate. (Laughs)"

"I can't wait."

Raymond sips his tea before switching gears to a more serious topic. Before he starts, he reaches across the table and breaks a piece of Roslyn's scone and eats it.

"About my cousin, Ana had Sean under surveillance. He met Mia and Mia became Keisha and eventually posed as his girlfriend. We were also slipping him subliminal messages using my voice as he slept."

"And why do that?"

"Initially, just my immature way to torture him and increase his guilt about leaving me to die. I came to realize that there was no way he could have stood up to Grann or his father, even if he didn't agree with their

tactics. But when I told Ana and her staff that Sean talks in his sleep, she said let's take advantage of that."

"How so?"

"They thought under the right circumstances or if prompted, he may give up secrets. We tried to use it to our advantage. (Sips his tea) I felt guilty after his personality shifted. (Solemnly) I didn't see that coming. I just hope I get the chance to help him before his alter ego gets him killed."

"Life is an endless cycle of uncertainty Ray. We can only hope that the very thing that changed him may bring him back."

"Let's hope so."

[Same day, noon with the twins]

Ana listens to Mia and Meck as they explain how Donnie came up missing before he was found hanging half beaten at that warehouse. Mia is talking…

"We checked on Donnie and when we got word that he was awake, I was able to talk with him before the local P.D could get to him. But I'll get back to that." (Points at Meck)

"He left me in San Jose, counterfeit cash in hand and headed back home. Once back in Colver, we sent him to a warehouse that provided equipment that he could purchase to start his dispensary business. That way we could provide proof of him using the money. We set the warehouse up with surveillance and were prepared to collect the cash and video as evidence."

"Meck, did he visit the warehouse and did he use the money?" Ana asks.

"Yes, on both."

"Did we collect the marked bills and acquire the video evidence?"

"Again… yes on both."

"Where did we lose track of him Mia?"

"It was two days after that. He was sitting on a bench in that neighborhood park he spends so much time in. I was told that a day later

he was interviewing a kid that survived Stacey Hunter's raids and then vanished shortly after that."

"How'd you find that out Mia?"

"I went to the park as Keisha to check his progress on his dispensary. One of his guys told me how no one had seen him since talking with that kid. Ana, shortly after came the news coverage with Donnie hanging from his wrists at the back of that abandoned shipping dock."

"Was Donnie able to describe or give any info about this guy he spoke with or how he was abducted?"

Mia looks at her brother. She begins to speak again but stops abruptly as if what she was going to say was interrupted with a new thought.

"Donnie was startled when I walked into his hospital room. He asked what brought me there and I put him at ease by telling him I came to check on the progress of his new business. He tried to smile but quickly stopped because of the pain. I then softly asked what happened to him. Ana, he told me that he was talking with the kid the other guy mentioned. Said he was doing a side walk interview. Hoping to steal him away for his new venture. They started walking towards a nearby corner store. The kid deflected when asked any questions about the robbery or being invited to work for Stacey Hunter. The short walk brought them to the entrance of the store and he asked the kid to wait outside as he went in to buy a soda. Donnie said he felt something sting him. He looked around and noticed a few bees flying around and thought nothing more of it. As he approached the register to pay for his drink, he felt a bit woozy. Donnie recalls coming out the door, squeezing his drink tightly and collapsing to one knee. He heard the kid tell someone he needed help and after that he blacked out. He woke up hanging by his wrists and to his people being killed. They were hung alone side of him as two others were spraying graffiti. He watched bodies being carried into the building. No one spoke. Nothing was ever said to him. People in masks would spin him, punch him, and hit him with bats. He was struck

with any weighty objects they could find. This went on for days. He also mentioned watching the sun rise and set three times. After that he barely remembers the sirens, ambulance or the doctors."

(Wearily)

"Oh my! That is a lot to have suffered and witnessed. Not to mention the only one to have survived it."

The room gets quiet as Ana rises from her seat and paces in front of her window.

"Meck I sense you have another concern."

"With Donnie laid up, I don't see how we can lure Stacey Hunter out using the plates or the counterfeit money. He had to see the news footage. He's probably laying low and being overly cautious about his next moves."

"Has anyone and that includes our personnel, the local police or any informants put eyes on Stacey Hunter?" Ana asks.

"There were a couple of 911 calls of someone suspiciously sifting through the rubble of Robert Kingsley's businesses. When the police arrived at each property, the man they encountered presented a badge and told them he was a fire investigator. Once he presented them with what seemed like the proper credentials, the police dismissed it and let him get back to work. But when I checked with the city, the only two investigators working for the fire department are Japanese-American and Caucasian. Both men with ten or more years of service."

"So, Raymond was right!" Mia shouted. "He's looking for the vault."

"And he obviously has not found it." Ana replies as she continues to pace.

"So…what now boss? What do we do?" Mia eagerly asks.

"We need an ID of that kid Donnie met with. Meck, check with the local police and see if a sketch artist was sent to Donnie's room. If not, have one sent to the hospital. Get us someone to look for. We need to quickly locate this kid and find out what or who he knows."

[Ana's phone rings.]

"Grainger here... uh-huh... Yes, I'm listening. Yes, I understand. This could be a problem. It will definitely complicate things. I'll discuss it with the team and we'll come up with a plan"

[Ana hangs up]

[Sacred Heart church 5pm]

Maya sits comfortably on the steps of the church. The evening wind blows her hair as she zips up her jacket, pulls a hat from her pocket and puts it on. She makes a couple of adjustments with her hair as Justin; her new second in command makes the short climb towards her. With a hand gesture she offers him a seat but he declines. He stops and stands on the concrete step that gives them both direct eye contact.

"That was good work grabbing Donnie and helping me see it to completion. Not many have the resolve or the mental strength to move on from it. What we did would haunt most people. How are you?"

"Except for my lady's snoring, I'm sleeping like a baby. I saw a movie once that said: some people deserve to die. Don't seem so surprised that I've been sent to do the killing: That put things in perspective for me. So, I'm good."

"You have been an asset and I don't want to lose you. (Justin fidgets) I'm worried Donnie might out you. We have to assume he's told the police that you were the last man with him. So, unless he's bad at describing accurate facial features, let's assume they know what you look like and will try to find you."

"Am I in danger?"

"If you were with me, you'd never get the chance to ask. In your current situation, only if you're arrested. They'll question you. Even pressure you. They may even violate your rights to get answers. But if they can't tie you to anything you should be fine. I just don't want to take that chance. So, here's what I want you to do. I need you to lay low for a few months. Get out of the state until this blows over. I doubt Donnie will turn snitch but

who knows what he'll do after what we did to him. Let's hope he packs up and starts new somewhere else. Again, I just don't want to take any chances."

"No, no…I get it."

[Maya's phone rings]

Justin stands and looks around as she answers her cell phone. Maya's facial expressions say much more than she ever did. With the wind blowing the strands of her hair not covered by the hat and the phone to her ear, she listened to four words that would change what she was initially saying to Justin. Maya hangs up her phone, looks towards the sky and sighs loudly and angrily. She lowers her head and rubs her eyes before taking her right hand to her forehead and doing the sign of the cross.

(Abruptly)

"Change of plans, you can't leave. I have to go see our boss who is the Kingsley's matriarch. After I do that, there is something dire we must take care of."

CHAPTER TWENTY-TWO

Setting the scheme

IT'S SEVEN IN the morning and the curtains are closed in Roslyn and Raymond's downtown Colver hotel room. Roslyn opens her eyes to a partially blurry view of Bane staring her in the face before rolling to her right. She adjusted herself until her head found her husband's chest. Raymond had just thanked the front desk for the wake-up call before moving his left arm to receive the inbound Roslyn. She nestles in by laying her left arm across his abs and her left thigh across his leg. Her eyes innocently drift upwards as she softly asks, "What are you thinking about? Whatever it is has been causing you to toss and turn all night."

(Strokes her hair)

"I think about this uneven, crooked road to redemption. (Softly) Shit, no one tells you that you'll suffer more along the way before any wrongs are ever righted. (Pauses) ***If****... it happens at all."*

"What are your expectations Ray? Deep down there must be something you desire. I hope you're not setting yourself up for an emotional letdown. (Rubs his leg with hers) How do you want this to end?"

"People romanticize daily about what they want and are often disappointed with the outcome. I want... (Drifts to silence briefly) I want to help Sean if I can but it may be too late for that. For the rest of my family, jail is preferable. Grann told me once that no one is too old to pay for their

sins. Whether it's within the penal system or with their lives, she's always preferred the latter. Honestly, I'm personally torn between the two."

"You couldn't possibly want to see your grandmother die?

Raymond reaches alongside of the bed with his right hand and begins to pet Bane.

"A little of column "A" ... a little of column "B". Who knows? (Breathes deeply) You, this dog and Sean may be the only family I have left. I'm not sure what I want but I'm concerned more importantly how it happens to work out. My uncle and my grandmother became dead to me after I realized they tried to kill me. It's hard to brush that off. They're just two criminals that need to be brought to justice in my eyes. The sooner I can put them behind bars and place the headache of my family's history behind me, the sooner we can build a normal life for ourselves Roz."

"What about your cousin? What about Sean's current mental condition?"

"I've been thinking about that. How do we coax Sean out of Stacey Hunter? How do we find them to be able to even try? The more I think about it, only creates more head pounding questions. I'm preparing myself for the eventuality that I may never find peace or the justice that I'm expecting."

Roslyn presses up against Raymond before giving him a half body hug.

(With sincerity)

"The peace you need will come. I'm sure of it. Justice on the other hand is not always balanced."

[9:00am]

Maya approaches Grann who is comfortably swaying on her porch swing. "Take a look at those two bottles over there child." Grann howls pointing at Maya as she reaches the steps.

"The thought of someone lurking around my house when I'm not here

infuriates me. Not to mention being coy about taking my only son. (Agitated) Oh, hell has definitely frozen over if he thinks he'll get any money out of me."

Grann rattles on. Her angry tirade would have been another two minutes if Maya didn't look for the right opportunity to interrupt.

"G-ma, G-ma! (Waving her hands) How are we going to handle this?"

"First with a revered grace and then we'll finish with unbridled violence! Make him think he's getting what he wants and then castrate the MOTHER FUCKER!"

"Who are you barking about? Who has Mr. Kingsley?"

"The bane of your existence since you came to help me, Stacey Hunter."

Grann stops swaying and takes a deep breath.

"If you look closely at that bottle child, there was a phone number put on the label. I called that number and that son-of-a-bitch smugly answered. Tells me he has my son and asks if I'm willing to negotiate to get him back."

"He obviously wants money."

"And a hell of a lot of it child. He set two prices. One, if Robert is harmed and the other if we want him unharmed. You know, I hate when people try to fuck with me. It is common knowledge that he had to hurt him to get him out of that hospital. That bastard just laughed and set his price. Maya this business isn't humane and the day you fall for some infant bullshit, is the day you shouldn't be in this line of work anymore."

Grann grabs a bag that was on the porch next to the swing and tosses it over to Maya.

"Take that with you."

"Where am I going?"

"You're going to meet him at 1 o'clock at the Peaceful Serenity cemetery in one of the mausoleums. Inside the grounds, take the first right and then the next left before looking for the second building. It's the bigger of the two. The best spot, the best advantage point is where my husband lays. Look for Mason "Big Mo" Kingsley. Find him and take your stand. Don't let that

Mother Fucker walk out of there with my money! I want him dead. But most importantly, secure my son. Then play on his ego and get close if he lets you. Slip out that little Derringer you have and put a .22 bullet between his ribs. Make sure the rest of your people are targeting any strays. Pop him, drop him, grab the money and get the hell out of the there. Kate is driving me crazy with questions. I haven't told her. She thinks I sent him out of town. Bring Robert here as quickly as you can."

"Yes Ma'am."

Grann sighs before respectfully nodding her head to assure she had nothing more for Maya. Maya grabs the bag, pulls her cell phone from her pocket and calls Justin as she exits the yard.

"It's me. Grab two reliable trigger-happy guys and meet me in front of the church in 45."

[10:00am Ana meets with her team]

"We have the necessary paperwork to exhume Cassie Reynolds remains. The coroner's office will meet us at the burial site and take possession from the Peaceful Serenity staff. Roslyn, I want you there just in case Raymond's aunt shows up to post a protest. (Ana pulls paper from a folder) Here's a copy of the paperwork in case you have to show her that it's all legal. Ray, I need you waiting in the shadows. Pose as a grounds keeper and secure the perimeter. Mia & Meck, I want you to be bookends next to the coroner. This extraction should be fairly easy. Never the less, I want us all to be ready for anything. Are there any questions?"

"Why won't they already have the casket out and ready when we arrive?"

"Yes, that would have been better for us Meck but the coroner and the cemetery staff could not get coordinated. Also, there is a process for lowing it from the wall. We can't cut corners. Every step is being documented. It's all by the book. And the book opens at 1pm."

Ana becomes uncharacteristically quiet for a brief awkward moment, as if she was searching for the right words. She walks to the center of her living room and sits directly across from Raymond. The room is quiet and filled with anticipation waiting for Ana to speak.

"The second thing we need to discuss is an unexpected wrinkle and it has been added to our list of tasks to complete. This will happen after recovering the remains of Ms. Reynolds. Ray…this may be harder for you than anyone else. (Pauses) There is no way to sugar coat this. Robert Kingsley is missing from the hospital."

[Assorted mumbling]

(Angrily)

"You have got to be ***fuck'en*** *shitting me! When?" Raymond shouts.*

"It's been about 36 hours now. The powers that be want us to locate him and find him fast. They believe his life is in danger."

"Do they have any information? Anything to go on?"

"Ray, hospital security footage only shows a nurse wheeling him down to the patient pickup & drop off area. The nurse that brought him is not on the nursing staff and the car that he was put into did not have any licenses plates."

"So now we are drug enforcement agents and missing persons as well?"

"Mia, their mindset is that this unfortunate incident is directly related to our case. So, we will have to address it."

"There could be an endless number of suspects. My uncle has a lot of enemies."

"But how many would actually take action against him?"

"That is a good question, Roslyn. Not many would. Not many have." Raymond says frustratingly shaking his head.

"I'd bet pennies for pussy that it's someone we are already looking for."

"Wow! Mia, that was colorful."

"Thanks, big brother. Participation doesn't have to be boring. But how many of you are thinking the same thing?"

Mia smiles sarcastically at Meck. Raymond shakes his head, rubs the back of his neck and leans back into the chair. Ana leans back as well before speaking again.

"So, our plan doesn't change. If we find Stacey Hunter, we find Sean. Find either and we may find Robert Kingsley. Ok gang, first things first. Let's get after it."

[11:15 Sacred Heart church]

Maya approaches the steps of the church where Justin and two others are waiting. She's wearing military camouflage pants, boots, a green turtle neck shirt and a black tactical gun vest. Maya has a look in her eye that anyone who has intentionally and consciously killed before could recognize. She was discreet but intensely focused. After grouping her crew into a half circle, she stepped in close so only they could hear what she has to say.

"Once we're on the cemetery grounds, Justin will pull over and let the both of you out. Then cut across the plots and position yourselves across from the two mausoleum entrances. (Abruptly) Better yet, get out of the car and hang back until you see us go in. The sight of two young black men visiting a loved one may look suspicious. In my experience Ya'll will do funerals and burials but rarely visit graves. On second thought, just hang back and keep anyone from ambushing us. If you didn't know, this is a recovery operation! Our boss is our priority. Let's try to bring him back unharmed. That's first. The second is not to allow Stacey Hunter to leave the grounds with our ransom money. If it has to get bloody, hold out until Mr. Kingsley is secure and out of the building. Once he's clear, we'll let loose if we have too."

"So once Mr. Kingsley is safe…that's when we go on the offensive?" One of the guys asks as Justin curiously looks at Maya.

"Not exactly. (Points) You both will be outside so I expect you both to

take out any potential threats while we are inside. But do it quietly. Early gunfire may complicate things. These types of exchanges typically never go as planned. No one has any trust and aren't willing to show any. Someone always tries to alter the deal and that just drags it out longer than necessary. Initially I want him to feel like he has the upper hand. Let's not tip ours showing concern for the money. If I can't get close enough to him to drop him with a single .22 shot, I have employed an outside hitter who will recover the money. Now I can't tell you what we may be walking into. I've seen situations like this expose the best and the worst in someone. If you believe the strong will survive…then survive. Again…our focus is Mr. Kingsley. Are we clear on that? (Heads nod) Then let's go!"

CHAPTER TWENTY-THREE

Hooker's Swallow

[Noon]

THE SKY IS gray and filled with dark clouds ready to drop more rain. The cemetery staff of Peaceful serenity was expecting to have a busy day. With three burials, the police's exhumation and an intrusive ransom exchange. Carson Watford, the facilities coordinator was hoping the day would be business as usual but that was until he received word from the grounds crew that last night's rain fall caused two of the newly dug plots to implode. This misfortune caused his crew to have to re-dig those plots which began to jeopardize the daily schedule. Especially with the city's coroner van pulling onto the property forty-five minutes earlier than expected. Carson approaches the van and taped on the window. While waiting on the driver to acknowledge him and roll down his window, no one noticed an old Crown Victoria station wagon driving pass them with a wooden crate hanging out the back of it.

"I'm terribly sorry but you're an hour or so early and my staff isn't available yet."

"I'm just the driver. The rest of the team has already gone up to the Mausoleum. They will wait for you and your staff there. With it raining, I will bring the van over once the team is actually ready for me."

"That will be fine." Carson responded after nodding, lightly tapping the side of the van and heading back to the office as the rain begins to fall again.

The station wagon moves through the property too fast for the wet pavement. Sliding unsafely onto the grass as it maneuvers around a few of the tighter turns. The crate bounces around, hitting against the sides of the wagon before the vehicle skids to an abrupt stop. "You guys get the crate out of the back while I go inside and take a quick look." Stacey says as he jumps out of the car and uses his jacket to protect himself from the rain. Once out of sight, Stacey's guys sloppily mishandle the crate onto a cart and try to catch up with him.

[12:15]

Inside the crate and with the drug still in Robert's system, he subconsciously drifts into an old memory. A hazy image reveals Robert and Kate standing silently with his hand interlocked with Kate's. She leans into him engulfed with sorrow over her sister. The hall of the mausoleum echoes with Kate's sobbing as her sister's coffin is placed into internment. But unbeknownst to Kate, Robert's smile is conniving as the marble with Cassie's name is secured by the cemetery staff.

"Come on love, nothing we can do for her now." Robert says softly as he tries to coax Kate towards the exit.

(Crying)

"No! Not yet Robert. I want to leave some flowers. It's what Cora would've wanted to do."

"Excuse me, can you wait a moment?" Robert asks of the staff before turning to Kate. "Ok. You take the car over to the flower stand while I speak with the director for a moment."

Kate walks outside to the car as Robert pulls the director back to the area where Cassie was just placed.

"Is there something else I can help you with, Mr. Kingsley?"

"After we leave today, I need you to straighten out the name plates. This one with Cassie's name should be where you placed Kimber Kelly's. I need you to swap them."

"I'm sorry, did we make an error? I believe everything for both of your loved ones was done as you requested."

"It's a bit complicated. It's not your mistake. (Sighs) Cassie's family wanted her to be buried but Cassie wanted to be cremated. Cassie worked for me and made me promise if anything were to happen to her that I would carry out her wishes. But…still find a way to appease her relatives. That casket you just placed is a visual comfort for the family. Cassie and Kimber were friends and died together. Kimber's wishes were to be cremated as well. Kimber's family volunteered to pick up Cassie's ashes when they picked up Kimber's and somehow Cassie's ashes ended up in Kimber's vault."

"And Mrs. Kelly's ashes?"

"They are sitting on a mantle in her parent's home."

"This does seem complicated."

"Here's what I want you to do. Leave the nameplates where they are. But once we're gone, I'll pay whatever payroll or overtime is needed to swap the empty casket and the urn with Cassie's ashes. That way Cassie's remains will be where the family expects them to be."

Robert reaches into his pocket and pulls out his money clip. He pulls off four-hundred-dollar bills and hands it to the director.

"This is for your trouble."

(Hesitant)

"O-kay."

"Is there a problem with what I want you to do?"

"Mr. Kingsley… not at all. Once you leave, I will switch the casket that you say is empty with the urn that actually has Mrs. Reynolds's ashes."

"That is exactly what I would like. Please bill me for any additional hours you use to get this done."

"Yes sir, we'll take care of this for you right away."

The director steps away as Kate walks back up with flowers in hand.

"These are the only flowers they had that I liked. They will have to do for now."

"They are fine Kate. They look fine. I'm sure Cassie would've loved them."

The hazy images of his past fade as Robert becomes conscious. Still groggy with a dry mouth, he opens his eyes. It's dark but he could hear muffled voices nearby. He listens. Trying to pick up any indication of where he might be or who he was delivered to. Nothing he could hear was clear enough to make out. Instead, he tries to move but any movement was constricted. His arms and legs were strapped down to whatever cramped box he seemed to be enclosed in. The muffled voices began again but this time they were followed with a lot of jerky movements.

"Hey Hunt…is this it? Because this motha-fucka is heavy. Normally there are six pushing something like this."

"That crate is on a dolly with wheels and we still have business to deduct once we find where we're s'posed to be. So why are you fuck'en whining? That's not a coffin so we don't need four other useless motha-fuckas with that box, just you two lazy bastards. Shit, so do me a favor, shut the fuck up and push the crate!"

[1pm]

Maya & Justin stand quietly near the resting place of Big 'Mo" Kingsley, Maya standing about 2ft in front of Justin. The rain rhythmically hits the building as the fluorescent lighting attempts to take the darkness from the hall. Justin's eyes are closed but he stands with his feet shoulder width apart and with his left hand clasped to his right wrist comfortably in front of him. He speaks to Maya but doesn't open his eyes.

"It's quiet at first and then it begins with a bit of whistling air before

the words become clear for me. Right now, I hear something or someone. It may be more than one voice but I'm listening."

Maya respectfully remains silent so she wouldn't break his concentration. She was curious, a street thug hearing the voices of the dead. This wasn't the first time she's seen this behavior from Justin. He did a similar thing in the abandoned depot warehouse. He closed his eyes and opened himself up to the spirits. It was there the voices of men were yelling out in pain. Begging for second chances and pleading for another chance for redemption. But with their deaths came judgment and, in their pain, the realization that it is too late for them now. The Promised Land had escaped the men laid out on the cold concrete of that warehouse floor. That's what Justin told Maya at that time but now she waits for him to tell her what he hears the spirits saying now.

"The spirits are restless. Maya they are pleading loudly. They say this is not the place for what is about to be done. This unrest will affect someone's immortality."

Maya's looks over her shoulder towards Justin at the moment he opens his eyes. Her expression was as if she said; what's done is done. Maya rotates her head back towards the empty hall, shrugging her shoulders and she solemnly says, "It's already too late for the lot of us. There's no hiding from judgment. It should be a short time standing at the gates before I plummet to hell. I cannot say enough Hail Mary's to fix all the wrong(s) I've done. (Looks back at him quickly) I can accept that. (Angrily) What I can't accept…are people who are late!"

Down the hall and around the corner, Ana, the twins and the coroner are waiting as well. Hoping the cemetery staff will show at any moment, Mia turns her attention and boredom to the coroner and decided she'd pry a little.

"So, I have to ask, why did you come today? They could've picked up the body and delivered it to you. Does being here feel odd?" Mia asks.

"With the rise of how cool they make us look on TV, I decided to get out of the office for a change of pace."

"That thought is interesting because you can always count on something to go excitingly wrong on TV. Are you ready if something does?"

"It's unlikely that anything will. Things happen on dramas to ramp up the action or the emotion of a scene. The real world isn't always so melodramatic or exciting. So, I find it unlikely. But to be out of the office, on a field trip if you will, is a break in the monotony that I need."

(Jokingly)

"Oh hell, I think you just jinxed yourself. (Leans over to Meck) He clearly doesn't know his odds have changed just being around us."

"Us! You do mean…you! If we had a seventies TV show it would be called 'Loose cannon & the cleanup man'. Your tag line would be, "Have a short fuse, get a fast boom" and your nickname would be Torch."

(Excited)

"Ooh, ooh because everything blows up around her?"

[Laughing]

"Precisely! The coroner hit that one on the head." Meck says smiling at his sister.

The hall is filled with laughter as the cemetery's manager approaches the group.

"Good afternoon, everyone. I'm sorry if we've kept you. It's been a busy morning. Thanks for your patience. My staff is here and will have what you've come for ready to transport shortly. (Points) If I could have all of you stand over here so we can get started."

Two men come into the area with a scissor lift wide and long enough to fit a single casket. Attached to the lift is a metal stand that would fit one staff member. With the lift in position and one of the staff ready to go up, they began the process to extract Cassie's remains. Everyone else turns their attention to the rain. Watching through the huge windows as it comes down heavily.

{The exchange}

The hall near Maya and Justin was quiet until the rattle and squeak of an unbalanced wheel broke the silence. This noise disturbed the music of the rain against the roof and was the indication that Stacey Hunter had finally shown up.

(Echoing)

"I think it's over here. Yea, there it is."

"There's nothing more annoying than someone who can't show up on time." Maya said sounding upset.

"I do believe this is my meeting. It starts when I'm ready for it too. Who gives a shit if you had to wait! I was kind enough to let your people pick the spot and now I see that that was a mistake. (Scoffs) Big Mo Kingsley, I know a little of his history. He was good at baiting people. Making them think they were getting what they wanted but effectively duping them out of much more. King of the bait and switch is what they used to call him. If your people think they can use this place or his history as a tactic then they are gravely mistaken."

"I hate to interrupt you from quoting the back of your drug dealer trading cards but I don't care to hear about the Kingsley family back story. Let's just get down to business."

The crate sudden comes into view and Maya could hear mumbling coming from it.

"The deal was...the cash for Mr. Kingsley. But I've been giving it some thought and now I'm going to amend the deal."

Maya looks back at Justin. "What did I tell you. No fucking surprise." (Turns back as Stacey continues.)

"I'll let you keep the cash. Call it relocation money. I want you and

what's left of the Kingsley clan to forfeit any rights to any territory holds they have in this city. Pack up and leave or I'll kill any remaining signs of business prosperity they think they have left. Their kingdom has crumbled around them and it is time for me to rise from the ashes."

"Last I heard your entire crew was found dead in a warehouse. You actually think we're almost out of business? You might want to reconsider that notion."

"Rebuilding a crew will be easy. How many people will work for a crew that has to pay ransom to get their leader back? It seems you've lost credibility on these streets. Retirement is a way for the Kingsley crew to save face and to ride off into the sunset with a little dignity. If I've gotten to him once, I can definitely do it again. And next time, ransom won't be an option. So, what's it going to be?"

"That's awfully cocky of you."

"It comes with having the upper hand. So…?"

"Yet another thought you need to reconsider. There's only one man who can agree to what you want and you'll have to take 'em out of that box to find out. But I think you already know what his answer will be. Money may be the only thing you walk out of here with. (Smiles) But even I'm curious what Mr. Kingsley will say. (Smirks) Open the box."

Stacey Hunter signals his goons. They take two cordless drills from beneath the cart and remove the screws holding the lid on. Once the lid was removed, they cut the straps going through the sides and under the bottom of the crate that were restraining Mr. Kingsley. "He may be a bit feeble fella. Help lift him out of there." Stacey's goons raise him up, lift him out and supported him once he was on his feet. Robert Kingsley raises his head and his eyes pop out now that he realizes that he was delivered to his son.

"Are you surprised at your surroundings? Wondering who I am or are you relieved you're still alive? I want to take a minute and speak with you. Actually…propose something. I was telling soft kitty over there that I'm

willing to fore-go your ransom if you retire and turn your territory of this city over to me. I hate to put you on the spot but I'm gonna need an answer."

Robert lifts his head and with a dry, raspy voice, forces out an emphatic, "NO!" Stacey Hunter shrewdly smiles before drawing his gun and putting it to Robert's head.

"Relax soft kitty, don't do anything you may regret. I just want to appeal to his better judgment. (Winks at Maya) This will only take a moment. Mr. Kingsley I'll get right to the point. I could just kill you and take every inch of city territory you're respected in but that wouldn't be advantageous. But if I assumed control because you handed it over to me then I wouldn't have to fight for it after you were dead. Your long hospital stay has caused you to lose perspective, control and profits in this city. It's time for you to call it quits. So again… what's it going to be?"

(Rough & silent)

"Still… no!"

(Aggravated)

"He's going to make me take his life. (Points) Maybe you'll want to save his life."

Stacey Hunter looks optimistically at Maya before taking his thumb and slowly bringing the hammer back on his gun. The slow clicks cause Robert to flinch as Stacey pushes the barrel into his temple. Maya's expression may show her nervousness but her mannerisms are calm. She unnoticeably throws her left hand back and quickly shakes it as instruction for Justin not to move or pull his gun.

"Maybe I haven't made this personal enough. So…let me appeal to your humanity soft kitty. You've got to feel something within you that would keep me from pulling this trigger. Something personal? Maybe some gut feeling or something biological?"

"What are you babbling about? You aren't making any sense. The man

gave you his answer. But if you shoot him, you will also die in this hall today."

"Look, I'm just trying to clear the air here. You must have felt a hole in your life all these years. And what I'm about to tell you is the very reason you would want to keep him alive." (Pushes gun into his temple again)

"WHAT THE FUCK ARE YOU TRYNG TO SAY?"

"I'm saying, this piece of shit …is your father. What would you do to save your father?"

"You must mean…my boss! My father died the year that I was born. Fuck that bullshit you say'en! I have no emotions you can manipulate."

"Is that what you were told?"

With the gun in his right hand and still pointed at Robert's head, Stacey reaches into his pocket with his left hand, pulls out a piece of paper and reads from it, loudly.

"Maya Sharice Sullivan, born July 10th, 1995. Mother, Evelyn Sullivan and it says here…father, Robert Kingsley."

It is silent as he looks back and forth between the two of them.

"By the looks on both of your faces, neither of you knew. (Looks between them again) You know what…you're welcome! I bring broken families back together. (Pauses) But my fucking question still hasn't been answered. Do you want to keep your daddy alive?"

"Alive, yes, I do. That other bullshit, only a fool would believe. There could be anything written on that paper. It doesn't make it true."

"I got this from the hall of records. You can do the same thing if you don't believe me."

Justin clears his throat attempting to get Maya's attention.

"Sully, the spirits say it's true." Maya looks back at Justin and cuts her eyes at him.

"I don't want to hear that nonsense right now. Not right now. (Turns back to Stacey) You want to turn this mausoleum into the O.K. corral?

Because we can! Or...you can take this ransom money; give me Mr. Kingsley and we can do a standoff in the middle of town some other day. Believe me I want nothing more than to deliver you to the gates of Hell myself. (Puts down her gun) What's it going to be Mr. Hunter?"

Stacey smirks before slowly un-cocking and lowering his gun from Robert's head. "Let's do it!" He yells impulsively.

"Send your boy behind you midway between us and I'll send one of mine with Mr. Kingsley."

Maya nods in agreement because she knows she's a much better shot than Justin. She stands ready to fire if she has too but keeps her weapon at her side. With Mr. Kingsley's arm over one shoulder, one of Stacey's henchmen walks him out to meet Justin. Justin comes around to Kingsley's right side to support him with the left side of his body and hands the money bag to the goon with his right hand. After taking the bag, Stacey's goon lets Kingsley's weight rest on Justin and begins too slowly back away.

"I'm not as weak as they think. Give me your gun and then get down when I tell you too." Robert tells Justin.

Justin doesn't hesitate. He reaches with his right hand into his open jacket, pulls his gun from the holster and Mr. Kingsley discreetly takes it with his left. "Get down, now!" Justin drops to the floor as Robert rotates over him and fires on the henchman that was backing away with the bag and the one standing near the crate. He fires two shots and puts a bullet each between both of their eyes. The gunshots were loud and before Stacey's henchmen's lifeless bodies could hit the floor, he turned and ran. Maya, just seconds from pulling the trigger on Stacey was startled when Robert moved in front of her yelling, "NO! YOU CAN'T SHOOT MY SON!"

(Frustrated)

"WHAT! Are you kidding me? Justin, get Mr. Kingsley out of here. I'll get Stacey and the money."

Maya side steps Mr. Kingsley, hits the nearest exit and gives chase to Stacey Hunter.

Down the hall, Ana, the cemetery staff, the twins and the coroner all hear the gunshots. Ana draws her weapon and sends the twins out to check the surrounding area as Roslyn calls the dispatch of the Colver police department to report the shots and ask for backup. At the same time the cemetery staff had lowered Cassie's casket and was moving it to the coroner's cart for transport. It was only moments after, Stacey Hunter came hauling ass from around the corner and plows into the coroner. Slamming himself and the coroner into Cassie's casket and knocking it off the cart and to the floor. (Everyone gasps) Stacey quickly finds his way to his feet and runs out the door into the rain. Ana addresses her team through her earpiece. She instructs the twins to go after Stacey and Raymond to back them up. "Copy that!" Raymond answers as he handcuffs one of Maya's henchmen, leans him against a headstone before standing and looking for where the twins would be in pursuit. He sees no one.

Back near Big Mo, Justin grabs the bag and follows Robert Kingsley in pursuit of Stacey. With gun in hand and still weak in the legs, Robert stumbles at a moderate pace up the hall and around the corner. He turns the corner, stops abruptly, stumblimg back as he runs right into the waiting barrel of Ana's gun. "Drop the gun! Drop it… NOW!" Ana yells as she moves her gun between Robert and Justin. Robert lowers his arm and releases the gun. The clunk was loud as the steel hits the marble floor. "You…drop the bag, come from behind Mr. Kingsley and both of you put your hands in the air."

{The Chase}

Maya instinctively took the faster exit from the building expecting Stacey Hunter to make his way outside. She was right. The heavy rain splatters off of her gun vest as she holsters her weapon and starts to run.

Initially she slips on the asphalt road but gains her footing and invokes her old track skills when she sees Stacey stumble out of the other entrance. He sticks to the road because he lost his footing when he tried to run across the flat headstones and the grass. He doesn't look back so he doesn't see Maya coming up behind him.

*"There!" Meck hollers to Mia as he points out Stacey Hunter running away from the building. The twins are startled when they see Maya high stepping passed them, knees high and arms swinging. They instantly join the foot chase. Mia, unlike her brother dresses more casually and was wearing suitable shoes to run in. It was amazing how fast Meck was moving in his semi-casual dress shoes on a wet surface. Mia yells "**Stop**" several times. Maya snaps her head around rapidly when she hears the yelling. But seeing them doesn't slow her momentum. Stacey nervously looks over his shoulder after feeling some pain in the leg that Sean injured back in his basketball days. That old injury began to slow him down. With Maya in full stride, she was easily catching up. As she ran, a sudden curiosity made her wonder who these two chasing she and Stacey might be and why. Maya made a snap decision on whether catching Stacey was worth it, especially not knowing who the two trailing her was. Now side by side with Stacey and hearing how out of breath he was, she reaches out and viciously shoves him. He stumbles from the asphalt onto the grass and slides across a flat, slick headstone before tumbling into a freshly dug grave. His momentum forces him to go face first into the furthest corner of the rain-soaked dirt before falling backward into the plot. Maya never looks back. She kicks into another gear. Believing no one could catch her on foot, she heads for the exit of the cemetery.*

The twins slowed to a stop after seeing Stacey Hunter plummet into the open ground. They both stand hunched over, breathing heavily as Meck peers into the hole.

(Huffing)

*"Damn! Is she an Olympic athlete? **Fuck** she's fast! Who was **that** gazelle?" Mia asks Meck.*

(Out of breath)

"No clue. But...clearly, she's in better shape than the both of us. (Pants) Could you see her clear enough to make an I.D.?"

*"Yeah... (Still out of breath) fast-**ASS**-bitch! (Pauses) High stepp'en Ho! Or try...Bitch with a blurr!"*

"I get it Mia; you couldn't see her."

*"Ya **think**!"*

Meck smirks at his sister's response as he straightens up and looks into the grave.

"What do you see?" Mia asks.

"He's moving...a little. He looks to be in some pain."

"How are we going to get him out?"

"Let's not worry about that just yet. It doesn't look like he'll walk that off right away. Let's see if he can get to his feet. Then we'll figure it out."

{Getting answers}

Robert and Justin stand against the wall handcuffed as Ana & Roslyn carefully sift through the items in the open casket. Mr. Kingsley avoids the open questions from Ana and also making any longing eye contact with Roslyn. The cemetery grounds were now filled with the flashing sirens of police cars and the lights could be seen through the windows of the mausoleum. Raymond was outside explaining who he and the thug tied up near one of the headstones are. The twins and the cemetery grounds crew were pulling Stacey Hunter out of the six-foot-deep plot which is proving to be challenging with the rain and the mud. The coroner limped his way down the hall to help the crime scene investigators secure the area where Stacey's henchmen lye dead. The cemetery seemed to be overrun with police personnel.

Robert Kingsley remains quiet because he recognizes Cassie's casket and his vault lying open on the floor. His calm expression hides the rage of anger he has for the old administration of the cemetery because his request to move the casket had not been carried out. Knowing his rights, he bottles his anger, looks uninterested and remains silent when any question or comment are thrown his way.

"Look here Ana, look at the name on the side of the casket. It says Hookers Swallow."

"A name like that sounds disrespectful but why do you think all this Stuff is in here and Ms. Reynold's remains are not, thoughts Roslyn?"

"Some time ago my home was broken into and a wall in the basement was spray painted with the words NOT HERE. I believe someone was looking for a vault that Raymond's father DL Kingsley was supposed to have. I think this open casket may be (Points at Robert) his secret vault."

The two ladies continue to sift through jewelry, gold in different forms, bricks of plastic covered money, copies of deeds and important papers until… Ana reaches into the box with a pen and pulls out a gun. She turns, giving a derisive smile at Mr. Kingsley as the weapon is placed into a plastic evidence bag.

"You can stand there Mr. Kingsley with that pompously smug expression but you and I both know who the contents of that box belongs to. Your overwhelming silence right now tells me you know enough about the law to remain quiet. Say nothing so you won't incriminate yourself. And that's fine, that's your right. But I must remind you that there is no statute of limitation on murder."

Robert Kingsley cut his eyes, giving her another uninterested look before sniffing and then heavily exhaling.

"Just let me know when I can call my lawyer." Robert says with an air of indignation.

Ana looks directly at Justin but points towards Mr. Kingsley who still looks uninterested in anything being said.

"I hope you're watching and listening. The guilty ones stay quiet and always have good lawyers. That's why he can afford to stand there as cocky as he is. (Pauses) It won't take very long to change his blank expression to a worried one. The truth is Mr. Kingsley is just one ballistics test away from being charged in an old murder case. I'd be equally concerned what the GSR results will be for the two men lying dead down the hall. Right now, you're an accessory to that crime. And men like the man you're standing next to don't usually share expensively good lawyers. But we'll get to the bottom of what happened here today, one way or another."

Robert mouths the words, "you'll be ok" to Justin before leaning back against the wall.

The twins placed handcuffs on a dazed Stacey Hunter just after the cemetery crew helps get him out of the hole. His face, hands, and clothes are covered with mud. With a tap on his arm, they lead him back down the road towards the mausoleum. They enter just as Ana was finishing her comments about ballistic results to Robert Kingsley. Roslyn stands surprised as Stacey Hunter walks passed her as if she's a stranger.

"What's his deal?" Ana asks looking back at the twins.

"This is your runner, Ana." Meck responds.

"Well, what happened to him?"

"He was being chased by another woman who shoved him into an open grave."

"And the woman?"

(Making hand movements)

"I'm sorry but ***that*** *bitch,* ***that*** *bitch was way too fast to catch. She got away." Mia said as she moved to stand next to Roslyn.*

Ana studies Stacey Hunter's blank expression. He appears to be dazed. His eyes are opened wide and they move slowly around the room.

"Do you need medical attention?" Ana asks.

Stacey doesn't respond. He remains silent and with his wrists handcuffed, uses his shoulder to wipe some of the mud from his face before looking towards Ana and shaking his head as if to say no.

"If you're medically sound then I must ask why were you running and who was the woman chasing you?"

Stacey glances at Robert and Justin before turning his gaze from anyone. He looks at the floor and says, "Last I knew, running through a corridor isn't a crime."

"That may be true Mr. Hunter but the reason that caused you to run could be nothing or anything up to accessory to a crime. Your cooperation right now could set you free or keep you in cuffs. (Pauses) At this point we have nothing on you but we're trying to understand why two men are dead and why you were being followed by ***that*** *man with a gun in his hand. I'll wait. It's a relatively easy question."*

Stacey squints his eyes and smashes his lips together before rolling his eyes. It was Justin that impulsively breaks the silence.

"He was trying to get ransom money for returning Mr. Kingsley. Then he tried to flee."

Mr. Kingsley nudges Justin with an elbow and mumbles, "She's fishing. Keep quiet. You're not helping."

"I didn't hear what was just said but no worries, we'll sort out the truth. And we'll do it person by person, question after question…as long as it takes."

"Is this the beginning of your, we believe in justice speech?" Robert says sarcastically. "Because I'm not interested."

"Actually, it's the beginning of the…it's time to send folks to jail speech."

Ana stops talking because Robert turns white as a ghost. He suddenly starts shaking and was stepping backwards into Justin who wouldn't allow him to move. Stacey's eyes settle between angry and confused as he looks at Robert.

"What the fuck are you doing? Is he cowering? What the fuck is that? (Looks around) He's acting as if he's seen the second coming of Christ. All because one man walked into the area? What da fuck!"

Raymond, wearing cemetery work gear, walked into the mausoleum and asks Roslyn what he'd missed. She smiles as if enjoying a guilty pleasure as she peeks around him. Taking in the moment to enjoy Robert's frightened reaction.

"I'll get you caught up later babe. Right now, you're missing your family reunion." Roslyn says as she points.

Raymond's turn towards his uncle was slow and dramatic. He was focused on his uncle only. Paying no attention to Stacey Hunter for the time being who seemed to be confused by Robert's fear. Stacey initially decided to remain silent, watching Ana and everyone else as Raymond walks slowly towards Robert.

(Under his breath)

"No, no…it can't be. It…can't…be."

"Uncle Robert," Raymond began, "It's time for you to answer for the attempt on my life. You stood watch as I was held down and Grann injected me with a lethal dose of something that would've killed me. You stood by and listened as she belittled my father's existence and tried to snuff out mine. He may not have been her son but he ***was*** *your brother. And true to your nature, you turned your back on him and me as well. Just loose ends to you and Grann both I suppose."*

(Mumbling)

"You flat lined. I saw it. You took your last breath. You can't be real."

Raymond scoffs and takes steps towards his uncle. Robert can barely look at him but tries to find the courage to do so. Raymond walks to him and pushes a single finger into the middle of his chest and increases the pressure.

"Can you feel that? Am I real enough to you now? I doubt this pressure is anything like what my father felt when you tied him to that truck and pushed him into that brick wall until it collapsed. Oh, I'm real."

"I…I…"

Robert looks to be in shock and just lowers and shakes his head back and forth. Stacey Hunter on the other hand is disgusted by the exchange between Robert and Raymond. He stands in disbelief that this man whose territory he wants to take, is reduced to a babbling mess by a man who seems to work for the cemetery.

Stacey stands in awe. Looking at the man he expects to dethrone. Cowering and appearing to be timid and weak in his eyes by an unknown gravedigger.

"Am I missing something? Who the fuck ***is*** *this guy? The fright on Kingsley is real right now. Wha-da-fuck?"*

"Must be frustrating not knowing who I am. Who you are or what's been driving you to go head to head with this man."

(Pointing at Robert)

"I ***know*** *who I am!" Stacey responds confidently.*

"Do you? It doesn't explain the lapses in your memory. The flashes of a life you don't remember as your own. Childhood memories, moments of regret that would wake you up in the middle of the night. Take a good look at me, and then tell me if you don't know who I am."

The area falls silent as Stacey shrugs off any notion of recognition.

"Like I said…I don't know you but I would like to know why he's afraid of you."

"Easy answer…there is guilt driving his fear. But you seem to be suppressing your guilt. (Turns) Do you know who ***she*** *is?"*

Raymond points at Mia who's standing next to Roslyn.

"The Sista or the Senorita?" Stacey asks.

"The Sista!"

"That's the chick I kicked out of my apartment. She had made herself at home, if I recall. (Pauses) Stacey Hunter doesn't have live ins."

(In Keisha's voice)

"I didn't mean enough to you to be memorable? I thought what ***we*** *had was special? Did you love me at all…Sean?"*

Meck looks over at his sister with his lips twisted as Roslyn leans in and says, "What was that?" Mia under her breath tells Roslyn she was just trying to ramp up the drama. Roslyn whispers, "I don't think they'll need your help." Stacey's only reply to Mia was repeating part of what he'd already said and then he turned his attention back to Raymond.

(Inquisitively)

"I never got your name."

"You can't remember? It's Raymond Kingsley."

"Ok, I heard you call him uncle, so obviously you're related. Still doesn't explain his fear. But earlier you mentioned suppressing guilt. Guilt is a festering wound. I don't do guilt. It weakens you. Just as I'd imagine fear would."

Raymond looks at Stacey as if what he just said sounded ridiculous.

"You can't just shut it out. To think so is reckless. It unnoticeably gets to you. It's being able to handle a full range of emotion that completes a man. Anything less…you'll always be divided."

"What's that got to do with ***his*** *reaction to you? He's frightened shitless over there."*

"Everything… in my eyes. Your reaction to seeing me should be similar to his. Full of fear and remorse. It was your guilt that kept you up at night. That was until you suppressed it and unleashed your anger for Robert Kingsley."

"With Kingsley it was just business. There's no emotion involved."

"I doubt that! You've been upset with your father for a long time. Did he force you to be in the hospital and make you stand with the family…

against me? I'm sure my cousin didn't want to hold me down while they tried to kill me. I'm confident they lied about something to get you to prove your loyalty. If only to satisfy Grann. I believe you said…see you in the morgue before you walked out. It didn't sound like you meant it by the way you looked at me as you walked away."

Stacey closes his eyes and shakes his head like he's rejecting what he is hearing.

"I have no memory of that. I was never involved."

"Of course, ***you*** *weren't Stacey but Sean Reynolds was. Your hands, which are his hands… they shook as you held me down. You looked away as our grandmother injected me. You kept looking over to your father for emotional approval. I believe the comments you made going out the door were intended to secure your father's belief in your abilities. Show him there's no part of the business you can't handle after a deed like that one. (Gives a shameful look to his uncle before turning back) You felt guilty! And after playing your part in killing me, you suppressed it. During my funeral you put on the same bullshit emotional show to appease your father. Now, look at me and tell me again that you don't know who I am!"*

Stacey's eyes remained closed and he began to mumble incoherently.

"Feeling hot. (Grunts) Head hurting. (Impulsively angry) ***This isn't real!****"*

(Intensely)

"You're just a manifestation of who your father wished you would be. YOU KILLED ME! YOU BURIED MY VERY EXISTANCE! You went against every instinct you had. Only to gain the approval of a father that would never offer it to you. (Loudly whispered) ***You suppressed it.*** *Something inside you decided you'd rather destroy him rather than wait for his praise."*

Stacey moves in small steps in the same 4ft space and breathes as if he's going to hyperventilate. He lowers his chin into his chest and continues to breathe heavily. He grunts, then shouts, "I'm not who you think I am. I'm not who I was."

"Then who are you? Do you even know anymore? Have you submitted to your alter ego? I'm not sure the cousin that I've been through so much with even exists anymore. If he does...you should know who I am!"

Stacey's head moves back and forth. The incoherent mumbling ceases. Suddenly the heavy breathing stops and he exhales as if a dying man was taking his last breath. He stands with no movement for a single minute as everyone witnesses the silent physical inner struggle. The tenseness and the aggression in his posture changes and he stops moving. As he takes a deep breath, his eyes open slowly. Sean looks around with an expression of bewilderment. Wondering where he is. Why he is in handcuffs and why his father was leaning against a nearby wall wearing cuffs as well. As he turns and sees Raymond, his eyes widen briefly before lowering his head in shame.

(Solemnly)

"I know who you are Rizzo. Out of different wombs but share the same tomb is what we used to tell each other. But my relief to know you're alive doesn't lessen my regret of being in the hospital room that day. I was told that any family member could share your fate if the family felt betrayed. And just as I stood by and did nothing to help you, my father did the same to me when I was presented with choosing the family's honor over you. Night after night I relived those moments and it kept me up. I could hear your voice some nights and it haunted me."

Robert looks at his son with a raging disappointment, feeling that Sean's said much more than necessary. He shakes his head and hopes that his son would notice the signal to remain silent. There's no way to describe the unconcerned, disobedient, non-compliant expression Sean exhibited as he looked directly at his father. And he held his ill-tempered glare until his father looked away. Sean then turns away and smiles when he sees Roslyn. Even in handcuffs he discreetly waves hello to her.

"Keisha! Is that Keisha over there?" Sean eagerly asks.

"Yes and no." Ana begins. "She is one of our undercover agents who shadowed you. You came to know her as…Keisha."

"Oh-kay, now that makes a lot of sense to me now. It also clears up a lot of confusion about intimacy with her."

Sean looks over at Mia who has turned away from everyone and is whistling casually. Roslyn turns and chuckles to herself at Mia's reaction. Sean returns his focus to his cousin after cutting his eyes at his father who's smirking as if someone got one over on him.

(With sincerity)

"There are plenty of gaps in my memory but regarding what I can remember, I would be remised if I didn't actually say…I'm sorry. I repeatedly wondered how I was able protect you on the street that night only to let you be harmed by the family…by me. I failed you Rizz and I don't think I can ever square that with you. I let down my guard and set aside my morals. What little wasn't shamed out of me. And for what! To be replaced, belittled, untrusted, set up and forgotten. That isn't how family should be. I hope one day you and I can be the family we used to be."

"With time…maybe we will."

Sean looks down at the handcuffs before raising his arms. He uses his shoulder again to dislodge some more mud. He turns to Ana and with an innocence in his face she's never seen and tone that in his voice that sounds different from Stacey, Sean asks, "Does anyone have any aspirin? My head is pounding right now. And… maybe someone can explain how I got here. Why I'm in cuffs and why I'm covered with mud."

"All questions asked or answered from this point will be done at the precinct. We'll find our answers in the interrogation rooms. Then we'll see who has what to say. I hate to break up the reunion but it's time to take folks to jail. (Looks around) Let's load 'em up."

CHAPTER TWENTY-FOUR

The ugly truth

A WEEK HAS PASSED and with Raymond & Roslyn back in his parent's home, their home, Roslyn opens the door for Ana who's visiting.

"Bane… go sit down somewhere."

"He doesn't frighten me. He's alright Roslyn. (Smiling) Hey Ray."

"Hi Ana, come on over and have a seat."

Ana, Roslyn and Bane make their way to the den where Raymond was toying with a guitar and all make themselves comfortable.

"I wanted to come by and give you both an update on where the state stands with the open cases against your family. But first, I'm wondering Roslyn, how does it feel to be back in the field?"

"It's nothing big. I'm posing as part owner of a smoke shop just twenty miles out of Colver. It's interesting. Some of the local thugs are trying to threaten us because were legally hurting their sales and others are illegally growing and are trying to do some backdoor sales with us. We're trying to follow them back to their grow houses. It's more so surveillance but I'm ok with that."

"And how's the desk job Ray?"

"It's taxingly boring but I'm too high profile to put back into the field. Especially now that the world knows that I'm alive. But if I can get this job preparing new undercover agents, I'll be just fine."

"I'm glad life is normalizing for you both. (Pauses) Well I've done enough stalling. It's time I get down to it. I'll start with your uncle. He was charged with killing the two men at the cemetery. His prints were found on the gun we took from him when he rounded that corner. Robert Kingsley will also be charged with the murder of your aunt Cassie. Ballistics came back from the gun found in the overturned casket. The bullet markings match the one's removed during her autopsy. Her murder case will be closed and he'll stand trial for all three."

"I'm sure prison will be just as comfortable for him as the outside was. He knows a lot of people and has a lot of connections."

"We did some more police work and learned that your aunt Cassie used the name Kimber Kelly when she worked for your uncle. He had her remains cremated and placed her ashes across from where we extracted the casket under that name. The cemetery has removed the Kelly nameplate and replaced it with Cassie's."

"That's good to know. I'll let both of my aunts know."

"As you know, Sean has been put in a secured mental facility. How's your cousin doing?"

"We went to visit with him the other day but weren't able to see him." Roslyn added.

"Yea Ana, we were told he seems to be going back and forth between the two personalities. We caught him as Stacey Hunter and when he saw me, he started yelling, fuck you gravedigger. Kingsley may be afraid of you but I'm not. (Gestures in disbelief) So, as he became increasingly angry and more aggressive the staff of the hospital asked us to leave."

"I'm sorry to hear that, Ray. I hope he can make some positive progress and you both can repair that relationship."

"Thanks for that, I hope we can as well."

"Right now, they don't think he's lucid enough to stand trial. Not as

an accessory for the attempt on your life and not for kidnapping his father as Stacey Hunter."

"I wouldn't press those charges against him anyway. I know he was coaxed to be there. It's my grandmother that needs to be arrested for that. You know, with everything going on its not surprising that she has up and disappeared."

"Well, that brings me to the bad news Ray. Your grandmother hasn't vanished. She is now a federal witness under their protection."

Raymond and Roslyn look at each other. Roslyn's mouth hangs open in shock and Raymond's expression comes accompanied with an unsurprising hunch of his shoulders.

"What's her angle Ana?"

"She turned witness against your uncle. She is claiming that the family's crime organization was being run by him. She's also saying the attempt on your life was orchestrated by him and she was threatened into playing her part. She's promised them recorded evidence to support her position. She is currently under witness protection until the trial and we have no way of knowing where she is."

"It wouldn't be my grandmother if she didn't have an exit strategy. We were always told to be ready for any eventuality. I wonder how Uncle Robert feels about it."

"What about the woman that was chasing Stacey. I mean…Sean?" Roslyn asks.

"She's a ghost. No one knows who she was and the one person who does know would only give up information about Stacey collecting ransom for Mr. Kingsley."

"So, my grandmother is going to get away Scot free? Then disappear."

"It all depends on the deal she made and whether she sticks to it. Anything could happen. She could refuse to testify or suddenly claim a loss in her memory. I've seen all kind of reasons witnesses don't make it to the

stand. And from what I've learned about her, I'm sure she's figuring a way to get out of it. I'm sorry Raymond."

"Don't be Ana. (Looks at Roslyn) I have the people in my life that means the most to me. That's all I need."

[In an undisclosed home in the Midwest]

Grann sits in one half of a duplex, rocking in a chair when there's a knock at the door. When she looks out of the peep hole, she sees a nicely dressed young woman with pamphlets and a bible in her hands.

[Door opens]

"How may I help you?"

"I'm wondering if you have time to discuss Jehovah and your relationship with God. Here with me, I have text that could bring you closer to our Lord and savior."

"Why don't you come in and we'll talk about it. I'm Georgia-May Jefferies. My family calls me Tinky, Tink for short. You may call me Tink. Please…come sit with me out on the back deck."

"Yes ma'am, thank you."

The two ladies step out of the sliding door and find two patio seats to comfortably rest on in the sun.

"I'm glad you found me Maya. We can only talk outside. I think the house is bugged. Did you get my instructions?"

"Yes G-ma I did and everything is ready. Here's the drug you asked for. Take it; they'll pronounce you dead and I'm already set up to collect you from the morgue. All you have to do is give the word and we'll set this escape plan in motion."

"Good…good."

"G-ma, I have to ask…Is Robert Kingsley really my father?"

"Yes, he is. Your mother felt underappreciated by your father. When he started spending so much time with the sisters and eventually fell hard for Kate. Your mother, she never told him she was pregnant. Your mother also

made me promise to never tell him…ever! That's one reason I've looked over you all these years. Deep down you are a Kingsley through and through. You've proven that with how you've handled yourself and this mess."

"But I still have one thing left to do G-ma. (Rubs her hands together) Kill Stacey Hunter."

"Sorry love, you're not going to be able to do that."

"What do you mean? Why not?"

"The man that tried to ransom your father, the man you were chasing in the cemetery… is actually Sean Reynolds…your brother."

"He was who I was looking for all along. How can that be?"

"He has some kind of mental thing and thought he was someone else."

"He was damn convincing at it. But if you had pictures in your house, I would have known what he looked like."

"I don't keep photos child, I know what ya'll look like."

"Besides my auntie and you, I haven't had much family G-ma. I hope I can get the chance to know my father and brother."

"To do so you'll have to visit the prison and the loony bin. But that will have to wait for now. We need to talk about rebuilding this family's empire. When we land where we're going, I want to hit the ground running. You'll know how to set up and runs things but you'll still get your direction from me."

"I'm in. G-ma."

"But first child there's something in Colver I need you to do. (Taps the chair with her hand) You have a niece named Cee-Jay that Sean's mother is caring for. I've talked Kate into placing her into an afterschool program to ease the stress of having to care for her. I did so before her father was in a mental hospital and her grandfather entered a prison. (Clears her throat) I want you to take the time to go and mentor her. Kate will welcome your help, any help. Then we can start preparing Cee-Jay to support our business. Let's help her with her confidence, eliminate any fears of trying new things

and teach her to rely on herself and her wits in a pinch. Be the hero, not need one. The same way I taught you. (Winks) The Kingsley women have always been the strength of this family and will continue to be. I know what it's like to start from nothing. If my years have taught me anything, it's how to bounce back and build it faster. And it won't be long before we rebuild this family's strength and fortune. We'll start over with you & I and make it strong again. Fortune is always with whoever is willing to sacrifice for their cause. It's no accident that I continue to survive. (Smiles sinisterly) It's almost time to put the pieces in place. I've heard death is only the beginning. We start in seven days."

AUTHOR'S NOTES

FOR THOSE WHO really know me, know that at any moment something strange is usually brewing inside me. I may not always say what I'm thinking but the smirk on my face often drives you to ask me about it. You do... at your own risk.

Rarely dirty, often silly, sometimes profound but always something I'd hope you would say is entertaining. I am the victim of an over-active imagination. More times than I'll admit, it's a gift that has reached out and tortured my friends and family. It's an affliction that I am happy to be stuck with.

There is a certain pleasure I receive when I watch the expressions on the faces of those who are listening to me tell one of my stories. It doesn't take much to get me going. Most often it only takes one smile, a partial smirk or even someone reacting by saying...What? I'm looking for a reaction. Either you're confused by what I've said or shocked that I've said it. Regardless ...the door is now open. Open for me to test my limits to entertain you. How far can I get before you decide you can't hear anymore, before the back of your neck is hurting from laughter or until the intrigue has fully captured your attention? Whether you realize it or not, that's exactly what I'm looking to do. No matter how I'm able to do it. Whether it's in the form of a joke, a short story or quick quip. I've said before that there's an entirely different world going on inside my head. a place where the folks in it tell me their stories and I in turn want to share them with you. There have often been moments in my life where inspiration engulfs me. Violently sweeps me away like the funnel of a hurricane. Holding me suspended until the churning of my mind finds peace and my ideas/thoughts manifest into something special. And you know it's something special if you're able to entangle someone else's attention with what you have created. That's what I want my work to do. To make you laugh, make you think, make you angry, even make you want to love or hate the characters you come to know.

I appreciate you taking the time to step out the boundaries of the real world and taking a look at some of the lives that are living inside my mind. I can only hope that they will affect you the way they have affected me. With long nights, frustrating days, confusing thoughts, and moments of inspired exhilaration. I used this work as an opportunity to better myself as a writer. Trying to push myself and my limitations so that the next story will continue to test my imagination. Producing work that will not only entertain you, but also bring a sense of satisfaction to myself. Art often imitates life...and our lives, whether fact or fiction ...is art.

Let's imagine that it's your favorite kind of day. You are alone or maybe with a friend. A few of my favorite pieces of work are lying somewhere close to you. The atmosphere is the perfect condition for you to concentrate on my words. I hope you take a seat and study what you see. Let it consume you, if only for a moment. Take your time...enjoy yourself.

My head is bowed, and hands are at my chest in a praying position

You have no idea how much I appreciate you taking the time to support me. Thank You...Thank You So Much.

For those who need a push to tell their own story.
You can't be afraid to express yourself.
Find freedom in your words.

M. Rashid

For everyone who allows me to untie the knots in my creative process...

Readers notes

Made in the USA
Las Vegas, NV
04 November 2022

58742323R00333